THE STARSHIP IN THE STONE

THE STARSHIP IN THE STONE
BOOK 1

M.R. FORBES

Published by Quirky Algorithms
Seattle, Washington

This novel is a work of fiction and a product of the author's imagination.
Any resemblance to actual persons or events is purely coincidental.

Copyright © 2025 by Quirky Algorithms
All rights reserved.

Cover illustration by Tom Edwards
Edited by Merrylee Lanehart

CHAPTER 1

The polished brass plate beside the door read "Ashworth, Tilling & Associates - Solicitors at Law" in an ornate font more suited to the Victorian era than modern Manchester. Beneath the firm's name, small gold letters declared "Est. 1773," lending an air of old-world authority to the already imposing glass and stone facade.

Bracing against the chill wind that whistled between the buildings, Thomas pulled the hood of his sweatshirt up around his face. There was nothing he could do about the elements while he was riding—he couldn't afford to cover his peripheral vision unless he wanted to end up in the hospital again—but once he dismounted his bicycle, all bets were off. The cotton helped keep the rain off his face and hair, making him at least ten percent more presentable—a half-drowned rat instead of one dead in the water—to his next customer.

His military-style boots squeaked against the marble floor as he entered the building's lavish lobby, the sound echoing off the vaulted ceiling like an accusation. The security guard, a burly man with salt-and-pepper hair and the bearing of an ex-military officer, gave him the once-over, a wide grin spreading across his face.

"Evening, Thomas," he said. "I see you still haven't taken my advice on upgrading your wardrobe. Brighter colors and some reflective tape would go a long way to keep you out of trouble."

"And I never will, Barry," Thomas replied. "The risk is half the reward."

"So you say, but I seem to recall your wrist in a cast not too long ago."

"That wasn't from riding. That was from an awkward punch at the gym. How are Olivia and the kids?" he asked, changing the subject.

"They're doing just fine."

"Glad to hear it."

Thomas moved on from the guard, crossing the rest of the distance to the receptionist desk near the back of the lobby. The woman there had already risen to her feet, smiling in greeting.

"Evening, Thomas," she said warmly. "Another late pickup? I swear you spend more time here than some of our junior partners."

"Hey, Miranda," Thomas replied, flashing her a charming smile. "You can blame Mr. Tilling for that. Anyway, the office's business keeps me well fed."

"You wouldn't know it by looking at you," Miranda answered, referring to his extra-lean, athletic frame. "Are you sure you've eaten lately?"

"Are you asking me out to dinner?" Thomas joked in reply, drawing a slightly embarrassed laugh.

"Ah, Thomas. Always a cheeky rascal. I'm old enough to be your mum. What would she think?"

"I don't know. She's on the other side of the Atlantic, and probably too high to remember that I even exist.

Anyway, if Mr. Tilling is true to form, I have a deadline on whatever it is he wants me to deliver this time."

"Right," Miranda said, returning to her seat. Her fingers moved efficiently across her keyboard, the click-clack of the keys a familiar rhythm. Her expression turned more professional as she messaged with the solicitor. "Mr. Tilling is expecting you. Seventh floor, end of the corridor. You know the way, I'm sure."

"I think I've worn a path," Thomas answered, already heading for the lifts. "Thanks, Miranda. Stay warm tonight. It's getting nasty out there."

"You're the one riding a bike around Manchester in this weather," she called after him. "Be careful!"

The lift area was clad in mirrored walls, fragmenting his reflection into a dozen angles. He realized the black hoodie with the black cargo pants tucked into his black socks made him look like a cat burglar, but fashion meant little when dodging traffic at midnight. Besides, the pants were comfortable and practical—after all, the last thing he needed was loose fabric catching in his bike chain— and he liked the look.

He wanted to strike an air of danger and menace to keep people at arm's length. He'd had enough complications back in the States. Now, he just wanted to do his job, earn enough honest money to survive, and otherwise stay under the radar.

The lift arrived with a soft chime more suited to a five-star hotel than a law office. Inside, three people in expensive suits shifted to make room for him, though one—a woman in her fifties with perfectly coiffed silver hair—clutched her designer handbag a bit tighter. Thomas nodded politely, suppressing a grin at their discomfort. "Lovely evening, isn't it?" he said cheerfully, partly to ease the tension and partly because he enjoyed watching them squirm.

The woman with the handbag managed a tight smile, her knuckles still white around the leather strap. "Rather nasty actually," she murmured in an accent that hinted at private schooling and country estates.

"Quite," muttered one of the men, his attention fixed firmly on his phone's glowing screen. Likely a junior partner, he wore an expensive but not quite bespoke suit. "Though I doubt many are out for pleasure in this weather."

The third occupant, an older man with a red face suggesting too many liquid business lunches, simply grunted and stared at the floor numbers ticking upward.

The lift stopped at the fourth floor, and the doors opened onto a hushed corridor lined with dark wood panels and oil paintings of stern-faced solicitors from centuries past. Everyone filed out with barely concealed relief, leaving Thomas alone as he walked down the corridor. Their eyes followed him, judging his untoward presence in their hallowed halls.

Mr. Tilling's office lay behind a heavy oak door all the way to the far end, its frosted glass panel emblazoned with "Senior Partner" in gold leaf. Thomas knocked twice, the sound sharp in the tomblike quiet of the corridor.

"Enter," called a cultured voice from within.

The office was true to form for the senior partner of a highly successful and historic solicitor's office. Leather-bound books lined the walls in perfect alphabetical order. A mahogany desk, so massive it nearly took up the back wall, rested on the far side of the room. Behind it, a view over the Thames showcased the city's twinkling lights. The air smelled of ancient leather, old paper, and expensive cologne.

If this were his first time here, he would have waited outside the door rather than put his wet boots on the thick carpet, but he'd been here often enough to know that Mr.

Tilling cared much more about efficiency than the cost of having his carpet steam-cleaned every week.

"Mr. Tilling," Thomas said, approaching the desk. "Good to see you again, sir."

Tilling, a rail thin man with wire-rimmed glasses and gray hair, looked up from his computer, the screen's light reflecting off his lenses. "Ah, Mr. Drake. You as well. Thank you for coming on such short notice." His voice held the same distinguished tones as his colleagues, but there was a hint of something else—perhaps Liverpool—carefully masked by years of polish. He reached into his desk drawer, withdrawing a thick manila envelope. "This needs to be delivered to 23 Chancery Lane, Suite 405. Mr. Harrison will be waiting to sign it. Once he does, bring it straight back here."

Thomas pulled out his phone and entered the address on his mapping app. Way downtown. A twenty minute ride. "How long do I have to return it?"

"Ninety minutes," Tilling replied. "But there's a bonus waiting for you if you're back within an hour."

Thomas grinned. "I can do an hour, sir, as long as Mr. Harrison is there when I arrive."

"He ought to be."

"Then consider it done. Guaranteed delivery in ninety minutes or you get a full refund. Standard rate okay? That's sixty quid, plus the after-hours surcharge."

"Yes, yes, of course," Mr. Tilling said, waving his hand dismissively. Money was never a concern with him. He wrote something on a Post-it note in precise, angular handwriting and stuck it to the envelope before holding it out across his desk to Thomas. "Please ensure Mr. Harrison signs on the marked pages. There are three spots requiring his signature."

"I'll let him know," Thomas replied, tucking the envelope securely into his messenger bag. "Is there anything else I can do for you, sir?"

"That's all for now." Mr. Tilling glanced at his Rolex. "Whatever happens, I must have these documents back no later than eight p.m. for filing first thing tomorrow morning. They're very important."

"No problem. I'll have them back way before eight," Thomas said, patting his bag. "Safe and signed."

"I don't doubt it, which is why I requested you specifically," Tilling replied, already turning back to his computer screen. "Be a good chap and close the door on your way out."

"Yes, sir."

Thomas retraced his steps from the office, the lift car empty this time as he rode it back down to the lobby. He waved goodbye to Miranda as he hurried for the exit.

"Have a good evening, Barry," he said, giving the security guard a a friendly two-fingered salute.

"Be safe out there, Thomas," the guard replied, opening the door for him.

As he exited the building, the blustery night air—carrying the scent of more rain and the ever-present bouquet of petrol fumes and wet people—hit Thomas like a sharp slap in the face. Already mentally mapping out the quickest route through the city's maze of streets and alleys, he was pretty sure he wouldn't need the directions on his phone's map app, but he had them just in case.

Avoiding the worst of the pedestrian traffic, he stepped over pools of rainwater and went to where he'd locked his bike to a lamp post.

While most couriers used electric bikes these days, he still preferred his practically-ancient-but-reliable fixed-gear Specialized Langster. He couldn't argue that the e-bikes were faster in a straightway and a lot less effort to ride, but they were magnets for thieves. His Langster, on the other hand, had enough battle scars to discourage anyone with bolt cutters to snip his cable and take off with it. Besides, his bike had better maneuverability and control than electric bikes, and he enjoyed the exercise that hard pedaling provided.

The Langster's matte black frame was virtually invisible in the darkness, but the reflective strips on the tires caught the streetlight like tiny lightning bolts. They were the only reflectors he could bring himself to utilize. The bare minimum. Barry wasn't the first person who had suggested he had a death wish riding around like a pedaling ninja, and he couldn't completely refute the idea that he did harbor somewhat of a self-destructive urge. He refused to wear a helmet, while some couriers even wore elbow and knee pads. He did often wear gloves, but they were more to keep his hands warm.

Life had been hard from the day he was born, and sometimes he just didn't see the appeal of trying to live more of it. It felt...pointless.

Thomas unlocked the Langster from the post, muscle memory guiding his hands as he stowed the locking cable in his bag. Swinging into the saddle always boosted his adrenaline. He looked for the next open space between cars before pushing off into traffic.

The evening rush hour had faded, but the streets were far from empty. Black cabs prowled for fares, their golden "TAXI" signs glowing like cat's eyes in the darkness. Red double-deckers still dominated the lanes, their windows bright with interior lights, while tourists wandered obliviously, their attention fixed on their phones as they searched for the next pub or posed for their next selfie.

Thomas wove between vehicles with practiced ease, ignoring the occasional angry honk from drivers who thought bikes didn't belong on "their" roads. A courier on a bike was practically invisible in Manchester traffic—just another ghost in the machine—slipping through gaps that cars couldn't navigate.

"Oi! Watch it!" shouted a cabbie as Thomas squeezed past his door, close enough to feel the heat from his engine.

"Sorry!" he called back, not meaning it.

Left at the next junction, straight through two sets of lights, then a quick right down a side street that would save him a few minutes. He knew every shortcut in central Manchester, every alley and cut-through that could shave precious seconds off his delivery time.

The bike responded to the slightest shift of his weight as he leaned into turns, tires humming against the wet tarmac. Wind whistled past his ears, carrying the city's familiar symphony of engines, sirens, and fragments of conversation. A group of pub-goers spilled onto the pavement ahead, their laughter echoing off the buildings as they stumbled up the sidewalk arm-in-arm.

"Bike! Coming through!" he shouted, hopping his bike up over the curb onto the sidewalk and swerving around them without breaking rhythm.

"Bloody cyclists!" someone yelled, but Thomas was already gone, their surprised shouts fading behind him, lost in the urban cacophony. He pushed harder on the pedals as he approached a green light that was about to change.

He checked his photoluminescent watch dial. Thirteen minutes to reach Chancery Lane. Plenty of time for the delivery and return journey, assuming everything went smoothly. Which, of course, meant it wouldn't. Life always had a way of throwing unexpected obstacles into his path, from the untimely death of his father when he was only eight months old, to being arrested and spending five years in juvenile detention.

Spotting a suitable light pole near his destination, Thomas brought the bike to a controlled stop, his breath forming short clouds in the cold air. The street was quiet here, most of the offices already closed for the night. The only sounds were the distant hum of traffic and occasional flickers of movement behind darkened windows where cleaning staff worked their way through empty buildings.

As he wrapped his cable around the bike's frame and the lamp pole, connecting the locking ends, a muffled cry came from the narrow alley behind him. He froze, his whole body tensing. It could be nothing more than somebody banging his knee against the door frame as he left his office building for the night. Then again, at this time of night, most of the white-collars had already gone home or left for one of the pubs a few blocks to the east.

It was none of his business either way. He had a delivery to make, a deadline to meet. And he was so close; he could see 23 Chancery two buildings away.

The cry—this time panicked and afraid—came again, and Thomas' jaw clenched.

In his thoughts, his past rushed up to meet him like an old friend. The prison rehab program and his mentor's voice in his head, swearing to him that one day he would have a chance to make up for his violent beginnings. The promise he'd made to do better. To help rather than harm. All those hours of training, learning to channel his anger and focus his energy in the right direction.

"Damn it," he muttered, checking that his bag, on a long strap slung across his chest, was properly closed. The envelope inside it would have to wait.

Some things were worth being late for. Some promises meant more than others.

He moved toward the alley's entrance, his boots soft on the wet pavement. The gloom between the buildings pulsed with quiet menace, but he stepped into it anyway.

The darkness swallowed him whole, the weight of the buildings pressing in on either side of him, watching to see what he would do next.

CHAPTER 2

The dark maw of the narrow alley stretched ominously between the backs of the old brick buildings, their walls pressing in on either side, their weathered surfaces still holding the day's dampness. Thomas' heart hammered against his ribs as he edged forward, barely daring to breathe. Each footstep felt like a thunderclap, though he barely made a sound.

Ahead, the noises grew clearer—harsh, excited breathing, fabric scraping against rough brick, a whimper quickly stifled. A man's voice, thick with malice, cut through the darkness like a twisted blade.

"Listen carefully, sweetheart," he growled, the words slithering through the shadows ahead of Thomas. "I'm going to take my hand off your mouth. If you make a sound —any sound at all—I'll stick you right here and leave you to bleed out with the rubbish." The knife in his hand caught a sliver of light from the street, its edge gleaming with malevolent promise. "Nod if you understand me."

The woman stayed perfectly still, pinned against the wall by his bulk. Even from the edge of the alley, Thomas could see her eyes wide with terror, the whites vivid in the dim light. She managed a tiny nod, and the man slowly removed his meaty hand from her mouth, leaving a visible dirty smear on her face.

Thomas' pulse roared in his ears as he watched. The woman remained dead silent while the man's free hand began to roam. His fingers pawed first at her necklace, ripping it free of its clasp, before moving on to the engagement ring on her finger. The woman pressed herself harder against the wall, as if trying to sink into the brick itself. A small sound— halfway between a sob and a hiccup– escaped her, and the knife twitched closer to her throat.

"What did I say about noise?" he hissed, his face inches from hers. "Don't test me."

Thomas pulled his hood lower, trying to control his breathing as he crept closer. Sweat trickled down his spine despite the cold. His mentor's voice echoed in his head: "Violence should always be the last resort, but when it's necessary, make it count. And Thomas? It's about control. Control your fear. Control your anger. Control your breathing. Above all, control the situation."

An experienced Marine, his mentor had served in some pretty ugly and dangerous places, but Thomas wasn't sure he'd ever had to stalk a knife-wielding maniac in a dark alley. He pictured Vin in his head, handling the situation. Controlling his fear. Making moves count.

He had to do the same. This woman was in trouble, and he was the only one there to help her.

Six feet away now. Five. Tension coiled in Thomas' muscles like a spring wound too tight. One wrong move and—

His foot connected with something solid. A discarded beer bottle. Time slowed as he watched it roll, hearing every click and scrape of glass against the pavement. The sound might as well have been an air raid siren in the confined space.

The attacker's head snapped around, momentarily distracted. "Who's there?" he barked, squinting into the darkness where Thomas stood frozen.

The woman seized her chance, drawing in a deep breath and letting loose a piercing scream that bounced off the alley walls like a pinball. The sound stabbed through Thomas' skull, setting every nerve ending alight.

"You bitch!" the attacker snarled, gaze whipping back to her.

The knife flashed downward in a savage arc, and the scream turned into a wet gasp as the blade sank into her abdomen. His other hand shot out, catching her across the jaw with enough force to snap her head back against the bricks with a sickening crack. She crumpled to the ground like a broken doll.

"Now look what you made me do," he spat at her unconscious form. Then he turned toward Thomas, the knife dripping blood in the dim light. "And you, mate. Whoever you are, you should've kept walking."

Thomas was already moving, blood pounding in his ears. Three quick steps brought him within range, and he launched himself at the man, driving his shoulder into his midsection. They crashed to the pavement together, the impact driving the air from both their lungs. The knife skittered away into the darkness.

The attacker—he could feel the man's heavy mass as they rolled across the wet asphalt—was much bigger than Thomas. They traded blows in the confined space. The man's fist caught Thomas in the ribs, a sledgehammer blow that sent lightning bolts of pain through his chest, but he managed to get his knee up between them to knock him away.

"This ain't your business!'" the attacker spat, scrambling to his feet. Blood trickled from his split lip where Thomas' elbow had caught him. "You thinking you're some kind of hero or something?"

Thomas didn't answer, focusing instead on his stance, keeping his guard up the way he'd been taught. His hands shook slightly as he raised them, too filled with adrenaline to speak.

The attacker charged forward with a roar, throwing wild haymakers that would have ended the fight if they'd connected. Thomas slipped the first punch and blocked the second, countering with a quick jab to the man's solar plexus that made him stumble back, wheezing.

"Fucking hero," the attacker gasped, but uncertainty crept into his voice. This wasn't going the way he'd planned. "I'll teach you to interfere."

He feinted left, telegraphing his move so clearly it had to be intentional, but Thomas anticipated the deception. He sidestepped and countered with a sharp right hook to the attacker's jaw, followed by a quick uppercut that sent the man staggering backward. Thomas pressed the advantage, launching a series of rapid punches—a left jab to the ribs, a right cross to the temple, an uppercut to the chin—each one connecting with precision. The attacker grunted, struggling to keep up as Thomas attacked, success breeding confidence in Vin's training.

Still on the defensive, the attacker swung wildly, but Thomas ducked under the blow, pivoting to drive his elbow into the man's side. The attacker wheezed, doubling over, and Thomas followed up with a kick to the gut that dropped him to one knee.

The attacker let out a roar of frustration and swung his arm in a wild, desperate arc. Thomas dodged it easily, but his foot slipped on the wet pavement. The attacker saw his chance, lunging forward and driving his shoulder into Thomas' midsection. Thomas lost his balance, and they went down hard, Thomas' back slapping hard against the pavement. His head cracked against the ground with enough force to make his teeth rattle, the taste of copper flooding his mouth where he'd bitten the inside of his cheek. His head swam.

"Not so fancy now, are you?" the attacker sneered, straddling Thomas' chest. His weight crushed the air from Thomas' lungs. The stench of stale cigarettes and cheap beer washed over him with each of the man's excited breaths as his meaty hands found Thomas' throat and began to squeeze..

Spots danced at the edges of Thomas' vision. He tried to buck the man off. His fingers clawed at his meaty hands, seeking pressure points that should have made him release his grip, but nothing worked. The black spots bloomed larger, Thomas' lungs burning for air. One of his hands fell limply to the asphalt. His fingers brushed something cold and metallic. The knife. His fingers scrabbled for the handle, closing around it. He didn't think. Couldn't think. Just as tunnel vision began to close in, pure survival instinct drove the blade upward, finding the soft spot just under the attacker's ribs.

The man's grip on Thomas' throat loosened. "What..." he managed as he looked down in surprise. His weight shifted, becoming heavier as his muscles went slack.

Thomas rolled away as the man toppled sideways like a felled tree. The knife clattered from his trembling fingers as he sucked in great gulps of air, each one feeling like swallowing broken glass. For a moment, he stared at the knife where it had landed in a puddle that was rapidly turning red. Beside it lay his attacker—motionless, eyes wide and staring at nothing. A dark stain was spreading rapidly across his shirt, feeding the bloody puddle.

"Oh, damn," Thomas whispered, scrambling backward, out from under the dead weight of the man's legs lying across his. He didn't stop until he hit the wall. "Damn,

damn, damn." His hands shook so badly he could barely pull out his phone. The man's blood smeared across the screen as he tried three times to unlock it before finally managing to dial 999.

"Emergency. Which service do you require?" The woman's calm voice seemed to come from another world entirely.

"P-police," he croaked, his throat feeling now like he'd swallowed sandpaper.

"Police emergency, what is the location of the incident?" a second dispatcher asked.

"Uh…" Thomas' lips froze over as the adrenaline began to fade, leaving him shivering. "Twenty Chancery Lane. The alley. A woman was stabbed and needs medical assistance. Her attacker is dead."

He ended the call before the dispatcher could ask any questions. He didn't want to get any more involved in this than he already had. He just wanted to get the contents of Tilling's envelope signed and bring it back to the solicitor. He was supposed to stay out of trouble, and this was the total opposite of that. But he couldn't leave the woman without at least checking on her.

Bracing a hand against the wall, Thomas pushed himself to his feet, fighting a wave of dizziness as he stumbled over to where the woman lay. She was unconscious, her head slumped to one side. He felt for a pulse at the side of her neck. It was steady under his fingertips, but blood was spreading across her cream-colored blouse from the stab wound, turning it a horrible dark red.

"Hold on," he told her, though he doubted she could hear him. His voice cracked as he continued, "Help is coming. Just hold on. I'm sorry I wasn't faster. I'm so sorry."

Sirens wailed in the distance, growing closer with each

passing second. The sound snapped him back to reality. He needed to get out of there.

Returning to his feet, he sprinted back to the mouth of the alley, returning to his bicycle. His hands fumbled at the lock's combination, his gaze lifting to the end of the street where the flashing lights of the responders reflected off the windows. He managed to get the lock off, quickly scanning the lamp posts for cameras. He didn't see any. Not surprising. He doubted the man would have been so bold to attack someone where he could be so easily seen and recorded. In the aftermath, it was good for him.

He didn't have to go far. Just thirty feet more, to the entrance of 23 Chancery. Rather than taking precious time to lock up his bike, he dropped it on the asphalt, ducking into the building as the first police car and ambulance rounded the corner. The vehicles raced past before coming to a quick stop while he watched through the window, his breath still ragged. He exhaled in relief as the constables leaped from the car and entered the alley, the paramedics right behind them.

He had done his good deed for the day. Maybe he had even started to make up for some of the bad things he had done.

CHAPTER 3

Thomas burst through the door of Suite 405, messenger bag clutched so tightly against his side his knuckles had gone white around the strap stretching across his chest. His hands still trembled, adrenaline making his movements jerky and uncoordinated as he approached the receptionist's desk.

The receptionist, a woman in her mid-thirties with carefully styled auburn hair, looked up from her computer. Her fingers stopped mid-keystroke as she took in his appearance. "Can I help you?" she asked cautiously.

"I have a delivery for Mr. Harrison," Thomas managed, his voice coming out in a harsh rasp that made him wince. Each word felt like swallowing broken glass. "From Ashworth, Tilling & Associates."

"Oh, my goodness," she said, standing up, her eyes widening as she noticed the blood on him. "Are you alright? You look terrible. Should I call someone?"

"I'm fine," Thomas cut her off, forcing a wan smile that probably looked more like a grimace. "I just took a spill off my bike. Nothing serious. Is Mr. Harrison still here? I'm on a bit of a deadline."

She hesitated, concern warring with professional courtesy on her features. Her hand hovered over the phone. "Are you sure? You really don't look well. We have a first aid kit. I could—"

"Really, I'm fine," Thomas insisted, cutting her off. "The truth is, Mr. Tilling offered me a bonus to get these papers signed and back on his desk in under an hour, and I could use the quid. I rushed to get down here, fell off my bike." He shrugged. "It happens. But I really just need Mr. Harrison's signature and I'll be on my way. I'm sure you're eager to go home tonight, too."

She pressed her lips together, clearly wanting to say more, but she finally relented. "Yes, he's expecting you. Through there." She pointed to a door left ajar, warm light spilling out into the darkened office. "But maybe stop at A&E on your way home?"

"Thanks, I'll think about it," Thomas lied, already moving toward Harrison's office, his wet boots squeaking on the polished floor. He knocked twice on the door frame before entering, the sound sharp in the quiet space.

The office was smaller than Tilling's, but similarly appointed with dark wood and leather. Mr. Harrison sat behind his desk, peering at a computer screen, the air reeking of furniture polish and the pipe sitting in an ashtray on the desk beside him. Unlike Tilling's carefully maintained silver hair, Harrison's was a shock of unruly white that made him look like an aging rock star who'd traded his leather pants for a proper suit.

"Mr. Harrison? I have a delivery from Ashworth, Tilling & Associates."

Harrison looked up, his expression shifting from mild annoyance at the interruption to alarmed concern. "My word, man. Are you alright? You look like you've been in quite a scrape." He stood up, pushing his chair back. "Sit down before you fall down. Sharon!" he called toward the outer office. "Bring the first aid kit!"

"No!" Thomas said quickly, perhaps too forcefully. He modulated his tone. "I mean, thank you, but that's not necessary. I fell off my bike. The weather's nasty out there. The documents just need your signature in three places." Unfastening his bag, he pulled the envelope from his bag, hands still shaking slightly as he placed it on the desk. A small drop of blood–not his–had soaked through the manila paper, creating a dark stain like an accusing fingerprint.

Harrison's eyes narrowed, taking in Thomas' disheveled appearance, the visible tremor in his hands, the way he couldn't quite meet his gaze. "Are you sure it was just a fall? Your neck looks rather…well…it looks like someone tried to strangle you."

Thomas' hand flew to his throat, covering the bruises he knew must be forming. "The pavement was wet," he replied, willing his voice to stay steady. A siren wailed outside, making him flinch. "I think I twisted my neck when I hit. The, uh, signatures, sir? I'm trying to make it back to Mr. Tilling within the hour."

"Bollocks," Harrison said bluntly. "I've been cycling in Manchester for thirty years. I know what bike accidents look like. No, you've been in a proper fight." He leaned forward, lowering his voice. "I heard sirens outside. You don't have anything to do with that, do you?"

"What? Of course not, sir," Thomas replied too urgently.

"Well, then did someone attack you? Perhaps I should call the police?" He started reaching for his desk phone.

"No!" Thomas again said too quickly. He forced himself to take a breath. "No, really, sir, I'm fine. Just embarrassed, that's all. The signatures are marked with tabs. Please, I really need to get these back to Mr. Tilling."

Harrison continued studying him for a moment longer. "Yes, well, I suppose it's none of my business," he said, reaching for the envelope, his expression making it clear he still wasn't convinced. He broke the seal and removed the stack of papers, efficiently flipping through them before uncapping an expensive-looking fountain pen and signing where indicated. Each scratch of the nib against paper felt like it took an eternity. Thomas fought the urge to look over his shoulder, half-expecting police to burst through the door at any moment.

Through the window behind Harrison's desk, he could see the reflection of blue and red emergency lights painting the buildings across the street. His palms grew slick with sweat as he waited, his messenger bag suddenly feeling like it weighed a ton.

"There we are," Harrison said finally, returning the papers to the envelope. "All signed and..." He paused, frowning when his gaze landed on Thomas' hoodie. "Is that blood?" he asked, pointing to a dark stain where Thomas' attacker had bled onto him.

"What? No. It...it's probably just some grease or oil that was on the roadway. Since you have so much cycling experience, I'm sure you know how filthy the roads are." He snatched the envelope back perhaps a bit too forcefully. Some of the papers slipped, and he had to juggle to keep them from spilling onto the floor. "Thank you, sir. Have a good evening."

"Now, wait just a minute," Harrison started to say, rising from his chair.

Thomas was already out the door, practically running through the outer office. His heart hammered as he hit the emergency stairwell, taking the steps two at a time. The frantic percussion of his boots on the metal stairs echoed off the concrete walls, a match to his racing pulse.

The lobby was mercifully empty. Through the glass doors, Thomas could see the flashing lights of the emergency vehicles reflected off the wet pavement, creating a strobing effect that made his head spin. Two police cars and an ambulance blocked most of the street, their lights painting everything in alternating shades of red and blue. He needed to get to his bike and get the hell out of there without drawing attention. But he couldn't go out on the street like this.

Thomas ducked into the men's room, locking the door behind him with trembling fingers. The fluorescent lights hummed overhead, harsh and unforgiving as he examined himself in the mirror. His reflection looked like something from a horror film. Blood was smeared across his sweatshirt in dark patches, and bruises were already forming around his throat in the shape of thick fingers. No wonder Harrison had been suspicious.

"Damn it," he whispered, touching the marks gingerly. They were tender, and he knew they'd look worse tomorrow.

Working quickly, he stripped off his hoodie and turned it inside out, hiding the worst of the stains. His t-shirt beneath was relatively clean, just some wet spots from the rain. He splashed water on his face and hands, scrubbing away any visible traces of blood. He also zipped his hoodie to the top, which covered most of his throat so long as he didn't stand in direct light.

"Just get back to Tilling," he muttered to his reflection. "Get paid. Go home. Forget this ever happened."

As if he could just forget that he had killed someone.

Again.

At least this time the bastard deserved it.

The lobby doors felt impossibly heavy as he pushed through them into the night air. The rain had picked up again, a fine mist that hung suspended in the glow of the street lamps. His bike lay where he'd dropped it, the frame gleaming wet in the emergency lights. He hurried to it and started lifting it upright.

"Oi! You there!"

Thomas froze, one hand on his bike's handlebar. A constable was walking toward him from the direction of the alley. He was young, probably not much older than Thomas himself, with the eager look of someone new to the job.

Run, every instinct inside him screamed. But he knew that would only make things worse. Instead, he forced himself to stay still, carefully wiping his face of all expression and adopting what he hoped was a casual posture. "Evening, officer," he managed, proud that his voice remained steady.

"Did you see or hear anything unusual in the last half hour?" the constable asked. "We've had an incident."

Thomas shook his head. "No, sir. I just got here about five minutes ago. I heard the sirens on my way in, and wasn't sure what they were about. I had to get some papers signed." He patted his messenger bag. "Mr. Harrison in Suite 405. What's happened?"

The constable's eyes narrowed slightly as he took in Thomas' inside-out sweatshirt and the way water had plastered his hair to his forehead. "A man and woman were attacked in the alley. You're sure you didn't hear anything? Any screams, maybe?"

"Nothing," Thomas said, fighting to keep his voice level. "Are they okay?"

"No. The man's dead. The woman was stabbed and traumatized." The constable's gaze dropped to Thomas' hand where it gripped the handlebar. "Is that blood?"

Thomas looked down, his stomach lurching. He'd missed washing off a smear of dried blood on the side of his hand "Oh, yeah. Fell off my bike earlier. Bit slippery tonight." He forced a self-deprecating laugh. "That's why I turned my sweatshirt inside-out. Got blood on it. Can't have clients seeing me looking like that, yeah?"

"Right," the constable said slowly, lifting a notepad from

his pocket. "I'll need your name and address, in case I have any additional questions."

Thomas' heart rate kicked up another notch. "Constable, I'm not a witness to whatever happened in the alley. I didn't see or hear anything, and I really need to get going. I've got ten minutes to get these documents back uptown if I want my bonus. It's been a rough night already with this weather and taking a spill. Please? I really don't want to lose out on that extra quid. I could really use it."

The constable studied him for a long moment, pen hovering over the notepad. Thomas held his breath, trying to project an air of harried innocence. Just another courier having a bad night, nothing more.

Finally, the constable lowered his pad. "Alright, get on with you then. But be careful out there. Weather's only getting worse."

"Yes, sir. Thank you," Thomas said, already swinging onto his bike. "I'm very sorry that anyone was hurt. I hope you sort out whatever happened."

He pushed off before the constable could change his mind, pedaling perhaps a bit faster than necessary. The bike's tires cut through puddles, sending up spray that soaked his legs, but he barely noticed. His mind raced faster than his legs, replaying everything that had happened in the alley. The woman's terrified eyes. The flash of the knife. The sick feeling as he shoved the blade into the man's flesh. The blood that he wouldn't be able to remove completely until he tossed his blood-stained clothes out and jumped in a hot shower.

The ride back to Tilling's office passed in a blur. He barely registered the traffic, operating on pure muscle memory as his thoughts chased themselves in circles. By the time he reached the familiar glass and stone facade of Tilling's building, his legs were burning and his lungs felt like they might explode.

Barry looked up from a book of sudoku puzzles as Thomas entered. "Blimey, lad. You look like you've been through the wars."

"I fell off my bike," Thomas said, the lie automatically coming easily now. "The weather's terrible."

"Well, this is Manchester," he replied. "Comes with the territory, I suppose. Are you hurt?"

"No. Just my pride." Thomas shook his bag. "I just need to drop these papers off with Mr. Tilling." Thomas managed a weak smile before glancing down at his watch. "Barely gonna make it back in time for my bonus" Grinning, he started walking backward. "Gotta go."

"Alright then, maybe take it easier on the way home, yeah?"

"Yeah," Thomas agreed, turning to hurry for the lifts.

Miranda looked up at him when he approached. She immediately started to rise, mouth opening to speak, but he waved her off.

"I'm fine," he said before she could ask. "Just a fall. Nothing serious. Mr. Tilling is expecting me."

"He is," she agreed, returning to her seat. "Go on up."

"Thank you."

Thomas could feel her worried expression follow him all the way to the lift. He rode it up in tense silence, checking the time again. He had less than a minute to get the documents back to Tilling and earn his bonus. He knew the man well enough to know he wouldn't give him any leeway.

He ran from the lift the moment the doors parted, sprinting down the hallway to Tilling's door. He knocked once before entering, not waiting for a response.

Tilling was still at his desk, exactly as Thomas had left him. He barely glanced up as Thomas placed the signed envelope in front of him.

"Ah, excellent. Just under the wire too, I see." He

reached into his drawer and withdrew a smaller envelope. "Your bonus, as promised." Tilling finally looked him over thoroughly as he held out the envelope, his eyes widening slightly behind his glasses. "Good lord, what happened to you?"

"Fell off my bike," Thomas said for what felt like the hundredth time. "Thank you, sir." He accepted the envelope, pocketing it without checking the contents. "Will there be anything else?

"No, that's all for tonight."

Thomas was out the door before Tilling could ask any more questions. Taking the stairs rather than waiting for the lift, he returned to his bike, exhaling a built up huff of stress as he got on his bike and slowly pedaled off.

His flat was only fifteen minutes away by bike, but it felt like it might as well be on the moon. Not only was he exhausted, every shadow held potential threats, every passing police car with a siren on made him cringe.

When he reached his building, the familiar smell of curry from the Indian restaurant next door wafted up the stairwell as he climbed to his third-floor flat. Usually that mouth-watering aroma made his stomach grumble with hunger, but tonight, his stomach turned at the very thought of food.

His hands shook so badly he could barely get his key in the lock. Inside, he dropped his bag by the door, kicked his boots off and draped the sweatshirt he'd turned inside-out over the radiator before collapsing on his sofa. He didn't worry about the rest of his dirty, wet clothes damaging the threadbare hunk of junk. He just wanted to rest a few minutes before stripping and getting into a hot shower. As hot as his shower would get, anyway.

The events of the night played on repeat in his mind like a horror film he couldn't turn off until his phone buzzed in his pocket. Probably another delivery request. It wasn't as if his mother would ever call him, and he had no other family or friends either here or in the States. Of course, he'd had friends once. The wrong kind. The kind he had left America to get away from.

He ignored the call, staring instead at his hands. They looked normal enough, if a bit scraped up from the punches he had thrown. The same hands he used to carry packages and fix his bike chain. The same hands that had just ended a man's life.

He was sure he should have felt guilty—should have felt something—but he was numb. Perhaps he was destined to be a heartless killer no matter how hard he tried to be one of the good guys.

Somehow that made it all seem worse.

Another police siren wailed in the distance and Thomas tensed. He waited for the sound to draw closer, but it faded away, leaving him alone with his thoughts in the darkened flat.

He was free and clear. No one had connected him to the incident. He should have felt relieved.

Instead, he waited for the other shoe to drop.

CHAPTER 4

By the next morning, the drip of water from Thomas' rain-soaked pants had soaked his socks. From there, it had formed a dark puddle on the hardwood floor, spreading outward from his sofa like a stain similar to the one on his conscience.

His boots lay where he'd kicked them off, leaving dirty streaks across the floor. The wet sweatshirt he'd draped over the radiator had left an odor of ozone in the air, mixed with the unmistakable smell of dried blood and Manchester's perpetually stale dampness.

He hadn't moved since collapsing onto the sofa the night before, his mind replaying the events in the alley like a broken film reel. The woman's terrified eyes. The flash of the knife. The sickening resistance as he forced the blade through the man's skin and into his flesh. The weight of his attacker as he slumped sideways across him, his eyes going blank as he died. It had gone on, his thoughts blending together into one steady stream of mental self-flagellation until, at some point, exhaustion had won out over anxiety and he'd drifted into a fitful sleep.

A sharp knock at the door finally jolted him from the

last vestiges of that sleep, even the watery morning light filtering through the threadbare curtains seeming too bright to his newly opened eyes. He blinked, focusing on the shadows that had spread across the floor to the peeling wallpaper. His attention finally landed on the water-stained ceiling. As he sat up, his throat screamed in protest, the bruised skin and tissue having turned into a stiff collar of pain. The next thing he was physically aware of was how stiff and uncomfortable his dry, sweat and dirt-stained clothing felt against his skin.

More knocks sounded, more insistent this time.

"Just a minute," he called out, his voice raw and scratchy. Each word felt like regurgitating broken glass.

His muscles protesting every movement, reminding him of each punch thrown and received the night before, Thomas pushed himself up from the sofa. Through the window, he could see it was still raining, a proper Manchester morning that perfectly matched his mood. The knock came a third time as he approached the door, giving him a start.

The peephole revealed two people—a man and woman—standing in the hallway, both in plain clothes but carrying themselves with unmistakable authority. The woman was short with close-cropped gray hair and reading glasses hanging from a chain around her neck, her weathered face suggesting decades of service. The man was tall and lean, his dark skin contrasting sharply with a crisp white shirt visible beneath his sport coat, his bearing parade-ground quality.

Thomas' heart began to race. He had spent enough time in trouble with the law to recognize them as detectives.

His gaze darted to the window leading to the fire escape. He could slip out, be three streets away before they realized he wasn't home. But then what? Besides, the fire escape creaked like a rusty hinge. They'd hear him for sure.

Plus, there was always the chance they had uniformed bobbies waiting at street level for him to take a powder.

He'd wanted to avoid police attention, but it was obvious that wasn't going to happen.

Taking a deep breath that did nothing to calm his nerves, Thomas opened the door, trying to project a calm he didn't feel. The bruises on his neck felt like they were glowing like a neon sign. "Can I help you?"

The woman smiled, but it didn't reach her eyes. Her gaze swept over him, taking in his rumpled appearance and the visible marks of violence. "Thomas Drake?"

He nodded, his throat suddenly dry.

"I'm Detective Inspector Rhodes," she said, showing her warrant card with practiced efficiency. "This is Detective Sergeant Patel. May we come in? We'd like to ask you a few questions."

Thomas stood frozen for a moment longer before stepping back, gesturing for them to enter. "Yeah. Sure. This is about last night, right?"

"It is," Rhodes replied as she and Patel entered.

His tiny flat suddenly felt even smaller with the two detectives inside. They took in the sparse furnishings—the ratty sofa and the two milk crates serving as a coffee table and the unpaid bills on it, and the bicycle parts scattered in one corner like mechanical confetti.

"Sorry about the mess," he said automatically, closing the door. "I wasn't expecting company."

"Clearly," Rhodes replied dryly, eyeing the dirty boot prints on the floor.

"How did you find me?"

"The constable who encountered you outside 23 Chancery spoke with Mr. Harrison after you left. It seems he was quite concerned about your appearance last night. Then we contacted your employer, Quickr Couriers. They were very helpful in providing your address."

"Of course they were," Thomas muttered. He remained standing by the door, unconsciously positioning himself between the detectives and his escape route.

"Perhaps you'd like to sit down?" Rhodes suggested, though her tone made it clear it wasn't really a suggestion. She perched herself on the overstuffed arm of his second-hand chair, her casual pose at odds with her alert eyes.

"Right. Sure." Thomas plopped down on the sofa, the springs creaking in protest. The events of the previous night—the woman's muffled screams, the glint of steel in the darkness, the wet sound of the blade finding its mark—once again crashed over him. "There's no sense in lying," he decided aloud, the words hanging in the air thick as smoke. "I killed the man in the alley. I didn't mean to, but he was strangling me." He pulled down the collar of his shirt, revealing the dark bruises that wrapped around his throat like a macabre necklace. "I couldn't breathe. The knife was just...there. On the ground. I grabbed it without thinking. It was his knife; he dropped it after he stabbed the woman and we first started fighting."

"Start from the beginning," DS Patel said, pen poised over his notebook. "What brought you to that alley in the first place?"

Thomas leaned forward, elbows on his knees, clasping his hands. "I was making a delivery for Ashworth, Tilling & Associates. Legal documents that needed signing. I'd just locked up my bike when I heard..." He swallowed hard. "I heard a woman cry out. From the alley."

"And you decided to investigate?" Rhodes asked, her tone neutral.

"Yeah. Maybe I should have called the police first, but..." Thomas shrugged. "There wasn't time. He had the knife to her throat. Said he'd kill her if she made a sound."

"And why didn't you say anything to the officer who questioned you last night?" Patel asked.

Thomas laughed bitterly, the sound rough in his bruised throat. "I had a nice bonus riding on getting those papers back to Mr. Tilling within the hour. A hundred quid." He pointed to the open envelope on top of his stack of mail. "It might not sound like much to you, but..." He gestured around the shabby flat. "...it is to me. Besides that..." He trailed off, his past like a sudden invisible noose around his already bruised neck.

"Besides what?" Rhodes prompted.

"I have a record. In the States. I came to the UK for a clean slate, and the last thing I wanted was to get in any trouble here." The words came out in a rush, like ripping off a bandage.

The detectives exchanged a look that spoke volumes. "Tell us about your record," Rhodes said, her voice carefully neutral.

"I don't know. I feel like maybe I should ask for legal counsel right now."

"That's certainly within your rights, Mr. Drake," Rhodes said.

"I mean, my record's not really relevant to this, is it?"

"You were the one who brought it up," Patel reminded him. "We wouldn't know anything about it otherwise."

Thomas shifted his position, dropping his head into his hands, scrubbing his face before lifting his head again. "I guess it doesn't matter." He sighed out some of his tension. "My father was American," he began, each word feeling like gravel in his throat. "He was in the Air Force, stationed at RAF Menwith Hill. He met and married my mother here in Manchester, and she went back to the States with him when he transferred home. I was born there, in New York. I have dual citizenship. Anyway, my father died in a car wreck not long after I was born." He swallowed hard, once again feeling the familiar regret over losing a father he never had a chance to know. "Mom...she ended up in a downward spiral. Got into drugs, lost her job, and turned to the streets to get by. My aunt took care of me for as long as she could, but by the time I was seven, I was basically raising myself. At thirteen, I fell in with a local gang. At the time, I thought they would be the family I never really had."

Thomas pulled his collar aside again, this time revealing a small tattoo just below his collarbone–a simple stylized sword, the lines crude and slightly blurred. "For initiation, they made me kill someone. They picked the target, I..." His voice cracked. "I cut his throat. Some kid from a rival gang. I didn't even know his name."

The silence that followed felt thick enough to cut. Rain drummed against the window, providing a somber backdrop to his confession.

"How long did you serve?" Patel asked finally.

"Five years in juvenile detention," Thomas replied. "It would have been longer if I'd been tried as an adult. I got lucky, I guess. If you can call any of it lucky."

Rhodes leaned forward slightly. "That's quite a story, Mr. Drake. It might help explain why you didn't come forward last night. But it doesn't paint a very reassuring picture regarding your involvement in another violent death."

The implications of her words hit Thomas like a physical blow. This was his past rising up to strangle his future, just like the hands around his throat the night before. Exactly what he'd feared.

"I'm not that person anymore," Thomas said. "The detention facility had this program with the local VA– veterans mentoring young offenders. That's where I met Vin." A ghost of a smile crossed his face despite the gravity of the situation. "Master Gunnery Sergeant Vincent Martinez, United States Marine Corps. Combat vet." Thomas shook his head, lost in the memory. "He saw past what I'd done, saw something in me that I'd never seen in myself. The first thing he ever said to me, before he even told me his name, was that I wasn't who circumstances told me to be. That I was destined to do great things and leave a positive mark on society." Tears welled at the memory. "Of course, I didn't believe him then, but in time, I started to buy into all of what I initially thought was his bullshit." He chuckled softly, remembering Vin.

"Tell us more about him," Rhodes prompted, her expression softening slightly.

Thomas stood and walked to the window, shoving his hands into his pockets to watch raindrops race down the glass. "He became the father I never had. Taught me discipline, self-defense, how to channel my anger into something productive. But more than that..." He turned back to face the detectives. "He taught me about consequences. About responsibility. About being the kind of man who stands up when others need help."

"Is that why you intervened last night?" Patel asked.

"Yeah." Thomas absently rubbed his bruised throat. "When I heard that woman scream...I couldn't just ignore it and walk away. I couldn't call you guys and leave her in danger while she waited for you."

"Where is Sergeant Martinez now?" Rhodes asked.

Thomas' jaw clenched, old pain flickering across his features. "He's dead. Lung cancer. From all the toxic shit he breathed in from burn pits during his deployments. He fought it hard, but..." He trailed off, swallowing the lump in his throat. "After he died, I just wanted to get away from the memories. Mainly, I wanted to get away from the gang who still thought I belonged to them. I thought Manchester would be far enough away to start fresh."

"Until last night," Patel observed, closing his notebook.

"Yeah. I wanted to do something good, you know? Help someone who needed it. Then when it all went sideways, I got scared, but I swear, I didn't do anything wrong. That bastard stabbed her before I could get to him, and then he tried to kill me." He lifted his head to make the bruises on his throat stand out. "I have visual proof of that."

"That someone choked you is undeniable," Rhodes agreed, getting to her feet. "And personally, I believe your story."

"But?" Thomas said.

"But I'd still like you to come down to the station."

"Why?"

The detectives exchanged a look before Patel spoke. "We have a bit of a problem, Mr. Drake."

"What kind of problem?"

"The woman you claim to have helped," Rhodes said carefully. "She's out of the hospital now. Her knife wound was superficial. Didn't hit anything vital, so all she needed was some stitches."

"That's good news, right?" Thomas asked, though his stomach was already knotting with dread.

"We showed her a photo of the man you claim attacked her," Patel explained. "She couldn't positively identify him."

A cold shiver ran through Thomas. It figured the woman couldn't remember who had attacked her. If she had, the conversation would be over. The detectives might chastise him for playing vigilante, but he would have still saved her life.

"He slammed her into the wall hard enough to knock her out," Thomas said. "She probably doesn't remember anything clearly."

"*Someone* slammed her head into the wall," Patel corrected.

"And you think it was me?"

"I didn't say that. I said we can't be completely sure it was the man we found dead of a stab wound in the alley."

"Which is precisely the problem," Rhodes said. "Without her ability to ID the perpetrator, we need a deeper investigation to be absolutely certain about what happened in that alley. You're part of that investigation."

"And a prime suspect, right? My prints are all over that knife."

"As are his," Patel countered. "We're not rushing to any judgments here, Mr. Drake. You're a person of interest right now, nothing more. The other man has a record of his own, and it suggests your version of events could be accurate, but we need to do this properly. If it happened as you say, we should be able to sort everything out before teatime."

Thomas sank back down onto the sofa, feeling the walls of his new life, as meager as it was, beginning to crumble. "Am I under arrest?"

"Not at this time," Rhodes replied. "We're hoping you'll come in voluntarily to help us clear this up."

Thomas looked around his small flat. It wasn't much, but at least he had earned it with honest, hard work. Work Vin would have been proud of.

"Since I'm not under arrest, can I meet you there in an hour?" he asked finally. "I need a shower, and..." He gestured at his rumpled clothes. "I want to look presentable."

The detectives shared another look before Rhodes nodded. "One hour, Mr. Drake. Don't make us come looking for you again."

"I won't," Thomas promised. "I didn't do anything wrong. I have nothing to hide."

"If that's true, you also have nothing to worry about."

"Here's my card," Patel said, placing it on the milk crate. "The address is on there. Ask for either of us at the front desk."

"We'll see you soon," Rhodes added.

Thomas nodded, walking them to the door. As it closed behind them, he leaned his forehead against it, letting out a shaky breath. His hands trembled as he looked at them.

The clock on his microwave blinked 8:47. One hour. Sixty minutes to decide whether to trust the system or run. Sixty minutes to choose between standing up for his decision to help the woman, come what may, or abandon everything he'd built here.

He walked back over to the window and watched the detectives getting into an unmarked car. They weren't posting anyone to watch him, at least not anyone obvious. They were giving him enough rope to hang himself, trusting him to make the right choice.

He straightened and exhaled sharply. Squaring his shoulders, his decision made, he moved more confidently through his flat as he headed for the bathroom.

He knew exactly what he had to do.

CHAPTER 5

The Greater Manchester City Centre Police Station loomed like a sentinel on the edge of the bustling city core, its exterior a blend of modern practicality and subtle nods to the brutalist architecture of the past. Large, rectangular windows punctuated the facade, each encased in dark metal frames that contrasted sharply with the light concrete exterior. The building's walls were smoothed and weathered, their uniform gray softened only by the occasional streaks of rain that, over the years, had etched faint lines down the surface.

A bold blue sign emblazoned with the insignia of Greater Manchester Police hung above the main entrance, its color standing out against the otherwise muted tones of the structure. Below, a set of automatic glass doors opened and closed with mechanical precision, swallowing officers, detectives, and the occasional subdued suspect into the depths of the station. Outside, sturdy concrete planters lined the walkway, filled with hardy shrubs impervious to the city's rain-soaked winters and indifferent to its rare, sunny spells.

Fifty-eight minutes after detectives Rhodes and Patel

had left his flat, Thomas stood in front of the imposing building, his boots planted on rain-slicked concrete. Rain pattered against his clean but threadbare hoodie, rolling off the fabric in steady rivulets.

He had lingered in the shower, hoping the warm water would calm his frayed nerves and allay his fears about a suddenly uncertain future. He wished he'd had something more sedate to wear to the station than another one of the black hoodie/cargo pants combos that made up his entire wardrobe. Money was just too tight to waste on a variety of colors when practicality would do. The bruises around his throat felt even more tender, throbbing in time with his pulse. He caught himself touching them nervously and forced his hand back down to his side.

He left his bike standing upright in one of the racks near the building, the locking cable wrapped around the frame and the rack but not fully clasped, just in case. He couldn't really see a scenario where he would actually try to run from a police station—that would be insane, right?—but old habits died hard. Back in New York as an adolescent, using a similar tactic, he'd made plenty of quick getaways after shoplifting.

"Well," he muttered to himself, rolling his shoulders to release some tension. "Here goes nothing."

The automatic doors slid open with a soft hiss as he approached, warm air washing over him as he stepped into the lobby. It smelled of industrial cleaner and wet clothes, dozens of damp people tracking rainwater across the scuffed old linoleum floors. A steady stream of humanity—officers escorting handcuffed suspects, civilians reporting crimes, lawyers in expensive suits clutching briefcases like shields—moved through the space or sat in the waiting area.

A long, steel-framed reception desk dominated a cubicle of thick reinforced glass on the back wall of the lobby, a round speaker set into the center-front of the glass. An unsmiling male receptionist sat at the desk. Off to his left, a row of computer monitors also occupied the cubicle, flickering with scenes from around the station.

The waiting area—three rows of five uncomfortable-looking plastic chairs—sat off to the right of the cubicle, their garish orange color at odds with the somber atmosphere. Only a few people waited to be called through a metal detector fronting the adjacent hallway to see whomever they had come to see. Beside the waiting area were two standing-room-only holding cells, an obvious drunk sat on the bench inside one of them, passed out against the bars. Long, oily gray hair fell over his eyes, and drool strung from his open mouth down the front of his soiled pea coat.

Thomas walked up the speaker in the glass-enclosed cubicle. "Excuse me," he said to the receptionist. The words came out raspy, his throat still raw from the previous night's violence. "I'm here to see Detectives Rhodes or Patel."

He looked up from his computer, eyes narrowing slightly as he took in Thomas' appearance. "Name?"

"Thomas Drake. They're expecting me."

"Are they now?" He reached for his phone, but before he could make the call, Detective Rhodes emerged from a side door, reading glasses perched on her nose instead of hanging from the attached chain.

"Mr. Drake," she said, meeting his eyes over the top of her glasses. "I came out to see if you had arrived. Fifty-eight minutes. I appreciate your punctuality."

"Like I said earlier, I have nothing to hide."

"No need to strain your voice," Rhodes said, her tone gentler than before. "Those bruises look even worse in this light. Have you had them looked at?"

Thomas shook his head. "I'll be fine."

"Stubborn lad, aren't you?" She gestured toward the security checkpoint. "This way, please. We'll try to make this quick."

Thomas' skin prickled with apprehension as he followed her through the metal detector and down the corridor. He had expected to be taken to an interview room, maybe shown some photos or asked to give a formal statement. Instead, Rhodes stopped at a door marked 'Line-up Room A'.

"Hang on," Thomas said, taking a step back and pointing to the worrisome sign. "What's this about?"

Rhodes turned to face him, her expression carefully neutral. "I told you earlier, the victim couldn't positively identify her attacker. But she is feeling well enough to view a line-up."

"But that makes no sense." Thomas' voice cracked. "She never saw me. I came up behind her attacker. She was unconscious before—"

"Mr. Drake," Rhodes cut him off, "if your story is true, then this should be a mere formality. Unless there's something you haven't told us?"

"No, but—"

"Then you have nothing to worry about, do you?"

"Look, I know how this works. You're trying to trip me up, catch me in a lie. But I'm telling you the truth. That woman was attacked. I tried to help her. The guy had a knife—"

"And now he's dead," Rhodes finished for him. "And we need to be absolutely certain about what happened in that alley. This is the quickest way to clear everything up. When she says she doesn't recognize anyone in the lineup, you'll be out of this pickle." She pushed open the door. "After you."

Inside, five other young men stood in a loose group, all

roughly Thomas' height and build, all wearing dark hoodies and cargo pants. They turned to look at him as he entered, their expressions a mix of boredom and resignation. Thomas recognized the look. They were probably regulars, paid to stand in line-ups, chosen specifically to match his description.

He had a sickening feeling he was being set up.

"Number three position, please," Rhodes instructed, gesturing to a numbered mark on the floor. "Detective Patel will give further instructions through the speaker."

"This isn't right," Thomas said, but he moved to the marked spot anyway. "She was traumatized, knocked unconscious. Even if she did see something, her memory can't be considered reliable in a court of law."

"Are you a barrister now?" Rhodes asked, one eyebrow raised.

"No! I'm just saying she's likely confused. She—"

"Just do what you're told." With that, she turned and left him standing there.

"Face forward," a voice crackled through the ceiling speaker. "Everyone remain still and quiet."

Thomas stared at his reflection in the two-way mirror, trying not to fidget. The bruises on his neck stood out starkly under the harsh fluorescent lights, an angry purple collar mocking his claims of innocence. Would the woman be able to see them? Would that influence her choice? He should have worn a turtleneck or something to cover them up.

"Stop touching your neck," the voice commanded, making Thomas realize he'd been rubbing his throat again. He forced his hand down, clenching his fists at his sides and facing forward as directed.

Sweat beaded on his forehead despite the room's chill. He tried to breathe slowly, to project calm, but his heart wouldn't stop racing. Innocent people didn't panic during line-ups. Then again, innocent people didn't usually have juvenile murder convictions in their past either.

Minutes crawled by like hours. His legs began to cramp. An itch developed between his shoulder blades, maddening in its persistence. The fluorescent lights buzzed overhead, the sound drilling into his skull until he wanted to scream just to break the tension.

"Turn to your right," the voice instructed.

Thomas complied, along with the other five men. From this angle, he could see their reflections more clearly in the mirror. They really did look remarkably similar to him—same build, same style of clothes, even similar haircuts.

"Turn to your left."

Another synchronized movement. Thomas' mouth had gone dry. He could feel unseen eyes studying him from behind the mirror, weighing and measuring every detail of his appearance.

"Face forward."

More endless minutes ticked by. Thomas found himself counting his heartbeats, trying to focus on anything besides the growing certainty that something was very wrong. This felt less like clearing his name and more like a trap slowly closing around him.

Finally, the door opened. Thomas' heart leaped into his throat as Patel entered instead of Rhodes. The detective's expression was grave, and Thomas' blood ran cold when he saw the cuffs in his left hand.

"No," Thomas said, stepping back. "No way. She couldn't have picked me. She never saw me!"

"I'm sorry, Mr. Drake," Patel said. "But she made a positive identification. You're under arrest for assault and murder."

"This is insane!" Thomas' voice cracked with desperation. "I was trying to help her! The real attacker is dead. Check his prints, check his record!"

"We did," Patel replied, moving to stand in front of him. "His name was James Morrow. Long history of violence, including several sexual assaults. But then, you probably already knew who he was. What really happened in that alley, Mr. Drake? Did he renege on his promises to you? Did you want the victim all to yourself?"

"What?" Thomas cried. "I didn't know him! I was just making a delivery. I heard her scream—"

"Turn around, please," Patel interrupted as the others began to file out. "Hands behind your back."

Thomas' gaze darted past Patel to the door. He wasn't a large man. One good shove and—

"Don't," Patel warned, reading his expression. "You'll only make things worse for yourself."

"They can't get much worse," Thomas replied.

Then he moved.

He drove his shoulder into Patel's chest, sending him stumbling backward. Thomas followed through, running for the door and yanking it open. Behind him, Patel yelled for him to stop. Ignoring him, he burst into the hallway, nearly colliding with a uniformed officer carrying a stack of papers. Startled, the man jumped back.

"Stop him!" Patel shouted from behind.

Thomas didn't slow down as he burst into the lobby, both Patel and the officer in hot pursuit. He rounded a corner, his boots squealing on the linoleum as he changed direction and headed for a glass door he hadn't noticed on his way in. It looked to lead out to a parking lot.

An officer was just opening it, leading a handcuffed teenager through. Thomas put on a burst of speed. "Out of the way!" he yelled.

The officer's eyes widened as he pulled his charge aside. Thomas barreled past them and out into the rain. Behind him, he could hear shouting and the thunder of pursuing footsteps.

Thomas startled several civilians walking down the sidewalk as he raced around the corner of the building and sprinted for his bike. The wet seat gleaming in the gray daylight, he leaped onto it in one fluid motion. Muscle memory taking over, he kicked off and pedaled hard into traffic, his locking cable landing with a splash in a curbside puddle. A horn blared as he cut across two lanes, but he ignored it, focused only on putting distance between himself and the station.

"Stop! Police!" a bobby shouted behind him.

Thomas glanced back to see three officers running around the building after him, but quickly falling behind as he picked up speed. They would have other officers already running to their cars, pursuing him within moments.

He needed to disappear. Fast.

His experience as a courier kicked in, muscle memory and intimate knowledge of Manchester's streets taking over. The first rule of urban cycling: the shortest distance between two points wasn't always a straight line.

Sirens approached as he cut down a narrow walkway between two brick buildings. Barely wide enough for his handlebars, the alley opened onto a residential street he knew well. Hanging a sharp right, his back wheel nearly skidded out from under him. He immediately turned left into another passageway between buildings just as a police car screamed past the entrance. Its siren faded away as Thomas emerged onto the adjoining street. He needed to get somewhere with heavy foot traffic, somewhere he could get away from the cop cars after him and lose himself in a crowd.

Rain pelted his face as he wove through traffic, cutting between cars and ignoring angry honks. His legs burned from the effort, but adrenaline kept him pushing hard. Another siren wailed behind him, closer this time.

"Think," he muttered, scanning the street signs. "Think!"

He couldn't go back to his flat. They'd be watching it. Couldn't contact his employer. Couldn't access his bank account. He had a hundred twenty quid in his pocket, the clothes on his back, and no idea what to do next.

Manchester's Piccadilly Station lay just ahead. Trains meant crowds, multiple exits, potential escape routes. They'd watch the transport hubs, but not yet. Besides, he didn't have a choice.

A police car appeared at the intersection ahead, lights flashing. Thomas swerved onto the sidewalk, pedestrians scattering ahead of him. "Sorry!" he called out, genuine regret in his voice as an elderly woman dropped her shopping bag and fell against the building behind her as he blasted by.

He cut through a small plaza, tires slipping on wet stone. Another police car, visible between two buildings, zoomed past on the parallel street, traveling in the same direction he was. They were trying to box him in. If he could just get to the station; it was his only shot.

Thomas burst out onto London Road, into a sea of umbrellas and rushing commuters. The station's entrance beckoned a hundred yards ahead. Two police cars converged from different directions, sirens howling as they raced toward him.

He abandoned his bike mid-street, letting it clatter to the pavement as he sprinted for the station entrance. Behind him, he heard the screech of tires as the police cars stopped, doors opening, voices shouting for him to freeze.

The station was packed with travelers, a blessing in disguise. Thomas shouldered his way through the crowd, ignoring protests and dirty looks. His eyes desperately scanned departure boards. He needed a train leaving immediately.

"Platform 4 for the 10:47 service to Holyhead, calling at

Crewe, Chester, Llandudno Junction, and Bangor," echoed over the PA system.

Wales. Perfect. Different jurisdiction, different police force. Hell, it was a different country!

Thomas spotted the ticket machine, quickly purchasing a single one-way to Bangor. The machine felt like it took forever to process his payment, each second an eternity as he glanced over his shoulder, expecting to see police flooding into the station.

Ticket finally in hand, he hurried through the turnstile, taking the stairs to Platform 4 two at a time. The train stood ready, doors open, a few final passengers boarding. Through the windows of the station's glass roof, he could see the rain coming down harder, obscuring visibility. Another stroke of luck.

He jumped aboard just as the doors began their warning beep. Finding an empty seat in the rear carriage, he slumped down, trying to control his breathing. Through the window, he watched as two police officers entered the platform, scanning the crowds. They were too late. The doors closed with a soft hiss, and the train began to move.

Thomas' heart hammered as they pulled away from the platform. Through the rain-streaked windows, he could see more police cars arriving outside the station, lights flashing, but none of them could get to him now.

He slid lower in his seat, trying to make himself invisible as Manchester's familiar streets gave way to suburbs. His throat ached, his legs trembled from the escape effort, and his clothes were soaked through with rain and sweat. But he was alive. And free.

For now.

That didn't keep the reality of his situation from sinking in. He had just assaulted a police officer and fled custody. Even if he could somehow prove his innocence in the alley incident, he would still be in serious trouble. His chance at a normal life, the fresh start he'd worked so hard for, had evaporated like morning mist.

A woman sat down across the aisle, giving him a curious look. Thomas realized he must look a mess—soaking wet, breathing hard, probably wild-eyed with panic. He forced himself to sit up straighter, to appear casual, though his mind remained in a panic.

The train rolled on through the rain, carrying him away from everything he'd built in Manchester. But toward what? He had no plan, no resources, no allies. He was alone, just like always.

Well, not exactly like always. This time, he was a fugitive with the entire Greater Manchester Police force looking for him. And somewhere out there, a traumatized woman truly believed he was the one who had attacked her.

Thomas leaned his head against the cool window, watching raindrops race down the glass. What the hell was he going to do now?

CHAPTER 6

The train lurched to a stop at Bangor Station, the brakes squealing against wet rails. Thomas kept his seat while other passengers gathered their belongings and filed toward the exits, his hands clenched in his lap to stop their trembling. Through the rain-streaked window, he watched a mother help her young daughter button up a bright yellow raincoat, the child's excited chatter about visiting her grandmother carrying clearly through the carriage.

Normal people living normal lives.

Just yesterday, that had been him. Now he was a fugitive, running from both a murder charge and the consequences of assaulting a police officer. His throat ached where the dead man's fingers had bruised it, a constant reminder of how quickly everything had gone to shit.

The train car emptied until Thomas was alone. He stood slowly, moving to the window to scan the platform. No sign of police. Hopefully, word of his escape had yet to pass to neighboring areas.

"Ending service to Holyhead," the conductor called out. "All passengers must disembark."

Thomas pulled his hood lower and stepped onto the

platform. The storm that had chased him from Manchester had followed the train to Wales, the rain somehow feeling even colder here. Trying to look like just another commuter, he hunched his shoulders against the cold as he joined the flow of passengers heading for the station exit.

He had no plan. The decision to flee had been pure instinct, fight-or-flight response taking over when he saw those handcuffs in Detective Patel's hands. But now what? He couldn't go home. Couldn't contact anyone he knew. Couldn't use his bank cards or phone without leaving a trail. In fact, he needed to ditch his phone. Even turned off as he had it now, he was sure they had ways to track him through it.

His stomach growled, reminding him that he hadn't eaten since...when? Yesterday morning? Before everything went to hell.

A Tesco Express caught his eye as he exited the station, its fluorescent lights harsh against the gray day. He patted his pocket, feeling the remains of his cash. Even with the bonus from Mr. Tilling, it wasn't enough to last long, especially if he needed to keep moving.

"I'm sorry, Vin," he muttered, thinking of his mentor as he pushed through the shop's automatic doors. The old Marine had taught him better than this. But Vin had also taught him about survival, about doing what needed to be done when backed into a corner.

The shop was nearly empty, just a bored-looking cashier scrolling on her phone and an elderly man studying the ready-made sandwiches. Thomas pretended to browse the aisles while his heart tried to crawl up his throat. He'd sworn never to steal again after getting out of juvie. But desperate times...

He palmed two Kit Kat bars when the cashier wasn't looking, slipping them into his hoodie pocket. The chocolate would help with his blood sugar at least. His hand shook slightly as he grabbed a bottle of water from the cooler, which he paid for to avoid suspicion.

"Nasty weather," he said to the cashier as he handed over a few pounds, forcing a smile.

She barely glanced up from her phone. "Always is."

Outside, he ducked into a shallow doorway and unwrapped one of the candy bars, wolfing it down in three bites. The sugar hit his system like a shot of adrenaline, making him jittery. Or maybe that was just nerves. He was about to take a bite of the second bar when a police car cruised past, its blue light bar dark but still unmistakable.

Thomas turned his face away, though the officer didn't even look in his direction. Still, his heart didn't slow until the car disappeared around a corner. He couldn't stay here. Train stations would have cameras. They'd be able to track his journey, and Bangor wasn't big enough to hide in.

He needed somewhere quieter. Somewhere with fewer eyes.

A memory surfaced—a camping trip last summer, before the weather turned. He'd taken the bus to Llanberis and spent a weekend hiking around Snowdon. The little village had been peaceful, the kind of place where strangers were noticed but not necessarily questioned. More importantly, it was the kind of place where police presence was minimal.

The bus station wasn't far. Thomas kept to side streets, staying under shop awnings when possible to avoid the rain. Every passing car made him tense, every glimpse of blue sent his pulse racing. He found himself touching his throat constantly, feeling the tender bruises there. The dead man's final gift to him.

The woman's face flashed in his mind—her terror as the knife pressed against her throat, her unconscious form crumpling against the wall. How could she have identified him as her attacker? He'd never even seen her face clearly in the darkness. How could she have seen him? It made no sense.

Unless...unless she really believed it. Memory was funny that way, especially trauma. Maybe in her confused state, she'd merged her attacker with her rescuer. Or maybe she hadn't actually identified him at all, and the police were lying to pressure him into a confession.

Either way, he was properly screwed.

The bus station's worn concrete facade came into view, a relic of 1960s architectural optimism gone to hell. Thomas checked his watch. If the schedule hadn't changed since his camping trip, there should be a bus to Llanberis leaving in twenty minutes.

He was reaching for the door when movement inside caught his eye. Two police officers, a man and a woman, stood talking to the ticket agent.

Were they looking for him?

He couldn't risk it. He backed away from the door, looking frantically for options. A sign caught his eye: "Toilets→" Following the arrow, he found a separate entrance leading to the station's bathrooms. The smell of industrial cleaner, not altogether masking other worse things, greeted him as he pushed through the swinging door to the men's room. One of the fluorescent lights flickered and hummed, casting an eerie glow over the thankfully empty room. He took the opportunity to drop his phone on the grimy tiles and stomp twice on it to crack the screen, and then he buried it deep in the discarded paper towels almost filling the trash can.

Thomas hurried to lock himself in a stall, perching on the toilet lid with his feet up so they wouldn't be visible under the door. His breath sounded too loud in the enclosed space. Water dripped somewhere, each drop like a hammer blow to his nerves.

Minutes crawled by. He heard people come and go, the

door creaking on its hinges, paper towels pulled out of their dispensers, hand dryers roaring to life and then falling silent. His legs began to cramp from holding the same position.

Finally, he heard the announcement he'd been waiting for: "Service 85 to Llanberis now boarding at Bay 3."

Thomas cracked the stall door open, making sure the bathroom was empty. He moved to the main door and listened. No voices in the corridor. Opening the door a crack, he saw the police officers still at the ticket counter, but their backs were turned.

He slipped out of the bathroom, inching along the wall, his head down. The boarding area was through a side door, separate from the main waiting room. If he timed it right...he counted to three, then made his move. Quick steps took him to the side door. He eased it open just enough to squeeze through, then walked rapidly toward Bay 3, where passengers were already climbing aboard the bus.

"Ticket?" the driver asked as Thomas reached the steps.

Thomas fumbled in his pocket, producing the handful of notes he had left. "Can I buy one on board?"

The driver sighed the sigh of someone who dealt with this request far too often. "Five quid to Llanberis."

Thomas handed over the money, painfully aware of how little he had left. The driver printed a ticket and handed it over without looking up.

Thomas moved quickly to the back of the bus, taking a seat behind a large man whose bulk would help shield him from view. Through the windows, he could see the police officers emerging from the station. His heart nearly stopped as the female officer looked toward the bus, but her gaze passed over it without interest.

The doors hissed shut, and the engine rumbled to life.

Thomas didn't relax until they pulled out of the station, leaving the police behind.

The bus wound through Bangor's narrow streets before hitting the A4244 toward Llanberis. He had no idea what he was going to do when they reached his destination. Find somewhere dry to sleep, he supposed. Figure out his next move. Try to prove his innocence somehow, though he had no idea how to even begin.

But for now, he was moving. And movement meant survival.

As rain streaked the windows, turning the Welsh countryside into an impressionist painting of greens and grays, Thomas pressed his forehead against the cool glass. Exhaustion suddenly hit him like a sucker punch.

The bus curved around a bend, revealing the mountains ahead. Even through the rain, they looked massive and ancient, indifferent to the troubles of the small humans at their feet. Thomas watched them draw closer, remembering what Vin used to say about mountains—that they were good places to find perspective, to remember how small our problems really are in the grand scheme of things. Somehow, he doubted even these mountains could make his current problems feel small.

The adrenaline that had carried him through the morning began to fade, leaving him feeling shaky and weak. The sugar from the stolen Mars bars sat like lead in his stomach, shame mixing with fear and exhaustion into a toxic cocktail.

He thought of the woman in the alley again. Was she okay? Besides the physical trauma, what kind of psychological damage had the attack left her with? He had tried to help, had killed a man to save her, and now she thought he was the monster. The irony might have been funny if it hadn't ruined his life so quickly and completely.

A road sign flashed past: *Llanberis 5 km*

Thomas pulled his hood lower and tried to make himself smaller in his seat. Five kilometers to relative safety and meager survival. At least he would have time to relax enough to truly figure out what to do next.

The mountains watched impassively as the bus carried him deeper into their shadow. Somewhere up there, he hoped, answers waited. Or at least a place to hide while he looked for them.

He touched his bruised throat again, feeling the tender flesh beneath his fingers. It was a reminder that sometimes doing the right thing comes with a cost.

He just hadn't expected the cost to be quite so high.

CHAPTER 7

The bus wheezed to a stop in Llanberis, its air brakes cutting through the steady patter of rain. Thomas remained in his seat as other passengers filed past, watching through rain-streaked windows as they dispersed into the wet afternoon. The village—a smear of slate-roofed buildings pressed against the mountainside, their gray stone somehow both grim and welcoming against the backdrop of Snowdonia's peaks—hadn't changed much since his camping trip. Clouds clung to the summits like cotton, obscuring the highest points in a perpetual veil.

The driver's reflection appeared in the window beside him. "End of the line, mate."

Thomas stood, keeping his head down as he slipped past the driver and descended the bus steps. The rain had lightened to a fine mist, but the wind cut through his damp clothes like a knife, finding every seam and gap. His stomach growled, reminding him that two stolen Kit Kats weren't much of a meal. He needed real food, proper gear if he was going to survive out here. But his remaining cash wouldn't cover even basic supplies.

"Sorry, Vin," he muttered, shoving his hands in his

pockets as he walked. "I know you taught me better." The ghost of his mentor's disapproval lingered in his thoughts, adding to the increasing burden on his conscience. He'd sworn to both Vin and himself he would never go back to the life that had landed him in juvie, and here he was, unexpectedly forced back into survival mode. Into a downward spiral that would only lead to a bad end. The only question was how long it might take.

The village main street stretched before him, lined with outdoor shops catering to the hikers and climbers who used Llanberis as a base for exploring Snowdonia. In better times, he'd spent hours browsing their shelves, dreaming of proper expeditions when he could afford better gear. Now those same shops represented both temptation and danger.

Joe Brown's was closest, its windows displaying bright North Face jackets and gleaming camping stoves. Thomas' hands trembled slightly as he pushed open the door, a bell chiming overhead. The shop was warm and dry, smelling of new fabrics. Behind the counter, a man in his sixties with weathered features and calloused hands—Dylan, if he remembered correctly from his last time here—was adjusting a display of climbing harnesses, his movements suggesting years of practical experience with the gear he sold.

Thomas pretended to browse, working his way deeper into the store while keeping track of the clerk's position. The layout was typical of outdoor shops—clothing near the front, hardware toward the back, accessories filling the middle aisles. Turning his body to block the security camera's view, he slipped a lightweight black shell jacket off its hanger and into his hoodie. His heart pounding, he added several protein bars from a display in one of the aisles, then a Swiss Army knife from another.

"Need any help there, lad?" the clerk called out, his

Welsh accent thick and friendly. "You look like you could use some dry gear."

"Just browsing right now, Dylan," Thomas replied, his voice steady despite his racing pulse.

"Take yer time, then. Since ye know my name, I'm sure ye've been in before?"

"About a year ago," Thomas answered. "I bought some granola." He made a show of checking price tags. "Prices have gone up, I see."

"Aye, though ye won't find any better deals in town. Go on and check on the competition first if it makes ye happy. Ye'll be back."

Thomas smiled at him. "I'm afraid I'll have to take you up on that offer. I'm nearly skint as it is."

"Like I said, ye'll be back," Dylan answered, matching his grin. It was obvious he had no idea Thomas had nicked some gear from the shop's merch.

Thomas pushed through the door, bell chiming his exit. He walked casually until he was out of sight of the shop's windows, then ducked into an alley between two buildings. Hunkering down between two dumpsters, he pulled the stolen items from his hoodie and stuffed them into the yellow one on his right, carefully noting its location in the long line of multi-colored bins. Water dripped from a rusted gutter overhead, the steady plink-plink-plink matching his elevated heartbeat. One shop down, two more to go.

Cotswold Outdoor was busier, which worked in his favor. Thomas drifted through the aisles while two clerks helped a group of obvious tourists choose waterproof trousers. When he was confident no one was looking, he slid a lightweight sleeping bag under his hoodie and wrapped it around his torso, his hoodie large enough to conceal his sudden weight gain. In the next aisle, he palmed more protein bars, making quick use of his cargo pockets.

He also grabbed a pack of beef jerky and some trail mix, focusing on foods that wouldn't spoil and required no preparation. His technique was rusty—before today he hadn't stolen anything since his gang days—but necessity was proving to be an effective refresher course.

The third shop, a small independent outfitter, yielded some additional dried fruit and nuts, along with a large backpack that would hold everything he'd gathered. The shop smelled of leather and wax, reminding him of better days spent preparing for legitimate adventures. Now he was preparing for something else entirely.

His survival as a fugitive.

He retrieved the rest of his stolen goods from the dumpster, again hiding from view between the bins to carefully arrange everything in the pack.

The campsite where he had stayed during his last trip lay just outside of town, a sprawling collection of tents and caravans nestled against the mountain's lower slopes. Thomas walked its perimeter slowly, reminding himself of the layout and the locations of the shower blocks and storage areas. Most of the campers were out for the day, hiking or sightseeing, leaving their gear relatively unprotected.

He waited until a large family arguing over lunch plans distracted the site manager before slipping between the tents. His eyes darted from campsite to campsite, looking for easy targets. Success here would mean avoiding the need to enter any more shops, reducing his risk of being caught on camera or perhaps even recognized from news reports.

A folding chair sitting unattended provided cover while he worked, making it look like he belonged at that particular pitch. He moved efficiently between sites, years of courier work making him silent and quick on his feet despite his heavy boots. From one tent's vestibule, he liberated several packages of dried noodles and a tin of biscuits. Another yielded some cereal bars and dried fruit. He focused on items that wouldn't be immediately missed, taking one or two things from multiple sites rather than clearing out any single campsite.

The rain picked up again as he worked, driving most of the remaining campers into their tents or the site's small shop. Thomas used the weather as cover, moving more boldly now. His new pack slowly filled with his shoplifted supplies, until he had enough food to last a couple of weeks if he rationed it, along with a pair of full water bottles he could replenish from the surrounding lakes.

A row of bicycles leaned against a rack outside the visitor center, most secured with flimsy combination cable locks. Thomas selected an older mountain bike with an easier to pick padlock and chunky tires perfect for rough terrain. The frame was scratched but solid, the components well-maintained despite their age. He was glad now he'd thought to nick a pair of paper clips off the checkout counter at Joe Brown's. Bending them into two distinct shapes, he slid them into the lock. Holding one in place and twisting the other, it took only seconds to pick the lock, the skill's muscle memory returning as though he'd done it yesterday instead of six years ago.

Casting one last glance around to be sure he wasn't seen, Thomas mounted the bike and pedaled quickly away, cutting through town and setting out along A4086. He knew there was a larger, more remote campground about ten klicks down the road, where he could hopefully avoid attention and have access to additional necessities while he figured out his next move.

In the back of his mind, he could hear Vin telling him to turn himself in and give the process a chance to work. If he was innocent, they would figure it out eventually and he would be released.

He clamped down on that thought. Even if he could somehow shake the murder charge, he'd still assaulted a police officer and escaped custody. He should never have done it, but it was too late for second thoughts now.

He was so lost in his mental argument with the ghost of his mentor that he lost track of time and distance, and didn't notice the police car easing up behind him until its siren chirped. The sharp, electronic whoop echoed off the mountain, announcing his crimes to the wilderness.

The sound nearly caused him to lose control. He looked over his shoulder at the car. A hundred meters back, a second police car approached, its distinctive fluorescent yellow and blue checkerboard pattern unmistakable even through the rain. His hands tightened on the handlebars as he forced himself to remain calm, to think rationally.

They might not be after him. Local police couldn't have received word about a fugitive from Manchester. Not yet anyway.

The car's blue lights flashed once, and an officer's hand emerged from the passenger window, clearly gesturing for him to pull over.

Thomas cursed under his breath as he scanned his surroundings. A visitor center loomed ahead. More importantly, he could see a wooden sign pointing toward a hiking trail just beyond the building. A bright yellow warning notice was tacked beneath it, though he couldn't make out the words from this distance.

He forced himself to pedal casually toward the visitor center's parking lot, as if complying with the officer's signal. The police car followed, maintaining its distance. Through its rain-streaked windscreen, he could make out two officers inside, the driver speaking into his radio. That couldn't be good.

The visitor center's lot was nearly empty, just a few vehicles scattered across the wet tarmac. Thomas guided the bike between them, using their bulk to break the officers' line of sight. His pulse roared in his ears as he counted the seconds, timing his move.

Now.

He stood on the pedals and accelerated hard, cutting across the remaining space toward the trailhead, noticing the gate was closed. A small gap on the left side of it allowed just enough space for him to ride past, so long as he judged it perfectly. Otherwise, he'd catch his handlebars on the gate and tumble off into the valley below. It wouldn't do to end up with a broken leg. Or worse.

Behind him, he heard car doors opening, voices shouting for him to stop. The bike's front tire threw up a rooster tail of water as he hit a puddle, soaking his already wet clothes.

The warning sign came into focus as he approached:

DANGER: MINER'S TRAIL CLOSED DUE TO LANDSLIP
NO PUBLIC ACCESS

Perfect. That explained why the car park was so empty.

He tightened his grip on the bike's handlebars as he swung around the stone marker ahead of the gate. The tires nearly skidded out from under him, but he got the bike under control just before the edge of disaster, slipping past the gate with barely an inch to spare. He didn't slow, racing off down the crushed slate trail, which was just wide enough for maintenance vehicles.

Or a police car.

Thomas looked over his shoulder. The two cars had stopped at the gate, the officer on the passenger side of the first one exiting the vehicle with a megaphone. "Police! Stop!"

Thomas ignored his order, pushing harder on the

pedals. The bike responded beautifully, its well-maintained drive train purring as he picked up speed.

The trail's surface changed abruptly from crushed slate to a rough mix of gravel, larger protruding stones, and mud. The bike's front wheel bounced over a stone and caught a rut, the handlebars nearly jerking the grips out of his hands. He managed to hang on and keep control, but the near fall forced him to slow.

"The trail is closed! It's not safe up there!"

Thomas smiled as he followed the meandering path, the officer's acoustically amplified voice slowly fading behind him. *Not safe* was exactly what he needed right now. Fortunately, years of courier work had built up his stamina. If necessary, he could maintain this pace for hours.

The trail curved, taking Thomas out of sight of the trailhead and the officers. He maintained his pace for another hundred yards before allowing himself to slow. Sweat ran down his back despite the chill, his thigh muscles were burning, and his clothes were soaked through from rain.

But he was alive. And free. For now.

He pedaled along the trail as it wound around to a small body of water, ancient ruins resting beside it. The sight was amazing, and he instantly regretted having never visited this part of Snowdonia as a tourist. There was nothing he could do about that now.

He finally slowed as he came to a fork in the trail. The split followed either side of another body of water, the two trails probably meeting up again on the other end. The left fork was posted with the same sign as the one at the trailhead, but curiously, he didn't see any evidence of a landslide.

"Damn it," he muttered in disbelief as the distinctive thump-thump of a helicopter's rotors echoed off the mountainside. They were taking this more seriously than he'd expected. He needed to find cover. Quickly.

THE STARSHIP IN THE STONE

Along the left fork, just a short distance away, what looked like an old boathouse sat beside the lake. Thomas pumped his legs as hard as he could, racing toward the cover it promised, the sound of rotors rapidly increasing in volume.

He reached the locked door to the building, skidding the bike to a stop in front of it. He was thankful to have practiced his lock picking skills earlier because they came in even more handy now. He opened the padlock in seconds, pulling the door open and dragging the bicycle inside.

As he closed the door, he got a split-second glimpse of the helicopter coming over the nearest ridge. His heart caught in his throat. He'd expected to see a police chopper. Instead, what he readily recognized as an Army Chinook came into view.

The military couldn't be coming for him, he decided as he slammed the door closed. That was impossible.

Wasn't it?

CHAPTER 8

Thomas opened the boathouse door a crack and pressed his eye to it. His heart raced as he watched the massive Chinook descend, its tandem rotors throwing up a maelstrom of debris and water. Despite the haze surrounding it, Thomas could make out the distinctive olive drab paint scheme, the forward fuselage gleaming wet in the scattered light. The chopper's presence felt completely wrong, like finding a lion stalking through downtown Manchester.

Thomas remained certain this had nothing to do with him. There was no way anyone would send military assets after a murder suspect.

But then, if not him, what the hell was going on here?

The helicopter landed a short distance away. Its rear ramp descended before the rotors had fully spun down, disgorging six troops in full tactical gear. They spread out in a classic search pattern, their weapons held at low ready. Their movements spoke of extensive training and recent combat experience—not the typical behavior for weekend warriors of the regular army.

"Damn it." Thomas slammed the door shut. Spotting the

deadbolt, he slammed it into its corresponding hole in the wooden frame. "Think. Think!" Once one of those soldiers put his shoulder to the door, he knew the old wood wouldn't hold the deadbolt for long.

The boathouse interior closed around him like a tomb, decades of damp having worked deep into the stone walls. Shafts of weak light filtered through small holes in the weathered mortar, creating strips of illumination that turned the disturbed dust into dancing motes.

He turned away from the door, searching for...what? A hiding place.

The boathouse was tiny and long abandoned. His gaze skimmed the shadowed corners near the roof, whipping back and forth as they cycled toward the floor. Layers of dust except where his fresh boot prints had disturbed it, rat droppings, and cobwebs covered the walls and floor surrounding the rectangular opening over the water. A few relics—a moth eaten canvas tarp shoved haphazardly into one corner, a bungee cord hanging from a rafter, a metal gas can missing most of its red paint—remained from a bygone era, but what caught his attention was something that didn't belong. Something new.

"What the hell?" Was that a steel hatch set into the floor? The modern hardware, free of not only dust but rust as well, despite the damp environment, existed in stark contrast to the decrepit structure surrounding it.

"Clear the perimeter!" an outside voice commanded from much too close to the door. Behind Thomas, the door rattled on its hinges. "Corporal, get your arse over here! I need your shoulder."

"Yes, sir!"

Hearing the approach of running footsteps, Thomas moved quickly to the hatch, his hope for escape plummeting when he saw the electronic access panel on the lid.

His shoulders fell. The knocks just kept coming. Still, he grabbed the handle and pulled, just on the off chance... He about swallowed his tongue in shock when the lid lifted easily on well-oiled hinges, revealing a modern shaft lined with sheet metal, a sturdy metal ladder descending into darkness.

Despite what the well maintained shaft might lead to, Thomas didn't look a gift horse in the mouth. He yanked the flashlight he'd stolen from his pack and sent the beam down the shaft. It descended farther than he could see. The air rising from below carried a hint of ozone and something else. A scent he couldn't identify but that made the hair on the back of his neck stand up.

Behind him, a body connected with the door, rattling it violently.

Thomas swung his legs into the opening, finding the top rung of the ladder with his boots. He began to descend—one hand on the ladder, the other pulling the hatch closed above him—just as the door burst open and a soldier virtually fell into the boathouse. Thomas went absolutely still and listened, the scuffle of boots as the soldier regained his feet.

"Clear!" his muffled voice called out from above, followed by the sound of his boots moving across the wooden floor. "Someone was just in here."

"Did they escape through the hatch?"

"Looks like it, sir. Footprints lead up to it," the Corporal answered.

"Get it open!" the officer behind him shouted.

Thomas swung his flashlight up to the hatch, spotting the locking mechanism. He reached up and turned it until it clicked loudly into place.

"I think he just locked it, sir," the Corporal confirmed.

"Bugger me! I find out who left that hatch open, I'll

skewer the daft sod. Inform command at once and get me the access code!"

"Yes, sir."

Thomas heard running footsteps leave the boathouse, but didn't wait to hear more. He descended as quickly as he dared, one hand gripping the flashlight while the other moved from rung to rung.

The shaft seemed to go on forever, the air growing cooler with each step down. Finally, when his foot found solid ground, Thomas swept the flashlight beam around, revealing a tunnel large enough to drive a small car through. The walls, floor, and ceiling were made of smooth concrete, and power conduits ran along the ceiling. Everything looked new, or at least well-maintained. The level of infrastructure—this was no makeshift mine shaft or emergency shelter—was staggering.

A clang echoed down the shaft, the hatch being thrown open above. Thomas didn't know how they had opened it again so quickly, and he didn't care. He picked a direction and ran.

"Movement in the tunnel!" the Corporal shouted, his voice bouncing off the concrete. "Subject is heading west!"

The tunnel curved gently to the left, maintaining its arc as it descended at a slight angle. The sound of pursuit—multiple sets of boots on metal as the Corporal and the officer, more soldiers behind them, descended the ladder, their bootfalls on the concrete growing louder behind him.

"This is insane," he gasped to himself between breaths. "What the hell have I stumbled into?"

The tunnel continued its descent, switching back on itself twice as Thomas delved deeper underground. His tired legs still burned from the earlier bike ride, but fear kept him moving. His flashlight beam bounced wildly as he ran, creating dancing shadows that made the tunnel seem to shift and writhe around him.

A fork! The main tunnel continued its curve while a smaller passage branched off straight ahead. Light spilled from that direction, along with the distant echo of machinery and the sound of boots scrambling across concrete..

"More troops coming up the main line!" a voice echoed from the smaller passageway. "Cut the intruder off at Junction Seven!"

With troops closing in on him from both in front and behind him, Thomas veered left, staying with the curving main tunnel. The floor sloped more steeply here, forcing him to watch his footing. Each breath came in ragged gasps, sending fresh pain through his bruised throat. The air, growing heavier somehow, was charged with something he couldn't identify.

As he risked a glance back over his shoulder, trying to gauge how close his pursuers were, his foot caught something—a bit of uneven floor, a loose stone, he never saw what—and he stumbled. His shoulder slammed into the wall, and suddenly he was falling sideways through an opening his light hadn't illuminated, the gap barely wide enough for his body to fall through.

Falling fast, his stomach leaped into his throat. Sharp rocks tore at his clothes, knocking the flashlight from his grip and slicing a stinging cut into his hand. Somewhere above, the light shattered, plunging him into total darkness. Knowing he was going to hit the ground hard enough to drive the air from his lungs, he pulled both his arms in, wrapping them around his ribs. But then, he was suddenly sliding on slick sheet metal. What had become a tunnel gradually changed direction, curving and widening into a slope that gradually bled off some of his speed.

He finally came to rest in a heap on a gentle, sandy incline, every part of him screaming in protest from the rocks he'd scraped past in his fall. Above him, boots thundered past his impromptu escape route, voices calling out coordinates and positions.

Trying to catch his breath, Thomas lay still until the sounds of pursuit faded away. Nothing felt broken, but he'd hit his forehead on the way down, and now a trickle of blood ran down off his brow into his left eye. He swiped it away with his sleeve, ignoring the cut. As his eyes adjusted to the darkness, he realized he was facing what looked like a cave entrance in the rocks. A faint glow emanated from it.

Carefully, he pushed himself to his feet and moved toward the light. The ground changed from sand to loose rock and began to slope downward at a steeper angle, leading him toward what looked to be a massive open cavern. For safety's sake, he crawled the last few meters toward it on his hands and knees, ignoring the sharp gravel digging into them.

A rhythmic pounding echoed from the cavern, accompanied by the whir of heavy machinery. As he neared the opening, the light from below grew brighter. And bluer. Voices carried up to him, too distant to make out words but clearly calling out instructions. The air began to grow fresher as well, but it was still charged with that same strange energy he'd sensed in the tunnel.

He stopped at the edge of an overlook and dropped to his belly, the bluish tint resolving into a shimmer that danced at the edges of his vision. He peered down over the precipice into a cavern so vast the far walls were lost in shadow, but in the center of the cavern, bathing in powerful flood lights mounted on tall poles, he found himself looking at the source of the blue light.

It was one of the most incredible sights he'd ever seen.

A hive of human activity, cranes, and excavation equipment surrounded what looked like a massive archaeological dig, but it was unlike any dig he'd ever imagined.

They weren't digging up ancient pottery or dinosaur bones.

Extending from the excavation like a monument to impossibility was the front half of what could only be a starship.

CHAPTER 9

The starship's surface was a dull silver, marked with strange symbols that Thomas could swear shifted and moved when he wasn't looking directly at them. Its elegant design was eerily reminiscent of a sword, suggesting a violent purpose. Even half-buried, it radiated a sense of power that made his skin prickle and his mouth go dry, probably because it was hanging open.

Teams of people in white protective suits swarmed around it, carefully removing centuries of accumulated soil and rock. Each time they cleared a new section, that strange bluish shimmer would dance across the surface before fading away. The vessel's hull responded to their touch as if it were somehow alive.

Thomas could do nothing but stare, unable to form the thoughts to express the swirling maelstrom of emotions playing through his mind. The implications of what he was seeing crashed over him in waves. This wasn't just some secret military project or archaeological find. This was something…else, that in an instant, changed everything he'd ever thought he understood about humankind's place in the universe.

A group of soldiers in familiar tactical gear jogged past just below him, heading toward what looked like a command center set up near the excavation. Thomas pressed himself flatter against the rock, though he was invisible from their position.

"Section D is clear," one of them reported, his voice carrying clearly in the cavern's strange acoustics. "No sign of the intruder. He must have doubled back."

"Negative," a woman's voice crackled over their radios. "Motion sensors show movement in the northwest quadrant. Sweep that section again."

"The timing's wrong," another soldier said. "No way he could have reached the artifact yet. Focus on the upper levels."

Thomas' breath caught in his throat. They thought he was there intentionally—a spy or saboteur perhaps. That explained the military response to what should have been a simple police matter. He had stumbled onto something enormous, something perhaps world-changing.

And now he knew too much.

He nearly laughed out loud at his growing streak of amazingly bad luck. He wasn't just running from a murder charge anymore. He had fallen into something far larger and more dangerous than he could ever have imagined. The bruises on his throat suddenly felt trivial compared to what might happen if these people caught him.

He needed to find a way out of this place and forget he ever saw it. At this point, prison felt safer than his current predicament.

Still, there was something about that ship that kept his eyes shifting back to it every time they drifted away. A sense of hope and promise that had eluded him for pretty much his entire life. It was almost as though the strange craft was calling out to him.

That thought faded fast at the sound of footsteps—the

measured, professional stride of experienced soldiers—approaching his position from somewhere in the darkness. He could hear them getting closer. He could make out at least three distinct sets, accompanied by the soft clink of carabiners, the creak of combat boots, the whisper of fabric against kevlar—tactical gear—but he couldn't see them or even pinpoint the direction they were coming from.

"Section Echo-Seven clear," a voice murmured, close enough that Thomas could hear the reply through their radio.

"Roger that. Proceed to Echo-Eight and—wait." The transmission cut off abruptly.

"Sir?" the first voice questioned.

"Movement was detected in the northwest corridor. Multiple sensors were triggered in sequence."

"It could be another equipment malfunction. We've had issues with the EM field from the artifact."

"Negative. The pattern suggests fast human movement."

Thomas held his breath, pressing harder against the rocks beneath him. His legs tensed, as if to push off and run if discovered. Not that he had anywhere to run to. He was stuck right where he was, with no avenue of escape. No way to do anything but sit tight and hope he wouldn't be caught.

"All units converge on Northwest Three," a new voice commanded through the radio. "Possible intruder contact."

The footsteps that had been approaching his position from his left suddenly turned and moved away at a rapid pace, boots drumming against stone as the soldiers responded to the call. Thomas remained frozen in place, hardly daring to believe his luck.

It was good.

For once.

"Greetings."

The voice came out of nowhere. No—his spine prickled—it came from behind him. He flipped over on his back. "What the hell!" he gasped, heart hammering. Braced on his elbows, he stared up at a shimmering holographic orb composed of pure blue light and had suddenly materialized directly behind him.

"Be quiet!" the orb commanded. "I didn't just go through all that trouble of drawing them away from us for you to get yourself caught a nanosecond later."

"You're the one shouting," Thomas hissed through clenched teeth, trying to get his heart rate under control.

The orb rippled with laughter. "Foolish boy. I'm not actually speaking at all. I'm projecting directly into your mind. The soldiers can't hear me. Though they might hear you if you keep swearing out loud."

Thomas stared at the orb, trying to process this new impossibility. "I feel like I'm going crazy."

"You should be so lucky. Unfortunately for both of us, this is all very real."

"What..." He swallowed hard and tried again. "Who or what the hell are you?"

"My name is Merlin."

Thomas' eyes widened, his gaze flashing to the starship and then back to the hologram. This had just gone from crazy to full-blown, without-a-doubt, ready-to-be-committed-immediately insane.

"Merlin?" he said incredulously. "The wizard? As in, King Arthur?"

"You've heard of Arthur?" the hologram asked, surprised. "That fool man left me down here, you know. 'Don't worry,' he said. 'I'll bring back help,' he said. Guess what?"

"He never came back?" Thomas guessed.

"At least you aren't a total nincompoop. That's right. He never came back."

THE STARSHIP IN THE STONE 75

Thomas shook his head, wondering if he had hit it harder than he thought during his fall. "This can't be real. I'm hallucinating. Or concussed. Or both."

"I assure you, this is quite real," Merlin replied. "And I need your help."

Thomas coughed out a soft laugh that held absolutely no humor. "My help? I'm the last person you want help from. I'm being hunted by soldiers and police. I'm wanted for murder. I've already spent time in juvenile detention for killing someone else. I'm a mess. A no good loser. I'm in no position to help anyone."

"Hmmm," Merlin muttered before vanishing and once more leaving Thomas alone on the ledge.

Thomas exhaled sharply and shook his head. A hallucination. It had to be. He needed to focus. To find his way out of the cavern and—

"On the contrary," Merlin said, the orb reappearing as instantly as it had vanished. "I triple-checked my calculations," he went on. "You're exactly what I've been waiting for. The first person to come along in nearly fifteen centuries who can actually help me."

"Right," Thomas muttered, skeptically. "Because that makes perfect sense."

"Sarcasm is the lowest form of wit," Merlin chided before grinning, "though I do often find it quite enjoyable. You, my boy, need to get to the ship."

"What?" Thomas replied.

"This isn't rocket science." Merlin paused, turning to glance at the starship with a laugh. "Well, technically I suppose it is." He looked back at Thomas. "Here's the deal. Neither one of us belongs buried under solid rock that is itself buried under a lake. I can't get out of here without you, and you can't get out of here without me. Therefore, the most logical course of action is for us to work together. I'd write out the mathematical proof for you on the wall behind me, but I can't fool those soldiers forever. They're accustomed to my bored antics by now, so you need to decide immediately if you agree with my assessment of the situation and then take the appropriate action in response."

"I don't see how I can help you," Thomas replied. "I can't exactly dig you out of here."

"Number one, you wouldn't be digging *me* out. I'm connected to Excalibur, but I'm not Excalibur, per se."

Thomas laughed. "Come on. You're telling me that ship's Excalibur? The sword in the stone?"

The orb rippled again. "I imagine Arthur tried to explain that he had a starship, but your people, being relatively primitive, probably didn't understand what he was prattling on about, and when he drew a picture for them... well..." He motioned to the ship again. "...of course it resembles a sword."

"So, the starship in the stone," Thomas said, the words coming awkwardly out of his mouth. He shook his head. "I must be dead. The fall through the crevice was fatal. That's what this is."

"Number two, you don't need to dig the ship out. Excalibur can take care of that. Unfortunately, security protocols limit my ability to access those specific systems because I have no physical form. But you, as real flesh and blood, can bypass them. Are you coming, or what?"

Thomas glanced back over the ledge at the partially excavated vessel. The teams of scientists in their white protective suits continued to swarm around it like ants, protected by rings of armed soldiers. "Yeah, sure. Why not? All I have to do is stroll down there past the heavily armed military personnel who are actively hunting me. Piece of cake. Do you think I should wave and introduce myself, or just let them shoot me straight away?"

"If you're worthy, you'll make it," Merlin said. Then the hologram vanished again, leaving for good this time.

CHAPTER 10

"If I'm worthy," Thomas repeated incredulously. "If I'm worthy?" He touched his bruised throat, wincing. "Maybe that asshole cut off the flow of oxygen to my brain. Left me in a coma, and this is all hypnagogic bullshit."

He rolled back over, gluing his attention back on the starship. Excalibur? Really? Its hull continued to pulse with the same bluish light that had accompanied Merlin's appearance, as if it were calling out to him. Crazy or not. Concussed or not. In a coma or not...Merlin was right about one thing.

There was no other way out of here.

Either he made it to the ship and let this fever-dream fully into his psyche, or he went down in a hail of bloody gunfire.

"Section Echo-Niner clear," a voice echoed from below. "Resuming sweep of upper levels."

Thomas pressed himself flat against the gravel. "Thanks for nothing, Merlin," he whispered. "If you wanted us to be a team, it would have been nice if you had, I don't know, offered some actual help." But even as he said it, his eyes were scanning the cavern, looking for options. The excavation team had erected scaffolding along the wall off to his left, providing access to different levels of the dig site. If he could reach it and climb down...

Thomas traced potential paths to reaching the scaffolding. Most of the security focus were on the ground level, oriented inward toward the ship rather than up at the walls. Getting across the open ledge to reach the scaffolding would be the biggest challenge, but he was confident he could make it if he timed it right.

His attention shifted to the workers below. A group of scientists approached the ship with what looked like scanning equipment, their protective suits gleaming under the floodlights. The soldiers adjusted their positions to accommodate the new activity, creating a gap in their coverage.

"Now or never," he whispered. He took one last look at the impossible ship below, its partially excavated form radiating power. "If I die trying this, Merlin, I'm going to haunt your disco ball dreams."

He began inching along the ledge, staying low and testing each hand and foothold before committing his weight. The rock was wet in places, slick with mineral deposits that had built up over centuries. One slip would send him plummeting to the cavern floor, some thirty or more meters below, though he supposed the fall would at least solve all his problems.

Twenty meters to the scaffolding. Fifteen. The constant background noise of machinery and echoing voices helped mask the sound of any loose rocks he dislodged, but each scrape of his boot against stone sent his heart rate spiking.

A soldier below looked up, scanning the walls with professional thoroughness. Thomas froze, barely breathing, pressed as flat against the rock as he could manage. The soldier's gaze passed over his position and continued upward.

Thomas waited until the soldier turned away before moving again. Ten meters to go.

"Teams Three and Four, check in," a voice crackled over the radio.

"Team Three, Level Two is clear."

"Team Four, beginning sweep of Level—wait." A pause. "I've got something on thermal imaging. Northwest quadrant, bearing zero-three-five."

Thomas' blood ran cold. He was willing to bet that was exactly where he was clinging to the ledge. He looked frantically for cover, but found only exposed rock.

Then, inexplicably, multiple alarms began blaring from the opposite side of the cavern. Red warning lights started flashing, and a computerized voice announced: "Warning. Contamination detection. Warning. Contamination detected. All personnel, evacuate immediately. All personnel, evacuate immediately."

"What the hell?" someone shouted from below. "Somebody go check that out!"

"Teams Three and Four, shift your search to Sector Five," a commanding voice ordered. "All security personnel maintain positions around the artifact."

"Sir, shouldn't we evacuate?" someone asked.

"Only if you want to be on my shit list, Private. This is probably a false alarm, or even a pathetic attempt at a diversion. We'll wait for the techs to call it."

"Yes, sir."

Thomas didn't waste his chance. He covered the remaining distance to the scaffolding, leaping from rock-to-rock in a hurry, despite potential demise if he slipped and fell. It was still appealing than being shot and then falling.

Looking at the gap between the ledge and the scaffolding, it was a little over a meter, and he couldn't get a run at it. He tried to convince himself not to look down, but the temptation was too great. His stomach was already twisted into knots. Seeing the cavern floor below just added nausea to the mix.

Taking one more nervous breath, he gathered himself and leaped, stretching for the metal framework.

Each second felt like an eternity.

One second. Another.

His right foot connected and slipped off a beam. He reached, grabbing onto the beam just above his head. He swung from it by one hand, his feet scrabbling for purchase. One foot found the same beam he'd slipped from, and then his other hand grabbed hold, the framework cold and solid in his grip as he laid his forehead against it and released a relieved breath. Moments later, he moved to the nearest platform and looked down in time to see soldiers thundering past below, rushing to deal with whatever new crisis had conveniently manifested to cover his movement.

"You did that, didn't you, Merlin?" he whispered, not expecting an answer.

"Of course I did," Merlin's voice replied in his head, startling him. "Though my tricks are becoming less effective. I doubt I'll be able to get this kind of response again. You're doing great so far, by the way. Keep it up."

"Yeah, right. Through blind luck and your interference. Some worthiness test this is turning out to be."

"Who said this was the test?"

Thomas opened his mouth to reply, then closed it again. Below, chaos continued to unfold as teams of technicians rushed to deal with the environmental system failure. The soldiers maintained their positions around the ship, but their attention was divided now.

"I suppose you're not going to tell me what the actual test is?" Thomas asked.

Silence was his only answer.

"Right," he sighed. "Of course not. That would be too easy."

He studied the scaffolding, plotting a route down. The metal framework offered plenty of handholds, but also plenty of opportunities to make enough noise to be seen. He would need to time his descent carefully, using the confusion below as cover.

A new alarm—this one a deeper, more urgent tone—joined the cacophony, seeming to resonate through the cavern. The ship's hull pulsed in response.

"Well, that's probably not good," Thomas muttered.

"On the contrary," Merlin replied, suddenly back in his head. "It's exactly what we needed. Now, jump."

"What?" Thomas stared down at the thirty-meter drop. "Are you insane?"

"Trust me."

"I just met you!"

"And yet, here you are." There was definitely amusement in Merlin's tone now. "Sometimes the only way forward is to take a leap of faith."

"I hate you," Thomas said with feeling. "I truly, properly hate you."

"Our partnership doesn't require mutual admiration. Now jump!"

Thomas looked down again. The ship's hull was pulsing faster now, building toward something.

"This is completely insane," he said.

Then he jumped.

The sensation of falling lasted both forever and no time at all. Wind rushed past his ears, his stomach tried to climb up his throat, and his brain helpfully informed him of all the ways this was going to end badly.

Just before he hit the ground, the ship's hull flared with brilliant blue light. The same energy he'd been feeling all along reached out and caught him, cushioning his fall like he'd landed in mud. He hung suspended for a moment, wrapped in alien power that made every nerve ending tingle. Then he dropped the remaining meter to the ground, landing unharmed and on his feet.

"Intruder!" someone shouted. "By the artifact!"

Soldiers were already running toward him, weapons raised. He had maybe seconds before—

The ship pulsed again. A section of hull that had looked completely solid simply vanished, revealing a dark opening. Thomas didn't hesitate. He sprinted for it.

"Stop him!" a voice commanded. "Don't let him reach the artifact!"

Energy crackled around him as weapons fired. Pain blossomed in his left calf, and he stumbled forward, another round screaming by where his head had just been. He only had one avenue of escape. He took it as another round grazed his shoulder. He threw himself through the opening just as more security forces rounded the ship's nose and began firing at him. Behind him, the opening vanished, cutting off the bullets and plunging him into total darkness.

"Well," Merlin's voice said, "that was certainly smooth. Like an albatross coming in for a landing."

"I'm hit," Thomas hissed. "My right shoulder and the back of my lower left leg." Both were burning like wildfire.

"You say that like someone who's been shot before."

"Yeah, once. A long time ago."

"You aren't old enough for anything to be a long time ago."

"Nearly half my life counts, as far as I'm concerned."

"Fair enough. Would you like aid for your wounds?"

"Yeah, that might be nice. Am I safe now?"

Merlin's voice darkened as Excalibur's interior lights activated. "My boy, you have no idea."

CHAPTER 11

"What do you mean by *you have no idea*?" Thomas asked, his shoulder and calf throbbing in time with his elevated pulse, blood seeping through his clothes where the bullets had found their marks. His shoulder wasn't bad—just a deep graze—but the bullet to the meat of his calf was a through-and-through. While it had missed both bones, it had apparently grazed a bleeder. A small puddle of blood was forming beneath the wound, stark crimson against the pristine deck.

"The soldiers can't get in here, right?" Thomas asked, drawing his leg up to put pressure on his worst wound. He grimaced as he shifted just enough to put his back against the outer bulkhead.

He was in a loading area, the stark silver walls both ancient and brand new at the same time. There were no boxes, no equipment, nothing to indicate it had ever been used. Just clean lines and spotless surfaces that caught and reflected the soft illumination emanating from recessed panels in the overhead.

Thomas closed his eyes against the burning pain, "You

there, Merlin? You haven't left me here to bleed out, have you?"

"Where else would I be? I can't exactly leave."

Thomas released an exasperated breath. "Then answer my question. Can the soldiers get in?"

"No, they can't get in," Merlin confirmed, the orb flickering into existence in front of Thomas. "Though I imagine they're going to try even harder now that they've seen you enter. But that's not what I meant."

Although Thomas could see straight through the orb to the bulkhead, it was more solid now than it had been in the cavern. "Then what did you mean?"

"Let's get you patched up first," Merlin replied, his form rippling slightly as if caught in an unseen breeze. "Those wounds need attention. Wait here a moment." The orb vanished, leaving Thomas alone in the eerily silent hold.

"What the hell am I doing here?" he muttered to himself, head tilting back against the cool metal. He tried to relax to ease the pain. Whatever this was, it was better than being chased by police or soldiers. Whatever Merlin had meant, it certainly felt safe enough.

For now, at least.

His gaze drifted around the bay again, noting details he'd missed in his initial scan. The walls weren't completely featureless. Subtle patterns were worked into the metal, geometric shapes that shifted and flowed when viewed from different angles. And there was something else, a low vibration he could feel through the deck plates, as if some massive engine was idling deep within the ship's core.

Heavy footsteps interrupted his observations, echoing from somewhere deeper in the vessel. The sound grew steadily louder, accompanied by the whir of servos and the subtle clank of metal on metal. Thomas pushed himself back to his feet, using the bulkhead for support as a hatch at the far end of the bay slid open with a soft pneumatic hiss.

"Oh shit!" he yelped as a massive mechanical figure ducked through the opening. The robot or cyborg—or whatever it was—stood at least three meters tall, its broad frame suggesting immense strength. Its design reminded Thomas of illustrations he'd seen in old fairy tale books, like an ogre rendered in gleaming metal and composite materials. Blue light gleamed from its otherwise dark eyes, matching the ethereal glow that permeated everything connected to Merlin and the ship.

He subconsciously shoved himself back against the bulkhead, trying to shrink away from the mechanical monster. "Merlin," he whispered. "Where are you? Help."

"Got you," Merlin's familiar voice emerged from the ogre with a laugh. "This is one of my Ground Operations Logistics and Engineering Modules. GOLEMs, for short. I use this one for maintenance and heavy lifting, when a more substantial presence is required."

"You aren't funny," Thomas said, his heart still racing.

"I disagree," Merlin replied, a note of amusement in his voice. The GOLEM crossed the hold with surprising agility despite its size. "Now, let's get you to the regeneration pod."

"Regeneration pod? What's that?"

"Am I wrong, or is the nature of the device not self-evident in its name?" The GOLEM reached for Thomas with surprisingly gentle hands. "May I?"

Thomas skeptically eyed the massive metal fingers. Each one was thicker than his arm, capable of crushing him without effort. "Do I have a choice?"

"You always have a choice. But walking on that leg will only make it worse, and I'd rather not have to redecorate the corridors in Early Modern Hemoglobin."

"Your sense of humor needs work," Thomas said, but he nodded. "Fine. Just...be careful."

The GOLEM scooped him up as if he weighed nothing, cradling him against its chest like a child. Despite its intimidating appearance, its touch was delicate, carefully avoiding his injuries as it carried him from the cargo bay into the corridor.

"My name is Thomas, by the way. Thomas Drake. You never asked."

"I didn't, did I?" Merlin replied. "Where are my manners? I'm sorry, Thomas. My systems have become corrupted by age. I'm not the Advisor I used to be."

"You're an artificial intelligence, then?" Thomas asked.

"My intellect is real. Advisors are digitized copies of actual individuals, typically renowned for their specific skills and abilities. Well, their minds, anyway. I'm not living or breathing, but I do think like an individual, not like a machine."

"So there was a real Merlin where you come from, and they what? Scanned his brain, saved it to a server, and made copies?"

"A simplified but not incorrect sequence of events," Merlin agreed.

"It must be weird to be a digital version of a living person."

"I've never known any other existence. It's perfectly normal to me."

"What were the living Merlin's skills and abilities that you inherited?"

"Intelligence, for one. A quick wit. A sharp tongue. He was also a well known inventor and technologist. And a master of the arcane arts, of course."

"Hold up. You're claiming you're actually a wizard? Magic isn't real, you know."

"Did you believe starships were real thirty minutes ago?" Merlin asked.

"Well...no," Thomas admitted. "Good point. So what kind of magic can you do? Shoot lightning from your hands?"

"I'm an Advisor. The only hands I possess are attached to a mobile platform. Machines can't use magic."

"As a digital copy, aren't you by nature a machine?"

"Technically, yes, as the data that composes my existence is stored on physical media and runs through circuits. More philosophically, my digital self is more ephemeral."

"A long series of ones and zeroes."

"Precisely."

"So you're a master of the arcane arts who can't cast spells."

"Now you're catching on."

Thomas fell silent, trying to wrap his mind around the concept of the Advisor.

"This ship has four main decks," Merlin explained as they continued through the silver-walled passages. "Engineering and storage on Deck One, crew focused amenities like berthing, bathing, eating and voiding on Two, with the flight deck at the center of the ship on Three. There's living space for up to twelve additional crew, in addition to the captain."

Thomas looked around at the stark passages, noting more of those shifting geometric patterns worked into the walls. "Did Apple design this place? I feel like I'm trapped inside a MacBook."

"I don't understand that reference," Merlin said.

"Everything's just so...clean and silver," Thomas explained.

"The aesthetic is intentional. Clean lines make maintenance easier, and the patterns serve both decorative and practical purposes."

"What kind of practical purpose could weird moving shapes serve?"

"The patterns help regulate various systems, among other functions."

"Right." Thomas shifted slightly in the GOLEM's grip, trying to find a more comfortable position. "So where's the Round Table?"

"There are multiple round tables within the ship."

"No, I mean *the* Round Table. The one Arthur and his knights sat at and talked about…well…stuff."

"Again, there are multiple tables that meet that description."

"Never mind."

They reached a medical bay. The room was dominated by a large cylindrical tank filled with slightly luminescent blue gel that pulsed with its own inner light. Thomas couldn't begin to identify the various pieces of equipment lining the bulkheads.

"Here we are," Merlin said as they entered a small medical compartment that looked extremely sparse.

There didn't seem to be any medical implements like a stethoscope or blood pressure cuff around, not to mention any medications or bandages. There were no cupboards for storage, just four bare bulkheads and a clear, flat-bottomed tank in the center of the room.

"You'll need to remove your clothes," Merlin advised, the top of the tank rising as he gently lowered Thomas to the deck.

He stared dubiously at the tank. The gel filling it to the mid-point moved in ways that defied physics, swirling and flowing of its own accord. "You want me to get in that?"

"Unless you'd prefer to remain bleeding and in pain."

"So what is this? Some kind of super advanced bacta tank?"

"Another reference I don't understand," Merlin said.

"The regeneration pod is a sophisticated medical device that will repair your injuries at the cellular level. The process is perfectly safe, if somewhat uncomfortable at first."

Thomas continued to hesitate, watching the gel's hypnotic movements. "Will it hurt?"

"Less than being shot, I imagine."

A fresh wave of pain from his leg made the decision easier. Thomas stripped off his bloody clothes, wincing as the movement pulled at his wounded shoulder where the blood had dried, adhering his t-shirt to the wound. The cool air raised goosebumps on his skin, making him even more aware of how exposed and vulnerable he felt.

"That's quite a scar you've got there," Merlin observed as Thomas' t-shirt came off, revealing the puckered flesh of an old wound—a permanent reminder of another bullet from an earlier time—to his abdomen.

Thomas touched the mark absently, remembering the burning pain, the taste of copper in his mouth, his mother's tears in the hospital. "I got caught in the crossfire during a gang shootout when I was seven. I nearly died." He laughed bitterly. "Maybe I should have. It might have saved everyone a lot of trouble. The funny thing is, I ended up joining the same gang as the guy who shot me. I killed someone so I could be part of it."

"I don't find that amusing."

"No, it isn't, actually. Look, Merlin. I don't know why you think I can help you when none of those soldiers out there could, but you mentioned being worthy, and you said getting to the ship wasn't the test. If this is about being pure of heart or something, you're going to end up disappointed whenever you put me to task."

"I disagree," Merlin said, his tone suddenly serious. "I believe you were meant for something greater. The calculations agree. That's why you're here. Now, get in the tank."

Thomas opened his mouth to respond, but the throbbing in his leg convinced him to save his questions until after he was healed. Still nervous, he stepped up and into the tank, the top descending and forcing him to lay back in the gel that came all the way up to his chin. It was surprisingly warm, with an odd tingling sensation. It felt almost alive, as if it were reaching out to examine him with millions of microscopic fingers.

Seconds later, more gel began pumping in from below. "Uh, Merlin?" he said, growing fearful. "What is this?"

"Just relax. You'll be fine."

Panic seized him as the gel around his face started encroaching on his mouth. He pounded on the lid with his good arm, ancient survival instincts screaming at him to get out. "Wait! I can't breathe in this stuff!"

"Actually, you can," Merlin replied calmly. "The liquid is oxygenated. Just relax and breathe normally."

The gel rose up over his mouth, heading for his nose. When it reached his nostrils, pure instinct made him hold his breath as it completely covered his face. He held his breath for nearly a minute before his chest burned so badly he couldn't stop himself from inhaling. The gel flowed into his lungs as easily as air, oxygenating his blood directly. When he exhaled, the material swirled around over his head in strangely mesmerizing patterns. The sensation was profoundly odd but not unpleasant.

"Try to relax." Merlin's voice came through clearly despite the liquid medium. "The process works better if you're calm. Let the nanites do their work."

"Nanites?" Thomas tried to ask as a profound weariness began creeping over him. His eyelids grew heavy as the warmth of the gel seeped into his very bones. He felt disconnected from his body, floating in a sea of blue light that pulsed in time with his slowing heartbeat.

The last thing he heard before drifting off was Merlin's

voice, distant now as if coming from the bottom of a deep well: "Sleep well, Thomas. We have much to do when you wake up."

His dreams were filled with swords in stones and knights riding alien six-legged horses. And through it all, a burgeoning sense of purpose he'd never felt before, called him toward something both ancient and new.

A destiny he'd never asked for and couldn't seem to escape. And maybe a chance to be more than the sum of his mistakes.

CHAPTER 12

Thomas awoke slowly, his mind struggling to break free from his strange dreams, both surreal and all-too-real. He expected to find himself still floating in the regeneration pod's warm embrace. Instead, he felt soft sheets against his skin and a plush mattress beneath him. His eyes fluttered open, taking in unfamiliar surroundings both alien and oddly welcoming.

The room was large and curved, following the ship's hull contours. Unlike the sterile corridors and medical compartment he remembered from earlier, this space had character—personality even. The walls were still that distinctive silvery metal, but here they served as a backdrop for an impressive collection of weapons that could only be described as exotic. Blades of various lengths and designs hung in careful arrangements, their surfaces seeming to drink in the light rather than reflect it. The center mounting point of the primary display was conspicuously empty, drawing his eye like a missing tooth in an otherwise perfect smile.

"What is this place?" he muttered, pushing himself up to

sitting position. His voice came out clear and strong, free of the rasp that had plagued him since his encounter in the alley. His hand flew to his throat, fingers probing gently where brutal bruises had been just hours before. The skin felt smooth and unmarked, with no trace of pain from the violence that had put him on his current path.

Intrigued, Thomas lifted the luxuriously soft blanket covering him and examined his shoulder and leg where the bullets had struck. Both areas were completely healed, not even a scar remaining to show where the wounds had been. "I'll be damned," he whispered, shifting his attention to his abdomen. He ran his fingers over the spot where the ugly scar from his old bullet wound—the one he'd carried since childhood—should have been. It was completely gone, vanished as if it had never been there, leaving only perfect, unmarked skin. He'd lived with that mark for so long it had become part of his identity, a constant reminder of just how close he'd come to death as a child.

An unexpected wave of sadness washed over him. Its absence felt almost like losing a familiar friend, but if surrendering his scars was the price of survival, he wouldn't complain.

Beyond the weapon displays, shelves lined the walls, holding artifacts from alien worlds. Strange devices, with purposes he couldn't begin to guess, sat alongside ancient-looking leather-bound books, their spines marked with glyphs he didn't recognize. A computer terminal and curved monitor dominated one section of wall, currently displaying a feed from outside the ship. Thomas watched teams of technicians continuing their careful excavation work, while further in the background, the soldiers he had evaded getting chewed out by a twerp in a tweed suit.

A government official, he supposed.

Sliding to the edge of the bed, his bare feet found thick

carpeting—or something similar to carpet, though the fibers shifted to comfortably cradle his feet. A plush chair sat nearby, made of a slightly more solid version of the regeneration gel. A stack of neatly folded clothes rested on it.

Thomas stood, pleasantly surprised to find his body completely free of pain and stiffness. He couldn't remember the last time he'd felt this good.

The clothes fit perfectly, though their style left something to be desired. "I look like I'm cosplaying at the world's fanciest Renaissance Faire," he muttered, examining his reflection in a section of the bulkhead.

The fabric was impossibly soft and light, with a subtle shimmer that reminded him of fish scales catching sunlight. The cut and design suggested medieval nobility—a doublet over a fine shirt, thankfully leather-like pants instead of hose, and an upgraded version of his combat boots. In comparison to the loose tie-string undershorts, he much preferred his boxer briefs. The materials and craftsmanship were clearly far beyond anything Earth could produce, but he supposed an alien starship wouldn't carry hoodies and cargo pants, and his had been a total loss.

Looking around at the bulkheads, Thomas tried to find the way out. He didn't see any seams or indications of a hatch anywhere. Pacing the perimeter, he ran his hands along the smooth metal, assuming maybe an invisible door would open up at his proximity. It didn't. His heart rate picked up, but he refused to panic outright. Merlin hadn't gone through the trouble of healing him just to stick him in a bedroom with no escape.

Had he?

Thomas' gaze wandered back to the weapon display, to a longsword mounted on the right side of the collection. Its design was elegant yet practical, the blade tapering to a needle-sharp point while maintaining enough width to deliver devastating cuts. The crossguard curved slightly toward the blade, and the grip was wrapped in some material that shifted colors as he watched.

Unable to resist, Thomas lifted the sword from its mounting. He expected it to be heavy, but the weapon's weight felt as though it were made of plastic, perfectly balanced in his hand. He gave it a few experimental swings, appreciating the whisper of its edge through the air.

"I would be careful with that if I were you," a familiar voice said as the previously invisible hatch slid open. Merlin entered, this time inhabiting a humanoid GOLEM that stood roughly Thomas' height of six feet. Its design suggested a suit of armor more than the ogre-like maintenance platform from earlier, though its eyes still maintained that distinctive blue glow. "That blade can separate your arm from your body with barely a touch."

Thomas carefully returned the sword to its mount. "This was Arthur's quarters, wasn't it?"

"These are the captain's quarters," Merlin corrected, moving further into the room. "Though I don't think Arthur will be needing them anymore. Fifteen hundred years is a long time, even for an Ursan."

"Ursan?" Thomas asked.

"Arthur's, and once my, race," Merlin answered. "Of course, you wouldn't know that humans come from the same evolutionary path as the Ursan. You're a bit behind, civilization-wise. Though, I did analyze your clothing, and it doesn't have much in common with my last sample. You've come a long way, my boy."

"So you're saying Ursans are humans?"

"Not exactly. But we do share the same general appearance. There are subtle differences, of course. You have larger ears and more body hair, for example. But it would take a trained eye to spot the variance."

"So what happened?" Thomas asked. "I mean, what

brought you here? Clearly you didn't intend to end up buried under a Welsh mountain for fifteen hundred years."

"Walk with me," Merlin said, gesturing toward the hatch. "How are you feeling?"

Thomas followed the GOLEM into the corridor, noting that this section of the ship felt warmer, more lived-in than the areas he'd been in before. "Better than I have in years," he admitted. "Maybe better than ever. Whatever that regeneration pod did, it fixed more than just the bullet wounds."

"The nanites repaired all detected damage, from recent trauma down to cellular degradation." Merlin led him past several closed hatches. "This is Deck Two, where most of the crew amenities are located. The galley is through there," he indicated a larger hatch, "heads and showers in that section, additional crew quarters along here. As for what happened…we'll get to that in due time."

They continued along the corridor until they reached a solid wall of softly glowing blue energy. Thomas pulled to a stop, but Merlin gestured him forward. "Through here."

"Through the glowing wall of death? Are you sure?"

"Quite sure. It's perfectly safe."

Thomas took a deep breath and stepped forward. A tingling sensation washed over him, like static electricity dancing across his skin. Then he was through, standing in a completely different corridor.

"Did we just teleport?" he asked, looking back at the energy field.

"Something like that," Merlin replied. "We're on Deck Three now. I fixed the transport field to take us here, but normally you would think about the deck you want to travel to as you enter, and that's where you'll arrive."

"Crazy," Thomas muttered.

"There's nothing crazy about it. The science behind it is all thoroughly documented."

They turned a corner and entered what Thomas knew

could only be the flight deck. He stopped in the doorway, his breath catching in his throat as he tried to absorb the impossible sight before him.

The circular chamber was dominated by twelve enclosed pods arranged in a perfect circle, each one crafted from the same silvery metal as the ship's hull and topped with clear canopies. In the center of the ring, a holographic representation of space hung suspended, stars and nebulae slowly rotating in an ethereal dance.

But it was the command pod at the rear of the circle that drew and held his attention. Unlike the other stations, which were relatively uniform in design, it was a work of art. It rose from a raised dais like a flower reaching for the sun, its base crafted from the same silvery metal but with more pronounced geometric patterns that flowed up the structure like living vines. The interior of the enclosed pod in the center of the design had to be formed from the same gel-like substance he'd encountered before, but it was darker, almost black, with streaks of that familiar blue energy dancing through it. The canopy swept up and over in a graceful arc, creating a cocoon that somehow managed to look both ancient and futuristic at the same time.

"Are you sure this isn't the Round Table?" he asked, approaching the nearest pod. "It's amazing."

"I'm appreciative of your admiration. It is truly a flight deck fit for a king."

"So Arthur was a king where you come from?"

"Yes. *The* King of Avalon. An entire galaxy."

Thomas ran his hand along the pod. From this angle, he could see how the patterns in the base weren't just decorative. They pulsed with power, feeding energy up into the pod itself. "How does it work?"

"It is similar to the regeneration pod," Merlin explained, "though in this case, it uses a different gel as the medium. The gel puts the pod's occupant into a trance of sorts, which allows them to interface directly with the ship's core—its primary computational cluster, to which I am also bound. The crew essentially becomes one with the ship, sharing thoughts and coordinating actions at the speed of thought. The command pod provides the deepest connection, allowing direct control of all the ship's systems simultaneously, that is..." The GOLEM's head tilted slightly. "...if you're worthy."

Thomas quickly stepped back from the pod. "So that's the test? To see if interfacing with the ship will drive me insane?"

"No."

"But you just said—"

"Being worthy is about more than the control interface."

"I appreciate how you're being so consistently vague about the whole thing."

Merlin chuckled. "In due time, my boy."

"I knew you were going to say that." He eyed the pods again. "So each person controls different aspects of the ship?"

"Not exactly. Each mind becomes an added partition to the whole, perfectly merged, perfectly synced. All minds control all actions at all times."

"Which is why you called the core a cluster?"

"The regeneration pod must have also done some fine work on your mind," Merlin commented. "Precisely. Though of course, the Captain has the power to override control at any moment. When fully crewed, the ship's operations become almost symphonic, twelve minds working in perfect harmony. It's rather beautiful to behold."

"I can imagine," Thomas said. "The crew...did they have to prove themselves worthy?"

"Of course."

"Were they good people?"

"How do you define 'good,' Thomas?" Merlin asked, his

mechanical features somehow managing to convey genuine curiosity.

"I don't know. Someone who's honest. Someone who protects the innocent. Fights for justice. Maybe someone who wants to leave the world better than they found it."

"And you don't think you could be such a person?"

Thomas' hand drifted to his throat where the bruises had been. "I killed a man two days ago."

"To protect an innocent," Merlin pointed out. "That seems rather good to me."

"I've killed before that," Thomas said quietly. "For much worse reasons."

"And yet here you are." Merlin gestured at the massive viewscreen dominating the forward wall, where the teams of scientists, work crews, and soldiers continued their work outside. "Of all the humans who have lived and died since we crashed on this world, you are the first to be invited into the ship itself. Do you think that's merely coincidence?"

Thomas' attention was drawn back to the holographic display at the center of the ring. Stars wheeled and danced, galaxies spun in stately procession, and somewhere out there was wherever this ship had come from. "I think I was running for my life and got lucky."

"Luck," Merlin said, "is often destiny in disguise."

"Now you sound like a fortune cookie." Thomas turned back to face the GOLEM. "I get the impression you didn't intend to come to Earth. So what happened? How did the most advanced thing I've ever seen end up here, buried and forgotten?"

Merlin's mechanical form sighed, though that should have been impossible. The blue glow of its eyes dimmed slightly, as if recalling painful memories. A metal hand reached out to touch the captain's pod, the gesture somehow conveying deep loss. "That," the Adviser said, "is quite a story."

"I'm not going anywhere," Thomas replied. "And I think I deserve to know what I've stumbled into."

"You do." Merlin moved to stand beside the holographic display. A wave of his armored hand and the star field changed. "I suppose it's time I explained the nature of my dilemma."

CHAPTER 13

"The Draconites," Merlin began, his voice taking on a storyteller's cadence, "were once our greatest allies," he said as the starfield shifted and coalesced into new patterns. The blue glow from his eyes dimmed further, suggesting deep contemplation or perhaps regret.

The hologram shifted again, showing beings that made Thomas' breath catch. They possessed large, scaled heads with an elongated snout lined with razor sharp teeth, horns that grew in an array of patterns, and eyes with vertical pupils that glowed from within. Thomas could only describe them as humanoid dragons.

They carried an intelligent look in their eyes that fit perfectly with the rich finery they wore about their upright-standing bodies. Muscled arms ended in manicured three-fingered hands, while they eschewed boots for their visibly powerful claws. Both sexes displayed humanlike gender characteristics beneath their clothing, though the females appeared in a range of colors and hues, beautiful in their variety. The males on the other hand were larger and obviously stronger, but much more limited in their coloring.

"They're beautiful," Thomas said, leaning closer to study the details. "Do they have wings?"

"No," Merlin answered. "But that doesn't make them any less dangerous. Like all advanced species, they had their political factions. The majority wanted to maintain our alliance. But there were others, led by Morgana, who believed they were the dominant power in our galaxy, and destined to rule it alone."

"Morgana was a Draconite?" Thomas asked. "In the legends, she's Arthur's half-sister."

"Yes, she was a Draconite. And one of their most powerful."

The hologram shifted again, focusing on a female figure whose presence dominated the space even in recorded form. A midnight blue, she had specks of white across her scales, giving her the appearance of a star field in the sky. Her eyes, a bright orange, flared like the sun. She had short horns that curved only slightly toward the center of her forehead, and were tipped in gold.

"And yes, she is related to Arthur," Merlin continued. "The Draconites are masters of biological manipulation. In fact, they were once full dragons, until they utilized nanites to mold themselves into more humanoid forms."

"Why would they do that?"

"They found their size and form limiting for space travel. Of course, there are still pure dragons out there, but they don't have the same power or influence as the Draconites. As for Morgana, she was created by combining the DNA of Arthur's mother Igraine, Queen of the Ursan, and Lethar, the Draconite king. She was meant to be a bridge between our kind." The mechanical form's shoulders slumped slightly. "Instead, she became the weapon that tore us apart."

The hologram expanded, showing a pristine, jewel-like planet hanging in space. As the hologram zoomed in further, it revealed the planet's surface to be covered in elegant spires and graceful architecture that grew from the land itself rather than being built upon it. Massive arched structures rose into the clouds, adorned with stained glass that caught and reflected sunlight in brilliant cascades. Gardens and parks filled the spaces between buildings, creating a harmonious blend of nature and civilization in which multiple species lived.

"Let me guess," Thomas said. "Camelot?"

"Correct," Merlin said softly. "The Ursan homeworld. The heart of our civilization."

Thomas stared in wonder at the holographic representation. "It's incredible. Those buildings..."

"The architecture was designed to capture and channel natural energy," Merlin explained. "The stained glass wasn't merely decorative—each panel was actually a sophisticated power collector. The spires you see weren't just beautiful, they were functional, helping to regulate the planet's weather and maintain perfect growing conditions for the gardens."

The view zoomed in again, showing streets lined with trees bearing impossible flowers—blooms that glowed from within, their petals shifting colors as they moved in the breeze. People of various species walked these paths in clothing similar to the outfit Thomas now wore.

"How many lived there?" he asked.

"At its height? Nearly a billion souls from a number of intelligent species, all living in harmony. Or so we thought." Merlin's mechanical features somehow managed to convey deep sadness. "Would you like to see how it ended?"

Thomas nodded, though part of him dreaded what was coming.

The hologram shifted again. Now the pristine planet was surrounded by massive ships—dark, foreboding vessels—all sharp edges with no visible weapons on their exterior. At their center was a flagship that dwarfed the others, its design suggestive of a massive dragon in flight.

"Morgana's assault fleet," Merlin explained. "She struck without warning, catching every race beyond the Draconite unaware. The planetary shields held at first, but..."

Thomas watched in horror as red energy surrounded the massive ships, belching out what looked like streams of fire. The energy tore through Camelot's defenses, the ships in orbit unable to match the sheer numbers of the Draconite fleet to overcome the sneak attack. The beautiful spires began to fall, their stained glass shattering in cascading waves of color that would have been breathtaking if not for the destruction they represented. The individuals in the gardens scattered, searching in vain for somewhere to hide as the gardens burned and the flowers turned to ash.

"How many..." Thomas couldn't finish the question.

"All of them," Merlin replied, his voice heavy with ancient grief. "Camelot was completely annihilated. Nothing was ever the same. Arthur..." The hologram shifted to show an Ursan in elaborate high-tech armor, his noble bearing obvious, even in the recording. "Arthur was off-world when it happened. As a prince, he was in the middle of his tour with the Royal Navy. His ship was responding to a distress call when Morgana struck. He heard the news from his superior officers. His parents, his sister, everyone he loved died on Camelot."

"What did he do?"

"What could he do? He became king and fought back. For years we waged war across the stars, trying to contain Morgana's expanding empire. Not satisfied depending on her own kind, she created others like herself—hybrid soldiers loyal only to her. Among them was Mordred."

"Arthur's son?" Thomas asked.

"Technically. She had secretly acquired Arthur's genetic material and combined it with her own. Mordred was her masterpiece. A being with both Ursan control of the arcane arts and Draconite strength and power." Merlin's mechanical form straightened with pride. "But Arthur refused to give up. With the help of the most powerful wizards and the most intelligent, learned scientists among the Ursan, Excalibur was developed, followed by a fleet of similarly advanced ships. With them, we began to push the Draconites back, reclaiming world after world. For a time, it seemed we might actually win."

"Until?" Thomas breathed.

"Until the ambush." The hologram showed a new scene. Excalibur flying alone through an asteroid field. "We were returning from a successful campaign when they struck. Mordred led the attack, his fleet the most elite among the enemy. We were caught between his forces and a spatial anomaly we believe was magically created."

Thomas watched as dozens of ships appeared from hiding places among the asteroids, already firing. Excalibur twisted and turned, juked and deked, avoiding what it could while its offensive blue energy blazed in return.

"Why were you out there alone?" Thomas asked.

"Arthur had sent the rest of the fleet to protect a convoy of refugees. Since there weren't supposed to be any additional enemy forces in the area—nor any anomalies like the one we encountered—we thought we could cross the field without incident." Merlin's voice carried a note of bitter remembrance. "Lancelot swore on it."

The hologram showed Excalibur taking multiple hits, its shields flaring as they absorbed impossible amounts of energy.

"Arthur realized we couldn't win," Merlin continued. "Not against those odds. We managed to open a wormhole. A desperate gambit. We didn't even know where it would lead—we just needed to escape before Mordred could bring his full power to bear."

The hologram showed space itself seeming to tear open, a swirling vortex of energy appearing just as Mordred's ship launched smaller multifaceted vessels that headed straight for Excalibur.

"We entered the wormhole just as the first boarding pod would have reached us," Merlin said. "The portal collapsed behind us, cutting off pursuit. But the battle had damaged our primary systems. We lost control during transit and crashed here, on your world. The impact drove us deep underground, and the geological instability of the region caused us to sink even further over time."

"What happened to Arthur?" Thomas asked quietly.

"He wanted to leave Earth immediately. But we couldn't. Not right away. The risk that Mordred might follow us, the damage his Draconites might do to this planet...Arthur was too compassionate to allow Earth to be laid to waste. Instead, he decided to venture out into your world in hopes of finding a means to communicate with our forces. I don't really know how he planned to accomplish that. But that was the last time I saw him."

"He never came back? Not even once to check in?"

"No. I monitored the surface as best I could through the ship's damaged sensors. I watched as centuries passed, as your civilization slowly grew around us. But he never returned."

Thomas absorbed this in silence, watching the hologram return to its default star field display. Finally, he asked, "So why me? Why now?"

"Because you're the first person in two thousand years who might be able to help," Merlin replied. "The first person who may be worthy."

"You've said that so many times. How do you know I'm worthy?"

"You possess the same qualities Arthur possessed—courage, compassion, intelligence, and most importantly, a desire to rise above circumstances to become something greater."

Thomas laughed bitterly. "You obviously have the wrong guy. I don't possess those qualities at all."

"No? Because your mother was addicted to drugs? Because you killed someone as part of a gang initiation? Because a traumatized woman mistook you for her attacker instead of her savior?"

"How do you know all of that?" Thomas whispered, his breath stolen by surprise. "I didn't tell you any of that."

"I scanned your mind when you entered the cavern," Merlin answered. "I know everything about you. I've checked the algorithms multiple times. The outcomes don't lie."

"I don't believe that."

"Why is it so hard to believe you could be a good person? Your mentor, Vin, certainly saw it in you."

"He changed my life. Anything that's good in me came from him."

"No. He helped you understand who you are. The real you, unencumbered by circumstance. You proved it to yourself when you tried to help that woman. Things didn't go as you planned; they went as fate intended."

"I don't believe in fate."

"That doesn't mean it won't affect you."

Thomas paused, chewing on the idea for a moment. "And if you're right…if I am somehow worthy…what then?"

"Then we put you in the command pod. We reactivate Excalibur's full capabilities and escape this place. And then…" Merlin's mechanical eyes gleamed brighter. "Then we find out if Morgana's empire still exists out there. And if it does, we finish what Arthur started."

Thomas stared at the command pod, its dark gel rippling with streaks of blue energy.

"That's insane," he said finally. "I'm just one person."

"So was Arthur…once," Merlin replied. "Every legend has to start somewhere, Thomas. Why not here? Why not now?"

The question hung in the air between them, demanding an answer that Thomas wasn't sure he was ready to give. His thoughts flashed back to the alley the night before. He had gotten involved because someone was in trouble, and he'd felt compelled to help. Hearing Merlin's tale, knowing there was a galaxy out there that had fallen into darkness, the same feeling crept through every nerve, sending shivers down his body.

"You don't need to believe in fate to believe in destiny," Merlin added.

"I want you to stop scanning my mind," Thomas replied.

"I only scanned it that one time," Merlin said. "I can tell what you're thinking by your expression. Arthur's was similar."

Thomas exhaled sharply. This was beyond insane. At the same time, it felt…right. Besides, what else did he have to do with the rest of his life? Things hadn't gone so well for him on Earth. Maybe his luck would improve somewhere among the stars.

A sudden wave of excitement swept over him, along with a healthy measure of fear. "Well, you probably already know what I'm going to do, so why don't you start telling me how to go about doing it?"

CHAPTER 14

Thomas moved closer to the command pod, studying the intricate patterns that flowed across its surface. The dark gel inside left him feeling uncomfortable, though he already knew from the regeneration pod that it wouldn't hurt him.

"How did Arthur handle it," he asked, "the first time he interfaced with the ship?"

"Quite poorly, actually," Merlin replied, his mechanical form making a sound that might have been a chuckle. "He was sick for three days afterward, but he was determined. He kept trying until he mastered it."

"You said there were other ships like Excalibur. How did those ship commanders handle the interface?"

"Some slightly better. Most worse. There were a few fatalities."

"What?" Thomas said, pulling his hand away from the pod as though it were on fire. "And you want me to get in there?"

"Look..." Merlin moved to stand beside Thomas. His mechanical eyes studied him. "Would you prefer I lie to you? The interface is intense. Experiencing the universe through the ship's sensors, feeling its power as an extension of your own body can be overwhelming at first."

Thomas reached out once more, his fingers hovering just above the gel's surface. "And this stuff...it's what lets you connect?"

"Each of the semi-viscous fluids on board Excalibur serve a different but similar purpose. The gel in the regeneration pod is teeming with nanites, using the gel as both a power source and a means of receiving instruction. This gel amplifies the electrical signals that pass between neurons in your brain, sending them to the ship's systems as control instructions. It's bi-directional, so your brain can also receive inputs directly from the ship."

"What other fluids are there?" Thomas asked.

"One to control the buildup of heat. Another to transfer energy to the hull. A third to clean yourself off at the end of a long day."

Thomas glanced sidelong at the GOLEM. "You might think you're funny. You aren't."

"I'm amused," Merlin answered.

Before he could say anything else, a distant boom echoed through the ship's hull, making Thomas jump. "What was that?"

"It appears your successful entry has upset the status quo," Merlin replied. "The weasel in the suit outside is getting frustrated with his team's lack of progress," Merlin replied. "They've started using explosives, trying to breach the hull."

"Can they?"

"No, but they can further drain the remaining energy stores from the reactor. When that happens, we'll both be stranded here." Another boom emphasized his point. "Worse, we'll lose our shields, and once that happens…"

"It means we're running out of time," Thomas finished. "Who is that guy, anyway?"

"He works for what I've taken to be a mercenary outfit known as Matrix Dynamics. They're leading the operation to excavate and study the ship."

"I've heard of those guys. I've seen them in the news. They aren't mercenaries though, they're government defense contractors. They've been touting some breakthrough technologies they're working on, raising a lot of money from the industry."

"Curious. I'm willing to bet that these technologies will only come to fruition should they succeed in their goal of entering the ship."

"How did they even find you down here?"

Merlin didn't respond, instead motioning to the command pod. "We should accelerate our timeline."

Thomas stared at the GOLEM. "Merlin, what did you do?"

"Why do you think I had anything to do with it?"

"Because that was one of the worst efforts to change the subject I've ever seen."

He responded with a sigh. "Very well. I may have made an effort to communicate back to Avalon. But I had no other choice. The ship's reactor was only estimated to last fifteen hundred years. When the ship's power does run out, I die. Self-preservation is as much a part of my nature as anyone else's."

"So they intercepted your communication?"

"It's encrypted, of course. But they picked up the signal. I had to use a high-powered quantum burst, and I suppose your kind has gained the technology needed to detect it, but none of that matters now that you're here."

"Doesn't it though?" Thomas asked, unconvinced. "How do I know I'm supposed to be here and not that I was just in the right place at the right time. You needed someone down here who isn't with Matrix Dynamics, and I fit the bill."

"I told you, the—"

"Algorithms don't lie," Thomas interrupted. "Maybe not. But how can I be sure that you don't? You're still derived from an organic mind."

Merlin glared at him, glowing blue eyes practically throwing sparks. "We need to get out of here, Thomas. The sooner the better."

Thomas paced away from the pod. "You really do suck at lying."

"Very well," Merlin growled angrily. "I never ran your profile through the algorithms. I have no idea if you're worthy or not. But my instincts tell me you are. If you aren't, we're both in deep trouble anyway. You can't argue that."

Thomas spun around, jaw clenched. He wanted to be angry because he'd started to actually believe in himself. Instead, he deflated. Merlin was right. He couldn't argue his crappy situation.

"Yesterday I was just a courier trying to stay out of trouble. Now you want me to do what? Become some kind of space knight."

"My boy, I don't want you to become anything," Merlin corrected. "I want you to be who you truly are. The person you could be if you stopped letting your past define your future."

"And who is that exactly?"

"I don't know. That's entirely up to you." Merlin gestured at the holographic display. A quick tip of his head and scenes from the war—massive fleets engaged in battle, worlds burning, civilizations falling—filled the display. "But I do know this...somewhere out there, Morgana's empire might still exist. They might have spread across countless galaxies by now, subjugating new species, destroying more worlds. Or perhaps they were destroyed themselves. Either way, don't you want to find out?"

Before Thomas could answer, another detonation rocked the ship.

"Power levels are decreasing," Merlin observed. "We probably have a few hours at most before we're dead under water, as it were. Once the shields are gone, they'll tear this ship apart trying to understand its secrets. And all of Arthur's sacrifice, all that we fought for, will be lost forever."

"No pressure then," Thomas muttered. He turned back to the command pod, studying its graceful lines and flowing patterns. "If I say yes...if I try this...what's the worst that could happen?"

"Oh, any number of terrible things," Merlin replied. "The neural interface could overwhelm your consciousness, leaving you a drooling vegetable. The ship's systems might reject you violently, causing massive internal hemorrhaging. Or you might succeed in connecting, only to find the responsibility of commanding a starship too much to handle, leading to a complete mental breakdown."

"You're really bad at selling this, you know that?"

"If it's any comfort, should the system leave you incapacitated, I am willing and able to end your life quickly and peacefully."

"Thanks, I guess," Thomas replied. "And if it works? If I can actually connect with the ship?"

"Then you'll experience something no human ever has—the ability to touch the stars themselves." Merlin's mechanical form straightened. "You'll have power beyond anything your species has yet achieved, and the responsibility that comes with it. You'll have the chance to make a real difference in the universe, to fight for something greater than yourself."

"And maybe find out what happened to Arthur?"

"After fifteen hundred years..." Merlin's voice trailed

off. "...he's most likely long dead and decomposed, but we can find out what happened to his kingdom. His legacy."

Another detonation rocked the ship.

Thomas looked at the command pod again, remembering the woman in the alley. He'd acted then without thinking, rushing in to help someone who needed it. Maybe this wasn't so different. Maybe this was just helping on a larger scale.

Or maybe he was about to make the biggest mistake of his life.

"Alright," he said finally. "I'll try."

"Excellent!" Merlin crowed. "I knew I could count on you."

In front of Thomas, the command pod pulsed with blue energy, as if acknowledging the choice that had just been made. "So, what do I do? Just hop in? Or do I need to get naked first?"

"Not this time," Merlin replied. "The gel is too thick to permeate your clothing and has hydrophobic qualities that will allow you to leave it behind when you emerge."

Thomas glanced from the GOLEM to the pod one last time. Then he strode back to it. "Do you really think I'm worthy?" he asked. "Be honest, this time."

"Honestly, Thomas, I don't know," Merlin replied, approaching him, "but more importantly, do *you* think you're worthy?"

Doubts flooded Thomas' mind, and he started to back away from the pod. Maybe he shouldn't do this after all. Maybe it would be better if Matrix Dynamics gained control of the ship. Maybe—

His panicked thoughts ceased, and he froze when the pod's canopy lifted up. Inviting him to take the leap. What if he took this chance and it opened a whole new world... no, a whole new galaxy to him? Considering his circumstances, what did he really have to lose?

He turned to Merlin and asked him one final question. "If I do this and make it out the other side with my mind intact, will I know how to fly Excalibur?"

"You'll just have to wait and see."

Merlin shoved him backward into the gel.

It caught him gently, pulling him in as the canopy began to close. "Merlin, you son of a—

"Let's just get on with it already, shall we?" Merlin interrupted. His blue eyes narrowed, taking on a reddish hue.

CHAPTER 15

Thomas thrashed in the thick liquid, his movements sluggish and uncoordinated. Useless, his boots slid against the smooth walls of the pod as he tried to push himself up and out. The gel clung to him, trying to hold him back and keep him within the pod with a persistence that sent shivers down his spine.

"Merlin!" he bellowed. "Let me out!" He slammed his fist against the curved canopy, but the soft material absorbed the impact without so much as a shudder. The holographic displays beyond the pod's clear surface looked distorted through the dark liquid, making Merlin's mechanical form appear to waver and dance like a mirage.

Panic clawed at his chest as the gel reached his shoulders, its strange warmth making it feel invasive, almost predatory. The fluid moved with purpose, tendrils of it wrapping around his arms when he tried to push against the sides of the pod. He quickly pulled them back down, folding them protectively across his chest.

"Relax," Merlin's voice echoed in his head, maddeningly calm. "Fighting only makes it worse."

"Easy for you to say!" Thomas snarled, twisting his body

in another attempt to break free. The effort left him exhausted, his muscles burning from fighting against the gel's inexorable pull. "You're not the one being eaten by alien Jell-O!"

His heart hammered as the fluid crept up his neck, its touch sending electric tingles across his skin. He tried tilting his head back, keeping his face above the surface, but the gel followed relentlessly. When it reached his jaw, despite knowing he was going to be able to breathe the gel in without problem, the primal terror of drowning bypassed all rational thought..

"I can't," he gasped, pressing himself against the back of the pod in a futile effort to gain another few seconds of air. "Merlin, please!" He'd changed his mind. He didn't want to do this. He wanted out.

The gel touched his lips, and Thomas clamped them shut. It rose over his mouth, and he tipped his head back, taking a deep breath and holding it as it covered his nose. He could feel it probing, seeking entry, patient and unstoppable as the tide. Seconds passed. A minute. His lungs began to burn, spots dancing at the edges of his vision as his body demanded oxygen. He fought against the instinct to breathe, knowing that if he opened his mouth or breathed through his nose, the strange fluid would pour in.

His chest finally spasmed as his body betrayed him, forcing his mouth open in a desperate gasp for air. The gel rushed in, flooding his mouth and nose, flowing down his throat. The strange warmth spread through him. He drifted from pure panic into a strange twilight state between waking and dreaming. For a moment, he almost relaxed.

Then the information hit.

It was like the entire internet downloading directly into his brain, all at once. Each new system added to the overwhelming flood of data. Sensor data—temperature readings from every point on the hull, structural integrity reports from thousands of monitoring points, power fluctuations from the reactor core, and astronomical calculations from the navigation computers—crashed like a tsunami into his consciousness.

He could see in every direction simultaneously through external cameras, the images overlapping and blending in his mind until he couldn't tell up from down. He felt the vibrations of Matrix Dynamics's explosions through hull sensors, each impact sending confused signals through his nervous system. The taste of ozone from electrical systems filled his senses, while quantum calculations from the navigation computers sent strange mathematical patterns dancing through his thoughts.

"Too much," he tried to scream, though no sound emerged. "Make it stop!"

"Focus," Merlin commanded. "Don't try to process everything at once. Take it one system at a time."

But how could he focus when every neuron was firing at once, when his brain felt like it was being pulled in a thousand different directions? The ship's primary processing unit thrummed through his consciousness like a second heartbeat. Its quantum core performed calculations that threatened to drive him mad if he looked at them too closely.

Another explosion rocked the ship. This time, Thomas felt it as actual physical pain, as if someone had struck him with a sledgehammer. The sensation was so unexpected, so intense, that he lashed out instinctively. Energy coursed through the hull, systems responding to his distress by sending a feedback pulse that knocked Matrix Dynamics's demolition teams off their feet.

"Good!" Merlin praised. "You're beginning to understand."

But Thomas wasn't understanding. He was drowning in an ocean of input, each new wave threatening to completely pull him under. Shield harmonics screamed through his mind like feedback from a broken speaker. Weapons systems primed and reset themselves, their potential for destruction leaving an acrid taste in his mouth. Life support metrics scrolled past his consciousness in an endless stream of data that meant everything and nothing at once.

His mind raced faster, trying desperately to process the torrent of information. Spots danced in his vision as memories began to surface, triggered by the neural interface attempting to integrate with his consciousness. The images came in violent flashes, each one more vivid than the last.

He saw himself at thirteen, the stolen knife heavy in his sweating palm as he waited in the darkness. The rival gang member walked past, never seeing death lurking in the shadows. The blade moved of its own accord, opening the man's throat in a spray of crimson. The memory was so sharp he could smell the copper tang of blood mixing with garbage from the nearby dumpster.

The scene shifted. Juvenile detention. The rage that burned in his gut day after day, the despair that threatened to consume him whole. The endless rhythm of meals, yard time, and nights spent in his small room, wondering if this was all his life would ever be. He remembered the taste of institutional food, the sound of doors slamming and locking, the feeling of walls closing in around him.

Then Vin appeared, as he always did, a lighthouse in the storm of Thomas' memories. The old Marine's weathered face creased with compassion rather than judgment as he spent hours teaching discipline, channeling anger into purpose. Thomas felt the weight of a practice dummy beneath his fists as he learned to fight with control rather than fury. He heard Vin's gravelly voice telling him he could be more, be better, if he only believed in himself.

"Who am I?" Thomas whispered into the void as the memories crashed over him. "What am I doing here?"

The gel pulsed around him in response, its strange warmth intensifying as more ship's systems came online. Each new connection felt like needles driving into his brain. He could feel himself starting to black out, darkness creeping in at the edges of his consciousness like ink spreading through water.

"I'm not worthy," he gasped, the words torn from his very soul. "I'm not..."

A fresh memory. The woman from the alley, her face contorted in terror as her attacker held the knife to her throat. He remembered the sick feeling in his gut as she crumpled against the wall, unconscious and bleeding, and then, for some reason, she had identified him as her attacker. Maybe she had seen something in him, some darkness he couldn't escape no matter how far he ran.

His body convulsed as the ship's weapons systems suddenly roared to life in his consciousness, unfolding like a deadly blooming flower. Energy weapons that could reduce cities to ash and defensive systems that could shrug off nuclear strikes. Enough raw power to level mountains. The weight of that destructive potential pressed down on him like a physical thing, threatening to crush him beneath its magnitude.

"Let go," Merlin's voice came to him through the maelstrom of data and memory, distant but clear as a bell. "Stop fighting it."

"I can't," Thomas replied, his consciousness fragmenting under the strain. "I'll lose myself." The fear in his voice was raw, primal, the terror of ego death, of being erased and replaced by something else.

"You need to lose yourself to find yourself."

The words struck something deep within Thomas, resonating with a truth he hadn't known he was carrying.

All his life, he'd been trying to be something, desperately searching for somewhere to belong. Each identity had been a mask, a role he played to survive or to please others, or to convince himself he was making progress, but maybe the truth was simpler. Maybe he didn't have to be anything at all.

"I don't know who I am," he admitted finally, the words carrying the weight of absolute truth. His voice cracked as he continued, "I don't know. I've never known. I'm not worthy. Not today. But...maybe I can be."

The moment the words left his lips, something fundamental shifted. The crushing pressure of information eased, becoming more manageable, as if his acceptance had unlocked some hidden strength in his mind. System after system aligned with his thoughts, no longer fighting against him but working with him. The ship's sensor data resolved into clear understanding rather than overwhelming chaos.

He could feel Excalibur now, not as an alien presence trying to consume him, but as an extension of himself. The reactor's pulse became his heartbeat, its core dancing in perfect harmony with his thoughts. The hull became his skin, letting him feel every vibration, every change in temperature, every touch against the ancient metal. The weapons became his hands, their deadly potential now a tool rather than a threat.

"There," Merlin said softly, satisfaction evident in his tone. "Now you're getting it."

Thomas opened eyes he hadn't realized he'd closed. Through the ship's external sensors, he could see the Matrix Dynamics teams regrouping, preparing to trigger more charges.

"Is this how it was for Arthur?" he asked, wondering if the ancient king had gone through the same transformation.

"Everyone experiences the interface differently," Merlin replied, his presence now a comfortable whisper in Thomas' mind rather than an intrusion. "But yes, I imagine it was similar. How do you feel?"

"Like I could touch the stars," Thomas answered honestly. The sensation was incredible. Power beyond anything he'd imagined. Yet somehow, it wasn't overwhelming him anymore. It felt right, as if he'd finally found something he didn't know he'd been missing. "What changed?"

"You did. The interface doesn't require worthiness in the traditional sense. It requires honesty, with yourself most of all. You stopped trying to be something and simply accepted yourself where you are right now."

Another explosion rocked the ship, but this time Thomas easily rode the impact, distributing the force through the hull structure. He could feel power building in the reactor, systems coming fully online for the first time in centuries. The sensation was intoxicating, like waking up after a long sleep, stretching muscles that had grown stiff with disuse.

"They're becoming quite annoying," Merlin observed dryly. "Perhaps it's time we did something about that?"

Thomas smiled, feeling the weapons systems humming with potential. The sensation was no longer frightening. Now it felt like slipping on a comfortable glove. "What do you have in mind?"

"I believe it's time we left Earth behind," Merlin replied. "The choice of how we do so is yours, of course. We could simply lift off, though that might cause some geological instability. Or we could make a more...dramatic exit."

Through the external sensors, Thomas watched Matrix Dynamics's teams setting up another round of explosives. The man in the tweed suit was gesturing angrily, his face red with frustration. The sight should have filled Thomas with anxiety, but instead he felt only a calm certainty. He wasn't running anymore. He wasn't hiding. For the first time in his life, he knew exactly where he belonged.

"Dramatic sounds good," Thomas said, feeling Excalibur's power building around him like a gathering storm. "Besides, I think it's time we showed them exactly what they're dealing with."

The ship's systems responded to his will, power flowing through ancient circuits that had waited two millennia for this moment. After centuries buried under a mountain, Excalibur was ready to fly again.

And Thomas was ready to fly with it.

CHAPTER 16

Through the external sensors, Thomas watched the Matrix Dynamics's demolition team plant what he was about to make sure was a final set of charges against Excalibur's hull. The sensation tickled, like ants marching across his skin.

Thomas flexed his consciousness, testing his connection to the ship's systems. Power coursed through neural pathways that felt both alien and familiar. The reactor thrummed in response, its quantum core spinning up to full capacity for the first time in centuries. Warning klaxons began blaring in the cavern outside as Matrix Dynamics's sensors detected the energy spike.

"They're scared," Thomas observed, chuckling to himself as he watched technicians all around the ship scramble away from the suddenly active vessel. The man in the tweed suit shouted into a phone, his face mottled with rage and fear. "They know the shit's about to hit the fan."

"Their instruments are detecting power signatures beyond anything they've ever seen," Merlin confirmed. "Would you like to give them something more substantial to worry about?"

Thomas' grin widened as he sensed the weapons systems powering up to capacity. A targeting reticle appeared in his mind, outlining the carefully placed explosive charges. "Can we disable those without hurting anyone?"

"Of course. Though I'm curious why you care about their safety."

"They're just doing their jobs," Thomas replied. "No need to hurt them."

He reached out through the weapons grid. Rather than attack the explosives, he did his best to poke them instead. Energy coursed through the hull, emerging as precise beams that struck each explosive charge in rapid succession. The devices sparked and fizzled, rendered harmless by the careful application of force.

"It's active! The artifact is active!" The Matrix Dynamics teams broke into runs as they realized their explosives had been neutralized.

Through the ship's sensors, Thomas could hear their panicked radio transmissions, one after another.

"Get EOD teams back! Now!"

"Sir, energy readings are off the charts!"

"Everyone clear the cavern! Emergency evacuation protocols! Move it! Move it! Move it!"

"Having fun?" Merlin asked, amusement obvious in his voice.

"A little," Thomas admitted. "But we should probably go before they bring in something bigger and badder than C-4."

He extended his awareness through the ship's structural systems, analyzing the rock surrounding them. Centuries of geological pressure had compressed the stone into a dense shell, but he could feel weak points where Matrix Dynamics's excavation had created stress fractures.

"The earth doesn't want to let us go," he said, surprised

by how naturally the technical analysis came to him. "If we push too hard, we could trigger a collapse that would bury half of Wales."

"Then perhaps we should ask politely," Merlin suggested.

Thomas felt the ship's gravity manipulation systems coming online, their quantum fields extending outward to envelop the surrounding rock. Instead of trying to break free by force, they could... "We can phase through it," he realized, in total awe of the ship's capabilities. "Use the gravitational fields to temporarily alter the molecular structure of both the ship and the mountain."

"Very good," Merlin praised. "Though I should warn you, it will take significant power, and we're already running on reserves."

"How do we refuel the reactor?"

"You already know."

Thomas found that he did. Solar radiation would give them a boost, though it would take hours to bring the reactor back to baseline. "Phasing through is better than causing an earthquake and killing people. Are you ready?"

"I've been ready for fifteen centuries."

The drive spooled up, its distinctive hum rising to a pitch that made Thomas' teeth vibrate. Energy coursed through the hull, creating a cascading wave of gravitational distortion that spread outward into the surrounding rock. Through the external sensors, he watched the cavern walls begin to ripple like water.

"Warning! Seismic activity detected!" someone outside shouted. *"The whole bloody mountain is shifting!"*

Thomas felt a moment of vertigo as reality bent around the ship. The sensation of passing through solid rock was indescribable, like moving through thick syrup while simultaneously being everywhere and nowhere at once. His consciousness expanded with the gravitational field, letting him feel every ton of rock they displaced. Every crystal structure they phased through.

Slowly at first, then with gathering speed, Excalibur began to rise. Not by breaking through the mountain, but by becoming temporarily part of it, sharing the same space for fractions of a second before moving upward. The sensation was dizzying, but Thomas maintained his focus, guiding them along the calculated course.

Five hundred feet to the surface. Four hundred. Three hundred...

Approaching the lake that had hidden Excalibur for so long, he could feel through the sensors the mountain's dwindling weight above them. Here, shot through with pockets of air and water, the rock grew less compressed. Less resistive.

Two hundred feet. One hundred...

The final layers of rock parted like curtains as Excalibur breached the surface of Llyn Padarn. Water cascading off her hull in sheets, the ship rose from the lake like some impossible sea monster, her silver hull gleaming in the afternoon sun. Thomas felt a surge of pure joy as fresh air touched the hull for the first time in two millennia.

"I suggest we don't linger," Merlin said. "Unless you'd like to explain this to the local authorities."

"Agreed." Thomas reached for the main drive systems, feeling them respond eagerly. He engaged them with a thought, lighting up the ship's tail in a flare of bright blue.

Excalibur rose into the sky like a sword drawn from its scabbard, her hull shedding the last drops of lake water as she accelerated upward. The sound of her engines—a rising chord that vibrated the air around them—was unlike anything Earth had heard in two thousand years.

As they passed through the clouds, breaking the sound barrier with an emphatic boom, Thomas took one last look at the world below through the ship's sensors. "Goodbye,

Earth," he whispered, feeling a strange mix of sadness and excitement. Everything he'd ever known—his flat, his bike, his simple life as a courier, even his estranged mother—was down there. But ahead lay the stars.

He could only imagine the mysteries beyond.

Feeling the ship's sensors tracking their ascent, he anticipated the energy of atmospheric friction hitting them in thirty seconds. Energy rippled across Excalibur's hull, creating a barrier against the coming heat.

Through the external sensors, Thomas detected multiple radar installations tracking them, military bases scrambling jets that would never catch up. He felt a momentary pang of guilt for the chaos they were causing, imagining the panic in various command centers as they tried to identify the impossible object launching from Welsh airspace.

"I'm picking up radio chatter from RAF bases," he said. "They're trying to decide if we're a threat."

"Are we?" Merlin asked, genuine curiosity in his tone.

Thomas considered the weapons at his disposal. He could wipe London off the map in an instant if he wanted. "No," he said finally.

The atmosphere began to thin as they climbed higher, bursting through the last wisps of clouds. Above them, the blue of Earth's sky gradually darkened toward the blackness of space. Below, the curve of Earth became visible, the blue and green beneath the clouds achingly beautiful. Thomas felt a sudden, profound appreciation for his homeworld, seeing it from this perspective for the very first time.

And perhaps the last.

The main drives reached full power, their song changing from a hum to a rising chord that echoed in the spaces between atoms. Stars loomed in the distance as the last scattered molecules of Earth's atmosphere fell away.

Thomas took one last look at Earth through the ship's sensors. Somewhere down there, a woman thought he was a monster. Somewhere else, Matrix Dynamics executives were probably having fits because their impossible prize had escaped. And in a thousand other places, people were looking up, wondering if they had just seen what they thought they had.

As Earth grew smaller behind them, Thomas' awareness expanded through Excalibur's sensor network like water through the roots of a tree. Colors he had no words for painted electromagnetic frequencies, quantum fluctuations, gravitational eddies and other non-visual measurements, turning it all into raw navigational data. The delicate web of human satellites and orbiting debris seemed primitive now, the radio chatter like whispers compared to the symphony of information flooding his consciousness. He settled into it, the flow quickly becoming more like a smooth lake than a turbulent river.

For the first couple of minutes, at least.

The first hint of danger came as a ripple through the sensors, a distortion radiating out from behind Mars. Thomas' newly expanded consciousness picked up three massive power signatures emerging from the planet's shadow. Pulled from Excalibur's ancient databanks, instant recognition of their power signatures coursed through his mind.

"Merlin," he said, tension and fear coiling in his gut, his heart rate leaping into overdrive. "I think someone in Avalon got your message."

"It appears that way," Merlin replied, his voice equally tense. "But it's the wrong someone."

CHAPTER 17

Thomas shivered at the sight of the Draconite warships, three small but still impressive destroyers accelerating on an intercept course.

Each vessel had the vague appearance of a dragon, with a sharp triangular bow flanked by a pair of protrusions resembling bent wings. Their surfaces reflected light as though they were covered in shimmering greenish-black scales, save for dark spots where internal weapon ports were positioned. With the neural link translating their presence into sensory input that transcended normal human perception, they tasted like burning metal and smelled like ancient leather.

"How did they find..." Thomas' question died in his throat as a warning flashed through his mind. The destroyers were powering up their weapons, the energy buildup like static electricity crawling across his skin. He didn't need to finish asking; he knew how they had found Excalibur.

Like Matrix Dynamics, they had picked up the message Merlin had sent in a desperate effort to save his existence.

Then, they'd waited.

Thomas reached out for defensive controls with his mind, but everything was happening too fast. Too many systems—power distribution, weapons targeting, shields, thrust, flight control—simultaneously demanded his attention. Each one required his input, and he had to manage them all alone, resulting in his unpracticed mind fumbling with the controls. He desperately tried to establish defensive coverage before…

The lead Draconite ship opened fire.

Red energy lanced across space faster than any human weapon could track. The beam struck Excalibur's port side and shattered against the shields. Even so, the impact translated through the neural link like a sledgehammer to his ribs.

"They've upgraded their weapons," Merlin commented as though it were a surprise. "This isn't good. Thomas, you need to get us out of here."

"Right," Thomas replied. "Here goes nothing."

His head began pounding as he tried to process the overwhelming flood of sensor data while simultaneously figuring out how to actually fly a starship. The neural interface translated his thoughts into action, but those actions weren't quite what he intended. Excalibur lurched to port as he overcorrected, the movement more violent than he expected.

"What are you doing?" Merlin demanded as they tumbled through space. "The controls respond to thought, not muscle memory. You're thinking like an Earth pilot."

"I'm not thinking like any kind of pilot!" Thomas snapped back, fighting to stabilize their flight path. The Draconite ships were gaining rapidly, their dragon-like forms growing larger in the sensor feed. "I deliver packages on a bicycle!"

He tried to level out, but without a proper reference point for *up*, he instead sent them into a wild spin. The neural interface translated the motion into a sensation of vertigo that made his stomach lurch.

"Stop trying to fly it like an airplane," Merlin advised, his tone managing to convey both amusement and concern. "There's no air resistance here. No gravity wells nearby strong enough to matter. Think in vectors instead."

"That would be great advice if I knew what the hell you were talking about!" Another attempted course correction sent them tumbling in a new direction. Through the sensor feed, Thomas could see Earth rotating past as they spun. The sight was simultaneously beautiful and nauseating.

"A vector is—"

"I don't need a physics lesson right now!" Thomas interrupted. "I need to figure out how to fly this thing before those ships catch up and obliterate us!"

The sensor feed showed the Draconite vessels spreading out into an attack formation, their weapons already charging. The neural interface translated the energy buildup into an uncomfortable prickling sensation across his skin.

"Perhaps if you stopped arguing and focused on the task at hand?" Merlin suggested.

"I am focusing!" Thomas mentally reached for the drive controls again, trying to find some stability in the chaotic tumble. Instead, he accidentally triggered the lateral thrusters, sending them into a roll. "Everything just keeps moving!"

"Of course it keeps moving. That's how space works. Objects in motion tend to stay in motion unless—"

"Merlin, I swear, if you quote Newton at me while we're about to die..."

A warning flashed through his mind as the lead Draconite ship fired again. Thomas reactively jerked away from the threat. The movement translated into another wild course change that sent them careening wildly in another vector as the energy beam lanced harmlessly past.

"Well," Merlin observed dryly, "at least you're making us a difficult target."

"That wasn't intentional!" Thomas tried to visualize their course, to think in three dimensions without reference points. It was like trying to swim in a pool with no water. "How the hell did Arthur handle this?"

"Much better than you, I must say. Though he did have some pilot training beforehand."

Thomas made another attempt at stabilization, this time managing to at least stop their spinning. The sensor feed settled enough to show him the Draconite ships had closed half their original distance. "Can't you help?"

"I'm an Advisor, not a pilot," Merlin replied. "I can tell you what you're doing wrong, but I don't have permissions to actually fly the ship."

"Then advise me! Tell me how to—"

His words cut off as the lead Draconite ship opened fire a third time. Once again, only their erratic movement saved them from a direct hit.

"Vectors," Merlin said quickly, "are simply directions of movement with speed attached. Don't think about up or down. Think about where you want to go and how fast. And remember, there's nothing to slow us down except us. So to fly in the opposite direction, you first have to come to a stop along your current vector to accelerate back the other way."

Thomas tried to wrap his mind around the concept while simultaneously watching the Draconite ships through the sensor feed. They were spreading out further, obviously trying to box Excalibur in.

"Where I want to go is away from them. Fast."

He reached for the flight controls again, this time trying to forget he had ever seen Star Wars. Instead of pulling back on a stick that didn't exist, he simply thought about moving away from the threat at maximum acceleration.

Excalibur's vectoring thrusters pushed them sideways until they had achieved the new vector. The main engines flared, blue energy pouring from the stern as the ship shot forward, finally moving in a straight line. The sudden acceleration pressed Thomas deeper into the command gel, which absorbed the majority of the g-forces.

"Better," Merlin said. "Though perhaps we could avoid traveling on a completely predictable vector?"

"One thing at a time!" Thomas replied. But he was starting to understand how the neural interface translated his intentions into flight control. The key was not thinking about how to make the ship do something, but simply thinking about what he wanted it to do.

Unfortunately, the Draconite ships were still gaining. Their drives burned like red stars in the sensor feed as they accelerated in pursuit, their formations tightening for another attack run.

"Those ships are faster than they should be," Merlin observed. "They've made significant improvements since the last time I encountered them."

"Great," Thomas muttered. "That's just great. Any other helpful observations?"

"Yes, actually. They're about to fire again."

Thomas reached for the flight controls, ready to attempt his first intentional evasive maneuver. He just hoped he could pull it off without sending them spinning off into deep space.

After all, how hard could it be?

The answer, as multiple energy beams cut through the space around them, turned out to be…very hard.

CHAPTER 18

The first beam of red energy passed Excalibur close enough for Thomas to feel its heat through the neural interface like a sunburn. He panicked, his mind jerking away from the sensation. Excalibur responded to his fear by lurching in three directions at once, the thrusters engaging erratically as his untrained thoughts triggered multiple systems simultaneously.

"That's not how you…" Merlin started to say, but another energy beam cut through space where they'd been a second before. "Though I suppose if it works…"

"Nothing about this is working!" Thomas felt the thrusters surge again as he tried to establish some kind of controlled flight path. Instead, the ship cork-screwed away from the attacking vessels in an uncontrolled tumble. "I can't make it stop doing that!"

"Perhaps because you keep thinking about what you don't want it to do, instead of—"

Three more energy beams sliced past them, the Draconite ships spreading out to create overlapping fields of fire. Thomas' attempt to dodge sent them into a wild sideways roll that somehow carried them between two of the attacks. The third beam grazed their shields, the impact translating through the neural interface like someone had punched him in the kidney.

"Damn it!" he cried, instinctively trying to curl into a ball. The movement translated into yet another erratic course change, sending them spinning away from the Draconite vessels. "Why does that have to hurt?"

"You're part of the ship, and the ship is part of you," Merlin explained as Thomas struggled to make sense of the tumbling sensor feed.

"Is that a bug or a feature?"

"I don't understand?"

"It's a terrible design!" Another attempt to stabilize their flight sent them pinwheeling through space. The sensor feed showed Earth, then Mars, then the sun, then the Draconite ships, all spinning past in a nauseating kaleidoscope. "I'm going to be sick."

"The gel will clear any expelled matter," Merlin said helpfully.

"That's not the advice I was looking for."

The Draconite ships had nearly caught up to them, their energy weapons preparing for another salvo. Thomas tried to focus on the flight controls, but everything kept moving. He couldn't tell which way was up, which way was forward, or how to make the spinning stop.

"Remember, don't think about the controls," Merlin said. "Think about where you want to go."

"Away!" Thomas thought desperately. "Far away!"

The main drive engaged, adding forward momentum to their already chaotic tumble. Now they were spinning and hurtling through space at ridiculous speed, like a thrown football with no aerodynamics to stabilize it.

"This is not optimal," Merlin observed as another energy beam passed through the space they'd occupied a second before. "Though I must admit, your random movements are making us rather difficult to hit. Perhaps you're a more skilled pilot than I realized."

"I'm not doing any of it on purpose!" Thomas felt the shields absorb another glancing hit, this one like a sharp jab to his collarbone. He flinched from the pain, accidentally triggering the lateral thrusters. Excalibur shot sideways while still tumbling, somehow avoided three more energy beams through pure chaos.

The Draconite ships adjusted formation again, trying to predict where their erratic target might go next. But there was no pattern to predict. Thomas was barely managing to keep them moving, let alone flying with any kind of purpose.

"We need to get out of here," he said, fighting down another wave of nausea as the sensor feed continued its wild spinning. "Can't we just...I don't know, teleport or something?"

"Actually, yes," Merlin replied. "I've already initiated the wormhole generator. But it will take approximately two minutes to power up."

"Two minutes?" Thomas watched the Draconite ships through the spinning sensor feed, their weapons charging for another attack. "We'll be dead in two minutes!"

"Then I suggest you keep doing...whatever this is...until then."

A countdown appeared in Thomas' mind, the seconds ticking away with agonizing slowness. All they had to do was survive for two more minutes. Judging by the energy building up in the Draconite weapons, that would be much easier said than done.

Thomas didn't pay attention to the status of the wormhole generator. He was too focused on the Draconite ships and his desperate attempts to gain some kind of intentional control.

Red energy lanced past Excalibur again, missing only

because he'd fired the ventral thrusters while trying once more to guide the ship where he wanted it to go.

"One hundred and ten seconds to generation," Merlin announced.

"Don't count. It's distracting!"

Another energy beam struck their shields, the impact hitting Thomas like a baseball bat to the ribs. He gasped in pain, unconsciously trying to protect his midsection. The movement translated into a wild spiral that somehow carried them between two more energy beams.

"Perhaps greater distraction would lead to better results. Shall I put on some music?"

Thomas perked up. Now that was something that might actually help. He'd often listened to music while riding through Manchester. He'd always felt the beats helped add a rhythmic flow to his pedaling. "That's not a bad idea. Do you have Earth music?"

"Yes, though I was only able to collect limited samples due to the damage to the ship's receivers."

"I'll take what I can get."

Music suddenly blared in Thomas' mind.

Bagpipes.

"Turn it off!" Thomas cried.

"You just said—"

"Forget what I just said. That's not music!"

The bagpipes stopped as quickly as they'd started. In their sudden absence, Thomas managed to level their roll and alter the ship's vector, switching direction as the latest Draconite attack speared the area around where he might have otherwise been.

"You did it!" Merlin praised.

"I did, didn't I?" Thomas answered. "Maybe I'm starting to get the hang of this."

With his newfound confidence, he mentally reached for the weapons controls, hoping to return fire. But coordinating weapon systems while flying proved to be a level of difficulty he wasn't quite ready for. His first shot went wide, disappearing into the void. His second missed by even more. Worse, Excalibur lost the smooth flight path he'd gained.

"Perhaps we should focus on staying alive," Merlin suggested as another barrage of energy beams filled the space around them.

"I am focusing!" Thomas tried to stabilize their flight again, but only managed to change the axis of their latest tumble. The Draconite ships had nearly reached them, their dragon-like forms growing larger with each passing second. "Why won't they just leave us alone?"

"They've waited a long time for this moment," Merlin replied. "Why would they give up, especially with victory so close at hand?"

"You don't think I can keep evading them," Thomas accused.

"You've proven that you can evade them, but only accidentally. Mathematically speaking, the chances of that continuing are like winning a game of dice."

"You have dice in Avalon?"

"Doesn't everyone have dice?"

The lead ship fired again, its energy beam passing so close that Thomas felt its heat on his own skin as the actual heat registered on Excalibur's hull. He instinctively jerked away from the sensation, sending Excalibur into another uncontrolled maneuver that somehow carried them to relative safety.

Even so, Merlin was right. Their luck was bound to run out, probably before the two minutes to wormhole generation were up.

"Eighty seconds," Merlin said.

"I told you to stop..." Thomas cut his words off as multiple energy beams converged on their position. Two missed completely, but the third struck their shields amidships. The impact felt like someone had dropped a car on his chest. His vision blurred as pain shot through his entire body.

Warning signals screamed through his mind. *Shields fluctuating, power distribution systems struggling to compensate, hull temperature rising from the direct hit.* He tried to make sense of it all, but the data crashed against his consciousness like waves against a shoreline.

"Sixty seconds," Merlin announced, his voice tense. "Perhaps try to avoid being hit again?"

"You try flying this thing!" Thomas watched helplessly as the Draconite ships moved to surround them, their weapons charging for what would likely be a killing blow. He gathered his thoughts, forcibly calming his mind for a couple of seconds. The ship leveled out again, but at the worst possible time.

"No! Don't fly straight!" Merlin shouted.

But Thomas had an idea. Probably a stupid one, but maybe one crazy enough to work. Sensing the buildup of energy on the Draconite ships, he had a feel for when they would release it in their direction. He waited for that moment to come before releasing the tidal wave of chaos in his head, where he tried to make multiple maneuvers at once under the heading of *anything to not die*.

Excalibur responded by executing a maneuver that would have been impossible in atmosphere and might have been impossible in space too if Thomas had known any better. They shot straight up relative to their previous course while simultaneously spinning end over end and sliding sideways.

The Draconite ships fired, their energy beams converging on the space Excalibur had occupied a heartbeat before. Thomas felt the heat of their passage through the neural interface as the weapons crossed paths behind them.

"Forty seconds," Merlin said.

Thomas didn't bother responding. The Draconite ships were already reorienting themselves for another attack, their weapons cycling faster now. He could practically feel their frustration through the sensor feed, their increasing desperation to destroy their target translating into more aggressive tactics.

Energy beams lanced out from all three ships simultaneously. Thomas' panicked reaction sent them tumbling through the barrage like a thrown playing card, still avoiding direct hits through a combination of luck and pure accident.

"Twenty seconds!"

A glancing blow struck their shields like a knife between Thomas' ribs. He cried out, accidentally triggering multiple thrusters at once. Excalibur shot off at an angle he didn't even have words to describe, tumbling, sliding and rolling all at the same time.

"Ten seconds!"

The Draconite ships tried to stay close, but struggled to match their maneuvers to Excalibur's. Rather than attempt to keep up, they focused on their weapon systems. Thomas felt the energy spike through the neural interface. As far as he could tell, they were going to fire everything they had, filling space with so much energy that even his random movements couldn't save them.

"Five seconds!"

Thomas caught glimpses of the attacking ships through the sensor feed, their hulls rippling with power, their formation tightening for a final coordinated strike.

"Three!"

Energy began to cascade from the Draconite vessels, the beams reaching out like the claws of some enormous predator.

"Two!"

Thomas felt reality beginning to bend around them as the wormhole generator reached full power. But the enemy weapons were going to reach them first.

"One!"

Space itself tore open in front of them, revealing a whorl of even darker energy ahead just as the energy beams converged on their position. Thomas felt the weapons' heat through the neural interface, like standing next to an opened blast furnace.

"Now!"

Thomas threw every bit of his mental energy into the thrusters. Excalibur shot forward, diving into the wormhole's maw. Reality twisted around them as they entered the tunnel, the Draconite ships' final attack tight on their tail.

The wormhole collapsed behind them, cutting off the beams and further pursuit.

Somehow—through fate maybe, though Thomas remained reluctant to believe in such a thing—they had made it.

CHAPTER 19

Reality snapped back into focus like a rubber band, the wormhole spitting Excalibur out at the same velocity with which they'd entered. His mind spun as the neural interface processed the transition, sensor data flooding his consciousness in a jumbled torrent.

"Woooooo! We made it!" he cried, trying to pump his fists in the gel, only to have them bump up against the transparent lid. "Where are we?"

"Somewhere in Avalon," Merlin replied, his tone suggesting his answer should be sufficient.

"That's helpful," Thomas said. "Isn't Avalon a galaxy?"

"It is. With over four thousand habitable worlds spanning millions of light years."

The numbers involved boggled Thomas' mind. Thankfully, didn't need to wrap his head around the sheer scale right now.

"So...could you be a bit more specific about where we are in Avalon?"

"No."

Thomas waited for elaboration, but none came. "What do you mean, no?"

"I mean exactly what I said," Merlin answered. "I don't know where we are."

"But you know we're in Avalon."

"Yes."

"How?"

"The coordinates I entered into the wormhole generator are in Avalon."

"And I assume since you don't know where we are, that means we haven't reached those coordinates."

"Correct."

"Then how do you know we're in Avalon?"

Merlin didn't reply right away. The GOLEM went still, as though he had vacated it to check on something. Like where the hell in the universe they had wound up.

"I've confirmed we're in Avalon," he announced when he returned.

"Just like you confirmed that I was worthy?" Thomas asked.

"You are worthy."

"You didn't know that before you shoved me into the command pod. I could have died, by the way."

"Yes, you could have. But you didn't. Neither of us did, and we have you to thank for it, even if you are the worst starship pilot I've ever seen."

"You could be nicer to the guy who just saved your life."

"I am grateful, my boy. You've nearly matched my expectations so far. I presume you'll continue to do so. As for how I know we're in Avalon...the sensors are registering magical distortion. Someone needs to be using magic to create distortion, and since humans don't have the faintest clue about what real magic is, it can't be them. Thus, Avalon. You can sense it for yourself, if you don't believe me."

Thomas mentally absorbed the sensor data, focusing on

magical distortion readings. Sure enough, they were greater than zero, though not much, wherever they were. "Okay, I accept that we're likely in Avalon. Why didn't we reach the coordinates?"

"I've spent the last fifteen hundred years buried under a mountain. As I mentioned earlier, some systems remain damaged despite my best efforts at maintenance."

"So you're telling me we just jumped into a wormhole with no guarantee of where we would come out?"

"Would you have preferred to stay and be destroyed by the Draconites?" Merlin asked. "Because that was our only other option."

"No, but—"

"The wormhole generator did what it was designed to do, which is more than I honestly expected given its condition. We're alive, and we're somewhere in Avalon. That's better than being dead on Earth."

Thomas absorbed this, watching distant stars wheel past as Excalibur continued moving along their exit vector. "I suppose you have a point. Now, what do we do? We can't just drift around hoping to stumble across something familiar."

"Actually, that's exactly what we're going to do," Merlin replied. "Though preferably with less drifting and more controlled flight. Speaking of which, perhaps you'd like to stabilize our course? We're still spinning rather dramatically."

"Really? I hadn't noticed."

"That's because the gel absorbs ninety-eight percent of your inertia. Otherwise, you'd be splattered against the canopy."

"So if I want to get out of this pod, I need to level us off."

"Internal inertial dampening will still lessen the pressure, but it's highly recommended."

Thomas mentally reached for the flight controls, trying to remember how he'd managed to level out during the battle. His first attempt sent them into an even tighter spin.

"Not like that," Merlin chided. "Remember what I said earlier?"

"I remember you trying to give me a physics lesson while we were being shot at," Thomas replied, making another attempt at stabilization. This time he managed to at least slow their rotation. "Which wasn't particularly helpful."

"On the contrary, you performed quite well once you stopped trying to fly like you were in atmosphere."

"I performed quite well at randomly flailing through space," Thomas corrected. He finally managed to bring them to a relatively stable orientation. "None of that was skill."

"Sometimes the best skill is knowing when to embrace chaos," Merlin said sagely.

"That doesn't even make sense." Thomas studied the sensor feeds, trying to find something—anything—that might help them get their bearings. "So what's wrong with the navigation system? Can we fix it?"

"Many things, and probably not quickly," Merlin replied. "I had planned to enlist your aid to effect repairs while still in the cavern, but Matrix Dynamics's efforts to breach the hull somewhat accelerated our timeline."

"They did seem pretty insistent about getting in."

"Yes, well, who wouldn't want access to technology far beyond their current capabilities? Though I suspect they would have been disappointed by what they found."

"Why's that?"

"Because the majority of Excalibur's systems aren't purely technological," Merlin explained. "They're a blend of science and the arcane."

"Wait. I know you mentioned that the original mind

you're copied from was a wizard, but the ship is magical, too?"

"Probably not like whatever you're thinking. Excalibur is imbued with enchantments, not reliant on spells."

"So how does it work?" Thomas asked. "The wormhole generator, for instance?"

"It works quite well when it isn't damaged."

"That's not what I meant. How does it actually function? What's the underlying mechanism?"

"It uses magic."

"Yes, but how does the magic work?"

"I don't know," Merlin admitted. "It just does."

"That's not very scientific."

"Hence why we call it magic." Merlin's tone suggested he was enjoying Thomas' frustration. "If we understood how it worked, it wouldn't be magic anymore, would it?"

Thomas started to argue, then stopped himself. His head had begun to throb, and exhaustion was creeping in around the edges of his consciousness. The neural interface felt heavier somehow, as if the gel itself were growing thicker.

"Okay, one other magic-related question. Do wizards use staffs or wands?"

"It depends on the wizard."

"What did the living version of you use?"

"I had a staff and a wand. But I didn't need them to use magic. Devices like those only serve to amplify the energy. Obviously, a staff is bigger than a wand and thus offers greater amplification. Why do you ask?"

"Just curious. One more question?"

"Go ahead."

"Can I get out of this thing now?"

"You need to set it to autopilot first. That will keep us on our current vector."

"You had to say vector there, didn't you?"

"Yes."

Thomas set the autopilot with a thought. "Okay, now will you let me out?"

"You don't need my permission. Open the canopy and climb out."

Thomas glared at Merlin's GOLEM through the gel. "Could I have done that at any time?"

"Of course. You're in the command pod. What do you think the word 'command' means?"

Thomas sighed, feeling especially weary. "I need food. And a nap."

He pictured the pod opening. The canopy lifted with a soft hiss, the dark gel receding from around his head and shoulders. He tried to sit up, but his arms felt like they were made of lead. His second attempt had him leaning over the side of the pod, his lungs expelling the gel, before the flight deck started spinning.

"I don't feel so good," he managed to say before he got a leg over the side and started to slide. He would have fallen face-first onto the deck if Merlin's mechanical form hadn't caught him.

"Easy there," the Advisor said, effortlessly supporting Thomas' weight. "The first neural interface session is always the most difficult. Though I must say, you're handling it better than most. Arthur was completely incapacitated for several hours."

"Really?" Thomas asked as Merlin helped him stand. He noticed his clothes were completely dry despite being submerged in the gel. Even his boots were untouched. "You aren't lying to make me feel better?"

"Of course not."

Thomas' eyes narrowed at the GOLEM, certain Merlin was in fact lying. Regardless, he decided to accept it as truth. His ego needed a boost right now. "I can't believe I actually survived a space battle."

"Neither can I, to be honest," Merlin said.

"Thanks for the vote of confidence." Thomas' stomach growled loudly. "Is there food somewhere? Real food, not more gel?"

"The galley is one deck down. Do you think you can make it?"

"I think so." Thomas took one shaky step, then another. His legs felt steadier with each movement. "Though I wouldn't mind if you stayed close, just in case."

They made their way to the transport field, Thomas leaning on Merlin's mechanical form occasionally when vertigo struck. The tingling sensation of the field was barely noticeable compared to the lingering effects of the neural interface.

The galley turned out to be a surprisingly spartan space, with enough seating for a full crew of thirteen positioned around a small round table. A machine resembling a coffeemaker rested on a counter against the far bulkhead.

"What would you like?" Merlin asked as Thomas dropped into one of the seats.

"What do you have?" Thomas replied.

Merlin's mechanical form moved to the coffeemaker device and tapped on the top of it. A moment later, he returned with a small, pink, translucent cube.

"What's that?" Thomas asked suspiciously. "Because it looks suspiciously like gel to me."

"A nutrient cube. Concentrated sustenance. It contains everything your body needs to replenish its energy stores."

Thomas took the cube dubiously. "What does it taste like?"

"There's only one way to find out."

Thomas sniffed the cube. It had no discernible odor. Shrugging, he took a small bite.

His eyes widened in surprise. "Coffee and caramel?"

"I suppose," Merlin replied. "The cube is formulated so

that it will provide whatever taste you find most appealing at any given moment. It's easier to ensure you'll receive proper nutrition that way."

Thomas finished the cube in three bites, already feeling better. The fog in his mind began to clear, replaced by a surge of energy. He stood up, surprised by how good he felt.

"That cube is amazing! I'm starting to like magic. I don't even need a nap now. We should get back to the flight deck and…"

The world tilted sideways as vertigo struck. His legs buckled, and he found himself looking up at Merlin's mechanical face from the deck.

"It appears you may have suffered some negative side effects from the neural interface. I believe another trip to the regeneration pod is in order."

Thomas couldn't argue with that. He couldn't argue with anything at all, since unconsciousness claimed him before he could form a reply.

CHAPTER 20

Thomas' eyes fluttered open. Once again, he was in Arthur's...no, the captain's quarters, naked under the soft blankets. A shrinking part of his psyche lamented that everything from the alley to now hadn't been a dream.

He sat up slowly, waiting for a round of dizziness that never came. He felt so much better, he only now realized how much of a toll the neural interface had taken on him. Still, the effort hadn't killed him. Somehow, for some reason, the ship had found him worthy. He still couldn't quite believe it. Maybe that was part of the damages Merlin had mentioned. Speaking of which...

"Merlin?" he said softly, looking around the room for the Advisor's golem. "Are you here?"

No answer. Thomas exhaled, grateful for a few minutes alone. It was all so much to take in, and had happened so fast. If this was actually real...

His gaze shifted to the collection of alien weapons. If this was real, there was an entire race of mutant dragon aliens who wanted Excalibur and anyone associated with it very dead.

Strangely enough, Thomas was okay with that. Vin had urged him to fight for the common good, instead of for himself. Maybe this was his chance.

With Merlin elsewhere, Thomas climbed out of bed, put on the clothing the Advisor had left for him—in a deep red this time instead of blue—and made his way to the bulkhead where he had seen the invisible hatch open earlier. He had thought the regeneration pod healed him well the first time, but somehow he felt even better now.

Or maybe just...different.

Standing off against the visually seamless wall, Thomas considered how he might convince it to open. He remembered what Merlin said about the teleportals, as he spontaneously decided to call them. Think where you want to go.

He thought about the bulkhead opening, and his desire to exit the quarters. His face split in a wide grin as the wall parted smoothly. Maybe he still couldn't fly the ship in a straight line, but at least he could open a door. He would take victories—no matter the size— wherever he could get them.

Stepping out into the sterile corridor, he had to decide where he wanted to go. He remembered the route from the room to the flight deck, and that he had walked past the galley on the way there.

His stomach rumbled at the thought of another nutrition cube. His brain agreed, with a force that left him wondering if the little pink gel cubes could become addictive.

He navigated the ship's passageways on his own, his courier's experience memorizing paths and directions coming into play. Within no time, he stepped into the galley and approached the cube machine. A tap of the lid, and the machine made a short whirring sound before delivering a single square of too-pink deliciousness.

"Ahh, there you are."

Thomas flinched in response to Merlin's voice directly

behind him. He whirled around, hands up in a fighting position, growling when he saw the GOLEM. "How did you sneak up on me like that?"

"You were too focused on your nutrition cube," Merlin replied. "How do you feel?"

"Surprisingly well. Even better than the first time." Thomas lowered his hands and reached for the cube.

"It's not wise to use the pod too often, as it can cause genetic degradation over time. But in this case, I believe it was justified. The nanites understand your ability to interface with the ship, and will have reconfigured your brain to strengthen your connection."

Thomas had been raising the cube to his mouth. He paused, eying the GOLEM. "Hold up. You're saying the nanites modified my brain?"

"Of course. Genetic modification is the primary purpose of the technology."

"I thought the pod only restored my body to prime condition, not that it would turn me into a mutant."

"It's not a mutation. Mutations are chaotic and uncontrollable."

"Like my mom," Thomas joked, though it fell flat on the Advisor. "So what would you call it, then?"

"An enhancement. Though technically, they are restoring your physical capabilities to the ideal. They couldn't strengthen your neural pathways if you didn't possess the genetics to do so in the first place."

"I guess that makes sense." Thomas took a bite of the cube. "Oh man, pumpkin spice," he said after he chewed and swallowed. "Is it okay if I get addicted to these?"

"No. Too much of a good thing is never a good thing."

"Well, how many can I eat in a given day?"

"I would advise no more than six. The cubes are intended as a temporary replacement for real food."

"I'll try," Thomas promised, devouring the rest of his

cube. "I forgot to ask before. What was Arthur's favorite flavor?"

"Mutton."

"And yours?"

"Mead. Specifically, Camelot's Finest." Merlin sighed. "I miss eating. And I miss Camelot. Speaking of which, it's obvious the Draconites are still in the picture, and strong enough to have had ships waiting for us on liftoff. Clearly, the loss of Arthur and Excalibur had a devastating effect on the war effort."

"Do you think they turned the tide again? I hate to say it, but what if the Ursan were wiped out instead?"

The GOLEM's eyes dimmed and its head lowered. "Then it is a very dark time for Avalon." It perked up again a moment later. "But I refuse to give in to despair. I've waited a long time to get back home."

"A really long time," Thomas agreed. "Humans didn't even have gunpowder yet, and you were already flying around in magical starships. I can't even imagine what the Avalon galaxy might be like now."

"It hasn't been as long as you might think," Merlin answered. "And one thing humankind will learn if they survive long enough is that once you've mastered most scientific avenues, the pace of change slows considerably. The problems you're trying to solve, the things you're attempting to prove all become so complex they may not be solvable at all. While the Draconite ships we encountered were more powerful than in my past experience, they didn't look or act significantly different."

"Can you give me an example of a complex problem?"

"Of course. Identifying the underlying nature of magic."

"But then it wouldn't be magic anymore."

"No, which is of course why it was and likely still is such a well-funded pursuit."

"But that would kind of take all the fun out of it, wouldn't it?"

"Indeed. Personally, I prefer that the arcane remain arcane. As I like to say, a life without mystery isn't a life worth living."

"I'll eat to that," Thomas said, reaching for the cube maker.

Merlin put his hand over the top of the device, preventing him from touching it. "Pace yourself. Too many too fast will send you to the head with severe cramping in no time."

Thomas pulled his hand back. "Fine. What did you mean when you said it hasn't been as long as I might think? I think it's been fifteen hundred years, because that's what you told me."

"A reasonable but incorrect assumption."

"I'm confused."

"Time dilation, my boy. Created by the effects of the many celestial vagaries in the ten billion light years between Earth and Avalon. I spent fifteen hundred years buried under that lake. It's been a little over one hundred years here."

Thomas paused to consider this. "So you're saying time is fifteen times slower here than in the Milky Way?"

"In its most basic explanation, yes."

"So if I stay here for ten years, it will be one hundred fifty years later on Earth."

"Your math skills are astounding."

"That really works out in your favor, doesn't it?"

"Of course. I truly enjoyed wallowing underground for centuries while Morgana and her ilk waged war against my people."

"I mean, you spent all that time trapped on Earth but you haven't lost that same amount of time here."

"It's a double-edged sword, but I suppose you're right."

"So what do we do now? You might be able to live for another fifteen centuries, but I don't want to float aimlessly out here forever."

"Obviously," Merlin replied. "I propose that our next step should be to confirm the situation in Avalon. To do that, we would need to figure out where we are, and utilize that information to make our way to somewhere useful. At that point, perhaps we can gather the means to effect repairs on the ship at the same time we gather additional information."

"Propose?" Thomas asked. "Why don't you just do it?"

"I'm an Advisor, remember? I advise. I don't have the ability to act without the permission of the ship's captain, who at this specific point in time happens to be you."

"When you put it like that, I get the feeling there's mutiny somewhere in my future. A trade-up for someone more worthy, maybe?"

"I don't have the capacity to mutiny against the ship's captain. But that doesn't preclude you from being captured or killed and someone else taking your place. I'm not your friend, Thomas. I'm your Advisor."

"Right. Were you Arthur's friend?"

"No."

Thomas frowned. The speed and tone of the answer left him more certain that he could pick up on Merlin's lies.

Possibly sensing this, Merlin added more of an explanation to his answer. "As an Advisor, it's my duty to provide you with the most complete selection of options to any given situation. Closeness begets bias, which can affect that duty."

"You may be digitized, but you still came from a living mind. Bias is unavoidable."

"I came from a living mind, but as a digital copy, I'm

still subject to certain controls," Merlin reminded him. "Arthur was the ship's captain, nothing more. As are you, now."

"To be honest, that's kind of cold."

"Yes, well, it is what it is."

"So, I guess we should go with your proposal. How do we do that?"

"I'll take care of the details. I suggest you return to the command pod and practice your flight control skills. Now that your neural pathways are more hardened, you might find it easier to handle multiple tasks simultaneously."

"Yeah, I definitely don't want to rely on chaos and luck to survive another run-in with the Draconites. How long do I have to practice?"

"A day at least. The perfect opportunity for you to further acclimate."

"That sounds like a plan. And how long before it's safe for my stomach to eat another cube?"

Merlin shook his head. "You definitely don't look like someone who always thinks with their stomach."

"I usually don't, but then, nothing in Manchester is anywhere near as good as those cubes."

"I would wait at least four hours. If you'll excuse me." The glow faded from the GOLEM's eyes as Merlin abandoned it in the galley.

Thomas stared at it a moment. Even though its physical appearance hadn't changed, he wondered why it had lost its sheen of intelligence and animation simply by its digitized consciousness having vacated the premises, so to speak. If nothing else, he would think it would still possess some inherent mechanical ability to follow orders.

Shrugging, he glanced longingly at the cube maker before exiting the galley and heading for the closest teleportal to the flight deck.

It hadn't escaped him that Merlin had vanished without offering any kind of detail on exactly how he planned to go about confirming the situation in Avalon.

He suddenly felt queasy, and he was pretty sure it wasn't from the nutrition cube. Exactly what had he just given Merlin permission to do?

CHAPTER 21

Thomas stood in the doorway to the flight deck, one hand resting on the smooth metal frame. His gaze wandered across the twelve pods arranged in their perfect circle, each one a masterpiece of engineering designed for a full crew working in perfect harmony. The silvery surfaces caught and reflected the light from the holographic display at the center, stars and nebulae dancing in an eternal cosmic ballet. Streaks of blue energy occasionally rippled across the metallic surfaces like lightning spiking in distant clouds.

The first time he saw them, the sight had filled him with wonder. Once they'd been occupied by Arthur and his closest and most trusted companions. Standing here now, alone, those empty pods, waiting for a crew the ship might never see again, only emphasized how empty the flight deck felt.

The familiar weight of loneliness settled over him like a lead blanket. Even in his gang days, when he'd been surrounded by others, he'd never truly belonged. They had accepted him, sure, but only after he'd proved himself willing to kill. That wasn't belonging. That was just mutual exploitation dressed up as brotherhood.

Vin had been different. The old Marine had seen past his walls, past his anger, past his mistakes. For a few brief years, Thomas had felt like he at least had one person who cared about him. He could still hear Vin telling him he was meant for better things. But then cancer had taken him away, just like a car accident had claimed his dad and drugs had turned his mother into the walking dead. In Manchester, he'd lived on the edges of society, delivering packages and avoiding connections. His bicycle had been his only constant companion.

Now here he was, on an impossible adventure, the captain of not just a starship, but the legendary Excalibur that myth had reforged as a sword.

Alone. Captain of a crew of one, his only company a digital copy of a real person who had made it crystal clear they would never be friends. He wasn't even here because Merlin wanted him here. He was here because he was convenient. And necessary.

No matter what, Thomas believed Merlin would replace him at the drop of a hat or the wave of his stupid magic wand or staff, given a chance. The Advisor needed help to save Avalon from the Draconites. That was the biggest joke of all. Whether the ship thought he was worthy or not, he could barely help himself.

He turned away from the pods. There was no point in practicing for a future that didn't need him. One that would be better off without him. Maybe he could help Merlin get the ship somewhere useful as they planned and then resign his post. Someone else could take over while he made a new life for himself in a new galaxy. He'd be out of trouble, and Merlin could find someone who could do more than fly Excalibur like a drunk. A win-win for both of them, if he had ever seen one. At least nobody here would give a crap about his past here. Even if they did, he could fabricate a new one.

Why did that thought make him feel like a slacker? A quitter? Temptation and a sense of responsibility...of duty as Vin had put it, turned him back toward the pods. Why was he having such a hard time letting go?

Because he wanted to matter, and he knew he might never get another shot. And in any case, what else was he going to do? The Draconites would find them eventually. It would be better to at least try to make something of this impossible situation. Maybe he could prove worthy of Vin's faith in him, even if he still couldn't believe in himself.

The dark gel rippled as he climbed into the pod, its surface tension breaking and reforming around his body like living mercury. The material was almost eager to welcome him, and now he welcomed it, too. He settled back against the contoured surface, thinking the canopy closed. It sealed with a soft hiss.

This time he didn't fight as the gel rose around him, letting it flow into his mouth and nose without resistance. The taste was neutral but the texture was strange—thicker than water but thinner than syrup, with an almost electric quality that made his tongue tingle. Funny he hadn't noticed that before.

The neural interface engaged more smoothly than the last time, sensor data flooding his consciousness in organized streams rather than the previous chaos. But his dark thoughts followed him into the connection, tainting the pure data with doubt and uncertainty. The ship's systems felt distant, held at arm's length by his own insecurities.

"Come on," he told himself, reaching for the flight controls. "You can do this. Just remember what Merlin said. Think in vectors."

He tried to visualize their current trajectory, breaking it down into its component parts like Merlin had suggested. All the physics he'd barely paid attention to in school—

velocity, direction, and angular momentum—suddenly seemed vital.

His first attempt at maneuvering sent them into a wild spin, just like before. The sensor feed blurred as stars wheeled past, their light breaking into rainbow patterns through the gel. His stomach lurched despite the inertial dampening.

Your technique needs refinement. He heard Merlin's voice in his head from wherever he was.. *Try to think mathematically. Break down the movement into discrete vectors.*

"Right," Thomas muttered. "Discrete vectors. Sure."

He tried again, this time attempting to calculate the exact thrust needed to change their course. The result was even worse—now they were spinning in two axes simultaneously while still moving along their original course.

Perhaps if you visualized the force diagram... Merlin suggested.

The comment gave him pause. He wasn't having a real conversation, and yet his imagination had suggested something he'd never heard of before. How was that even possible? He decided it must have something to do with the neural interface.

"And what the hell is a force diagram?" he replied.

The representation of all forces acting on the ship at any given moment. If you can understand the underlying physics—

"Your way isn't working for me," Thomas interrupted, trying desperately to stabilize their course. He overcorrected, sending them tumbling in yet another direction. The sensor feed showed them practically tied in a knot, their course resembling a drunken butterfly's flight path. "There has to be another approach."

The laws of physics aren't negotiable, Merlin replied, a note of frustration creeping into his voice. *Space flight requires precision. Mathematical understanding. You can't just feel your way through it.*

"Watch me," Thomas shot back. But his next attempt at course correction only made things worse. Stars blurred past faster now, their light stretching into streaks that made his head spin. Warning indicators flashed through his mind as the ship's stabilization systems struggled to compensate for his erratic commands.

Perhaps we should try a different exercise, Merlin suggested diplomatically. *Something simpler to start with.*

"No." Thomas forced himself to take a mental step back. "I'm just going about this wrong."

I've been trying to tell you that.

"That's not what I mean." Thomas released his mental grip on the controls. Try as he might, he wasn't able to force the ship to follow vectors because he didn't really understand the concept. And right now, he felt like he was fighting against the ship as though it were a stubborn mule.

He needed a new approach.

Vin had taught him to fight, but the old Marine had also taught him when to take a step back and center himself. Thomas did that now, focusing on his calm, giving up control and opening himself to the ship. He let the sensor data come to him, to flow through his mind instead of trying to grab hold of it and read it all. He was only one person, he couldn't process everything at once.

But he didn't need to process everything.

Rather than trying to capture the flood of data, he ignored the vast majority of it, turning his attention to the things he needed to fly the ship. At first, nothing changed. The ship continued its chaotic tumble through space, sensor data crashing against his consciousness like waves against the shore. Then, like switching from standard definition to crystal clear 4K, everything suddenly snapped into focus.

The data feeds fell into the background, while the visual stimuli merged cleanly with external-facing systems. The thrusters. The shields. The weapons system.

Interesting approach, Merlin observed. *Though I'm not sure—*

"I've got this," Thomas interrupted, mentally reaching for the flight controls again. This time, instead of thinking about how to fly, he simply thought about flying. The difference was subtle but profound, like the gap between reading about riding a bike and actually riding it and feeling the balance of his body on the seat.

Excalibur responded instantly, her course smoothing out as if she'd never been tumbling at all. Thomas sent them through a series of gentle turns, marveling at how natural it felt now that he'd stopped fighting the interface and trying to force Merlin's technical approach.

Better, Merlin admitted grudgingly. *Though your technique is highly unorthodox.*

"Story of my life." Thomas executed a more complex maneuver, rolling the ship around its longitudinal axis while maintaining their vector. He wobbled some, losing balance and threatening to lose control before leveling out. "Besides, isn't unorthodox exactly what we need right now?"

Perhaps. A pause. *Though I still think you should learn the proper—*

"Let me guess. You're going to suggest more vector calculations?"

The mathematics of space flight are not arbitrary.

"Neither is intuition." Thomas guided them through another series of maneuvers, each smoother than the last. The ship responded as if it had been waiting for him to stop overthinking. "Sometimes you have to feel your way forward."

Is that what you were doing during our escape from Earth? Feeling your way forward?

"That was pure panic," Thomas admitted. "This is different. I'm not fighting the ship anymore. We're working together."

The ship is a machine, Merlin said. *It doesn't work with you. It responds to your commands through the neural interface.*

"Says the digital consciousness living inside it."

That's different.

"Is it? Maybe you've been looking at this the wrong way for the last fifteen centuries. Maybe all that time alone has made you forget what it's like to trust your instincts."

I highly doubt that.

"And yet here we are, flying in a straight line for the first time since I took command. Face it, Merlin. Sometimes the unorthodox approach works better than the scientific solution."

A fortunate accident, Merlin replied, a note of approval beneath the dismissive tone. *Though I suppose results do matter more than methodology.*

"If we call it magic, does it make you feel any better?" Thomas asked, knowing that was as close to a compliment as he was likely to get. He continued practicing, pushing himself and the ship through increasingly complex maneuvers. Each success built his confidence, while each minor failure taught him something new about Excalibur's and his capabilities.

Hours passed, marked only by the steady pulse of the reactor through the neural interface. Finally, fatigue began creeping in around the edges of Thomas' consciousness. The sensor feeds started to blur, their crisp data growing fuzzy around the edges like an old photograph.

"I think that's enough for today," he said, guiding them back to a stable vector. His mind felt worn down, and he wanted another nutrition cube.

Agreed. You've made considerable progress.

Thomas thought the pod open, the gel receding as the

canopy lifted with a soft hiss. This time when he climbed out, his legs felt much steadier beneath him, though they remained a bit wobbly. His clothes were once again perfectly dry despite being submerged in the gel, but his skin tingled slightly as if he'd been floating in carbonated water.

Merlin's GOLEM waited nearby, a nutrition cube held in its mechanical hand.

"I heard you talking to me even though you weren't here," Thomas said. "Was that real or my imagination?"

"I've only been watching you for a short while," Merlin replied, offering him the cube. "The rest was all in your head."

Thomas didn't sense any insincerity this time. He supposed he had heard what he believed the Advisor would say and acted against it. Whatever the circumstance, it had worked.

"Thanks for the nutrition." Thomas accepted the cube gratefully, already anticipating its flavor. "How's our plan coming along?"

"I've repeated the message I transmitted from Earth," Merlin replied, his mechanical form shifting slightly in a gesture Thomas was beginning to recognize as discomfort. "I'm hoping it will be received by an acquaintance of mine."

Thomas paused with the cube halfway to his mouth, sudden suspicion replacing his anticipation. "Acquaintance? After over a hundred years? Isn't that a bit optimistic?"

"Mortality is a complex subject when dealing with advanced civilizations composed of multiple intelligent life forms," Merlin replied evasively. "Some beings can be quite long-lived."

"And some digital beings apparently can't give straight answers." Thomas lowered the cube. "What about the

Draconites? They intercepted the same message when you transmitted it from Earth. What's to stop them from..." Thomas trailed off, realization hitting him like a bag of bricks to the face. "Merlin, what did you do?"

"Why do you think you've been practicing your flight control?"

CHAPTER 22

"What the hell, Merlin?" Thomas cried. "I didn't agree with you repeating the same mistake you made on Earth. You know, the one that nearly got us killed."

"Actually, you did agree. You gave me permission to carry out my proposal to gather our bearings and then navigate to somewhere useful. By sending out the message, one of three things will happen. One, my contact will arrive and help guide us to the nearest safe harbor. Two, the Draconite will arrive and attack us. Only this time we'll be ready, and can trace their wormhole distortion to presumably occupied space. Three, both the Draconite and my contact will arrive at the same time, in which case we'll have a fighting chance to defeat them in combat, especially now that you've practiced."

"I practiced doing loops and figure-eights, not getting into another firefight."

"Your methodology for controlling the ship appears sound. I have every confidence in you."

Thomas' face twisted. "That makes one of us."

"Considering the three options, two of them benefit us,

which means the odds are in our favor. Vis a vis, it was a logical step to take to achieve our determined goals."

Thomas glared at Merlin's GOLEM. "Did you get beat up a lot in school?"

"I don't see what school has to do with it. In any case, finish your cube and—"

Merlin was cut off by alarms blaring across the flight deck.

"What is that?"

"Hurry. Back in the command pod."

Thomas' heart pounded as he lunged back to the pod, jumping on the step and pirouetting in the air to fall backward into the gel. "Your contact or the Draconites?" he asked before his face was submerged.

"It's unclear," Merlin replied. "But an unexpected wormhole just opened nearby, hence the alarm."

Thomas sank into the gel, once more merging with the ship's systems. Repeating the procedure a second time within a few minutes proved harder than he expected, leaving him disoriented when he most needed to get settled. Sensor data flowed into his brain, and he struggled to center, letting it come to him instead of reaching for it. He had only practiced once, when everything was calm. How was he supposed to relax when they were likely about to be shot at again?

Through the neural interface, Thomas immediately felt the wormhole, the sensation like static electricity crawling across his skin. The sensor feed showed reality bending around the anomaly, local space-time warping as something massive pushed through from elsewhere. A wave of spatial distortion radiated outward from the tear, sending ripples through the sensors that made Thomas' teeth ache.

"Here we go," he muttered, already reaching for the flight controls. This time the ship responded smoothly to his thoughts, accelerating toward the distortion. The main drive thrummed through his consciousness as power built in the engines, their song rising in pitch as they pushed harder. If they were about to face more Draconite ships, he figured it was better to meet them head-on. If it was Merlin's contact instead...well, better to go shooting past than be caught flat-footed.

"An interesting tactical choice," Merlin observed, his tone suggesting he found Thomas' aggressiveness both concerning and amusing. "Though perhaps not the wisest."

"You're the one who set this up," Thomas replied, pushing the engines harder. Blue energy poured from Excalibur's stern as they accelerated. "Besides, they won't expect us to attack first."

"There's usually a reason for that."

Three Draconite destroyers emerged from the wormhole, their scaled hulls drinking in the starlight. Thomas recognized them as the same class of vessel they'd encountered off Earth, though these looked like newer models. Their dragon-like forms seemed to ripple as they oriented themselves, energy building along their hulls in preparation for a fight. The neural interface—a pressure against his consciousness that set every nerve ending tingling with alarm—translated their presence into pure menace.

"Of course it's Draconites," Thomas said. "I guess it was too much to hope that it might be your mysterious contact."

"The odds were in our favor," Merlin replied, though he sounded less certain now. "Though perhaps I miscalculated."

"Oh, now you reconsider your math?" Thomas complained.

"It's not as if we had a wide array of options to choose from. This was still the most prudent course. And from my perspective, it beats being dissected by Matrix Dynamics."

Thomas didn't waste any more time arguing. He pushed Excalibur into an attack run, targeting the lead destroyer before its crew could fully react to their presence. Energy built along the ship as he lined up his shot, the sensation translating through the neural interface as a tingling in his fingertips. The targeting sensors painted the enemy vessel in his mind.

Still orienting itself, its crew likely surprised by their bold maneuver, Thomas focused on the lead Draconite ship, letting himself feel the connection with Excalibur's weapons rather than trying to force it. The firing solutions resolved themselves in his mind like pieces of a puzzle falling into place. With just a thought, a shot of blue energy lanced out from Excalibur's bow.

The beam struck the lead destroyer along its port side, burning through unprepared defenses and scoring a deep wound. The destroyer's hull sparked and buckled, molten metal streaming into space like blood from an arterial artery. Secondary explosions rippled along its length as internal systems overloaded and Thomas caught glimpses of atmosphere venting from multiple breaches.

"Got him!" Thomas exalted as they screamed past the wounded ship, close enough that he could make out individual details of its scaled surface through the sensor feed. "Damn, that felt good!"

"Impressive," Merlin admitted, genuine surprise in his tone. "Your unorthodox approach appears to have some merit. Though now the other two know we're here."

As if to emphasize his point, space lit up around them as the trailing destroyers opened fire. Red energy beams sliced through the void directly behind them, their passage leaving trails of ionized particles that tasted like copper in Thomas' mind. He threw Excalibur into an evasive maneuver, trying to maintain the initiative while the wounded ship fell behind.

The neural interface gave him a perfect sense of Excalibur's movements as he juked and rolled, each course change smoother than anything he'd managed in their previous encounter. That didn't mean his flight patterns were smooth. The ship rolled too far or jerked too hard, but like the first time the chaotic movements served to throw off the enemy's aim. Still, the Draconite ships stayed with them, their attacks becoming more coordinated as the crews recovered from their initial surprise.

"At least they can't coordinate their fire as well with only two ships," Thomas said, flailing around another barrage. The maneuver carried them between the beams with room to spare, though he could feel the heat of their weapons like a sunburn on his skin.

"You're getting better," Merlin commented. "The time you spent practicing appears to have paid off."

A glancing hit struck their shields, the impact translating through the neural interface like a punch to the shoulder. He grunted in pain but maintained control, the sensation accompanied by cascading warnings about power fluctuations and shield harmonics. Thomas couldn't quite process it all as he broke right to avoid the follow-up barrage.

"Maybe I spoke too soon," Merlin grumbled. "You're about to fall right into their kill zone."

The destroyers split their formation, trying to catch Excalibur in a crossfire. Thomas sensed them taking up positions to either side of Excalibur, hulls glowing with building energy. Merlin was right. And they were running out of escape routes.

"They're more aggressive than the first group," Thomas said.

"These crews appear to be better trained," Merlin agreed. "Though I suppose that's to be expected. The ships we encountered off Earth were likely the closest responders."

"Any chance of opening another wormhole?"

"We could," Merlin replied, "but without knowing where we would come out, it would only put us back to square one. I would need to send another transmission to begin assessing our new position, and we'd be in the same situation as we currently are, only more beaten up."

"So what are we supposed to do?" Thomas threw them into another spinning dive as both destroyers opened fire. Their energy beams burned past Excalibur, the overlapping attacks creating a lattice of deadly light that filled space around them. "I can't do this all day."

"No, you aren't nearly skilled enough to continue to avoid their attacks," Merlin agreed. "I'm analyzing their wormhole signature. If we can maintain our structural integrity long enough, I'll complete the trace back to their point of origin. Then we can open a wormhole."

"What about the damage to the navigation system? Won't the wormhole we create end somewhere other than the coordinates you enter?"

"Yes, and we can use that to our advantage. The distortion over distance will be minimal compared to tunneling from Earth to Avalon. We'll emerge near the Draconite patrol's origin, but not right on top of it. Beneficial in case they came from, say, a Draconite assault platform."

"Assault platform?"

"A military asset. Either a super dreadnought, space station, or the like."

"What if we emerge too near to something like that?" Thomas asked. The idea of coming face-to-face with something Merlin referred to as a super dreadnought sent shivers of fear through him that translated into a suddenly erratic flight pattern that came just in time.

A coordinated attack from the Draconites sent a spread of energy beams lancing out from different parts of their hulls. The unpredictable movement from his emotional instability sent the first few shots arcing past. Still, several more hits struck their shields in rapid succession. The impacts were like body blows through the neural interface, driving the breath from Thomas' lungs. Warning indicators flashed through his mind as the shields threatened to fail.

"How much longer do you need to finish the trace?" he asked, struggling to control his trepidation.

"Longer than we likely have," Merlin admitted. "You're just not ready for this yet."

"That's what I've been trying to tell you since you beckoned me into this ship!"

Thomas let go of the flight controls, ready to accept defeat. Excalibur flew in a straight line while the Draconites lined up the killing blow.

"What are you doing?" Merlin asked, desperation in his tone.

"I quit."

CHAPTER 23

"What?" Merlin cried. "You can't quit."

"Why not? I'm in the command pod, remember? I can do whatever I want."

"Thomas, I apologize. I should have allowed you more time to practice and become accustomed to flying the ship. I should have offered you lessons in combat tactics and maneuvering. I should have been patient, instead of too eagerly rushing to rejoin whatever might be left of the fight against the Draconite. A fight that may in fact be long over. You were correct when you suggested that I used you to escape Earth. I did use you. But I also scanned your mind. I know that you needed to leave that place as much as I did. And I'm absolutely certain that given time, you have enough fortitude, courage, strength, and compassion to not only become equal to Arthur, but surpass him. None of that can happen if you give up now."

Thomas didn't know how much of Merlin's speech was true and how much came from self-preservation. He had only seconds to decide whether to accept the Advisor's words or allow them to be destroyed. His entire life had been a waste to this point, spent bouncing aimlessly from one kind of trouble to another. It was so damn hard for him to believe in himself, but he wanted to believe so much that he was ready to accept Merlin's estimation, even if the digital consciousness didn't believe a single word of it.

Before he could do anything, a new sensation crawled across his skin through the neural interface. The familiar static-electric feeling of another incoming wormhole made every nerve ending tingle with alarm.

It burst open like a flower blooming in fast motion, its edges ragged and unstable compared to the Draconites' precise tears in space-time. A new ship emerged—smaller than the destroyers, its hull the color of weathered iron. Like Excalibur, its design reminded Thomas of a sword that had seen centuries of hard use. Age and battle damage marked its surface, leaving it looking more like a rusted relic than a viable warship.

Any thoughts about the vessel's apparent state of decay vanished as it moved. Despite its ancient appearance, it accelerated with impossible grace, executing a complex series of maneuvers that made Thomas' best efforts look even more pathetic than he already knew them to be.

The Draconites took the newcomer seriously as well. They immediately broke off their attack on Excalibur, likely assuming they could come back to finish them off later, since they were hardly a threat.

"Is that your contact?" Thomas asked as the sword-ship oriented itself. Unlike both Excalibur and the Draconite ships, the newcomer had more traditional gun batteries arrayed across its hull. At first glance, it hardly seemed like a fair fight against the sleek, scaled destroyers.

"I'm not certain," Merlin replied, something off in his tone. "Though the timing is rather convenient."

The sword-ship wasted no time announcing its intentions. It opened fire on the nearest Draconite destroyer with what Thomas took to be machine guns of some kind. The rounds glowed with a greenish hue, each one both a penetrating ballistic and a tracer. The pilot's aim was exceptional. The barrage swept across the destroyer, chewing through its shields as if they didn't exist and punching into vulnerable points along the hull. The destroyer tried to evade and return fire, but the sword-ship's pilot remained one step ahead.

Thomas watched as the ancient vessel rolled around the destroyer's counterattack while evading the second Draconite ship's energy beams, its movements precise but not impossible. The pilot used the destroyer's own momentum and bulk to his advantage, staying in positions where the Draconite ship's weapons couldn't easily target him, and the second destroyer couldn't get off a clean shot without risk of hitting the first.

"We should try to establish a line of communication," Merlin suggested.

"Right," Thomas agreed, thinking of sending a transmission across every frequency available. "Unidentified vessel, this is Excalibur. Are you friendly?"

No response came as the sword-ship continued its deadly dance with the enemy. The larger vessel's hull sparked and buckled where the machine gun rounds found their mark, atmosphere venting from multiple hull breaches. A lucky shot from the second destroyer scored a hit on the sword-ship's flank, but its pilot turned the damage into an advantage, using the impact to spin into a better firing position.

"Now that," Merlin observed as the destroyer finally succumbed to the relentless assault, "is how you pilot a starship."

"Thanks for the critique," Thomas muttered, watching the sword-ship engage the second destroyer. "They're still not answering our hails."

"Perhaps they're busy," Merlin suggested as the sword-ship dove through another barrage of energy beams. The pilot's skill was evident in every movement—each course change efficient, each attack carefully timed. They weren't performing impossible or overly complex maneuvers, just executing standard tactics with incredible timing and precision.

The second destroyer exploded as the sword-ship's weapons once again found their mark, its hull splitting along structural weak points. The scuffed and rusted vessel emerged from the explosion already turning, and Thomas felt a chill as he realized it was angling toward Excalibur.

And not in a friendly way.

"Merlin?" Thomas asked softly, growing nervous.

"Keep trying to make contact."

"Unknown vessel, we mean you no harm," Thomas strained. "Please respond."

No answer.

"Unidentified vessel, we surrender," Thomas tried. "Please confirm."

Still nothing, though the ship had burned its velocity away from them and had started accelerating on an intercept course.

"Merlin, about that wormhole..."

"Have you decided to unquit?" Merlin asked.

"Yes! What about the wormhole!"

"Almost there. Don't let him hit us."

"Are you kidding? He just made the two ships that were making me look like a joke look like jokes."

The sword-ship opened fire, its glowing rounds spewing toward them. Thomas threw Excalibur into an evasive maneuver, but their attacker read his intentions, adjusting his aim to where Excalibur would be rather than where they were. Only the oversteer from Thomas' panic saved them from a direct hit.

"Any time now!" Thomas shouted as another attack nearly vaporized them.

"Almost there," Merlin replied again, fascination creeping into his tone despite their predicament. "The pilot is very experienced. He knows what you're going to do before you do. And he'll no doubt rapidly adjust to your poorly refined vectors."

"I swear, if you ever say vector to me again..." Thomas trailed off as he attempted another evasive maneuver, pushing Excalibur's engines to their limits. The sword-ship stayed with them, but not quite perfectly enough to blow them to bits.

Not yet. But Thomas was sure Merlin had it right. The ship's pilot was learning. Biding his time.

"Unknown vessel," he tried one last time. "We are not your enemy. We don't want to fight. We'd really like to surrender! Please respond."

The sword-ship's only answer was another barrage of fire. Thomas rolled them through the attack, feeling the heat of near-misses through the neural interface.

"Whoever they are," Thomas said, executing another series of evasive maneuvers, "they really don't want to talk."

"So it would seem." Merlin's tone suggested he found this development both fascinating and troubling. "Though their attack pattern is...interesting."

"Great. You can analyze it after we escape. How's that wormhole coming?"

"Almost..."

The sword-ship suddenly slid sideways and rolled in a spiral, opening fire as it slipped laterally along Excalibur's path. Rounds zipped through space around them like a tightening, barbed wire noose quickly cinching shut. When it did...

"Merlin!" Thomas cried in desperation.

"Now!"

Space tore open in front of them as Excalibur's wormhole generator engaged once more. Thomas didn't hesitate, throwing them into the vortex at maximum thrust. Reality twisted around them as they transitioned, the sword-ship's final attack passing through the space they'd occupied a heartbeat before.

CHAPTER 24

When they emerged on the other side, Thomas kept the engines at full power for several minutes, scanning for signs of pursuit. None came.

"Well," he said finally, allowing himself to relax. Through the neural interface he could feel the strain they'd put on Excalibur's systems. While the shields had held throughout the battle, they would need time and starlight to properly regenerate. Fortunately, a star rested surprisingly close to their starboard side. "That was unexpected."

"Indeed," Merlin replied, unusually subdued. "That didn't go quite as I had planned."

"You don't say." Thomas cut the thrust and allowed them to drift on a stable vector, trying to ignore how badly his hands would have been shaking if they weren't submerged in gel. "That pilot was incredible. I've never seen anyone fly like that, even in video games."

"Yes. Their technique was...distinctive."

Something in Merlin's tone made Thomas pause. "You know who it was, don't you?"

"I have suspicions," Merlin said after a moment. "Though none I care to share without further evidence."

"More secrets?" Thomas felt his frustration rising. "That ship looked like it belonged in a museum, but its pilot wiped the floor with those Draconite ships before nearly destroying us. If you know something about who they are..."

"What I know and what I suspect are not the same thing," Merlin interrupted. "And neither will help us in our current situation."

Thomas started to argue, then stopped himself. He was tired, sore, and in no mood for Merlin's cryptic responses. The neural interface was beginning to feel heavy in his mind, fatigue setting in now that the immediate danger had passed.

"Fine. Keep your secrets. I'm getting out of this pod," he said, the dark gel receding and the canopy lifting in response to his thought command. "Try not to orchestrate any more battles without informing me first, okay?"

"As you wish," Merlin replied, his tone suggesting he found Thomas' attitude amusing. "Though you might want to remain ready. The day isn't over yet."

"What's that supposed to mean?"

"We've exited the wormhole into occupied space. I'm not entirely sure where just yet, but I'm analyzing the nearby star field. Once the analysis is complete, I'll know exactly where we are. In the meantime, it's unlikely but not impossible that a passing ship could stumble across us."

"I need to rest. And eat." He climbed out of the pod on shaky legs, his head spinning, but not so much that he couldn't remain upright on his own. That was a definite improvement.

"I agree with you on that. But first, we should discuss your desire to quit…"

"I don't want to talk about it."

"You nearly got us both killed."

"For one thing, you aren't alive, so you can't die. For

another…I don't know. Aren't you tired of being a failure? I know I am."

The GOLEM stared at him. "What did you call me?"

"A failure," Thomas replied. "You advised Arthur right to his doom. He ended up dying on Earth while his kingdom, his galaxy, was at war."

He regretted the comment as soon as it had left his mouth. The GOLEM's eyes dimmed, taking on an angry reddish hue.

"I'll allow you this one outburst," Merlin growled. "Because you aren't accustomed to the interface. But if you ever again suggest that I failed Arthur, I'll—"

"You'll what?" Thomas interrupted. "You can't fly the ship without me."

"No, but once we reach a populated area you can be replaced."

"Hasn't that been your plan all along?"

"Honestly, no."

Thomas couldn't keep the surprise from his voice. "You're joking, right? Haven't you been watching me out there?"

"Yes, Thomas, I have. What I see is raw. Very raw. But it also has potential. You may be ready to give up on me. You may be ready to give up on yourself. But I'm not giving up on you. I meant what I said when I apologized."

Thomas had opened his mouth to continue the argument. His jaw fell slack, all of the fight draining out of him and leaving him cold.

"Why?" he asked.

"Why what?" Merlin replied.

"Why me?"

"I don't know. Perhaps because you remind me so much of Arthur. Perhaps because I want another chance to make things right. You aren't wrong in your suggestion that I failed him. It's something I've had to live with for the last fifteen hundred years. Alone. You cannot imagine the difficulty."

Thomas' face flushed. His shoulders slumped. "Damn it. I'm sorry. I'm being an asshole. Maybe we can just drop this one? Maybe you're right, I'm just not used to the interface."

"Very well," Merlin agreed. The GOLEM turned to leave.

"Wait," Thomas said. "You really aren't going to tell me anything about that ship?"

"I've already told you my position on that matter."

"Right. Your suspicions. But you know, you could maybe try voicing them, instead of keeping them to yourself."

"Perhaps," Merlin replied after a long pause, "my reluctance to share certain information stems from uncertainty about its overall value."

"You mean you don't trust me?"

"It's not about trust. There are larger concerns at play."

Thomas laughed. "Larger concerns? Like getting shot at by ships that look like they shouldn't even be able to fly anymore? That pilot..." He trailed off, remembering how efficiently the sword-ship had dispatched the Draconite vessels. "He wasn't just good. He was trained. Really well trained. And highly experienced."

"An astute observation."

"And you know where he learned to fly like that, don't you?"

"What I know," Merlin said carefully, "is that we should focus on immediate concerns. The Draconites clearly maintain significant influence in this region of space. Their technological advancement suggests—"

"That ship was old," Thomas pressed, not letting Merlin off the hook. "Maybe as old as..."

He froze as the implications hit him. The sword-ship's design. Its projectile weapons. The pilot's incredible skill...

"No way," he whispered. "That's impossible."

"You're beginning to understand," Merlin said softly.

"That ship..." Thomas turned back to face the empty pods arranged in their perfect circle. Like pieces of a puzzle, details began falling into place in his mind. "It was from your time, wasn't it? From before..."

"The fall of Camelot?" Merlin finished for him. "Possibly."

"Oh, come on, Merlin." Thomas felt his fists clench at his sides. "That ship was ancient. And its pilot flew like..."

"Like someone trained in classical combat techniques?" Merlin finished. "Someone who learned to fly before neural interfaces were developed?"

"Like someone who helped develop those techniques in the first place."

The GOLEM's eyes flickered, though whether from uncertainty or something else, Thomas couldn't tell. "That would be quite impossible."

"Then how do you explain what we just saw?"

"There are many possible explanations. Perhaps the pilot learned from old training records. Or maybe they simply developed similar techniques independently."

Thomas crossed his arms. "And picked up an old junker starship from the scrapyard? You don't even believe the words not coming out of your mouth."

"What I believe is less relevant than…"

"Than what? The larger concerns you keep hinting at?" Thomas started to pace, his fatigue forgotten in the wake of growing suspicion. "That ship picked up your transmission, just like the Draconites did. Except, it's obviously not with them." Thomas paused, working through the problem while Merlin remained conspicuously silent. "Oh hell. The ship didn't come to fight the Draconites, they just happened to be in the way. It came looking for you. For Excalibur."

"Another interesting theory," Merlin said.

"Stop it!" Thomas slammed his fist against the nearest pod, the impact sending dull pain shooting up his arm. "Why do you have to be so damned secretive? That swordship has been searching for Excalibur since it disappeared. I'm sure of it."

"A hundred years is a very long time to maintain such a quest," Merlin observed quietly.

"But not impossible. Of course, the captain's not just looking for the ship, and he sure as hell isn't looking for me. He came for Arthur, didn't he?"

A heavy silence fell over the flight deck. Merlin's GOLEM remained frozen while the Advisor hesitated to answer.

"We don't have to be friends," Thomas said, remembering something Vin had told him the day they had met. "But if we're on the same team, then we damn well better learn to communicate with and trust one another. That's the only way this works."

Merlin still didn't answer. Thomas growled in frustration, pushing past the GOLEM on his way off the flight deck.

"Thomas, wait."

He turned around, glaring at the GOLEM, whose eyes had brightened back to their typical blue glow.

"Yes, he came for Arthur. And for me."

"You know who he is, don't you?"

"Not for certain, but I suspect."

"Who is it?" Thomas asked.

"As I mentioned, there's no sense in raising concern without confirmation."

"Who. Is. It?"

Merlin's golem slumped into a defeated posture. "I believe it may have been Lancelot."

CHAPTER 25

"Lancelot?" Thomas said, not as surprised as he might have expected. "Didn't you say Lancelot betrayed Arthur?"

"Not in so many words," Merlin replied. "I've long suspected he did. He informed us the path through the asteroid field was clear. Arthur trusted his word, and then we were attacked."

"That could all be circumstantial. It doesn't mean Lancelot told the Draconite you were coming."

"No, it doesn't. But only days earlier Arthur had discovered his wife was having an affair with Lancelot."

"Just like the legends."

"If you know about that, then Arthur probably told the story to someone on Earth at some point in time. In any case, he did what any man of his stature and standing would do. He challenged Lancelot to a duel over his and Guinevere's honor."

"Did Lancelot accept?"

"He did. But they had to wait until they were both out of the war zone to commence the duel."

"And Arthur was attacked before that could happen," Thomas guessed.

"Of course. Lancelot was the better pilot, but he feared Arthur's wrath, and he feared Excalibur."

"So get both out of the picture, steal the wife, and become king?"

"If Arthur were declared dead, Lancelot would have been able to position himself to gain the throne. But he always claimed he didn't want to be king."

"Yeah, well, men can do some crazy things over women."

"I was a living man once, too. I'm well aware."

"But if Lancelot did become king, he wouldn't be out here in an ancient ship, waiting for you to show up."

"Which is why I can't confirm my hunch. And why I didn't think any of this was important right now."

"I think it's still useful to know, if only because I need to be a lot more prepared if Lancelot is gunning for us."

"Yes, we both do."

"What about the contact you intended the message to reach? Who is that?"

"It's not really important right—"

"I thought we were on the same page with the whole communication and trust thing?"

"Fine, but I remain steadfast that it isn't important, especially since she never responded. I tried to contact Nimue, my...well, the original Merlin's former companion."

Thomas' face twisted as he tried to connect Nimue to what he knew of Arthurian mythology. He was sure she had played a role in the stories he had heard, but he couldn't quite place the name. "How do you know she's still alive after a hundred years?"

"If anyone would be, it's her. Back then at least, she was the most powerful wizard in all of Avalon."

"So if anyone could extend their life, it would be her?"

"Precisely."

"I'm sorry, if she's gone."

"Thank you, Thomas."

"So, you know where we are, then?"

"I do."

"So what do we do next?"

"We'll need to spend a few hours in proximity to the star to allow the reactor to recharge and the shields to regenerate. I suggest you use the opportunity to begin studying starfighter combat. There are tactical manuals available in the databanks. You can access them from the terminal in the library."

"The ship has a library? You never showed it to me."

"I scanned your mind. You only started reading when you entered detention, and you stopped as soon as you got out. I didn't take you as the sort who enjoys learning."

"I think that's all a matter of purpose and motivation. In juvie, it gave me something to do to pass the time. Out here, it might keep us both alive."

"If you're sure you want to live."

"I haven't always been sure," Thomas admitted, his voice softening. "I...well, you know. I almost killed myself once. After that night."

"Yes."

"Nobody tells you that downing half a bottle of Tylenol will only make you crazy sick."

"I'm not sure what that means. However, it's obvious the fates had a different purpose for you."

"There you go with fate again. You can believe whatever you want. But yeah, most of the time I'm grateful to still be alive. The rest of the time...I feel like the universe doesn't need me. That I'm a waste of space."

"It's understandable, given your upbringing. But also patently untrue. Maybe your galaxy didn't need you, but this one does."

"I guess we'll see about that."

"Yes, we will."

"And what about once the reactor and shields are ready? Do you have any idea where to go, since your ex is ghosting you?"

"I suggest Caerlyon," Merlin said. "It's a major trading hub within a short burst from here."

"Burst? Does that mean no wormhole?"

"Correct. A burst is acceleration fueled by the same energy that powers the weapons and shields. It allows Excalibur to travel faster than light more efficiently than via wormhole. It's especially suitable for relatively short range interstellar travel."

"How many light years to Caerlyon are we talking?"

"Seventy-four."

"In how long?"

"Seven and a half hours."

Thomas laughed. "It's crazy that seventy-four light years is short range."

"The wormhole from Earth to Avalon carried us over ten billion light years."

His laughter died off instantly. Even though he had already heard the number once before, it still left him in awe. "Now that's magic."

"In part, yes."

"So where's the library?" Thomas asked after he overcame his shock at the vast distance they had traveled, pretty much instantly.

Merlin's GOLEM gestured toward the door. "Return to the captain's quarters, then follow the corridor aft toward the stern. When you reach the entrance to engineering, turn right. It's the second door on the right."

"What's behind the first door?"

"The armory."

Thomas raised an eyebrow. "You have an armory? On a starship?"

"Of course. Did you think those weapons in your quarters were merely decorative?"

"Actually, yes." Thomas headed for the door, then paused. "Are you coming with me?"

"I have other tasks to attend to while the reactor recharges. The library's computer will respond to voice commands. I trust you can handle that without supervision?"

Thomas huffed "I think I'll manage."

He left the flight deck, making his way back through the now familiar corridors.

Following Merlin's directions, he soon reached the first of the two hatches. It was more heavily reinforced than the one a short distance ahead, larger rivets visible around the frame.

He approached it hesitantly. He knew he should go straight to the library and start studying tactics, but curiosity got the better of him. The hatch responded to his desire to open, parting with a soft hiss.

The armory was smaller than he expected—more like a walk-in closet—but it somehow managed to feel both ancient and cutting-edge at the same time. Racks of weapons lined the bulkheads, most of them melee designs that wouldn't have looked out of place in a museum of medieval warfare. While there was a mix of weapons like maces, halberds, pikes, and other assorted blades and blunt force instruments, swords dominated the collection, their edges catching and reflecting the soft blue lighting in ways that made them appear to glow from within.

"These can't all be just regular swords," he muttered, approaching one that particularly caught his eye. Its blade was forged from some dark metal that absorbed the light rather than reflecting it. The crossguard was oddly shaped, as if it had been made to match the look of Excalibur itself.

"They aren't regular swords."

Thomas jumped at Merlin's voice, though the Advisor wasn't physically present. "Are you really talking to me, or is this all in my head again?"

"How would you know the difference if I told you it was real?"

Thomas paused to ponder the question. "I wouldn't until I talked to you in a GOLEM form, I suppose."

"In any case, I can multitask. And I suspected you might get distracted here after I told you what was behind this door."

"Well, since you're here, what makes these swords special?"

"Not just the swords. All of the weapons in this compartment are imbued with various enchantments. That one you're admiring, for instance, can cut through most energy shields as if they weren't there. And it's made from fayrilite, which enhances magic and will never dull."

Thomas quickly stepped back from the rack. "Maybe I shouldn't touch anything in here."

"Probably wise, for now. Though I notice you're not asking why a starship needs weapons like this at all."

"You can't always be on the starship, right?" Thomas guessed, moving deeper into the armory. "Though I am wondering why there are so few ranged weapons." He gestured to a small rack that held rifles similar to the ones carried by Matrix Dynamics's mercenaries, though these were clearly far more advanced.

"There are rules to combat in Avalon, and nearly everyone follows them," Merlin explained. "It's about honor and respect, and it's been part of our history for thousands of years. Personally, I always thought it was foolish to limit your tactical options that way, but tradition can be a powerful force."

"I like it."

"You'll fit right in here, then."

"And die quickly if I get into a fight. I know some hand-to-hand combat. I don't know how to use any of these."

"If you survive long enough, you'll learn."

"Yeah, so what about the limited stock of guns, then? Is that a result of your opinion on the subject?"

"In part. But also, I said nearly everyone follows the rules. Those who don't are fair game to both rifles and ranged magic."

"Ranged magic? Like fireballs?"

"That's just one example. It's a simplified explanation. There are circumstances where the rules change, but for now, perhaps we should focus on your tactical education rather than my expounding on combat philosophy?"

"Yeah, you're probably right." Thomas took one last look around the armory before stepping back into the corridor. The second hatch opened at his approach, revealing a circular chamber that followed Excalibur's aesthetic of clean lines and flowing patterns. But where he had expected to find shelves of books, he instead found only a raised platform in the center of the room with a control podium in front of it. "Voice activated, you said?"

"Simply state what you wish to study," Merlin replied. "The computer will provide relevant materials."

Thomas stepped onto the platform. "Uh, starship combat tactics?"

The lights dimmed as a holographic display sprang to life around him. A familiar figure materialized—a tall, athletic man with sharp features and close-cropped dark hair. He wore what Thomas took to be an Ursan military uniform.

"Greetings," the figure said. "I am Sir Lancelot of the Avalonian—"

"Wait a second." Lancelot froze, his introduction ceasing mid-sentence. "Merlin, how is it that I can understand him? You're in my head, so it makes sense I can understand you. But what about everyone else? And don't say magic."

"But—"

"Seriously?"

"Excalibur, and most other locations in Avalon, are polyglot enchanted, but there are also digital translators that can do the trick. I'll provide you one if you ever need it."

"I guess that's good to know." Thomas refocused on the hologram. "Repeat and continue."

"I am Sir Lancelot of the Avalonian Star Knights. Welcome to basic starfighter combat."

The hologram showed Lancelot as he had been a hundred something years ago—young, confident, radiating the easy competence of someone who knew exactly how skilled they were. The same person who might now be hunting them in an ancient sword-ship.

"Hold up," Thomas said. The hologram again froze. "Merlin, is this going to be weird?"

"Only if you make it weird," Merlin replied. "Lancelot was the finest pilot in the fleet. His combat tutorials are still the best resource available."

Thomas considered this. "Even if he may have betrayed Arthur?"

"The betrayal doesn't change the quality of his instruction." A pause. "Though perhaps we should skip the section on loyalty and chain of command."

Thomas coughed out a laugh. "That might be a good idea. Continue."

The holographic Lancelot continued as if nothing had happened. "Today we'll cover basic combat maneuvering. Remember, effective combat, no matter what kind, isn't about how dramatic your moves look. It's about efficiency, precision, and understanding your enemy's capabilities as well as your own."

Thomas settled in to watch, determined to learn everything he could. They would probably encounter the swordship again, and if Lancelot or maybe one of his descendants was the pilot, he wanted to be as ready as possible.

Whether the knight had betrayed Arthur or not, his lessons might be the difference between survival and destruction. The irony wasn't lost on Thomas as he focused on the hologram's instructions, watching techniques demonstrated by the same pilot who had just nearly destroyed them.

Lancelot's hologram gestured, creating a tactical display of ships in combat. "Now, let's begin with basic attack vectors..."

CHAPTER 26

"Now watch closely," the holographic Lancelot said, his features intense with concentration. The tactical display showed two ships engaged in a complex dance through simulated space, energy beams crisscrossing between them. "Notice how the smaller vessel maintains optimal distance? This is crucial. By controlling the range of engagement, you force your opponent to either close with you on your terms or break off entirely."

Thomas leaned forward, fascinated by the interplay of the vessels. The display rendered their movements in perfect clarity, complete with color-coded vectors showing momentum and direction. After hours of study, he was finally starting to see the patterns Lancelot described.

"In this scenario," Lancelot continued, "the defending vessel appears outgunned. But watch..." He gestured, and the simulation slowed. "By maintaining proper distance and using their superior maneuverability, they can effectively neutralize their opponent's advantages. Every engagement has an optimal range. The key is finding it before your enemy does."

"And if they're faster?" Thomas asked, forgetting for a moment he was talking to a recording.

To his surprise, the hologram responded: "An excellent question. When facing a faster opponent..." Lancelot manipulated the display, adding a new scenario. "You must force them to sacrifice their speed advantage by controlling the engagement zone. Let me demonstrate—"

"Still at it, I see."

Thomas started at Merlin's voice, the hologram freezing mid-gesture. He turned to find the Advisor's GOLEM standing in the library doorway, a nutrition cube held in its mechanical hand. In the soft lighting, the golem's metallic surface seemed almost alive, shifting subtly as if breathing.

"These tutorials are incredible," Thomas said, accepting the cube. "The way it responds to questions, adapts to the student's understanding…it's like having a real teacher, not a recording."

"Portions of Lancelot's consciousness were digitized for the training curriculum," Merlin replied. "It responds as he would if he were actually here. Or at least, as he might have all those years ago. I must admit, I'm surprised by your dedication."

Thomas took a bite of the cube, his eyes widening at the explosion of flavor. "Mmm. This one tastes like the bangers and mash from 'Spoons." He savored the taste before continuing. "When I first came to the UK and started working as a courier, I spent weeks memorizing Manchester's layout. Every alley, every shortcut, every traffic pattern. Now that I've had some proper training, I realize this isn't so different. It's just in three dimensions. I even understand vectors now. How long have I been watching these tutorials anyway? Feels like I just started."

"Nine hours, fourteen minutes, and approximately thirty-eight seconds," Merlin replied with mechanical precision.

"What?" Thomas stared at him. "That's impossible. I haven't even gotten tired."

"The nutrition cubes help with that," Merlin explained. "They provide precisely what your body needs at any given moment. And time does tend to pass quickly when one is genuinely engaged in learning." The GOLEM's head tilted slightly. "Speaking of time, we're approaching Caerlyon."

"Already?" Thomas paused, a thought occurring to him. "Wait a minute. You told me you couldn't fly the ship, but you got us to our destination without any feedback from me."

"You're correct that I can't fly the ship," Merlin agreed, his GOLEM's eyes flickering slightly. "But there's a significant difference between initiating predetermined travel protocols and actual piloting. Wormholes and bursts are essentially just complex mathematical calculations executed through the ship's systems. Since you agreed to my proposal to travel to Caerlyon, I was able to run the calculations and initiate the burst myself."

"I guess that makes sense," Thomas said.

"If I couldn't execute basic navigational patterns, someone—in this case you—would need to be in a pod at all times. Which would make learning, sleeping, eating, or otherwise quite difficult."

"I get it," Thomas repeated. "I'm not complaining."

"Good. Perhaps you'd like to see Caerlyon for yourself?"

"I'm right behind you," Thomas replied, turning away from the projection. "I assume it won't lose my place."

"Of course not."

They made their way through Excalibur's corridors, their footsteps echoing off the metallic surfaces. Thomas found himself already anticipating the neural interface, his mind revisiting Lancelot's lessons about vectors and momentum.

When they reached the flight deck, Thomas crossed to

the command pod without hesitation, no longer afraid of the device. The command pod reacted in kind, welcoming him like an old friend, the dark gel parting around his body as he settled into position. The neural interface engaged much more smoothly this time, the pain and disorientation minimal.

"You seem to be getting the hang of things," Merlin observed.

"It's much better," he said, letting his awareness expand through the ship's systems. "Though I still can't monitor everything at once."

"That's why there are twelve seats. With a full crew, you could easily parse everything in realtime."

"Is that one of our goals, then? To pick up crew?"

"Perhaps, but until we know the score, it's unwise to put even the smallest trust in any stranger."

Thomas focused his mental energy on the external sensors, allowing them to flow into his mind and provide a composite image of Caerlyon. His breath caught at the sight.

The station was colossal, a breathtaking fusion of ancient grandeur and advanced technological superiority—a medieval castle reimagined for the stars. It hung in high orbit around a gas giant whose swirling storms painted the visible hemisphere in shades of purple and gold. Ships of various designs moved purposefully around it, their paths creating complex but orderly patterns in Thomas' mind.

Massive docking arms radiated from its central hub like the spokes of a wagon wheel, each one capable of accommodating vessels of all shapes and sizes. The docking arm surfaces gleamed with intricate engravings, as if to remind visitors that artistry could co-exist with utility. Not to mention magic.

From the station's sprawling surfaces, majestic towers rose into the blackness, their buttressed spires seemingly defying the weightless environment. Each tower was adorned with shimmering panels resembling stained glass, casting vibrant hues across the hull as they captured and refracted starlight. Flying buttresses arched gracefully between these structures, the antennae rising from them suggesting they were sensor systems cleverly disguised as architectural flourishes.

Along the station's outer perimeter, a shimmering energy shield pulsed rhythmically like a moat of pure light, guarding against the constant threats of space debris and hostile forces.

Despite it's majestic appearance, it wasn't the station or the volume of traffic that quickened Thomas' pulse. It was the vessels patrolling its perimeter.

"Draconites," he said, his mouth going dry. "They control the station?"

"So it would appear," Merlin replied, his tone darkening. "The political situation has clearly...evolved during our absence."

"How the hell are we supposed to reach the station?" Thomas asked, watching as a Draconite patrol ship intercepted and scanned an incoming merchant vessel. "The moment they spot us…"

"We aren't going to reach the station. At least, not in Excalibur."

"How else are we going to get there, then? Teleport?"

"That would be unwise, as it would badly limit our potential escape routes if the need arose."

"But you could potentially teleport from here to there?" Thomas asked with amazement.

"In some scenarios, yes. But not this one. You'll understand why shortly. First, we need somewhere to hide the ship." Merlin's GOLEM gestured to a small rocky planet visible through the sensor feed. "That should do nicely."

Thomas studied the barren world through multiple

sensor bands. It was barely large enough to qualify as a planet. It looked more like an asteroid that had been pulled into a stable orbit. But its position relative to Caerlyon was perfect.

"Good idea," he said, guiding them toward it. The movements felt more natural now, more like riding his bike through familiar streets.

"Your piloting skill has noticeably improved," Merlin observed.

"Those tutorials were thorough."

They maneuvered slowly but steadily to the rock, with Thomas using his improved skill to also keep a close sensor eye on the Draconite patrols. Twenty minutes later, Thomas successfully parked Excalibur close to the planetoid's surface on its dark side, keeping them well below any likely patrol routes.

"I did notice that Lancelot didn't include any lessons about hiding from superior forces," Thomas said as he cut the main thrusters.

"The Avalonian Knights didn't believe in hiding," Merlin replied, a note of what might have been nostalgia in his voice. "Though perhaps if they had..." He trailed off, then gestured toward the door. "Set the ship to autopilot and come with me. There are preparations to make."

Thomas did as Merlin suggested before climbing out of the command pod. He felt slightly dizzy as he stepped down, but regained his composure quickly. He was definitely starting to get the hang of the interface.

They made their way through the ship, surprising Thomas when Merlin stopped at the doors to the armory.

"It's best not to travel to potentially hostile places unarmed," he said, opening the doors.

Thomas stared at the racks of medieval armaments. "I don't think that's a good idea," he said finally. "I'm more liable to hurt myself with one of these than someone else."

He raised his hands, curling them into fists. "I'm safer with these."

The GOLEM's eyes flickered in consideration. "Likely a wise decision at this point," Merlin replied. "Though you should at least take an energy shield." He indicated a bracer resting on a nearby shelf. "The emitter is designed to be discreet while remaining instantly accessible."

Thomas lifted the device carefully. It was lighter than he expected, its surface etched with the same flowing patterns he'd seen throughout the ship. A small display showed shield strength as a percentage, currently reading 100%.

"How exactly does it work?" he asked, turning the bracer over in his hands. "I'm assuming it's not just ancient space magic."

"Actually, it is precisely ancient space magic, enhanced by technology," Merlin replied, somehow managing to sound both amused and serious. "Or perhaps it's the other way around. No matter. The principles are quite straightforward. Simply secure it to your wrist. The shield will activate automatically if it detects incoming threats, projecting a barrier of pure energy around you."

"And that keeps me completely safe?"

"From most conventional weapons, yes. Though I should warn you that the power supply is limited. The more hits it takes, the faster it drains." Merlin gestured at the dark-bladed sword Thomas had admired earlier. "And certain weapons, like those forged from fayrilite, can penetrate energy shields without issue. As can some forms of magic."

"Of course they can," Thomas muttered, securing the bracer to his wrist. It adjusted automatically for a perfect fit. "Should I wear armor too? Do the whole space knight thing?"

"Only if you want to stand out like a court jester in a

convent." The GOLEM's eyes flickered with amusement. "Come."

They returned to the cargo hold where Thomas had first entered the ship. This time, Merlin approached the bulkhead on the far side of the hold. When he neared, a section of the bulkhead parted. Thomas peered into the space beyond, his eyes widening at what he saw.

A small hangar contained a diminutive starship barely large enough for one person. Its design reminded Thomas of a hawk—all sharp angles and predatory grace, with swept-back wings that looked more suited to atmospheric flight than space. The craft's hull was a matte gray that shifted colors slightly as he looked at it. A familiar blue glow emanated from etchings along its fuselage.

"Is this a GOLEM?" he asked, noting the distinctive energy signature. "How many of these things do you have?"

"Enough," Merlin replied cryptically. "I constructed this one during my time in the cavern. It is unique, which means neither the Draconites, Lancelot, or anyone else will easily identify its origins or true nature."

"I'm impressed," Thomas said. "You've obviously been thinking about this for a while."

"I had centuries to consider various scenarios," Merlin said. "Though I admit, I didn't expect to be sneaking past Draconite patrols quite so soon after our emergence."

"What's our cover story?" Thomas asked. "I assume we're not just going to fly up and ask nicely to dock?"

"Actually, we are."

"Do you think that'll work?"

"My confidence level would be higher if we had any gold to help grease the gears, so to speak."

"Gold? Is that what you use for currency out here?"

"Among other precious minerals."

"Not digital currency?"

"There is a digital aspect. But the accounts are backed

by tangible goods. Unfortunately, even if Arthur's accounts still existed, we couldn't use them without drawing too much attention. I do have a small cache of physical coin you can use on the station."

"*I* can use? Don't you mean we?"

"If I meant we, I would have said we."

"So you're sending me onto the station alone?"

"Of course not. But the aim is not to draw attention. Which means you'll have to speak for yourself while I maintain a more subtle presence."

"I'm not sure what that means, but I don't think I like it."

"We don't have a choice." Merlin gestured toward the craft's open cockpit. "Shall we?"

Thomas approached the small ship cautiously. "You're sure about this?"

"Would you prefer to try reaching the station in Excalibur?"

"Point taken." He climbed into the cramped cockpit, finding barely enough room to sit comfortably. The controls looked similar to what he'd watched Lancelot use in his demonstrations. "Cozy."

"A smaller ship makes for a smaller, more nimble target," Merlin replied, his voice now coming through hidden speakers as the cockpit sealed around Thomas with a soft hiss. "Though I did include inertial dampeners. I assumed you wouldn't want to experience high-g maneuvers completely unprotected."

"How thoughtful of you," Thomas muttered, then tensed as the small craft lifted off. The external hangar doors began to open, revealing the star-filled space beyond.

"Are you ready?" Merlin asked.

Thomas gripped the edge of his seat as the tiny ship aligned itself with the opening. "Do I have a choice?"

"There's always a choice," the Advisor replied, amusement clear in his tone. "Though in this case, all the alternatives seem considerably worse."

"In that case, let's do this."

Inertia pushed Thomas back against the GOLEM's seat as the small craft shot forward into the void, accelerating smoothly away from Excalibur's hiding place and around to the visible side of the planetoid. He watched the massive station grow larger through the forward viewport, trying not to think about the many ways this could all go very wrong.

CHAPTER 27

Slipping deftly through the endless stream of traffic, Merlin's GOLEM ship glided through the organized chaos surrounding Caerlyon station. Thomas watched in awe as vessels of all sizes navigated the carefully orchestrated dance of arrivals and departures, each vessel a symbol of the incredible diversity of spacefaring cultures that called Avalon home.

His fingers traced unconsciously over the energy shield bracer on his wrist. The familiar weight of uncertainty settled in his gut–that same feeling he'd had his first day as a courier in Manchester, when the city's maze of streets and alleys felt impossibly vast and complex. But this was different. This wasn't just a new city to learn. This was an entirely new galaxy.

A massive ship passed above them, blocking out the stars. Covered in ornate spires and gothic architecture that defied the laws of nature, its hull was a monument to unnecessarily complex but visually incredible design. Gigantic burning braziers hung from chains along its flanks, their flames somehow persisting in the vacuum. Statues of armored figures stood an eternal watch from alcoves carved into the hull, their blank eyes seeming to follow their small craft as it passed beneath the behemoth's shadow.

The disturbed ions of the massive vessel's rear thrusters caused the GOLEM to shudder slightly, reminding him of how vulnerable they were out here.

"What the hell was that?" Thomas asked.

"A merchant vessel from the Druidic worlds," Merlin replied, his tone suggesting both fascination and mild disdain. "They're very high on themselves, aren't they? Magic users, all of them. In fact, they banish any offspring within their nations who aren't able to learn the arcane arts. Their ships have no energy shields. They use magic alone to protect them."

"They might be arrogant, but that ship is pretty cool," Thomas remarked. "When you say banish offspring, how old are we talking?"

"Most individuals with talent for the arcane begin displaying competency around puberty."

"That's still kind of young for someone to be on their own."

"Yes. Many of the outcasts end up on stations like this one, in gangs or as thieves and pickpockets."

"I can empathize with that."

"I'm sure you can. But that won't make it sting any less if they rob you, so beware."

"If they have their own worlds, does that mean they were never under Arthur's rule as king of Avalon?"

"All worlds and nations were under Arthur's rule back then, until the Draconite rebelled. The Druids refused to get involved, claiming their magic would give too much of an advantage to whichever side they joined." Merlin scoffed. "Cowards, all of them. Magic is powerful, but it isn't invincible."

"Couldn't Arthur just order them to join his side, as their king?"

"Perhaps, but Arthur wasn't that kind of king."

"Do you think the Draconite would have rebelled if he had been that kind of king?"

"I've often pondered that question," Merlin replied somberly. "I hate to admit that it's a distinct possibility."

On that note, Thomas returned his attention to the traffic around them. He watched as a squadron of smaller vessels shot past in tight formation. Each bore heraldic markings—crests and symbols—that glowed and pulsed in time with their power cores.

"Those weren't Draconite," Thomas observed, watching as the squadron executed a perfect turn that would have been impossible in atmosphere. The sureness of their movement spoke of extensive training and experience.

"No. The station serves as a neutral trading hub," Merlin explained. "While the Draconites control it, they allow most species to dock and conduct business. It's more profitable that way."

"So who were they?"

"Judging by the heralds, I believe they may be what passes for Avalonian Knights these days."

The answer surprised Thomas. "And the Draconites let them fly openly around the station?"

"Apparently. It would mean they're of little threat, which is a bad sign."

"Do you think their presence means that Lancelot may be here, too?"

"It's unlikely, but not impossible. Even if he followed the wormholes back to our starting place, he would have no way to know we would come here."

"Are you sure? Watching those training videos, he talks a lot about anticipating the enemy, based on subtle tells that often become apparent as an opponent flies. A slight dip before they vector to port, for example. What if he anticipated our move?"

"If we spend our lives casting glances over our shoulder in search of Lancelot, we'll never move forward. Besides, Caerlyon is one of the largest stations in Avalon. Even if he's here, locating us would hardly be trivial."

The traffic grew denser as they neared the station. Massive cargo haulers moved with ponderous grace while sleeker vessels darted around them like fish around a coral reef. Some ships Thomas recognized as obvious military design–all sharp angles and weapon ports. Others defied categorization, their forms suggesting organic growth rather than construction.

"Approaching vessel, identify yourself." The voice crackled through the comm system, making Thomas jump slightly. It had an artificial quality to it, as if the speaker wasn't entirely organic.

"I will handle this," Merlin said before Thomas could respond. "Personal vessel Cowardly Hawk requesting permission to dock. Single passenger, no cargo."

"Cowardly Hawk?" Thomas whispered in question.

"A non-threatening name is the first step to disarming the opposition," Merlin answered.

"Lancelot never said that."

"Lancelot doesn't know everything," Merlin snapped.

A tense pause followed, the silence interrupted only by the soft hum of their engines and the occasional crackle of static. "Cowardly Hawk, docking fees are two gold per day, please provide payment credentials and begin vectoring toward Gate Seventeen."

"Um, yes…about that," Merlin replied. "We've had a bit of a misunderstanding with our treasury and were forced to withdraw our assets. We're currently unbanked, you see, but we'll be happy to pay the fee to the gatekeeper directly." There was just the right amount of resigned annoyance in his tone, as if this were a common inconvenience.

Another pause, longer this time. Thomas' hands balled into tight fists, certain they were about to be turned away. Or worse, the Draconite patrol ships would advance on them. Through the viewport, Thomas watched a pair of them glide past, waiting for the moment they would change direction and come after them.

"Continue to Gate Seventeen," the controller said finally. "Failure to pay the gatekeeper will result in immediate arrest and forfeiture of your vessel. Is that clear?"

"Perfectly clear," Merlin replied.

The GOLEM adjusted course slightly, threading its way between larger vessels toward a space between two of the docking arms. Thomas couldn't help but notice how the traffic patterns shifted around the Draconite ships, other vessels giving them a wide berth like pedestrians crossing the street to avoid a gang of thugs.

"That was too easy," he muttered nervously.

"They process identifiers and visual data against a database of flagged vessels," Merlin replied. "As I said, this GOLEM is too new to be recognized. Once we returned clean records, as long as we're willing to pay the fees, they won't dig any deeper. Greater scrutiny is afforded to larger ships that might pose an actual threat."

"That isn't so different from Customs on Earth," Thomas said.

"Is that so? Many things truly are universal."

They passed through the station's shimmering shield barrier, the energy field parting around them like water. Thomas felt a slight tingle through the hull, reminding him of the shield bracer on his wrist. They continued past the ships attached to the docking arms, headed for an apparently force field protected hanger tucked within their armpits. It was a cavernous space beyond that could have swallowed Manchester Cathedral whole.

Various small craft were arranged in neat rows across the deck, their designs running the gamut from sleek and pretentious to slabs of scrap metal. Maintenance crews of various species—some human-looking, others decidedly not—moved between them. Robots reminding Thomas of mechanical spiders scuttled about their business, carrying cargo in their multiple arms.

Merlin guided them to an empty spot near the back of the hangar. After setting down, a panel in the cockpit slid open with a soft hiss, revealing a worn leather purse that looked like it belonged in a museum. "Take it," Merlin instructed. "You'll need coin for the docking fee and other expenses."

Thomas reached for the purse, then hesitated. The leather felt alive under his fingers, warm and supple despite its apparent age. "What about you? Are you just going to wait here while I get lost in this place?"

A smaller panel opened, and something small and metallic scurried out. Thomas recoiled in surprise, nearly dropping the purse before realizing it was another GOLEM, this one barely larger than his palm and shaped somewhat like a mouse. Its tiny blue eyes glowed with the same intelligence as Merlin's larger GOLEM forms.

"I'll be coming with you," Merlin said. "Though this form won't be of much use to you if you get into any kind of physical trouble. So, I recommend avoiding that at all costs."

"I'll do my best."

The GOLEM scurried up his leg and disappeared into one of his pockets as the cockpit canopy opened, allowing Thomas to stand.

"Are you ready?" Merlin asked.

"As I'll ever be."

He had barely climbed down from the GOLEM ship when a loud shout froze him in place.

"Oy! You there!"

The voice cut through the background noise like a knife. Thomas turned to find a stout female approaching, her heavy boots clanking against the deck plating. She barely came up to his chest, but her broad shoulders and muscled arms suggested she could probably bench press him without difficulty. Her face was weathered and lined, with a prominent nose and thick eyebrows that met in the middle.

"Landing fee's two gold pieces," she said gruffly, holding out a hand that looked like it could crush stone. "Pay up or get out. And don't try passing off any of that counterfeit shit. I can smell fake coin."

Thomas reached into the purse, trying to project confidence he didn't feel as he withdrew two small gold coins.

The hangar master snatched them from his hand before he could even offer them, sniffing each one before nodding in satisfaction. "Right then. How long you planning to stay?"

"I'm not sure yet," Thomas replied. "What if I need more than a day?"

She grunted. "Additional day rate is one gold piece. Since you don't have a treasury, you'll pay when you leave. Try to get out without paying, and you'll have to deal with the patrols outside. And if I were you, I wouldn't be too keen to test them." Without waiting for a response, she turned and stomped away.

"Charming woman," Thomas muttered under his breath.

"Focus," Merlin said. "We need information about the current state of affairs in Avalon."

"And how exactly do we get that?" Thomas asked quietly as he made his way toward the hangar exit.

"How do you think? We head to the nearest tavern."

CHAPTER 28

"The nearest tavern?" Thomas questioned dubiously. "Are you kidding?"

"Not at all. Some things are universal constants, regardless of species. Where there's trade, there's drink. And where there's drink—"

"There's loose lips. Okay, I get it."

"So what's the problem?"

"I just…I don't like drinking, and I don't like drunks. Hits a little too close to home."

"We need information, and we need to get it without being conspicuous. Listening in on inebriated conversation is our best avenue to achieve our goals."

"I told you, I get it. But I don't have to like it." Thomas paused. "I do have a question, though."

"What is it?"

"I take it you've been here before."

"That wasn't a question, but yes. From what I've seen so far, it hasn't changed much in the last hundred years."

"Then you know where we should start our quest?"

"Indeed. Just try not to stare too obviously at the others on the station. I know it can be tempting for someone who's never seen the varied beings of Avalon before. But it's better not to upset the wrong ones."

"Are they all humanoid, or should I expect something weird like a talking sloth or a blue squirrel? I just want to be prepared."

"They're all humanoid, as you put it. Or Ursanoid. But there will be Draconite present, I'm sure. And probably Fae —they're the most diverse in appearance, by the way—and Druids, Sidhe. And likely elves and possibly shape-shifters, but they'll look like any of the aforementioned races."

"And you want me not to stare?"

"Exactly. I want you to listen. We need to know more than just whether or not the Draconite are the dominant force in Avalon. We need to know who are allies, who are enemies, and who remain undeclared."

"Assuming there's still a war going on," Thomas said softly. "The Draconite may not have any enemies. In which case, your chance of changing the status quo is zero."

"There has to be a reason the Draconite are still looking for Excalibur," Merlin countered. "Even if there is no active fighting, they must believe Arthur's return could spark rebellion."

"How? It's been a hundred years. Wouldn't they expect him to be dead?"

"The Pendragon line was known for longevity. It's even possible Arthur's mother, Igraine, is still alive."

"But you don't want to contact her?"

"No. Whatever the situation, she'd be too risky to reach out to right now. In any case, we can argue possibilities all day. There's only one way to learn the truth."

"What's the name of the place we're looking for, again?"

"The Starforge Tavern," Merlin answered.

Following Merlin's directions, walking through Caerlyon station felt like walking through a fever dream filtered through Thomas' memories of wandering Manchester at night. The corridors twisted and turned like the back alleys he'd once known by heart, but instead of rain-stained brick and crumbling concrete, the walls were smooth metal etched with alien symbols he couldn't read.

Holographic signs floated at intersections, their alien script transforming into readable text as he approached, reminding him of the way street signs would emerge from the fog on particularly grim northern nights. Decorated with gothic arches that wouldn't have looked out of place in Manchester Cathedral, except for their barely contained energy, the ceiling soared overhead.

The station's inhabitants were even more surreal than the architecture. Beings of all shapes and sizes moved through the corridors with purpose, their clothing ranging from elaborate robes to practical spacer gear covered in tool pouches and mysterious devices. Thomas tried not to stare at a group of passersby, with skin tones ranging from pale yellow to a deep red. Their features were just different enough from human standard to be unsettling—too angular, too perfect, like marble statues given life.

"Left here," Merlin said from his pocket. "The Starforge should be just ahead. And try not to gawk quite so obviously."

"I wasn't gawking," Thomas muttered, though he knew he had been. "I'm just...adjusting."

"Adjust faster. We're trying to blend in, remember?"

Thomas spotted the tavern's sign—a holographic display of a bright star resting on an anvil, a hammer about to fall on it—floating in mid-air as it slowly rotated. The establishment's name was rendered in flowing script that reminded him of Celtic knotwork.

The tavern itself looked like someone had started with a traditional English pub before adding the latest technology to the environs. The windows were actual stained glass, but the scenes depicted starships in battle. Inside, dark wood panels lined the walls, though they were inlaid with strips of softly glowing material pulsing in time with the music drifting through the door. It reminded Thomas of medieval court music played on synthesizers.

"Don't just stand there," Merlin chided. "You're drawing attention. And fix your posture. You look like you're expecting someone to mug you."

"Old habits," Thomas replied, forcing himself to straighten up. He stepped into an atmosphere thick with conversation and the smell of unfamiliar food and drink. The interior was dimly lit but comfortable, with tables scattered across multiple levels connected by short flights of stairs. A long bar dominated one wall, its surface embedded with crystals that caught and reflected the light.

His attention was immediately drawn to a group of Draconites seated near the center of the room. They weren't in armor, but their presence was impossible to miss. Their scaled skin ranged from deep crimson to midnight blue, and their horns were decorated with metallic bands that glimmered beneath the overhead lights. One of them, a female whose scales had an iridescent quality like mother of pearl, laughed at something her companion said, revealing rows of sharp teeth that could probably tear through steel, and could definitely tear his throat out with barely any effort.

"I said don't stare," Merlin warned. "The last thing we need is to attract attention. Especially from that particular group."

"Right. Sorry." Thomas forced his gaze away, moving toward the tables. He found an empty one near the center of the first floor, close to the bar, where he could listen to the other patrons without being too obvious about it.

"Just sit there and try to look natural," Merlin instructed from Thomas' pocket. "I can monitor multiple conversations simultaneously."

Before Thomas could reply, a serving girl appeared beside him. She looked human at first glance, but there was something distinctly otherworldly about her features. Her skin had a faint greenish tint, and her hair moved as if stirred by a breeze he couldn't feel. She wore a simple skirt and white blouse with a red apron over it, matching the other servers in the tavern.

"What can I get you?" she asked, her voice coming out like a melody through a flute.

Thomas hesitated, taken by her ethereal beauty, until he felt Merlin crawl up his back under his shirt to whisper in his ear. "Order the house ale. It's safe for human consumption, and it's what most traders drink."

"House ale, please," Thomas managed.

She studied him for a moment, head tilting slightly. "First time on Caerlyon?"

"That obvious, huh?"

"Where are you from? You look like you've never seen a Draconite before. That's pretty hard to do, these days."

Thomas' face burned, and he offered a meek smile. "I'd rather not say."

He expected Merlin to chide him for the response, but the Advisor remained silent. The serving girl laughed at his non-response, revealing too-white teeth that almost glistened. "Don't worry," she said, "your secret's safe with me. So what brings you here, stranger?"

"Tell her you're a free trader looking for work," Merlin suggested. "It's a common enough cover story."

"I'm a free trader," Thomas said, hoping he sounded more confident than he felt. "Looking for opportunities."

"Aren't we all?" she replied with a knowing look. "Though opportunities are harder to come by these days, what with all the new regulations. Still, there's always work for those willing to look in the right places." She gave him a significant look that Thomas wasn't sure how to interpret. "I'll get your ale."

As she moved away, Merlin's voice came from his pocket again. "Good. Now be quiet and let me listen. There's quite a bit of interesting chatter, especially from that group of Druids in the corner."

Though it was hard not to stare at the variety of beings around him, Thomas stretched out one leg and slouched back in his chair, trying to look casual as he observed the room.. Without being obvious, he paid particular attention to the Druid men in dark robes. They all wore curiously serious expressions. At another table, a Draconite was deep in conversation with someone Thomas at first took for human—or Ursan—but as he looked closer, he noticed the man's lithe frame, boyish good looks, and the pointed ears jutting out from under his long blonde hair.

He stiffened. "My boy, are you reconsidering your desire to live?" Merlin asked.

"What? No. Why?"

"Because if you keep staring like that, you're going to get yourself killed. I can try to find another worthy champion, but you can't be resurrected."

Thomas lowered his eyes to the table. "You don't have resurrection spells here?"

"Nimue does, perhaps," Merlin answered wistfully.

The serving girl returned with his ale, served in a mug that looked like it was carved from a single crystal. The liquid inside resembled Earthen beer with a slight purple tint. "Cheers!" she said with a smile before moving on to another table.

Thomas took a cautious sip. The flavor was unlike any beer he'd had before—complex and slightly sweet—definitely not what he expected in a house brew. "Not bad," he said quietly.

"This is worse than I had hoped," Merlin said, interrupting his enjoyment of the drink. "The Draconites have consolidated their hold on most of the core systems. Those Druids I pointed out are discussing new trade routes to avoid Draconite checkpoints. Apparently, any vessel that hasn't been inspected before reaching its destination is subject to hefty fines and a thorough search."

"What are they looking for?" Thomas whispered into his mug.

"My guess would be everything and anything that could pose a threat to their control. Weapons, obviously. Magical artifacts. Communication devices that could be used to coordinate resistance."

A burst of bitter laughter from another table drew Thomas' attention. It was occupied by a trio of almost ethereal-looking humans with dark skin and hair, and perfect bone structure. They were wearing light robes that wrapped around their delicate bodies. "What about them?" he asked.

Merlin's voice grew darker. "Those Sidhe traders are talking about what happened to the Academy of Arcane Arts on Fentagel. The Draconites shut it down last month and arrested all the senior faculty." Merlin gasped. "And executed them," he added angrily. "It appears they may be systematically eliminating anyone they see as potential threats, even where no threats exist."

"Why would they do that?"

"The only reason I can surmise is that they aren't confident in their grip on power."

"That might be a good thing."

"For us, perhaps. Not for the dead masters."

"That trader at the end of the bar?" Merlin said, his voice leveling out again. "He's telling his companion about a fledgling settlement that was wiped out last week. Their only crime was their inability to pay their taxes."

Thomas absorbed this, his grip tightening on his mug. "What about the resistance?"

"There's no talk of it. No hint that anyone is still fighting against what appears to be absolute tyranny. From what I'm gathering, the Draconites have turned neighbor against neighbor, made everyone afraid to trust anyone else. That argument between those two by the kitchen? They're traders. The big one is accusing the other one of being an informant. It happens constantly now. The paranoia is..." Merlin paused as new conversations caught his attention. "There's more," he said after a moment. "It seems they're looking for something specific. Those mercenaries two tables over...they're discussing bounties. Enormous rewards for information about certain artifacts. Magical weapons, ancient technology. Anything that could be connected to..."

"To what?"

"To Arthur. To Excalibur. To me." Merlin's voice grew tight. "They're still afraid, Thomas. After all this time, they're terrified that Arthur might return. That the legitimate heir to Avalon's throne will one day reappear to challenge their rule."

"But Arthur's dead," Thomas whispered. "Isn't he?"

"Yes. But they don't know that. Symbols have power. Hope has power. That's why they're so brutal in crushing any hint of outside strength, like the school on Fentagel. They know that if people started believing again, if they thought Arthur's return was possible..."

He fell silent as a new group entered the tavern. More Draconites, in civilian dress but carrying themselves with obvious military bearing.

"Who are they?" Thomas whispered.

"I'm not sure, but it's obvious from everyone's reaction they aren't very welcome."

Thomas forced himself to remain casual, pretending to

stare down at his ale as if pondering something as the newcomers spread out through the tavern. He couldn't help but notice how conversations grew quieter, more guarded. The fear in the room was almost palpable.

"This isn't the Avalon I remember," Merlin said softly, real pain in his voice. "In my time, it was a place of wonders. Of magic and technology working in harmony. Different species living together, learning from each other. Now..." He trailed off as the tavern's atmosphere grew even more tense.

Thomas was about to respond when the room suddenly went from subdued to silent. The change was instant and complete, conversations dying mid-sentence as all eyes turned toward the entrance. His blood ran cold as he saw why.

Three Draconites filed through the tavern doorway like incoming storm clouds. Their armor looked like it had been forged from the scales of some ancient monster, all sharp angles and overlapping plates that hinted of violence to come. Long swords hung from one hip, sleek, high-tech pistols from the other.

"Who are they, Merlin?"

"Bad news. Security guards."

Thomas' heart hammered as their eyes swept the room before settling on him. For a moment that stretched far too long, he was sure they'd somehow tracked him from the hangar.

Everything was about to go sideways in the worst possible way.

CHAPTER 29

"Don't move," Merlin hissed. He'd skittered back down to his pocket, his tiny mechanical form vibrating against Thomas' leg.

The Draconites moved forward with the measured precision of apex predators, their armored boots clicking against the floor in perfect unison. Each step sent little jolts of panic through Thomas' system. His fingers tightened around his mug as they drew closer, his mind already mapping escape routes he knew he'd never reach in time.

"Are you sure I shouldn't run?" he muttered out as softly as he could.

"Not yet," Merlin replied. "I'll give you the signal."

The guards advanced on Thomas, their long faces invisible beneath dark, menacing visors. He did his best to keep his eyes fixed on his ale, matching the other patrons in the tavern. They couldn't know who he was. They had never seen him.

Had they sensed Merlin's GOLEM somehow? Did it give off some kind of unique signature?

The Draconite guards strode toward his table, their armored boots striking the floor with metronomic precision.

Each impact sent tiny vibrations through the deck plates that he could feel in his bones, like the drumbeat before an execution. Thomas fought the urge to shrink into his seat, his heart pounding so hard he was sure everyone could hear it.

His hands trembled as he set down his ale, the crystal mug making a soft click against the table's surface that was far too loud in the sudden hush that had fallen over the room. An electric charge coursed through the atmosphere, the calm before the storm that reminded him of the moments before he had been shot as a child. It was that same electric anticipation of violence about to erupt.

The guards reached his table. Thomas could smell something sharp and metallic—like copper mixed with an underlying reptilian musk—coming off their armor. Their visored helmets swept the room in perfect synchronization, faceless masks that somehow managed to project both authority and threat.

Thomas could barely breathe now, his entire body tense, his heart ready to rip through his chest, his legs practically begging him to use them, but he held his position, eyes remaining on his mug as he waited for Merlin's signal. Waited for the guards to stop and turn in his direction.

Except, they didn't.

To his immense relief, they continued past him toward the bar, surrounding an older man who sat alone nursing what looked like whiskey in a scratched glass. The man's white hair was like fresh snow, though his weathered features suggested he'd seen more than his share of hard winters. His clothes, while clean, showed signs of careful mending. Thomas took him as a trader, but one with very limited means.

Sensing the guards' approach, the man turned slowly on his barstool, facing them with an expression that made Thomas' chest tighten. He knew that look. He'd seen it in juvie, on the faces of kids who knew trouble was coming and had decided that fight was preferable to flight.

"Arlen Black." The lead guard's voice cut through the silence like a blade, his hissing accent casting the name like an accusation. "You are wanted for the murder of Strax Vilseth. Come quietly, or come deceased."

A bitter laugh escaped the old man's throat, the sound harsh as steel on stone. "Murder?" He set his glass down with exaggerated care. "Is that what you're calling it now?"

He stood, and Thomas noticed how despite his apparent age, he moved with the fluid grace of someone who knew how to handle himself. The guard's hand shifted slightly toward his weapon, but Arlen didn't seem to notice or care.

"That creature," the old man continued, his voice gaining strength, "was bleeding my people dry." His words carried clearly through the dead-silent room. He wanted everyone present to know what he had done, and why. "Do you want to know what your precious tax collector was doing? He took a widow's last coins, money she'd saved for medicine for her sick daughter. When she begged him to leave her just enough to buy the drugs..." He trailed off, his hands clenching into fists. "He laughed. The bastard said maybe she should have thought about that before having children she couldn't afford to keep healthy. But she was just fine before your queen decided she needed more. And for what?"

"Careful, old man," the guard warned, a pair of thick gauntleted fingers wrapping around his sword hilt. "Your words border on sedition."

"Sedition?" Arlen's laugh held no humor now, only raw pain and anger. "Look around you!" His arm swept out to encompass the tavern. "Look what you've done to Avalon! Our worlds lie in ruins while you gorge yourselves on stolen wealth. Our children starve while yours grow softer and more entitled." His gaze swept the room, taking in the diverse crowd that watched in tense silence. "How can I be a traitor to your queen, when she isn't my queen?"

"She is the Queen of Avalon. She is your queen." The lead guard raised his voice for the rest of the tavern. "She is queen to all of you, and you will respect and follow her commands."

"She's nothing but a traitorous usurper," Arlen spat. "There is only one true ruler of Avalon. Only one man I respect enough to follow. None of the rest of you will say it openly, but I know I'm not alone. His name is Arthur Pendragon. And by the fates, I know he lives. I know that one day, he'll return, and your precious queen will be left groveling before him."

"That's enough," the lead guard hissed. "We are the most superior species in Avalon," he said, his tone almost conversational. "Not the Ursan. Not any of the rest of you. The strong rule. The weak serve." He turned to address the room at large. "Remember this moment. All of you will be subservient, or you will face the same consequences as this man."

He nodded to one of his companions, who drew his sword with liquid grace. The blade's edge promised swift and final judgment.

Except Arlen—who had looked frail just moments before—simply wasn't there when the sword thrust forward. He moved like water around the attack, his body following paths Thomas' eyes could barely track.

Two daggers appeared in Arlen's hands as if conjured from thin air, their blades glowing with a soft blue light that reminded Thomas of Excalibur's hull. The weapons hummed with barely contained energy as they traced deadly patterns through the air.

"Do something!" Thomas hissed, already half-rising from his chair. His muscles tensed with the familiar surge of adrenaline, Vic's voice in the back of his head, urging him to do the right thing. "We can't just watch this!"

"Sit down!" Merlin replied, real pain in his voice. "Do you want them to kill you, too. And then what happens to Avalon's last hope?"

"But he's—"

"Watch," Merlin cut him off softly. "And remember. This is what we're fighting against. This is why we need to be smarter than our anger."

The old man fought with desperate grace, his daggers leaving trails of blue light that burned afterimages in Thomas' vision. Each movement spoke of years of training, of muscle memory honed through countless battles. For precious seconds, he actually held his own against three armored opponents.

Thomas recognized the look in Arlen's eyes—the calm acceptance of someone who knew they were already dead but had decided to make their ending mean something. He'd seen that same expression on Vin's face near the end, when the cancer was winning but the old Marine refused to go quietly.

The guards moved with practiced coordination, their armor turning what should have been killing blows into glancing strikes. Every time Arlen's daggers found a gap in their defense, the blades sparked harmlessly off energy shields Thomas couldn't see but knew must be there.

"Their armor," he whispered. "It's like my bracer..."

"More advanced," Merlin replied grimly. "The Draconites have had a century to improve the technology."

"The fayrilite sword…"

"Yes, but what good is a sword without a steady hand to wield it?"

Thomas glowered. Merlin was right. He didn't know how to use a sword, and his fists would do nothing against the powerful guards. He dropped back into his seat, angry and defeated.

The end came with shocking suddenness. Arlen had just executed a perfect spinning attack that would have opened two of the guards from hip to shoulder if their shields hadn't caught the blades. The third guard simply stepped inside his guard and drove his sword forward with mechanical precision.

The blade entered just below Arlen's ribs, angled upward toward his heart. The old man made no sound as he fell, his daggers clattering against the floor. Their blue glow faded as his blood spread across the worn boards in a slowly expanding pool.

Bile rose in Thomas' throat. He'd seen people die before—hell, he'd killed someone himself—but there was something especially horrible about the casual efficiency of this execution. The way the lead guard wiped his blade clean on Arlen's shirt, as if he were nothing more than a dirty rag.

"Remove this trash," the guard ordered, his tone suggesting mild annoyance at having to deal with such an insignificant matter. His subordinates lifted the body, carrying it from the tavern as if disposing of refuse rather than a person who had dared to stand against tyranny.

The moment they were gone, conversation resumed as if nothing had happened. Glasses clinked, deals were made, lives continued while a trio of servers scattered powder over the blood spill and it soaked it up without leaving any evidence of it ever having been there. Thomas noticed however that the laughter held a brittle edge of fear poorly masked by false cheer.

"Here, let me get you a fresh ale," a familiar voice said. The serving girl was back, already replacing his barely-touched drink. All traces of her earlier flirtatiousness had vanished, replaced by something harder, more cynical. "You look like you need it."

"Does that happen often?" Thomas asked, his voice rough with suppressed anger.

She glanced around before leaning closer, her voice dropping to barely above a whisper. "More and more these days. The Draconites have always considered themselves superior, but after winning the war...and time has only made them worse." She straightened slightly, wiping imaginary spots from the table. "They think because they've perfected their genetics that makes them better than everyone else. They'd be nothing without their nanites. And how can they consider their genetics so great when they're all such arrogant bastards?" She paused, eyes darting around the room, nervous about being overheard before continuing. "This is how life is now. And how it will be forever, I'm afraid." The resignation in her voice struck Thomas harder than any physical blow. These people had lost all hope.

And maybe they were right to.

Thomas stared into his fresh ale, seeing instead Arlen's face in those final moments. The dignity in his defiance. The acceptance of his fate, tempered with the determination to face it on his own terms. It reminded him painfully of Vin, of lessons learned about standing up for what's right even when victory seemed impossible.

"The thing is," the serving girl continued, her voice barely audible, "Vilseth deserved what he got. Everyone knew he was skimming, keeping part of what he collected. But even saying that could get you killed these days. But I'm sure you know about that. You live in Avalon, too." She straightened, plastering on a fake smile that didn't reach her eyes. "Can I get you anything else?"

"No," Thomas managed, though his throat felt tight. "Thank you."

Anger burned in his gut like acid. He hated the casual cruelty of the execution, hated the way everyone simply accepted it, but most of all he hated his own powerlessness to do anything about it.

"We've heard enough here," Merlin said quietly. "It's time to move on. Leave a silver for the drink."

Thomas nodded, dropping a silver piece on the table. The coin felt inadequate somehow. As he stood to leave, his gaze was drawn to the servers and the powder that completely vanished before his eyes, erasing all evidence of yet another small tragedy in a galaxy he had a feeling was way too full of them.

The corridor outside felt too bright after the tavern's dimness. Thomas walked without real purpose, barely registering the flow of beings around him. His mind kept replaying the scene—the old man's words, the guard's casual cruelty, the way everyone just accepted it as normal. It was like living in his apartment growing up, where his neighbors, and even his own mother, pretended not to hear domestic violence through the thin walls—all of them telling themselves it wasn't their problem.

"I understand how you feel," Merlin said as they moved through the crowded passage.

"Do you?" Thomas asked bitterly. "Because I feel useless. Weak." His hands clenched into fists at his sides. "Like there's no point in fighting back. Just like I did on Earth."

"That's exactly how they want you to feel," Merlin replied, real heat entering his voice. "How they want everyone to feel. But remember what you saw in there. Remember that one old man was willing to stand up to them, even knowing it meant his death. Remember that he invoked Arthur's name. He hasn't been forgotten, and that's good for us. As long as the rebellious spirit exists, even if the organized resistance is dormant, there's still hope."

Thomas absorbed this in silence as they walked, his jaw

clenched so tight it hurt. Finally, he asked, "What's our next move?"

"We keep gathering information," Merlin said. "We learn everything we can about what we're facing without drawing attention. There are a few more taverns we can visit and pick up on the conversation."

"And watch a few more people be executed?"

"I should hope not. But sadly, it seems the possibility always exists."

"And once we've learned everything we can?"

"Then we go shopping."

"Shopping?" Thomas asked, confused.

"We need parts to repair the damage to the ship. Thankfully, they're all rather small, but also quite critical to extending the lifespan of the reactor and correcting the variance in the wormhole generator, among other things."

"Do we have enough coin?"

"Judging by the stress these people are under, we may not. I hope so."

"Me too. What about after that?"

"We return to the ship and prepare to do something about all of this. Something they won't expect. If the flame of resistance is dead, then it's up to us to relight the fire. Of course, this is all just my advice. It's up to you to make the final decision."

Thomas nodded slowly, still struggling to believe that he could make a difference in anything. A big part of him wanted to give up. But there was a small part that didn't. His own personal flame that had ignited when he saw the glaive-ship stand against the Draconite before attacking them, and had been fanned when Arlen invoked Arthur Pendragon.

"Alright," he said softly. "Where do we go next?"

CHAPTER 30

The station's corridors were like the streets of Manchester, but where Thomas had once navigated through rain and fog, here he walked through a maze of technological wonders and alien architecture, surrounded by beings he could still hardly believe existed.

Even so, the events at the Starforge Tavern had dulled his entire view of Caerlyon station, wiping away its outward sheen and revealing the dark, ever-present threat beneath.

"The Starlit Crown is just ahead," Merlin said from his pocket. "Try not to look so nervous. You're drawing attention."

"I can't help it," Thomas muttered. "Every time I see a Draconite patrol, I feel like they can smell fear."

"They can, but barely contained fear probably isn't out of place around them. Just walk like you belong here."

"Easy for you to say. You're hiding in my pocket."

They reached the tavern, this one darker and grimier than the Starforge. The holographic sign flickered erratically, suggesting either poor maintenance or strangely deliberate aesthetic choice. Inside, the air was thick with smoke from some kind of herb that made Thomas' nose itch and his eyes water.

"Find a spot near those merchants," Merlin instructed, indicating a group of beings that were almost too attractive to be human or Ursan, as strange as that definition felt to Thomas. "Sidhe traders are always good for gossip."

Thomas worked his way through the patrons, careful not to bump into anyone who might take offense. He'd already seen how quickly violence could erupt here. Finding an empty table close to the Sidhe, he settled in to listen while pretending to study a menu projected above the scarred surface.

"...another attack in the Lanwyn Cluster," one of the merchants was saying, his voice carrying a musical quality at odds with his grim expression. "It's the third time this month."

"The Draconites are calling the attacks industrial accidents," his companion replied with a bitter laugh. "As if we don't know better."

"They have to," a third added. "They can't admit someone's intentionally attacking them. It's bad for morale."

Thomas leaned slightly closer, trying to catch every word while maintaining his facade of disinterest. A server—this one Ursan—approached, but Thomas waved her off with a shake of his head.

"You really think it's organized resistance?" the first Sidhe asked, lowering his voice. "I heard rumors of a ship bursting from out of nowhere, striking military targets and vanishing like some kind of ghost."

"Impossible," his companion scoffed. "There is no more resistance. These are probably just isolated incidents. Independent actors pushed too far."

"That's what the Draconites want everyone to think," the third said. "But three times? Disgruntled civilians can't pull that off. Whoever it is knows what they're doing."

"Could it be Lancelot?" Thomas whispered, barely moving his lips.

"Unlikely," Merlin replied just as quietly. "This isn't his style. He was always more direct in his approach."

They listened as the Sidhe continued their discussion, but the conversation soon turned to more mundane matters of trade routes and tariffs.

"It's time to move," Merlin instructed after some time had passed. "Most of the conversation here is similar to what we heard at the Starforge. We'll head to the Silver Chalice next. It's in the diplomatic quarter. A more upscale clientele, so we may pick up more nuanced information there."

Thomas stood, making his way back through the pub. They walked in silence for some time, leaving Thomas to continue processing all they had seen and heard so far.

None of it was good.

The Silver Chalice proved to be much more opulent than even the first establishment they'd staked out, its external facade decorated in large panes of intricately formed stained glass. Instead of a holographic sign, the central pane formed a huge silver chalice resting in a reptilian hand. That piece of glass looked newer than the panes flanking it, leaving Thomas to wonder if an Ursan hand had once clutched the chalice. Maybe even Arthur's hand.

Inside, the atmosphere was completely different from the Starlit Crown. The air was clean and cool, the lighting subdued but elegant. The clientele—beings in elaborate robes and formal attire—matched the setting, their conversations conducted in careful whispers.

"The bar," Merlin directed. "That group near the end. The ones in black. From the Druidic worlds. Diplomats, by their insignia."

Thomas found an open spot two seats down from them

at the bar. He ordered a house ale like before and settled in to listen. The Druids spoke in measured tones, their words clearly chosen with care, even in what they probably thought was a private conversation.

"...the Queen is getting increasingly paranoid," one was saying, his features set in lines of concern. "The increasing boldness of the attacks have her concerned Arthur may be behind them."

"After all this time?" his companion asked. "Impossible. Even for an Ursan..."

"I heard that she believes he found a way to extend his life. That he's been gathering strength in secret, waiting for the right moment."

"And what do you believe?"

A pause. "I believe she fears ghosts. But her fear makes her dangerous. The treaty that protects our interests grows weaker by the day. The worse things get, the more likely it is she'll look to consolidate her power, and that means—"

"Careful," a third voice cut in. "Even here, the walls may have ears."

Though his pulse had quickened at the mention of Arthur, Thomas casually sipped his drink. The Druid's words confirmed what they'd learned earlier. The Draconites's control wasn't as absolute as it appeared on the surface.

"The Draconites rule through fear and force," Merlin said later as they left the Silver Chalice, "but they've had to make concessions to maintain full control. The Druids have some autonomy through old treaties, but it's fragile. Draconite allies may be persuaded to change sides with the right incentive."

"And somewhere out there, someone is actively fighting back," Thomas added. "Maybe the fire isn't totally extinguished."

"A keen observation, my boy. If it remains smoldering, it

will be easier to reignite. Though we still don't know who's causing the disturbances." Merlin paused. "The next tavern I want to check out is in the merchant's quarter, on the far side of the station. It'll be faster to take a shuttle around the station than make our way through the passageways."

"Which way should I go?" Thomas asked.

Merlin directed him to the shuttle bay, a short walk from the Silver Chalice. They joined a large group of others in the corridors leading to the destination, leaving Thomas surrounded by an assortment of beings. He was beginning to acclimate to their not-quite-human looks and presence, his open gawking diminishing to more subtle glances to take in a new feature or two, comparing and contrasting with his own physiology.

The shuttle bay reminded Thomas of a dodgy taxi back in Manchester, the kind where drivers lounged against their vehicles eyeing potential fares with barely concealed desperation. Here though, the cabs were compact spacecraft designed to ferry passengers between the station's districts. They were all lined up in neat rows within a small hangar bay protected from the vacuum of space by a shimmering force field.

Thomas lined up in a queue with the rest of the passengers, finding himself placed between a green Draconite female in flowing robes and a male elf whose outfit resembled a flight suit. He did his best to remain inconspicuous as the line steadily advanced, at one point nearly tripping over his own feet to avoid stepping on the Draconite's thick tail.

"Where to?" the pilot asked as Thomas reached the front of the line. An Ursan, his weathered face and tired eyes immediately reminded Thomas of Arlen, making him wonder how many people had perished to the Draconite's cruelty already. How many more would die in the future?

"Merchant's quarter," Thomas replied.

"One silver," the driver said, surprised when Thomas retrieved the coin purse and paid him in legal tender. The man pocketed the coin and opened the door. "Hop in."

The shuttle was cramped and worn, with seats that had seen better decades. Thomas found a spot near a viewport that someone had tried to scratch their initials into, the transparent material marred with other nondescript scratches. It felt familiar somehow, this universal constant of public transport, where every surface bore the marks of countless passengers leaving their mark on the world.

"This is actually not that different from home," he whispered as they lifted off with a slight shudder. "Just cleaner than the Northern line."

Through the scored viewport, Caerlyon station revealed its true scale—a massive structure up close—that somehow managed to be both beautiful and forbidding. The shuttle wove between towers and buttresses, following well-designed pathways through the architectural maze. Other shuttles moved in familiar patterns, in a complex dance choreographed by necessity and routine.

As they circled the station, Thomas found himself wondering what his younger self would have thought of all this—the kid who'd literally killed to join a gang because he couldn't see any other options for family or survival. Now here he was, flying through space with an ancient digitized consciousness in his pocket, trying to figure out how to fight what amounted to an evil empire.

The shuttle docked a minute later, landing smoothly and letting them out before advancing to the waiting queue at this station. Thomas made his way from the bay, following the corridor away from the outer bulkheads.

"This next tavern is called the Magic Keg," Merlin said as the passageway opened up ahead of them, revealing a large concourse and a number of beings moving about. "It's the largest alehouse on Caerlyon, and at least back before the destruction of Camelot, was owned by an acquaintance of mine."

They exited the corridor onto the concourse. Immediately, Thomas caught sight of a dark blemish amidst the otherwise lively storefronts and shops that lined the cavernous section of the space station. "Whatever shop that was looks like it caught fire," he said.

"That shop was the Magic Keg," Merlin replied softly, sadness obvious in his tone. "And from what we've seen and heard, I'm willing to bet its destruction was no accident."

CHAPTER 31

Thomas spied a holographic placard floating in front of the wrecked alehouse. He approached it as nonchalantly as he could, reading it with a sidelong glance as he walked by.

CONDEMNED BY ORDER OF THE OVERSEER FOR HARBORING TRAITORS AND TERRORISTS

"Yes," Merlin said. "I can definitely imagine Jalisen granting succor to those the Draconite would deem traitors and terrorists."

"Jalisen is your contact?"

"Indeed. As fine a Druid as you would ever want to meet. Unlike his nation, he refused to remain neutral while Avalon was burning. He offered many a knight food and rest at the Magic Keg, including Arthur."

"Maybe we shouldn't be surprised it's gone, then."

"Perhaps I should be more surprised that it lasted as long as it did."

They moved on from the wreckage before drawing attention from the crowd of beings—Ursan, Fae, Druids and the like—their attire an eclectic mix of medieval tunics, thick robes, tight-fitting flight suits, and uniforms.

The rest of the merchant quarter opened before them, a

chaotic fusion of futuristic and the ancient, buzzing with life and commerce. Holographic advertisements floated overhead, their constantly shifting images reflecting off stalls fashioned from a combination of metal alloys and stone. The air was thick with the smell of foods he couldn't identify and stranger things he probably didn't want to know anything about.

"Remember why we're here," Merlin said as Thomas found himself drawn toward a stall where globes of pure light drifted like balloons, defying the station's artificial—and likely magical, Thomas realized—gravity. "We need parts for the ship, not—"

"Is that a magic shop?" Thomas asked about the stall. The elderly woman behind the counter had skin like burnished copper and short, thick silver hair. She smiled as he approached, and something about that smile reminded him of Vin, as if she too often saw potential where others saw only problems.

"Interested in the arcane, young man?" she asked.

"Thomas..." Merlin's warning was clear in his tone.

"What?" he replied under his breath. "Do you have a monopoly on magic?"

"This isn't why we're here."

"Excuse me," Thomas said to the woman, turning away from her. "Are you going to teach me magic?"

"Why do you want to learn magic?" Merlin replied.

"You said yourself that the ship uses both technology and magic. How am I supposed to truly master it if I don't understand both?"

"That's a more noble and logical reason than I expected. But you don't need to know anything about magic to use the ship's enchantments."

"What if I just want to know about magic? What if I want to become a wizard?"

"You have a lot more important things you need to

learn, and a lot more important things we need to accomplish together. Magic takes many years to master."

"You have to start somewhere."

"I'm sorry, my boy. But I don't think that's a wise use of your time."

"Is that your decision, or your advice?"

"Thomas…"

He turned back to the stall, addressing the woman. "I've never tried to do magic before. How hard is it to learn?"

The woman's smile widened slightly. "That depends on your aptitude. Not everyone is suited to become an acolyte. The first lesson is quite affordable, though. Just three silver for an introductory course on spell casting and enchantments."

"Thomas, wait," Merlin said.

"Excuse me," Thomas again said to the woman, turning away from her. He could only imagine what she might think of his strange behavior. "What now?"

"You don't need to pay for this woman's lessons. And you don't need me to teach you directly. The onboard library contains tutelage from the real Merlin, including an introductory lesson."

"Why didn't you say that in the first place?"

"I wanted to see how serious you were about learning. Though I maintain that you'll struggle to find the time to review the materials."

"We'll see about that." He turned back to the woman. "I'm going to do some more shopping and circle back."

"Two silver, then," the woman replied, still hoping to make a sale.

"I'll come back," he repeated, walking away before she could continue haggling.

The market seemed to stretch on forever, bustling with activity as beings shopped a wide array of merchandise from clothing to medicines, to robots, and more. The only thing Thomas didn't see were weapons, armor, or anything that would also be considered illicit on Earth.

Merlin guided him purposefully toward either a scrapyard, a repair shop, or both. Even from a distance, Thomas could make out stacks of used parts piled high behind a counter, a handful of smaller humanoids working to sort through it.

"The parts we need should be available here," Merlin said. "Assuming we can afford them."

From closer up, the scrap piles behind the counter of the shop looked even more chaotic and disorganized. A large, muscled humanoid with an oversized head and a pair of long teeth jutting out from his wide mouth sat among the chaos, massive hands delicately picking through the garbage for something of value.

"Tell me what we need," Thomas said before stepping forward to haggle for parts they desperately needed with coin they barely had.

"A quantum stabilizer core, seventh generation or earlier," Merlin recited. "Three phase-lock crystals, matched set. And a first generation variable distortion regulator."

Thomas repeated the items as he approached the shopkeep, who looked away from the scrap pile. Up close, the creature's skin reminded Thomas of Manchester's winter sky—a particular shade of gray-green that meant trouble was brewing. But his eyes held an intelligence that challenged whatever stories Arthur might have shared on Earth about ogres.

"Parts," the ogre said, his voice surprisingly soft for his massive frame. "Or repairs?"

"Parts," Thomas replied, forcing confidence into his voice. "I need a quantum stabilizer core, seventh generation or earlier. A—"

"Hah!" The ogre's laugh rattled tools on nearby shelves.

"Might as well ask for pixie teeth. That part has to be a hundred years old."

"But do you have one?" Thomas pressed.

The ogre's eyes narrowed. "I'll have to check the inventory. What else?"

"Phase-lock crystals. Three of them, matched set."

"Getting more interesting." The ogre leaned forward, intrigued. "Continue."

"And a first generation variable distortion regulator."

"Now that," the ogre rumbled, "is a very specific request. Very specific indeed. First generations are older than the quantum stabilizer you asked for. Give me a minute." He rose from his seat, towering over Thomas before lumbering out of sight.

"Why do I get the feeling he's going to tell the Draconite guards what we just ordered?" Thomas said.

"Random spaceship parts," Merlin replied. "Nothing more."

"Old random spaceship parts."

"We need them, my boy. It's a risk we have to take."

Thomas glanced around the market, trying to look inconspicuous as he hunted for Draconite guards. He didn't see any so far, at least.

The ogre trundled back to his seat and leaned forward onto the counter. "Today's your lucky day. We happen to have all three items in stock."

"Great. How much?"

"Thirty gold pieces."

"Hmm, we don't have thirty," Merlin said. "You have twelve left in your purse."

"Please don't call it a purse," Thomas whispered.

"What's that?" the ogre asked.

"Oh…uh…"

"Tell him the stabilizer's worth four at most, considering its age. I'm willing to bet it's been sitting in his scrap pile for the last fifty years."

Thomas relayed the message.

"That might generally be true," the ogre agreed. "But you need the parts, and two of them are rare finds. So… thirty."

"Six," Thomas countered.

"No."

"Suit yourself." Thomas turned away.

"What are you doing?" Merlin asked.

"Leaving."

"We need that part."

"We can't pay for it. Besides, I know how this game is played, at least." Thomas continued walking away.

"Hold on!" the ogre rumbled.

Thomas looked back at him over his shoulder. "Are you going to make a serious deal or are you just going to keep playing games?" he asked. "I want the parts, but I don't need them."

"Yeah, okay. Let's try again."

Thomas returned to the counter. "Six."

"Twelve."

"Seven."

"Ten, and you tell me what ship they're for. I want to know what's still around that takes such old tech."

"Ten, and I don't tell you anything."

The ogre grinned. "Deal." He extended a meaty hand that swallowed Thomas' whole. His grip was gentle as they shook on it.

Thomas counted out the coins and laid them on the counter, trying not to think about how little coin they had left. The ogre once more disappeared into the chaotic disorder of his shop. Thomas resumed lookout for incoming Draconite guards while he was gone, not finding any. A few minutes later, the ogre returned with a misshapen sack.

"Don't drop it," he advised as Thomas took the bag. "Some of these parts are…delicate."

"I know." Of course, he didn't, but the ogre didn't need to know that. The sack had to weigh at least thirty pounds, forcing Thomas to sling it over his shoulder as they hurried through the market, headed back toward the shuttle bay.

"You may have been right about the shopkeep," Merlin said suddenly. "I believe we're being followed."

CHAPTER 32

Thomas kept his pace steady through sheer force of will. He felt that familiar tightness in his chest, the same feeling he'd gotten running from the police in Manchester. "Damn it. I knew it."

"Regardless, we needed these parts. However, we can't lead them back to Gate Seventeen. If they see my other GOLEM..."

"So what do we do?"

"Fortunately, I have a schematic of the station stored in my memory. A benefit to being digital. Take the next left. There's a maintenance access way. A path less traveled."

Thomas turned casually, like someone who belonged there and knew exactly where he was going.

"Through that door up ahead," Merlin said. "Quickly."

Thomas reached the door, but it didn't open at his approach, or when he tapped on the control panel beside it. "Locked."

Merlin's GOLEM climbed out of his pocket. "Bring me close to the panel."

The GOLEM climbed onto his hand and Thomas extended it to the door controls. A flash of blue energy shot from the diminutive GOLEM's eyes into the panel, a wisp of smoke erupting from it. The door slid open, and Thomas hurried inside.

"The only problem now is we can't close it," he said.

"One thing at a time, my boy," Merlin answered. "Let's get far enough ahead of them that it won't matter."

The maintenance corridor—no architectural flourishes here, just bare metal walls lined with pipes and conduits—was a stark contrast to the main thoroughfare. Their footsteps echoed differently, making it impossible to tell how close their pursuers were.

Thomas followed Merlin's directions through the smaller corridors, checking over his shoulder every few seconds. He never saw anyone following him, but when the door ahead of them hissed open and a pair of Draconite guards stepped out, he knew they were in deep trouble.

"Run," Merlin cried.

Thomas didn't need to be told twice. He spun and sprinted back the way they had come until he reached a side passage, the sack of parts bouncing on his shoulder.

"Merlin?" he questioned meekly. He turned the corner just as an energy blast hit the bulkhead next to him, sizzling into the metal.

So much for following the rules of combat.

Survival instincts kicked in. He forgot about the weight of the bag as he sprinted down the corridor. He could hear the Draconite guards chasing after them, two pairs of footsteps joined by more.

"Shit!" he cried. "This was a bad idea."

"Left here," Merlin directed calmly. "Then second right. There's a secondary maintenance shaft that will take us down three levels."

Thomas followed the directions, his boots ringing on the metal deck plates. The new maintenance shaft—a vertical tube with rungs set into one side, disappearing into darkness below—turned out to be barely wider than his shoulders.

"Down," Merlin said. "Quickly."

Thomas swung onto the ladder one-handed, still clutching the precious parts. The sack was almost too wide to fit, and. caught on something as he started down. He held on tight and pulled, forcing the sack down with them.

Seconds later, he heard voices—sharp, reptilian sounds that needed no translation to convey their meaning—above. They were running out of time. And options.

The ladder felt endless, each rung slick with condensation that made Thomas' palms slippery, threatening his grip. The sack of components pulled him off balance, throwing him off his rhythm. His arms burned from the awkward descent.

"Keep going," Merlin urged. "Three more levels."

"Easy for you to say," Thomas gasped. "You're not the one doing all the work."

A metallic clang from above sent his heart racing faster. The guards were in the shaft now, their heavier forms making the whole structure vibrate. The darkness below promised either escape or a very long fall.

"There's a maintenance hub two levels down," Merlin said. "If we can reach it before they catch up..."

Thomas didn't waste breath responding. His world narrowed to the next rung, the next step down. The sack caught again on something unseen in the darkness, nearly jerking free of his grip. He couldn't lose these parts. Without them, Excalibur would eventually fail. Everything would have been for nothing.

Just like his whole life had been for nothing, before all this started.

The thought sent a surge of determination through his tired muscles. For the first time in his life, crazy as it all was, he had something to fight for. He wasn't giving that up so easily.

Harsh industrial illumination suddenly bloomed below, spilling from an open access way. Thomas could make out pipes and conduits, and what looked like maintenance robots scuttling along the walls like mechanical spiders.

"That's the hub," Merlin confirmed. "But we've got company coming up from below, too."

Thomas risked a glance down. More armored figures were emerging from another access shaft, their scaled faces turned upward. He was caught between them, like a rat in a drain pipe.

"Options?" he asked, trying to control his breathing.

"There's a horizontal shaft about three meters below you. It runs between the main power conduits."

"How wide?"

"Not wide enough for them to squeeze through in their armor."

The Draconites were closing from both directions, their movements deliberate and coordinated. They thought they had him trapped.

"Sometimes," he muttered, remembering Vin's words, "the only way out is through."

He took a deep breath, calculated the distance, and let go of the ladder.

The fall lasted less than a second, but time stretched as he twisted in the air. The maintenance shaft gaped before him—a black rectangle barely wider than his shoulders. He caught the edge with his free hand, muscles screaming as he dangled there. With a heave, he threw the sack into the shaft. Then, he pulled himself up and in behind it.

The space was even tighter than he expected. Thomas squirmed forward on his elbows, pushing the sack ahead of him. The walls pressed in on all sides, making each movement a struggle. Cables and pipes ran along the ceiling, occasionally dripping unknown fluids onto his back.

"Faster," Merlin urged as shouts echoed from the vertical shaft. "They'll figure out where you went soon."

"I'd like to see them fit through here," Thomas grunted, pushing himself forward another few inches.

"That doesn't mean they can't shoot you in the ass!"

"That's not very honorable."

"I hate to say it, but perhaps those old ways are as dead as Arthur."

Light flickered ahead. Another access point? Or just maintenance indicators? The shaft felt like it was getting narrower, though that might only have been his imagination. Or panic at work in his mind. It was hard to tell the difference crawling through a metal tube while being chased by mutant space dragons.

"This would be a really bad time for claustrophobia to kick in," he muttered.

"You're not claustrophobic," Merlin replied.

"No, but I'm starting to reconsider it."

A loud bang echoed through the shaft behind them, followed by cursing in what had to be Draconite. Thomas forced himself to move faster, ignoring the way the metal walls scraped against his shoulders. He could feel death breathing down his neck, and it had scales.

The question was, what waited ahead?

CHAPTER 33

Thomas squirmed forward through the maintenance shaft, feeling like a parasite stuck inside a monster intestine. His shoulders scraped against every seam connecting the sections of the shaft, his clothes scraping off rust flakes and decades of grime. The sack of parts bumped and caught on every protrusion, each snag threatening to trap him here while the Draconite guards closed in.

The air, tasting of metal and dirt, grew thicker as he crawled, the oppressive darkness broken only by occasional maintenance lights casting everything in sickly green shadows. Somewhere ahead, proper light spilled through what looked like another access hatch, but the distance was impossible to judge in the confined space.

"Almost there," Merlin said, the tiny golem's weight in his pocket a constant reminder that he wasn't completely alone in this mess.

"That's what you said two minutes ago," Thomas grunted, shoving the sack over another seam in the piping. His arms burned from the constant effort, sweat running into his eyes and making them sting. "And two minutes before that."

"Would you prefer I remain silent instead of offering encouragement?"

"I'd prefer not being chased by angry space dragons."

"Simply surrender and they'll stop chasing you."

"And skewer me instead." Thomas pushed forward another few inches, trying to ignore the way the walls seemed to close in with each movement. "No, thank you."

"A wise choice."

"Thanks for the advice."

Finally, mercifully, he reached the access hatch. It opened onto empty space, dropping away eight feet to a metal deck below. The room beyond housed what looked like massive air handling equipment, its huge ducts disappearing into the walls and ceiling. The machinery's constant drone would have covered any sounds of pursuit, if Thomas could have heard anything over his own pounding heart.

"Lower the parts first," Merlin instructed. "Then yourself."

"I know how gravity works, Merlin," Thomas muttered, but he followed the advice anyway. He maneuvered the heavy, awkward sack through the opening, his arms trembling from exertion as he leaned down, trying to minimize its descent to the deck. The weight of the bag threatened to pull him out with it. The strain on his shoulders felt like someone driving hot needles into his shoulder joints.

"Careful," Merlin warned as Thomas' grip slipped slightly. "Those components are irreplaceable."

"Unlike me, right?"

"While true, that's not what I meant."

Thomas let the sack drop the last few feet, wincing at the clang it made against the deck. The sound echoed through the space like a dinner bell, announcing their presence to anyone listening.

"I hope nothing was broken," Merlin muttered.

"I hope we can get out of this unbroken," Thomas replied.

He didn't have enough space in the shaft to turn around and put his legs out first, So he continued sliding forward, wedging his legs as best he could, his body pressed against the wall. As he extended out to his knees, the weight of his body overcame the friction of his pressure on the metal, and he slid the rest of the way out. Frantic, he turned as best he could to catch the brunt of the fall on his shoulder instead of his head and neck. Just barely, he managed to avoid landing on the sack of parts, fresh pain radiating from his neck all the way down his arm.

That's when he heard the hiss of a door opening at the far end of the room.

He rolled onto his hands and knees as three Draconite guards charged the room, quickly boxing him against the wall.

"Oh hell," Thomas whispered. "So much for your escape route."

"Indeed. This is less than ideal," Merlin observed.

The lead guard stepped forward, his helmet's faceplate retracting to reveal iridescent scales in shades of deep crimson surrounding narrow green eyes. "Surrender," he commanded. "You have nowhere left to run."

"If they take us," Merlin said, "they'll find me. And then we'll both be dead. Well, you'll be dead. I'll be erased."

Thomas knew he was right. He'd seen how the Draconites dealt with those who opposed them. Arlen's death—the casual brutality, the way everyone had simply accepted it as normal—was still fresh in his mind. He wanted no part of whatever passed for justice in this world.

He rose slowly to his feet, refusing to cower in front of the guards. "What do you want with me?" he asked. "I haven't done anything wrong."

The lead guard huffed. "If you're innocent, then why did you run?"

"Fear?" Thomas offered. It wasn't a lie, at least.

"You dimwits should know by now that running only makes it worse. What do you have in that sack?"

"I think you know what's in the sack."

"And why do you need those parts?"

"Why does anyone need parts for equipment typically found on a starship? Is that illegal?"

"No, but your selection is…intriguing."

"Is it illegal to own an old ship? I'm just a dimwit, it's the best I can afford."

The lead guard's mouth twisted in what might have been amusement, revealing rows of needle-sharp teeth. "Your needs are especially coincidental, to the extent of being suspicious. And running didn't help your case. Put your hands over your head. You will be strip searched."

"Wait, what?" Thomas said as two of the other guards took a step toward him. Strip searched or just searched, either way they would discover Merlin's GOLEM, and it would be game over. "Over my dead body."

"If that's how you prefer it."

Rather than approaching, the other guards spread out. Their blades whispered from scabbards, edges gleaming. Thomas had never faced opponents with swords before. His street fighting experience felt woefully inadequate as he watched them circle.

"This is your last chance to reconsider," the guard leader said. "Even the slightest display of intellect could save your life."

"I doubt that," Thomas replied, bending slightly to grab the sack of parts. He glanced at his bracer, putting faith in the idea that it would protect him. His only hope was to absorb their attack and push through them, then outrun them back to…wherever.

"Merlin," he whispered. "Any advice?"

"Try not to die," he replied.

"Not very help—"

The leader's attack—a lightning-fast thrust that would have skewered him if the shield hadn't activated—came without warning. Blue energy flared around Thomas as the blade struck, the impact translating through his body like being hit by a lorry. The sensation was completely alien, nothing like the familiar sting of fists he'd gotten used to growing up.

He stumbled backward, barely avoiding a second strike. The other two guards moved to flank him, the three of them like a well-oiled machine, their attacks coordinated to keep him off balance. Each swing of their blades carried lethal intent, the shield's constant flaring was all that kept him alive.

Thomas managed to dodge the next few slashes, but they were clearly toying with him, predators playing with their prey before the kill. "The shield won't last forever," Merlin warned as another blast of energy rippled through the protective barrier. "We need to get clear of them."

"Working on it," Thomas gasped, ducking under another swing that came so close he felt the displaced air ruffle his hair. He spotted what looked like an opening and threw a punch at the nearest guard's head, putting everything he had behind it just like Vin had taught him.

His fist connected with the guard's helmet with a satisfying crack. Unfortunately, the satisfaction lasted only until pain shot through his hand, his knuckles almost certainly broken. It felt like he'd punched a brick wall.

Stupid.

The guards pressed their advantage, forcing him toward a corner. Their blades sparked off his shield again and again, each impact draining its power. Thomas could feel the energy field weakening, becoming less stable with each hit. The blue glow was starting to flicker, like a lightbulb about to die.

He tried to break past them, but they moved too well together, blocking him. Every time he found what looked like an opening, another guard would be there to cut him off. They had him completely boxed in, their scaled faces showing no emotion as they prepared to finish him off.

The shield flickered again, more violently this time. Thomas raised his fists, ignoring the stabbing pain from his broken knuckles. He wasn't going down without a fight. The old him might have given up, accepting his fate. But something had changed since he'd found Excalibur. For the first time in his life, he had a purpose worth living for.

"Hold!"

The shout echoed through the room, startling everyone. Thomas looked up to see a figure standing in the open doorway. Clad in a dark cloak wrapped around his body, his face shrouded by a large hood, he gripped a pair of blades that glowed with the same energy Thomas had seen on Arlen's daggers in his gloved hands.

The guards turned to face the new threat, recognizing something in his bearing that told them he was the greater danger. They spread out again, trying to trap him between them.

"Who dares interfere?" the lead guard demanded.

The newcomer didn't bother responding. He threw open his cloak as he exploded into motion. A flash of blinding light from an amulet around his neck forced the guards to turn their heads, leaving them flat-footed when he reached them.

He flowed between the Draconites like water through rocks, his blades leaving trails of light as they wove through the air, his attacks finding gaps in their defenses. Even as the guards began to recover, their training and experience meant nothing against the stranger's speed and skill.

The first guard fell, his throat opened by a precise strike that somehow bypassed both his shield and armor. The second lasted barely longer, managing to parry two attacks before a lightning-fast combination left him crumpled on the deck, dark blood pooling beneath him.

The remaining guard attacked, his dual blades whistling through the air in perfect harmony. The stranger caught both swords in his crossed daggers, using his opponent's momentum to turn the Draconite aside, then deftly circled behind him, blades completing their deadly work.

It was over in seconds. Thomas thought he knew what violence looked like, but this was something else entirely. All three Draconite guards lay dead or dying on the deck, the newcomer standing over them.

The man turned to Thomas, his hood still hiding all of his face but his chin, making his intentions completely unreadable. "You should come with me," he said. "More guards will arrive soon."

CHAPTER 34

"I can't leave those parts," Thomas said, nodding toward sack of parts, still lying where he'd dropped it. His broken hand throbbed in time with his racing heart, but they couldn't leave without those components. Everything they'd risked would be for nothing.

The man's eyes narrowed slightly as he studied Thomas. "Most would prioritize their life over machine parts," he said. "But then, your interests seem different from the common free trader."

"Using that cover term is no accident," Merlin pointed out.

Thomas tensed. "You were following me?"

"From the moment you approached the Magic Keg," the man confirmed. "There was something about the way you reacted to the destruction of the tavern. You looked like someone searching for something, but not quite sure what that something was." His mouth quirked in what might have been amusement. "I must admit, I didn't expect you to lead me on such an invigorating chase."

Thomas scooped up the sack with his good hand, trying

to ignore how every movement sent fresh waves of pain through his busted knuckles. Each breath felt like ice in his lungs as the adrenaline began to fade, leaving him shaky and lightheaded.

"Should we trust him?" he whispered, watching as their mysterious rescuer went to check the corridor beyond. "He still hasn't lowered his hood. That's kind of suspicious, isn't it?"

"Given our options are rather limited at the moment," Merlin replied from his pocket, "I suggest we take what providence has provided. Though I find his observations concerning."

"In what way?"

"He suspects something, but he's too cautious to say it outright. We're all playing a game now. The question is which side he's on."

"If we're on the same side, then we'd be playing against ourselves."

"Precisely. Careful communication is essential."

"The path is clear," the man said. "This way."

They followed him into the corridor, leaving the dead guards behind. The passage was narrow and utilitarian, clearly part of the station's maintenance network. Their footsteps echoed off metal bulkheads despite attempts at stealth.

"When I saw the Draconite guards pursuing you, I knew my instincts were correct," the warrior said without looking back. "They honed in on you like flies to offal. You've managed to draw their attention rather quickly."

"Thanks for the help back there," Thomas said carefully. "But who are you? Why follow me at all?"

The man paused at an intersection, turning to Thomas as he lowered his hood. He had a handsome, angular face with high cheekbones and a strong jawline, beneath dark hair tied back in a topknot. His storm-gray eyes reflected both amusement and mystery, while a faint scar above one brow hinted at prior scrapes.

"My name is Amren. And you are?"

"Thomas," he replied.

"Well met, Thomas. As for why follow you..." He gestured for them to turn down another corridor, this one sloping gradually downward. The lighting grew dimmer, creating pools of shadow between aging fixtures. "Let's just say I've spent a very long time waiting for someone."

"Someone like me?"

"Someone who might have access to certain...things." Amren's voice dropped lower, barely above a whisper. "Things the Draconite desperately want to destroy. I watched you interact with Groz at Sucker's Surplus. That sack is very important to you, and I think I know why. They're very specific components, aren't they? Meant for a very particular vessel?"

Thomas felt Merlin's GOLEM shift in his pocket. The tiny mechanical mouse was obviously agitated, though whether from recognition or concern, Thomas couldn't tell.

Thomas forced himself to keep his expression neutral, though his heart was pounding again. Someone who knew more than they should, asking questions he couldn't safely answer, was exactly what they didn't need. The maintenance corridor suddenly felt more like a trap than an escape route.

"I don't know what you're talking about," Thomas said, trying to keep his voice steady. "I'm just a free trader who ran into some bad luck."

Amren's soft laugh held no humor. "Bad luck doesn't draw the immediate attention of the guards." He stopped again, turning to face Thomas. "But a ship thought lost to time? That would certainly get their attention."

"Listen—" Thomas started.

Amren raised a hand, cutting him off. "We should keep moving," he said, his voice dropping even lower. "The guards I dispatched were merely the first to arrive. More will come, drawn by their loss of communications." He gestured down the corridor. "I know a safe place where we can talk. Unless you'd prefer to take your chances with the Draconite?"

Thomas glanced back the way they'd come, weighing his options. The sack of parts felt heavier by the second, and his broken hand throbbed with every heartbeat. They were lost in the station's maintenance maze, being led by someone who clearly knew more than he should to who knew where.

"This feels like walking into another trap," he whispered.

"Perhaps," Merlin replied from his pocket. "But I'm intrigued to see where this leads. There's something about this Amren. Something familiar I can't quite place."

Amren waited for him to make his choice with patient intensity. His stance was relaxed but ready, like a coiled spring waiting to release. Everything about him spoke of careful control and deadly capability.

"Time grows short," he said. "The Draconite will have activated security protocols by now. Soon, every corridor will be monitored, every exit watched. Either come with me, or go off on your own, but decide now."

Thomas exhaled sharply. "Fine. Lead on."

Amren turned and continued down the corridor. Before long, they reached another intersection, and Amren paused again, head cocked as if listening. "I'm wondering, Thomas. Who guided you here? Who told you what to seek?"

Thomas felt Merlin's GOLEM go completely still in his pocket, its usual subtle vibration ceasing entirely. The tiny machine's weight suddenly felt like a lead bar against his leg.

"I don't know what you're talking about," Thomas replied, but the words sounded hollow even to his own ears.

Amren's expression softened slightly. "The thing about lies…they need to be at least minimally believable to have a chance of success." He gestured down another corridor. "This way. We're nearly there."

They descended deeper into the station's maintenance levels, the air growing cooler and heavy with the scent of machinery. Their path appeared random, and they stopped multiple times to allow maintenance robots to pass. But Thomas suspected Amren knew exactly where they were going.

"You said you've been looking for someone like me," Thomas said finally, breaking the tense silence. "Why?"

"Because I made a promise," Amren replied, "to someone who meant a great deal to me. I swore I would wait, and watch, and be ready." He glanced back, his eyes reflecting the dim light like a cat's. "When I saw you at the Magic Keg, I felt something I haven't experienced before. Something that was described to me by my father so that I would recognize it should it ever come."

"And what feeling is that?"

"Hope."

"Hope for what?"

"Hope that perhaps the time has finally come. That the wheel has turned once more. Tell me, Thomas, do you believe in destiny?"

Thomas hesitated. "I…I don't know. I didn't a few days ago. Now, I'm not so sure."

"I know exactly what you mean," Amren replied, stopping at a seemingly blank section of bulkhead. "But what matters now is what you know."

He pressed his hand against the wall, and a hidden door slid silently open, revealing a small room beyond. Inside, ancient-looking computers hummed softly, their displays casting blue light across surfaces covered in maps and diagrams of the stars.

"Welcome to my sanctuary," Amren said. "Now, shall we discuss Excalibur?"

CHAPTER 35

Thomas felt the blood drain from his face. The hidden room closed in like a cage, the humming computers a mechanical heartbeat counting down the remaining moments of his freedom. He couldn't fight Amren. The man would kill him in a heartbeat. There was nowhere for him to run. Not now.

But something in Amren's expression brought those thoughts to a screeching halt. The man wasn't threatening them. If anything, he looked hopeful, almost reverent.

"I never mentioned Excalibur," Thomas said. Growing up on the streets had taught him to trust his gut about people. Right now, his instincts were all over the place, like a compass spinning near a magnet.

"You didn't have to." Amren moved to one of the computers, his fingers dancing across ancient controls. He pulled up a schematic on a fixed display that Thomas recognized instantly.

Excalibur.

"These components you carry...they're not unique in and of themselves, but together...there's only one ship I know that might still exist and would use all three. A quantum stabilizer core, phase-lock crystals, a first-generation variable distortion regulator. The exact parts needed to restore some of Excalibur's most critical systems."

"Admit nothing," Merlin said. "Not until we know more. Ask him where he got that schematic."

"Where did you get that?" Thomas asked, pointing to the screen.

"An inheritance from my father," he replied.

"And who is your father?"

"He was Sir Bedivere." Amren's voice carried equal measures of pride and old pain. "He was there when Excalibur was built and fought alongside Arthur in the great battles. Until Camlan." He bowed his head, trying to hide his grief. "Mordred nearly killed him. The wounds never truly healed. We lost the battle, and soon after that the war, but he survived and made his way back here to Caerlyon."

In Thomas' pocket, the GOLEM stirred. The Advisor's next words carried a weight of recognition and remembered grief. "Amren speaks true," it said, poking its head up out of Thomas' pocket and wrapping its front paws, more like mechanical fingers, over the pocket's rim. "Bedivere was one of Arthur's greatest allies." The GOLEM climbed up out of the pocket and jumped to the counter beside the old computer, its blue eyes bright with emotion. "He was a dear friend of mine, and one of the finest knights I ever knew."

Amren looked up in surprise. "Merlin? Is it truly you?"

"It is. Though I never thought to meet Bedivere's son." The GOLEM's mechanical features somehow managed to convey deep feeling.

Amren grinned, pointing at Thomas. "I knew it. I knew you were different. Merlin, I...I can't tell you what it means to me for you to be here."

Thomas leaned against the wall, cradling his broken hand. The adrenaline was wearing off, leaving him exhausted and hurting, but he couldn't help being drawn into the weight of what was unfolding before him.

"We almost weren't. Thank you for coming to our aid. Please, tell me more about Bedivere. Clearly, he had a son after the war. What else?"

"He found what peace he could here, working at the Magic Keg. He met my mother there. She was a serving woman, kind enough to see past his scars, both physical and otherwise." His smile held echoes of old stories. "He trained me in the old ways when he could, taught me everything he knew about being a knight. He made me swear to watch and wait, to be ready when Excalibur returned. He was always so confident that it would. That you would. So much so that I always believed it, too."

"And did he..." Merlin hesitated. "Did he find happiness, in the end?"

"Some days were better than others. The pain never fully left him, and he carried the weight of our loss at Camlan until his dying day. But yes, I believe he found moments of joy. Particularly in raising me to be a knight." Amren's expression grew distant. "He spoke of you often, of Arthur, of what was lost. And the day it might all be restored." A sheen of fresh grief filled his eyes. "My father died never knowing what happened to Arthur, to the ship. What happened, Merlin? Why were you gone for so long?"

"We were ambushed," Merlin said, his mechanical eyes dimming with the memory. "Mordred had positioned his forces perfectly, hiding them within an asteroid field that Lancelot claimed was unguarded. We were pinned between his fleet and a destructive galactic anomaly. We barely escaped through a wormhole, but the battle had damaged our primary systems. We lost control during transit."

"Lancelot," Amren spat. "My father always suspected he was involved. You crashed, I assume. Where?"

"Ten billion light years away, on a planet called Earth."

Merlin's voice carried centuries of regret. "The impact drove us deep underground." He paused, and Thomas could hear the pain even in his artificial voice. "I wanted to leave immediately, to return to the fight. But Arthur refused. He feared that Mordred might trace our route and follow us to Earth. The planet was inhabited. Thomas is a human, from Earth."

Amren glanced at him. "So like us, but I could tell you weren't Ursan. I just couldn't figure out how that would be possible."

"Yeah, it's pretty crazy," Thomas agreed.

"The humans were more primitive when we arrived. Arthur feared that if Mordred followed us, he might lay waste to an innocent world to reach us, and he wouldn't allow it."

"That sounds like him," Amren said softly. "Always thinking of others first."

"He ventured out against my advice, hoping to find some way to contact our forces. To let them know we survived." Merlin's small form seemed to shrink further. "He never returned. I waited, watching through damaged sensors as centuries passed, as humanity slowly grew and developed around me. But he never came back."

"Centuries?" Amren said. "It's been a long time, but not that long. A little over a hundred years."

"Not on Earth," Merlin countered. "For me, it was nearly fifteen hundred years."

The silence that followed felt heavy enough to bend light. Thomas found himself completely caught in the gravity of the moment.

"All this time," Amren said finally. "All these years watching, waiting...and Arthur has been lost for centuries."

"I'm sorry," Merlin replied. "I know it's not the answer your father, or you I imagine, hoped for."

"No." Amren straightened, something of the knight he'd

been trained to be showing through. "But at least it's an answer to all our questions. And at least you're here. The Draconite have grown stronger, more brutal with each passing year. They claim their rule is absolute, ordained by destiny itself." His eyes found Thomas. "But now Excalibur has returned. And with it, perhaps hope."

Thomas shifted uncomfortably under that intense gaze. "I'm nobody special," he said. "I'm just...helping."

"The ship accepted you," Merlin pointed out. "Found you worthy. That alone makes you somebody special."

Thomas nodded, though internally he wasn't so sure. He was nothing compared to Amren, who had spent his entire life preparing for this moment.

"Amren," Merlin said somberly. "We know so little about the situation here, other than that it's exceedingly bleak."

"I'm sorry to say, the more I tell you, it only gets worse," he replied. "Merlin…" he trailed off, hesitant to reveal what was obviously bad news.

"Go on," Merlin said. "Spit it out."

"The Draconite have expanded their mastery over the nanites. With them, they can replicate almost anything we can do with magic. I fear it's only a matter of time before they begin outlawing the arcane and destroying everything and everyone connected to it."

"It's already started," Thomas said. "They closed a school for magic on Fendragel and executed the teachers."

"How do you know that?"

"We overheard some traders talking about it in the Starforge Tavern."

"That's terrible news," Merlin agreed, "but that's not the news you're struggling to reveal. Is it, Amren?"

"No," he admitted, sighing heavily. "Morgana is still alive. She remains the Queen of the Draconite, even after a hundred years."

A heavy silence fell over the small room. Finally, Merlin replied. "I see. And Mordred?"

"He lives as well. But he's not the same as he was back then. He's more nanite now than Ursan or dragon. He's more terrifying and dangerous than ever."

The GOLEM's eyes dimmed. "Then we certainly have our work cut out for us."

"Lancelot is still out there, too," Thomas said. "We ran across him when we first arrived. He destroyed a pair of Draconite ships, and then fired on us."

"Lancelot?" Amren said. "I was led to believe he was long dead."

"It was either him or someone he trained," Merlin said. "Perhaps a child?"

"Gawain? He would never attack Excalibur."

"You're in communication with him, then?"

"No, but from what my father told me of him, I could never imagine him doing such a thing."

"Neither could I," Merlin admitted. "But these are strange, dangerous times. Anything is possible."

"I suppose. Though I can't imagine why he would want to harm you. No matter what Lancelot might have done that led to your disappearance and centuries stranded on Earth, the last time anyone saw him, he was the most wanted fugitive in Avalon."

"It seems he may have chosen a new side," Merlin said. "His own."

"Perhaps," Amren agreed. "What's important now is that you're back. Even without Arthur, Excalibur remains a symbol among the beings of Avalon, as do you, Merlin."

"I'm only a shell of the real thing. Tell me, does my organic version still live?"

Amren shook his head sadly. "I'm afraid not. He refused to use his magic to extend his life further, after what happened at Canlan. Some called him a coward for taking the easy way out."

"If they knew him at all, they would know that decision wouldn't come easily. He was already nearly two hundred years old. That should be enough for anyone."

"Not Morgana, unfortunately."

Before the conversation could continue, a sharp tone sounded from one of the displays in the room. Thomas turned to it, pointing when he saw a squad of Draconite soldiers entering a corridor he assumed was nearby. "That looks like trouble," he said.

"It may be," Amren said. "The guards have ignored this part of Caerlyon's bowels for years. It only proves how badly they want to find you."

"Are we safe here?"

"Possibly, but if they do locate this place, there's only one way out. I used this location to watch and wait for you in secret, away from the prying eyes of the Draconite. Now that you're here, there's no reason to stay."

"Do you have a ship?" Merlin asked. "Ours only seats one."

Amren grinned. "Mine may be slightly bigger. It seats two. And hopefully, the Draconite have yet to implicate me in the deaths of their guards. It's treason, you know." He grinned as he leaned over his control board, entering commands. When he finished, he straightened and turned to Thomas. "We should go. We have five minutes to clear this area before the entire station falls into chaos."

Merlin hopped from the counter to Thomas' shoulder.

"We're right behind you," Thomas said.

CHAPTER 36

Thomas followed Amren through Caerlyon's maintenance corridors, the sack of parts bouncing against his back with each step. His broken hand, where he held it against his midsection, throbbed in time with his racing heart, sending fresh waves of pain through his arm every time he had to use it to steady himself against a wall. The ancient passages felt like a maze—all sharp turns and sudden drops—designed by a drunk architect. It made no logical sense.

"How much further?" he asked, his voice barely above a whisper.

"Not far," Amren replied. "Though getting there may prove interesting."

As if summoned by his words, heavy footsteps echoed from ahead. Thomas recognized the distinctive sound of Draconite armor before he saw them—that same measured cadence he'd heard in the tavern before they'd executed Arlen.

"Get back," Amren hissed, but it was too late.

Four Draconite guards rounded the corner ahead, showing no signs of hesitation as their swords whispered from scabbards with a sound that sent shivers down

Thomas' spine. They picked up their pace, charging down the passageway toward them, blades ready to strike.

"Stay behind me," Amren commanded, his weapons appearing in his hands as if conjured from thin air.

Thomas pressed himself harder against the bulkhead as Amren exploded into motion, countering the Draconite force with his own. His attack was pure poetry—each movement flowing into the next with deadly grace. Where Thomas had learned to fight in New York alleys, throwing wild punches fueled by fear and adrenaline, Amren had clearly spent his entire life mastering the art of combat under the tutelage of his father.

The first guard barely had time to raise his blade before Amren was past his defense, one dagger opening his throat while the other found a gap between armor plates. Dark blood sprayed across the corridor in an arterial arc, droplets shimmering in the overhead light. The second guard managed to parry once before a lightning-fast combination left him crumpled against the wall, his scaled features frozen in an expression of permanent surprise.

"Show off," Merlin muttered from Thomas' pocket, the tiny GOLEM's voice carrying a mix of approval and criticism.

"Do you know any other knights who could do better?" Thomas whispered back, unable to tear his eyes away from the fight unfolding before him. Part of him wanted to help, to prove he wasn't completely useless. But his throbbing hand reminded him what happened when street fighting met full body armor.

"A few," Merlin replied. "But they're almost all dead now. Some by choice, some by circumstance. All because they believed in something greater than themselves."

The remaining guards attacked together, their movements synchronized by years of training. Their blades wove complex patterns through the air, too quickly for Thomas to follow. But Amren knew what was coming ahead of time, anticipating the Draconite's maneuvers, his daggers trailing blue fire as they sought vulnerable points.

Each strike found its mark, multiple stabs overwhelming energy shields and bypassing armor in a blur. Thomas watched in horrified fascination as the man dismantled his opponents with terrifying efficiency. There was no wasted movement, no dramatic flourishes—just the pure craft of dealing death, honed to perfection.

Seconds later, it was over. Four more dead Draconite guards lay cooling on the deck while Amren was barely winded. He wiped his daggers clean with practiced efficiency, the gesture somehow more chilling than the violence preceding it.

"We should move," he said, already heading down the corridor. "More will come."

Thomas hurried to keep up, trying not to look too closely at the bodies they passed. They hadn't gone far when fresh shouts echoed from ahead, accompanied by an orange glow that cast strange shadows along the curved walls. The light pulsed with an organic quality that made Thomas' skin crawl, as if reality itself were being warped by whatever approached.

"Finally," Amren said, a note of anticipation in his voice that sent fresh chills down Thomas' spine. "I was wondering when they'd send a magic user."

"That's a good thing?" Thomas asked incredulously, unconsciously touching the shield bracer on his wrist.

"It means they're taking us seriously." Amren's mouth curved in a predatory smile that reminded Thomas he wasn't just dealing with the son of one of Arthur's knights. He was dealing with someone who had spent their entire life preparing for exactly this kind of fight.

The new group of guards rounded the corner ahead, led by a figure in elaborate robes whose hands crackled with barely contained energy. Thomas had just enough time to register the wizard's scaled features—more serpentine than the guards, suggesting more dragon DNA than Ursan—before a ball of pure fire roared down the corridor toward them.

His shield flared automatically, the blue energy field absorbing most of the heat. Even so, the temperature spike left him gasping, the superheated air searing his lungs. The smell of burning metal filled the corridor, the bulkheads blistering. Beside him, Amren's own defenses glowed as the flames washed over him, but he stood his ground, his enchanted daggers held at ready angles.

"Stay back," he commanded, his voice carrying an edge Thomas hadn't heard before. "This requires a more direct approach."

The wizard launched another attack, not fire this time, but pure magical force that left sparking trails in the air. Amren dodged with impossible grace, each movement carrying him closer to his target while the guards spread out to protect their spellcaster.

Amren rolled beneath another blast of energy that left scoring marks in the deck plating. He came up inside the guards' formation, his daggers already seeking vulnerable points. Two fell before they could react, their armor providing no protection against his enchanted blades. Dark blood painted the walls, a grim sample of his lethal skill.

The wizard snarled in a language Thomas couldn't understand. Power gathered around the spellcaster's hands, reality warping as he prepared to unleash something that would probably reduce them all to component atoms.

Amren was already there, moving faster than Thomas' eyes could track. One dagger swept up to intercept the gathering energy, the blade's own enchantments somehow containing the spell, while the other found the gap between the wizard's ribs. The spellcaster's eyes widened in surprise, his last spell dying uncast as he slumped to the deck.

"Rather anticlimactic," Merlin observed, though Thomas thought he detected a note of respect in the Advisor's tone. "It used to be difficult to dispatch any wizard who possessed a mote of skill."

"I inherited these blades from my father," Amren replied, wiping them clean on the wizard's robes. "He was gifted them by Nimue, to pass on to me. Designed for the sole purpose for which they're now being used."

Fresh shouts echoed from behind them. Thomas didn't need to look to know more Draconite guards were closing in. "We've got company," he said, unconsciously shifting the sack of parts to protect it with his body. After everything they'd been through to get these components, he wasn't about to lose them now.

"We do," Amren replied, those deadly daggers already returning to his hands. "Though they may find their timing...unfortunate."

Something in his tone made Thomas nervous. "What do you mean?"

"Remember when I said we had five minutes?" A predatory grin split Amren's face. "Time's up."

CHAPTER 37

The explosion, when it came, wasn't the overwhelming blast Thomas had expected. Instead, it started as a deep vibration that he felt through his boots, a subsonic rumble that built steadily until his teeth rattled. Then the corridor behind them lit up like a new sun had been born in the station's guts.

The shockwave hit a heartbeat later, a wall of superheated air that would have knocked Thomas off his feet if Amren hadn't grabbed his arm. Even through his shield, the heat was incredible. Behind them, screams of surprise and pain suggested the pursuing Draconites hadn't fared nearly as well.

"What the hell did you do?" Thomas gasped as Amren pulled him forward, away from the destruction.

"Created a diversion," the knight replied. "Though I admit, the yield was slightly higher than calculated. These old maintenance tunnels do tend to channel energy in unexpected ways."

"You're insane," Thomas said, but found himself grinning despite the situation. Maybe it was the adrenaline, or maybe he was finally starting to appreciate the absolute lunacy of his circumstances. Two days ago, he'd been delivering packages in Manchester. Now he was running through an alien space station while his new acquaintance blew holes in it.

"Hardly," Amren countered. "The explosion will force an evacuation of this section, creating confusion we can use to reach the hangar."

They rounded another corner, emerging into a wider corridor where emergency lighting strobed in time with blaring alarms. The deck plates vibrated beneath their feet as damage control systems engaged, trying to contain whatever havoc Amren's explosives had wreaked.

"The hangar's nearby," Amren said, leading them toward an increasingly crowded passageway. "We'll blend in with others trying to reach their ships. The evacuation protocols—"

He cut off as another group of Draconites rounded the corner ahead. But these weren't guards. They wore civilian clothes, and their scaled faces showed fear rather than aggression. They barely glanced at Thomas and Amren as they joined the flow of beings leaving the area, clearly more concerned with escaping whatever had caused all the fuss.

"See?" Amren gestured for Thomas to join the flow of beings now filling the corridor. "Just act like you belong."

"Right," Thomas muttered. "Belong. While carrying contraband parts and a talking robot mouse." But he fell into step with the crowd, trying to match their urgent but not quite panicked pace. "Did you actually damage the station? I mean, seriously damage it?"

"The charges were shaped to create maximum chaos with minimal structural harm," Amren replied as they joined the other evacuees. "The station will recover, though the Draconites may need to redecorate that section. By the time they realize the explosion was merely a diversion, we'll hopefully be long gone."

They continued with the crowds to the hangar bay, where organized chaos reigned. Beings of all descriptions hurried toward their vessels while station security tried to maintain some semblance of order. Warning klaxons continued to sound, their urgent tone adding to the general atmosphere of controlled panic.

"This way," Amren said, guiding them through the crowd and past the array of parked starships. Their crews were just beginning to reach them, the first of the ships rising from the tarmac and shooting through the gate and out into space.

Amren led them to what Thomas first took for a derelict ready for the scrapyard. Its canopy was scratched, its hull scarred and pitted, and its weapons mounts were barren, making it appear as dangerous as a geriatric cat with no teeth.

"How are we going to escape in this?" Thomas asked. "It doesn't even have any guns."

"Civilian ships aren't permitted to mount weapons," Amren explained. "I know she's not much to look at, but at least she has two seats." Amren pressed his hand against the hull, and a hatch in the side opened. "After you."

Thomas had just started toward the ship when new alarms began to sound. These carried a different tone—sharper, more urgent. The crowd's relatively ordered evacuation suddenly became something else entirely as beings broke into dead runs toward their vessels.

"What's happening?" Thomas asked.

"We need to leave," Amren replied. "Now."

They boarded the spacecraft, its small cargo hold and up front flight deck a patchwork of salvaged systems, each switch and dial looking like it had been harvested from a dozen different vessels. Some pieces bore scorch marks.

Others showed signs of hasty repair. It wasn't pretty, but there was something honest about it as if the ship had earned every scar and replacement part.

Thomas squeezed into the co-pilot's seat, keeping the sack of parts clutched awkwardly in his lap to prevent them from being tossed about if they needed to make any sudden maneuvers.

"Control, this is Gray Oath," Amren said into his comm, his voice carrying the precise tone of someone who'd made this request countless times before. "Requesting launch clearance."

Through the scratched canopy, Thomas watched other vessels lifting off in orderly sequence. A sleek merchant ship rose on columns of blue fire, followed by what looked like a private yacht. The traffic flow was smooth and professional. Routine.

"Negative, Gray Oath," a clipped voice replied. "Maintain position."

Thomas shifted uncomfortably as another ship received immediate clearance. "That can't be good."

"Indeed," Amren agreed. They watched seven more ships lift off before he keyed the comms again. "Control, requesting priority clearance. We have a situation on board."

"Maintain position, Gray Oath."

Amren's expression tightened. More ships lifted off, each departure like a personal rebuke.

"They're stalling," Thomas said softly.

"Yes. It may be they've decided they know who was behind your escape and the blast." Amren tried one final time. "Control, my passengers have a medical emergency requiring immediate—"

"Gray Oath, maintain position," the controller snapped. "Security teams are en route to your location."

At that, guards began pouring through the hangar

doors, carrying heavy weapons that sent a shiver down Thomas' spine. His broken hand throbbed in time with his racing heart as he watched them begin setting up firing positions.

"I don't suppose your shields can handle whatever those are?" he asked.

"I'm not waiting around to find out," Amren replied. His hands slid across his controls, ancient systems humming to life. The engine's whine rose to a pitch that suggested machinery being pushed well past its design limits. "Fasten your harness." Thomas made short work of it as Amren pushed the throttle forward.

The ship leaped from the deck, throwing Thomas back against his seat. His stomach lurched as they shot toward the thin force field between them and the hard vacuum of space.

The guards opened up with their heavy weapons, filling the air with crackling bolts of energy. Each impact was like someone hitting the hull with a sledgehammer, the shields flaring brightly around them.

"Gray Oath, you are in violation of station protocols," the controller's voice crackled through the comms, real alarm entering their tone. "Return to your assigned landing zone immediately or—"

Amren cut the channel as they reached the force field. For a terrifying moment, Thomas thought they weren't going to make it through. Then suddenly they were in space. Caerlyon station fell away behind them, its massive form already growing smaller as they accelerated into the void.

Warning indicators flashed as the ship's systems registered multiple craft accelerating from the station in pursuit. The comm crackled with demands for their immediate surrender, each one more urgent than the last.

"Now what?" Thomas asked, watching the tactical display as hostile contacts multiplied.

"Now," Amren replied, an increasingly familiar predatory grin spreading across his face, "things get interesting."

CHAPTER 38

Thomas watched the tactical display as Draconite vessels poured in pursuit from Caerlyon Station's docking bays. The larger patrol craft resembled abstract metal sculptures of swooping dragons, their wings swept aggressively back. The smaller fighters looked like individual claws, all sharp angles and dark metal, moving with predatory grace as they spread out into attack formation.

Amren pushed the ship's straining engines harder. The ancient machinery protested with worrying vibrations Thomas could feel through his seat, leaving him to wonder if abandoning the station had been the best idea. Maybe they could have found somewhere else to hide and wait for the dust to settle.

"I count six fighters and two patrol ships," Amren said. The tactical display showed their pursuers spreading out to box them in, their relative velocity indicators steadily climbing.

"Please tell me this ship is faster than it looks," Thomas replied.

"She may not be pretty," Amren replied, his hands on worn controls that looked like they'd seen much better days, "but she has a few surprises left." He threw them into a sideways roll as energy beams from the lead fighters sliced through the space they'd occupied moments before. The maneuver drove Thomas back into his seat, his stomach lurching as whatever kind of inertial dampeners were on the ship either struggled to compensate or were barely functioning.

The nearest beam passed so close he could feel a trace of its heat through the hull, the sensation sending shivers down his spine. Warning indicators flashed across the ship's console.

"Though I admit," Amren continued, his voice tight with concentration as he wove them through another barrage, "outrunning them may not be our best option."

A massive blast from one of the patrol ships lit up space around them, the energy discharge temporarily overloading their viewscreen's ability to compensate. Thomas blinked away the halos, his heart hammering as he realized how close that one had come to striking them.

"What other option do we have?" he asked, watching the tactical display as more ships launched from Caerlyon. "This ship doesn't even have weapons."

Amren's predatory grin returned, though his eyes never left his controls. "Are you sure about that?"

His fingers slid across a series of controls that looked particularly jerry-rigged, the connections held together with tape and crossed-fingers. Panels slid open along the ship's hull with a grinding sound that suggested rarely-used mechanisms, revealing weapon ports that had been carefully concealed beneath layers of cosmetic damage. The tactical display suddenly came alive with targeting data as systems Thomas hadn't even known existed powered up.

"Sneaky," he muttered admiringly.

"My father always said deception was a powerful weapon." Amren's grin widened as he threw them into a complex series of maneuvers, bleeding off velocity while simultaneously rotating to bring their weapons to bear. The move left Thomas' stomach somewhere behind them, but positioned them perfectly to engage their pursuers. "Now, let's give our friends something to think about."

Energy gathered in the weapon ports, building to a crescendo that made Thomas' teeth vibrate and sent static dancing across the instruments. The lead Draconite fighter had just begun to react to their unexpected course change when Amren opened fire. Brilliant green bolts of energy lanced out from their concealed weapons, catching the enemy vessel squarely in the bow.

The fighter's shields flared brilliantly as they tried to absorb the assault, but Amren's weapons proved stronger than they appeared. The protective barrier shattered like glass, letting the remaining energy tear into the hull beneath. Secondary explosions rippled along its length before it vanished in a final flash.

The remaining fighters broke formation, scattering in different directions as they realized their prey had teeth. But Amren was already moving, sending them through a series of rolls and slides that ignored physics entirely. Energy beams from multiple attackers crisscrossed the space around them, filling the void with deadly light that somehow always passed just behind or ahead of their position.

"You're good at this. Like, really good," Thomas said as they spiraled through another barrage that should have reduced them to atoms. Each near miss sent fresh jolts of adrenaline through his system, his body unable to decide if this was terrifying or exhilarating.

"I should be good," Amren replied, his attention never wavering from his controls. His hands moved across the battered console with practiced precision, each adjustment perfectly timed. "I've been practicing for this moment my entire life." He threw them into another sideways slide while simultaneously rotating to track a pair of fighters trying to flank them. The move should have been impossible, leaving Thomas wondering if some of the ship's systems were enhanced with more than just technology. "My father set up a simulator in the back of the Magic Keg, hidden behind crates of ale. I spent every free moment in that machine, running combat scenarios and studying historical battles."

"While other kids were playing?" Thomas asked. A massive blast from one of the patrol ships passed so close he tensed, certain it would envelop them in its fury and make a quick end of his existence. Warning indicators screamed as their shields struggled to dissipate the energy.

Amren remained unbothered, continuing to speak as he maneuvered. "While other children were learning trades or following their parents' paths, yes. But I was following after my father as well." Even as he talked, his eyes constantly scanned their tactical display, anticipating the enemy's next move. Another fighter exploded as his shots found their mark, the debris scattering across space like a handful of thrown confetti. "I swore to him on his deathbed that when the moment came, I would be ready. And here I am."

The four remaining fighters adapted their tactics, spreading out to attack from different vectors while the patrol ships held back. Through the forward viewport, Thomas watched energy building in the larger vessels' weapon ports, their heavy guns charging for killing shots if Amren made even the smallest mistake.

"Not that I'm complaining," Thomas said as they wove through another coordinated attack, his good hand gripping his armrest so tight his knuckles had gone white, "but why are you so much better than they are?"

"Because for all the Draconite's speak of being superior, they aren't," Amren replied, triggering another burst that stripped the shields from an approaching fighter. The vessel broke off its attack run, trailing plasma like blood in water from damaged systems. "These pilots learned to fly in academies, following procedures and protocols. They've never experienced a real battle, or likely even spoken to anyone who has. I learned through thousands of hours of practice, and by studying the techniques of the greatest pilots in history." The damaged fighter exploded as Amren caught it trying to retreat, the blast briefly illuminating their cockpit. "Including Lancelot."

"I started watching his old training videos," Thomas said. "I'm trying to learn. I have about three hours of experience."

"There's no better instructor than Lancelot," Amren answered. Fresh warning indicators flashed as the patrol ships began moving to cut off their escape routes. Amren executed another series of maneuvers, somehow keeping them away from the patrol ships' heavy weapons while simultaneously engaging the fighters. Despite the ship's compensators, the g-forces threatened to squeeze the breath from Thomas' lungs. "And if Excalibur found you worthy, then I'm sure you'll do well. You just need time and experience."

Two more fighters vanished in expanding balls of plasma, their pilots unable to match Amren's skill and experience. But the patrol ships were another matter entirely. Their heavy shields shrugged off attacks that had destroyed the fighters, while their weapons forced Amren to focus more on evasion than offense.

The ship groaned around them as Amren pushed it harder, the hull creaking like it might shake itself apart at any moment. Sweat beaded his forehead as he fought the controls, each maneuver becoming more desperate as the patrol ships pressed their advantage.

"I'm afraid fighting is no longer a viable option," Amren

said, his voice tight with concentration. "Their shields are too strong, and they're cutting off our escape routes." He threw them into another wild spin as coordinated fire from both patrol ships filled space around them with deadly energy. The tactical display showed their own shields weakening with each near miss, the protective field growing unstable. "I don't suppose you'd care to share Excalibur's coordinates?"

"Merlin?" Thomas asked. The Advisor had remained silent during the battle, though it didn't seem Amren needed quiet to concentrate.

"Yes, yes," Merlin replied, as if the question had ripped him out of a different stream of thought. "Of course." The golem emerged from Thomas' pocket and rattled off a series of numbers that meant nothing to Thomas.

Another blast from the patrol ships rocked their vessel, this one close enough to partially penetrate their failing shields. Warning klaxons blared as systems began to overload, the aged machinery protesting the abuse.

Amren entered the coordinates into his nav computer with one hand while continuing to evade with the other, his movements growing more desperate as their options diminished. "Hold onto something," he said, his expression grim. "I'm going to do a short-range burst."

The ship's engines changed pitch as Amren redirected power from weapons to thrust, and Thomas reached for an overhead strut supporting some of Amren's auxiliary equipment. Thruster sound rose from a whine to a scream that suggested components on the verge of failure. Sudden acceleration on a new vector pinned Thomas to his seat as they shot away from the patrol ships, quickly gaining unbelievable speed. Space itself bent around them as they pushed harder, faster, the ancient engines protesting with sounds Thomas had never wanted to hear from machinery keeping them alive in space.

"Will they be able to follow?" Thomas asked, watching the tactical display as the patrol ships fell behind.

"Not immediately," Amren replied. "But they'll track our burst signature. We won't have much time once we reach Excalibur."

The ship grew quickly in their view as they decelerated from the burst. Its silver hull gleamed in starlight, surface patterns shifting in ways that still made Thomas' eyes hurt if he looked too long. The sight filled him with equal parts relief and anxiety—they were almost safe, but the patrol ships would be right behind them.

"Um, Merlin, how are we supposed to dock?" Thomas asked, identifying their next challenge. "This ship's a bit large for the landing bay."

"Align beneath the hull," Merlin instructed. "I'll open a section for us." Even as he said it, a portion of Excalibur's hull spread aside, revealing the cargo bay.

"The patrol ships have already picked up our signature," Amren said, checking his displays. Red warning indicators flashed across the tactical screen, showing two contacts rapidly closing the distance. "They'll be here in minutes." He reached for a control panel between their seats. "Thomas, are you ready?"

"For what?" Thomas asked, still uncertain how they would get from one ship to another. His stomach clenched suddenly as the answer came to him, at the same time Amren pulled the lever between the seats.

The canopy explosively detached, spinning out into space. The sudden depressurization caught Thomas by surprise. His ears popped painfully as the last vestiges of atmosphere evacuated the cockpit. His throat constricted, leaving him unable to draw a breath.

Amren was already moving, releasing Thomas' harness and grabbing his arm. He pushed off from his seat with practiced grace, dragged Thomas with him, clutching the sack of components to his chest with his good hand as Amren pushed off his seat, propelling them upward toward the opening in Excalibur's belly..

The few seconds in open space felt like a panicked eternity. The void pulled at Thomas with hungry fingers while stars shifted crazily around him, his heart pounding so hard he thought it might burst. The sack of components threatened to slip from his grasp, their weight somehow both present and absent in the zero gravity.

Through it all, Excalibur's open bay beckoned like a promise of salvation. But the distance seemed impossibly vast, even though logically he knew it wasn't. Behind them, he caught glimpses of their abandoned ship, already beginning to drift away into the void. They were almost to the bay when the first patrol ship burst into normal space behind them, its weapon ports already beginning to glow with gathering energy.

Then they were through, tumbling into Excalibur's hangar bay as the hull sealed seamlessly behind them. They landed in an undignified heap as artificial gravity reasserted itself. Thomas lay there for a moment, just breathing, his injured hand screaming in protest at the rough treatment. They'd made it. Somehow, against all odds, they'd actually made it.

"Welcome aboard," Merlin said, his GOLEM crawling out of Thomas' pocket and landing on the deck.

"Thank you," Amren replied, already climbing to his feet. He offered Thomas a hand up, his eyes constantly scanning their surroundings with professional assessment. "Though I suggest we quickly make our way to the flight deck. Those patrol ships will be here soon, and I doubt they'll be happy about losing their fighters."

"Yes, we need to get moving," the Advisor agreed, the tiny GOLEM falling to the deck as Merlin's essence left it for Excalibur.

Still clutching the precious components, Thomas accepted Amren's hand up. "Right. Follow me."

The deck plates thrummed beneath their feet as they ran, a subtle reminder that Draconite patrol ships were closing in on them, weapons charged and ready.

Their brief victory might prove very short-lived indeed.

CHAPTER 39

Thomas led the way through Excalibur's corridors, the deck plates thrumming beneath his feet. Each vibration sent fresh waves of anxiety rushing through him.

"The flight deck is just ahead," he said, glancing back to make sure Amren was keeping up. Of course, he was.

An impact rocked the ship, nearly sending Thomas into a bulkhead. Only Amren's quick reflexes kept him upright, the man's strong grip steadying him before he could fall.

"We need to hurry," Amren said, his voice tight with urgency. "Those patrol ships pack enough firepower to crack this hull like an egg if they land too many direct hits."

They burst onto the flight deck to find Merlin's humanoid GOLEM already waiting by the command pod. The Advisor's mechanical features somehow managed to convey both urgency and welcome as they entered. The holographic display at the center of the ring of pods showed their situation—two Draconite patrol ships moving to destroy them—in stark detail. Their hulls were already beginning to glow with gathered energy.

"Quickly," Merlin said. "The patrol ships are—"

A massive impact made even Amren stagger. Warning

tones blared across the flight deck as systems struggled to compensate.

"That's not good," Merlin warned. "Without the repairs, we won't last long against sustained fire."

While Thomas hurried toward the pods, Amren had forgotten himself and froze just inside the entrance, his eyes wide as he took in the flight deck. The ring of pods. The holographic display at the center. The command throne. "It's exactly as my father described," Amren breathed. "The heart of legend itself. The place where—"

"Amren," Thomas began, recognizing the same sense of awe he'd felt when he first saw it, but they didn't have time for wonder right now. "We need to—"

Another hit rocked the ship, this one accompanied by the screech of straining metal that set Thomas' teeth on edge. The holographic display flickered ominously before stabilizing, showing their attackers moving into optimal firing positions and preparing another salvo.

"We need to hurry," Merlin reported, his mechanical voice carrying an edge Thomas hadn't heard before. "A few more hits like that will collapse the shields entirely."

Thomas turned to Amren. "You should take command. You're an actual warrior, trained for this. I'm just an Earthling in over his head. You've spent your whole life preparing for this moment."

"No." Merlin's voice cut through the chaos like a blade. "It has to be you."

"But he's been training his whole life for this!" Thomas protested, gesturing at Amren with his busted hand. "You saw what he did out there. He took out six fighters and escaped the patrol ships in a ship being held together with paperclips and hope. He's obviously more qualified than I'll ever be!"

The ship shuddered again as another blast struck home. The deck plates beneath their feet vibrated at a frequency that suggested something vital was about to give way.

"It doesn't work that way," Merlin replied, his GOLEM eyes flaring bright blue with intensity. "Even if Amren proves worthy—which isn't guaranteed—he would need time to acclimate. Time we very clearly don't have."

Another impact rocked them, this one powerful enough to send sparks cascading from overhead panels like a metallic waterfall. The holographic display winked out completely for several seconds before flickering back to life.

"We need to act now," Merlin said.

"He's right," Amren agreed. "I understand how this works better than you might think. The ship chose you, Thomas. That means something." He gave Thomas a gentle shove toward the command pod as another blast rocked the ship. "Now get in there and show them what you can do before they blow us all into atoms."

Thomas hesitated for just a moment longer, torn between his own self-doubt and the urgent need to act. His eyes met Amren's, finding nothing but calm confidence there despite their dire situation. Finally, he nodded and climbed into the pod, settling into the dark gel.

The canopy sealed with a soft hiss as the neural interface engaged. Sensor data flooded his consciousness, far more organized than during his first attempts but still overwhelming in its scope and intensity. They painted a grim picture, their shields flickering and unstable while the patrol ships hammered them uncontested, their defenses at full-strength.

Through the external feeds, he could see their weapons charging for what they clearly intended to be a final volley. The energy building translated through the sensors as a rising crescendo that set every nerve ending tingling with alarm.

"You can do this," Amren's voice came through the

canopy, steady and assured. "Remember what you learned from Lancelot's lessons. Trust your instincts. You're here for a reason."

Thomas reached for the flight controls with his mind. Feeling Excalibur respond instantly to his thoughts, the main drive thrummed through his consciousness as power built in the engines. His broken hand throbbed in sympathetic rhythm, a constant reminder of how quickly things could go wrong.

"Here they come," Merlin warned as both patrol ships opened fire simultaneously, their coordinated attack filling space with deadly energy.

Thomas threw them into a sideways roll, trying to minimize their target profile while bringing their weapons to bear. The maneuver was clumsy compared to Amren's grace—more like a drunk staggering than a dancer's pirouette—but it carried them clear of the majority of the incoming fire. Only a glancing blow found its mark against their failing shields.

The impacts translated through the neural interface like body blows, each one threatening to break his concentration.

"Their attack run left them vulnerable on their ventral side," Amren pointed out. "If you can bring our guns to bear..."

Thomas saw the opening and took it, sending a stream of blue energy toward the nearest patrol ship. His aim was off, the shot going wide, frustration building as he watched a potential killing blow miss.

"You're thinking too much," Amren advised, his calm voice a stark contrast to Thomas' rising panic. "Let the targeting systems do their work. Focus on positioning. Flow with the ship's movements instead of trying to force them. You can do this."

The patrol ships adjusted their tactics, spreading out to

catch Excalibur in a crossfire. Their next coordinated barrage filled space around them with deadly energy, the beams forming a lethal web designed to snare and destroy them.

This time Thomas was ready. He knew Amren was right. When he rode through the streets of Manchester to deliver something, he didn't think about every car, curb, and pedestrian. He just let his instincts and subconscious calculations guide him. He could do the same here.

He stopped trying to make the ship move the way he thought it should, instead letting his intentions flow through the neural interface like water finding its natural path. Excalibur responded instantly, sliding between the attacks with growing confidence. The movements still weren't pretty, but they were effective.

"Better," Amren said. "Now press the advantage while you have it."

Thomas targeted the nearest patrol ship again, this time letting the weapons systems guide his aim instead of fighting them. Blue energy lanced out from Excalibur's bow, catching the enemy vessel as it tried to adjust course. Their shields buckled under the assault, crystalline patterns of failure spreading across their surface like cracks in ice.

Then they broke through, tearing into the hull beneath. Secondary explosions rippled along its length, power systems cascading into failure. The patrol ship tried to withdraw, but Thomas stayed with them, pouring more fire into the wounded vessel until it vanished in a final, satisfying flash.

The remaining patrol ship broke off its attack, the ferocity of his assault giving the enemy pause. But Thomas wasn't about to let them escape. He pushed the engines harder, staying with them as they tried to withdraw. His next salvo caught them from behind.

The results were spectacular. The patrol ship's hull split

along structural seams as Thomas' fire found vital systems. The vessel's reactor went critical, the explosion briefly overwhelming the viewscreen's ability to compensate.

"Yeeeessss!" Thomas shouted, beyond excited to have earned some success. "I did it!"

"Nicely done," Amren said, real admiration in his voice. "A bit rough around the edges, but effective. Though I suggest we leave quickly. More ships will no doubt be on their way."

Giving more attention to the sensor stream, Thomas confirmed the statement. More ships were already on their way from Caerlyon, hoping to prevent their escape. He reached for the burst drive controls, feeling power building in the engines as Excalibur prepared for faster-than-light travel.

"Time to go," he said, trying to project more confidence than he felt.

"I can take it from here," Merlin suggested.

"It's all yours."

Stars blurred around them as they accelerated to burst speed, leaving Caerlyon and its pursuers far behind. Thomas' entire body immediately began trembling with releasing tension, the aftermath of combat leaving him feeling simultaneously exhausted and exhilarated. With a thought, he opened the canopy, stepping out of the pod and onto the deck.

"Well done, Thomas," Amren repeated, clasping him on the shoulder, a huge grin on his face.

"That wasn't exactly elegant," he replied. "Especially compared to you."

"Elegance is overrated," Amren replied with a small laugh. "Victory is victory, no matter how you achieve it. Though I noticed you've already started incorporating some of Lancelot's techniques. With practice, you'll improve quickly."

"Thank you both," Merlin said. "Amren, we wouldn't have escaped without your help. And with the parts we acquired, once we can effect repairs, Excalibur will be back to full operational capacity."

"I'm honored to serve," Amren said formally, though something dark passed behind his eyes. "Though I admit, this isn't quite how I imagined finally boarding the legendary vessel. I always thought..." He trailed off, unable or unwilling to finish the thought.

"You thought Arthur would be here," Thomas finished for him, understanding flooding through him as he remembered everything Amren had said about his father's faith.

"Yes." Amren's voice carried centuries of accumulated hope and disappointment. "My father always believed. He died believing." He straightened, visibly shaking off the moment of melancholy. "But this is what the fates have decreed. A new beginning, rather than trying to reclaim the past. I'm proud to stand with you, Thomas of Earth."

"Well, I'm certainly glad you're here," Thomas replied.

"Thomas, you should visit the regeneration pod to fix that hand," Merlin said. "Amren, when we arrive somewhere safe you can enter a pod and try to interface with the ship. Until then, let me show you to one of the open quarters."

"Thank you, Merlin," Amren replied. "Thomas, I'll see you again soon."

Both he and the GOLEM left the flight deck.

Alone with his thoughts, Thomas didn't head for the med bay right away. Instead, he stared at the circle of stations and the hologram floating in the center of them, a map of stars with their burst trajectory a blue line across the center.

As much as he wanted to believe the tapestry of fate had woven him tightly into it, he couldn't ignore the sense that his thread was close to its end.

CHAPTER 40

The regeneration pod's canopy lifted with a soft hiss, cool air brushing Thomas' skin as the healing gel receded. He lay there for a moment, flexing his newly-repaired hand and marveling at how the nanites had not only knitted the cartilage and broken bones back together, but did so without any residual stiffness or soreness. They had healed his other muscles as well, saving him from days of tenderness after the chase on Caerlyon Station.

Rising from the pod, he found fresh clothes—another set of medieval and sci-fi chic in a deep crimson that Merlin had apparently decided would be his signature color—waiting for him. Though he still wasn't entirely comfortable with the style, the doublet and fitted pants felt impossibly soft against his skin. The clothing looked like something from a Renaissance fair, but moved like high-tech athletic wear.

"Merlin?" he called out, but received no response. The medical bay remained silent. The emptiness felt oppressive after everything that had happened on Caerlyon.

Thomas made his way through the ship's corridors, his

footsteps echoing off the deck. The flowing patterns etched into the walls were more active than usual, energy pulsing through them like blood through veins. He checked the flight deck first, finding it empty, though a look at the holographic display showed him that they were no longer bursting through space, but were instead sitting motionless in the middle of nowhere. The ring of pods stood silent sentinel, their dark gel rippling occasionally with streaks of blue energy.

The library was similarly deserted, though he paused briefly to consider the collection of training materials he still needed to study. Lancelot's frozen hologram waited patiently to continue his lessons, but that would have to wait. Thomas had more immediate concerns weighing on his mind.

A faint mechanical whirring drew his attention as he passed engineering. The hatch stood partially open, spilling harsh white light into the corridor. Peering inside, Thomas spotted movement among the complex machinery—something serpentine and metallic weaving between components with precise grace. Its segmented body reminded him of a snake, but with multiple small manipulator arms that allowed it to grip tools and components with delicate precision. Currently, it was deep in Excalibur's guts, installing what Thomas recognized as one of the parts they'd acquired on Caerlyon.

"Merlin, I assume that's you?" he said, stepping into engineering.

The GOLEM's head turned toward him, familiar blue eyes glowing from its serpentine mechanical face. "This form is better suited for detailed repair work," the Advisor replied, his manipulators continuing to work even as they spoke. "The humanoid GOLEM lacks the dexterity needed for these particular repairs. How is your hand?"

Thomas flexed his fingers demonstratively. "Good as new. Maybe better." He watched as Merlin deftly connected a series of hair-thin wires to the component he was installing. "Those nanites are amazing. I can't even tell it was broken."

"The technology was revolutionary even in my time," Merlin said. "Though the Draconite have apparently advanced it further."

"Where are we, anyway?" Thomas asked. "I saw the star map on the flight deck projector. It looked like—"

"Nowhere in particular," Merlin interrupted, his snake-like form twisting to access another component. "Deep space, away from any inhabited systems. We'll need to decide our next destination once repairs are complete."

"Speaking of decisions..." Thomas leaned against a nearby console, choosing his words carefully. "I know we touched on this during the heat of the moment, but...don't you think Amren would be better suited to make them? He's clearly more qualified than I am." He gestured vaguely at the complex machinery surrounding them. "I mean, look at all this. I barely understand how any of it works. But he grew up with this technology, this culture. He's a better pilot, better trained, knows more about the galaxy..."

The GOLEM's head swiveled back, mechanical eyes fixed on him, work momentarily forgotten. "Is this about Amren's qualifications, or your own self-doubt?"

"What do you mean?"

"I mean you're still mentally hung up on your upbringing as an excuse for why you can't succeed." The snake-like golem fully turned to face him, tools temporarily set aside. "You look at Amren and see everything you think you're not—nobility, training, purpose. But you're missing what's right in front of you."

"Which is what?" Thomas asked, crossing his arms

defensively. "That I'm some courier from Earth who stumbled into all this by accident?"

"That you're exactly where you're meant to be." Merlin's voice carried centuries of certainty. "The ship accepted you, Thomas. It found you worthy. Not because of your skills or knowledge, or because of your lineage or how many gold pieces you have in your coffers. Because of who you are at your core."

"And who is that, exactly?" Thomas pushed off from the console, frustration building. "A street kid who killed someone to join a gang? Someone who couldn't even save his mother from her addiction? Who couldn't..." He trailed off, old pain threatening to surface.

"Someone who survived," Merlin replied softly. "Someone who was smart enough to listen. Who found the strength to change and try to do better. Someone who, despite everything life threw at him, never lost his fundamental compassion." The GOLEM's eyes pulsed gently. "You need to stop doubting yourself and begin believing. Things will only get harder from here, but that part of your life is over. It's time to turn the page."

"That's easy to say. But you saw Amren out there. The way he flew, the way he fought. He's literally been training for this his entire life. His father was one of Arthur's knights. Meanwhile, my father..." He shook his head. "Well, I don't even know who he was."

"Your past does not define your future," Merlin said, his serpentine form coiling slightly as if settling in for a longer conversation. "Do you think Amren's heritage makes him more worthy? That his training makes him better suited to command?"

"Doesn't it? He knows this galaxy, these people. He understands the politics, the culture. And he's an incredible pilot and fighter. We would be dead if not for him. I'm still trying to wrap my head around the fact that magic is real."

"You should know," Merlin said, his tone growing somber, "Amren entered the command pod while you were in regeneration."

That brought Thomas up short. Disappointment bubbled up. "Oh. So he's already prepared to replace me."

"Why so dour about it? I thought that's what you wanted?"

"What I want and what makes sense are two different things."

"So you want to remain in command of Excalibur, but you don't think you're worthy?"

"Why do I feel like you're leading me around by the nose again?"

"Answer the questions, Thomas."

"Well, yeah. I do want to stay on. Make a difference. I don't need to be in charge though. I just want to…belong. And no. I don't think I'll ever believe I'm worthy."

"Then it's a good thing it isn't up to you. Amren entered the command pod. He nearly died." Merlin's mechanical features somehow managed to convey genuine concern. "The neural interface rejected him almost immediately. If I hadn't been able to extract him quickly…" He left the implications hanging.

Thomas' jaw went slack. "What? How can he not be worthy? He's everything a knight should be."

"It may seem that way from the outside. But he's not everything a knight should be," Merlin replied. "He's too confident, too sure of himself. He's unwilling—or perhaps unable—to truly merge with the ship's systems. He tries to maintain too much control rather than working in harmony with Excalibur."

"I don't understand," Thomas said. "He's spent his whole life preparing for this."

"And that's part of the problem. He has very specific ideas about how everything should work, and how the ship should run. But the neural interface requires something different." Merlin's snake-like form lowered to Thomas' eye level. "It requires surrender as much as control. The ability to let go of preconceptions and truly become one with the ship."

"Like when I was flying," Thomas said slowly. "When I stopped trying to force it and just...let it happen."

"Exactly. You may lack formal training, but you possess something far more valuable—the ability to adapt, to learn, to grow." Merlin's manipulators gestured expressively. "Amren has spent his life learning to be in control. It served him well as a solo fighter pilot and warrior, but it works against him here."

"Could he learn? To let go, I mean?"

"Perhaps. He may yet prove suitable as part of the crew, one of the twelve. But he would need to sacrifice some of his autonomy, his need for control. I'm not certain he can do that, even when he might want to."

Thomas absorbed this in silence, watching as Merlin returned to his repairs. The serpentine GOLEM moved smoothly between components, each action precise and purposeful.

"Is he okay?" Thomas asked. "Amren, I mean."

"He's recovering in his quarters. The experience was difficult for him. Not just physically, but emotionally. Everything he believed about his destiny has been challenged. In some ways, he's the same as you. He likely believes he's a failure."

"I should talk to him," Thomas said, starting to rise.

"Give him time," Merlin advised. "He needs to process this in his own way. And you need to process what it means for you."

"What do you mean?"

"I mean that perhaps now you'll start believing in yourself." The GOLEM's eyes fixed on him again. "I've said it before. I'll keep saying it. You're here for a reason, Thomas. Not because you're perfect, or fully trained, or even ever much more than an adequate pilot. But because you possess exactly the qualities needed for what lies ahead."

Thomas felt something shift—not a dramatic transformation—inside him, but a small crack in the wall of doubt he'd built around himself. "I'll try," he said finally. "To believe, I mean. But it's not easy."

"Nothing worthwhile ever is," Merlin replied. "But consider this—every time you've truly needed to rise to the occasion, you have. Whether it was escaping the Draconite at Caerlyon or that first space battle. When it matters most, you find a way."

"Usually by accident," Thomas said, but there was less self-deprecation in his tone than before.

"The universe rarely deals in accidents," Merlin said. "Now, if you're done questioning your place here, perhaps you'd like to help me with these repairs? The sooner we finish, the sooner we can decide our next move."

Thomas found himself smiling slightly as he stood. "Alright. But I warn you, I know nothing about quantum stabilizers or phase-lock crystals."

"Then it's time you learned," Merlin replied. "After all, this is your ship. You should understand how it works."

As Thomas moved to help, he felt something—a sense of belonging, of purpose—he hadn't experienced in a long time. Maybe Merlin was right. Maybe it was time to turn the page on his past and focus on what lay ahead.

Even if what lay ahead involved fighting an empire of dragon-people who had mastered both technology and magic.

One step at a time, he told himself. Starting with learning how to fix a quantum stabilizer.

"So," he said, kneeling beside Merlin's serpentine form, "where do I begin?"

The GOLEM's eyes brightened slightly, and Thomas could have sworn he detected a note of approval in Merlin's mechanical voice as he began explaining the intricacies of Excalibur's systems. For the first time since boarding the ship, Thomas felt like he wasn't just along for the ride.

He was exactly where he was supposed to be.

CHAPTER 41

Thomas wiped the sweat from his forehead, grimacing at the black smudges the gesture left on his sleeve. After nearly ten hours helping Merlin with repairs, he felt like he'd been dragged through an oil slick, but the work had left him with a deep sense of satisfaction. Understanding how Excalibur functioned made him feel more connected to the ship, more worthy of his unexpected position.

"That should do it," Merlin's serpentine GOLEM announced, manipulator arms gracefully withdrawing from the final installation. "The quantum stabilizer is fully operational, and the phase-lock crystals are perfectly aligned. The ship's capabilities are nearly restored to peak efficiency."

"Nearly?" Thomas asked, stretching muscles cramped from hours in awkward positions.

"There are always improvements to be made," Merlin replied. "But for now, we've accomplished what was necessary. You should get cleaned up."

Thomas nodded, already anticipating a hot shower. "Thanks for teaching me about the systems," he said. "It helps, knowing how everything works."

"Understanding leads to confidence," Merlin replied, his mechanical eyes dimming slightly. "Now go. You smell like you've been swimming in reactor coolant."

In his quarters, Thomas peeled off his grimy clothes, selecting another crimson outfit from the wardrobe. The color was growing on him, though he still felt slightly ridiculous in the clothing. The shower lived up to his expectations, the hot water washing away not just the grime but some of his lingering doubts. His conversation with Merlin helped him see things differently. Maybe he wasn't exactly who he thought he should be, but he was right for Excalibur.

And Excalibur was right for him.

Clean and refreshed, he headed for the galley, his stomach reminding him that nutrient cubes weren't quite the same as real food. He was so focused on the promise of sustenance that he nearly ran into Amren as the other man emerged from a cross corridor.

"Thomas," Amren said, startled. The usually composed warrior looked troubled, his shoulders tense beneath his tunic. "I was just..." He trailed off, clearly uncomfortable.

"How are you feeling?" Thomas asked carefully. "After the command pod, I mean."

Amren's expression darkened. "Merlin told you."

"He mentioned it. Said it was rough."

"Rough." Amren laughed bitterly. "That's one way to describe it." He exhaled sharply, clearly frustrated by the outcome. "Do you know what it's like to spend your entire life preparing for something, only to discover you're fundamentally unsuited for it?"

"Not to the same extent as you might, but I have some idea."

"The interface..." Amren shuddered slightly at the memory. "It was like drowning. Like being crushed. I couldn't... I couldn't let go. Couldn't surrender control.

Everything I've ever learned, every instinct I've developed, fought against it."

"Merlin said something similar," Thomas said. "About how your training works against you here."

"My father believed in me," Amren continued, real pain entering his voice. "He was so certain I would play a vital role when Excalibur returned. But I failed. Failed him, failed myself, failed everything we worked toward."

"Maybe you're judging yourself too harshly," Thomas replied. "Merlin told me something earlier, that our past doesn't define our future. Maybe that applies here, too."

"How so?"

"Well, everything you learned, everything you trained for...it was all about being in control, right? Being the best warrior, the best pilot. But maybe this is about learning something new. Something different."

Amren's brow furrowed. "You sound like you speak from experience."

"I grew up on the streets," Thomas said. "I've done a lot of things I'm not proud of. Up until recently, like maybe an hour ago, I couldn't shake the feeling that my past defined me. That I could never be anything else, but then I talked to Merlin about it and now...I don't know. I always expected Merlin to be this wise old wizard with a long white beard and robes. It turns out this one doesn't even have a body, but he's still pretty wise. Maybe we both need to stop letting our past dictate who we can become."

Amren grinned, his expression thoughtful. "You make it sound so simple," he said. "But how does one simply discard a lifetime of training? Of preparation?"

"Not discard," Thomas replied. "Build on it. Use it differently." He gestured toward the galley. "I'm starving. Want to join me? We can talk more over nutrient cubes."

"I don't know what a nutrient cube is," Amren replied.

"Really? You don't know what you're missing. They're amazing. Come on."

They walked together to the galley. Thomas immediately retrieved two cubes from the dispenser, handing one to Amren before taking a seat at the small table. "Merlin says they have all the nutrition you need, plus they taste like whatever you crave most when you eat one."

Amren studied his cube before taking a bite. His eyes widened slightly. "Honeycomb bread," he said softly. "My mother used to buy it from a vendor near the Magic Keg. They went out of business when I was a teenager. I haven't had it in years."

"See? The cubes know." Thomas bit into his own, savoring the perfect blend of flavors that reminded him of his favorite curry shop in Manchester. "Listen, I've been thinking. Maybe we can help each other."

"How so?"

"Well, I need training. Real training, against a real person. And you need..." Thomas hesitated, choosing his words carefully. "Well, I don't know exactly what you need, but I need you."

"You want me to train you?" Amren asked, surprise evident in his tone.

"Why not? You're clearly skilled with weapons, and I have to learn. Who knows, maybe teaching will help you see things from a new perspective."

Amren considered this, taking another bite of his cube. "It would be an honor," he said finally. "Though I warn you, I may not be a very good instructor. I can only teach you the way my father taught me, and he was a difficult taskmaster."

"Good," Thomas replied. Vin had been hard on him, too. But for all the right reasons. As far as he was concerned, this would be the same. "I don't want easy. I want to learn everything I can."

"Then we'll start tomorrow. Basic sword handling first, then—"

He cut off as Merlin's humanoid GOLEM entered the galley, its blue eyes bright with purpose. "I'm glad to find you both here," the Advisor said. "Amren, how do you feel?"

"Well enough," he replied. "Thomas and I were just discussing his weapons training."

"An excellent idea. I'm sure you'll both find it rewarding."

"I know your physical form is a machine," Thomas said. "But you look like you want something."

"Indeed. I believe we should plan our next move."

"That's a good idea," Thomas agreed. "What are you thinking?"

"Let us start with what we know," Merlin said. "What we know is that the Draconite are aware of Excalibur. Sooner than I would have liked, but what's done is done. At least we brought its systems back to optimal performance."

"Word of your return will reach Morgana quickly, if it hasn't already," Amren said. "If she's like me, she'll immediately think Arthur has returned."

"Which perhaps we can use to our advantage," Merlin said. "But it's also a disadvantage."

"Moving freely will become much more difficult," Amren agreed. "Every Draconite patrol will be on alert, and it won't be long before her hunter-killers are searching for us."

"We also know that Lancelot is out there, and he may be looking for us, too," Thomas said.

"Not only Lancelot," Merlin said. "Many factions have different interests in this ship, especially for as long as they think Arthur resides on it. Half of Avalon will be looking for us."

"So what do we do?" Thomas asked.

"That's what we need to decide."

"If you want my opinion," Amren said. "I think the best place to start would be to enlist more allies. From what my father always told me, the more knights Excalibur has connected to her interface, the more powerful she becomes."

"That's right," Merlin confirmed.

"So we need crew who are suitable to become knights. Beings who remain loyal to Arthur despite the passage of years. We're also badly in need of a wizard."

"A wizard?" Thomas asked, interest peaking at the mention.

"Yes," Amren replied. "Preferably someone powerful enough to help disguise the ship."

"Is that possible?"

"With the right practitioner, yes," Merlin replied. "Though finding one we can trust won't be easy."

"What about Avalyeth?" Amren asked. "It's a Druidic world, technically allied with the Draconite but not closely watched. Many there still remember the old ways. They still honor Arthur's memory."

"And probably harbor those who oppose Morgana's rule," Thomas added. "But wouldn't that make it dangerous?"

"Everywhere is dangerous now," Amren replied. "At least on Avalyeth, we might find help."

Thomas remembered something else from their time on Caerlyon. "What about that mercenary job the Sidhe were discussing? The one about Morgana searching for some ancient artifact?"

Merlin's mechanical features shifted slightly. "Go on."

"Well, if she wants it, maybe we should try to get it first. Even if we can't use it, keeping it out of her hands seems worthwhile."

"An interesting suggestion," Merlin said. "Though perhaps we should focus on your training before attempting such missions. You've barely scratched the surface of what you need to learn."

"Maybe," Thomas replied. "But we can't hide forever. And if we're going to make a difference, we need to start somewhere."

"Perhaps you're right," Merlin answered. "Or perhaps our best approach would be to start harassing the Draconite. To strike out against them could start rumors that will remind the galaxy of Arthur. That in turn could bring the recruits we need over to our side before we need to convince them."

"Accomplishing two goals at once," Amren said. "But it could be risky for just the three of us to nip at the Draconite. Especially with Thomas flying Excalibur alone." He looked at Thomas. "No offense intended. But you can't deny your need to improve your skills."

"No," Thomas agreed. "You're right. It might be better to start by trying to expand the crew. And hire a wizard." He paused, remembering another snippet of conversation they had eavesdropped on. "Speaking of which, there's also the situation in the Lanwyn Cluster. Someone is attacking Draconite ships. Maybe we could bring them over to the cause? Maybe they have a wizard?"

"That could also be very risky. If someone is creating problems for the Draconite, I'm all for it. But we could end up in the middle of it, which I don't believe we're prepared for. And the odds they would have the kind of wizard we need are low."

"Yeah, I get your point," Thomas said. "Merlin, what do you think?"

"All of the options are on the table," Merlin said. "As captain, the final decision is yours."

Thomas looked to Amren. "You don't mind if I decide for all of us?"

"Why would I?" he replied. "You're the captain. You sit in the command pod."

Thomas sat back, considering their options. "It seems to me that Avalyeth is our best bet," he decided. "How long will it take to get there?"

"Through a wormhole?" Merlin replied. "A few minutes. With any luck, word of Excalibur's return hasn't reached that quadrant of Avalon yet. If it has, we may not get very far before we're forced to leave again, a Druidic world or not."

Amren rose from his seat, his earlier dismay having faded like the morning mist. "Then what are we waiting for?"

CHAPTER 42

The planet Avalyeth hung in space like a round emerald tinged with aquamarine, its surface a patchwork of deep greens broken by pale blue ribbons of rivers and lakes. Unlike Earth with its sprawling cities and industrial centers, the world appeared largely untamed, with no obvious signs of civilization visible.

"It's beautiful," Thomas said from the command pod, sensor data flowing through his mind as Excalibur approached an orbit. Through the neural interface, he could feel the planet's magical energy like a subtle heartbeat against his consciousness. "I can sense something…different about it."

"Avalyeth rests on a powerful magical energy stream," Amren explained, standing beside the pod. "The Druids chose to settle it specifically for that reason. They say the planet itself is alive with arcane energy."

"Which makes it an ideal place to find what we need," Merlin added, his humanoid GOLEM's eyes glowing softly. "Though landing won't be simple. The Druids are protective of their world."

"For obvious reasons," Amren said.

"Which is why Merlin fried the control boards for the oxygen scrubbers," Thomas pointed out. "It might have been better to break something that wouldn't kill Amren and I if you have trouble putting it back together again."

"The Druids would see through a simple mechanical failure," Merlin answered. "This will appear more urgent and legitimate."

"Yes," Amren agreed. "Because it is. I can feel the deterioration of the air in my lungs already."

"Unidentified vessel," a cold voice cut uninvited through their comms. "This is Avalyeth Control. You have entered restricted space. Identify yourself and state your purpose."

"What do we tell them?" Thomas asked.

"The truth," Merlin replied.

"Avalyeth Control, this is private transport Longstrider," Thomas replied, trying to keep the tension from his voice. "We're suffering from a critical life support malfunction. Requesting emergency landing clearance for repairs."

"Please transmit your system logs and carbon dioxide reports immediately," Control replied.

"Go ahead," Merlin prompted before Thomas had to ask. With a thought, he gathered the data and passed it to orbital control.

A long pause followed. Thomas tensed, ready to engage the thrusters and orient to enable a burst if they needed to make a quick escape.

"Longstrider, you are cleared to land in Quarantine for inspection," the controller finally responded. "Escort ships are being dispatched to guide you. Any deviation from this course will be considered hostile action."

"Understood, Control."

No sooner had Thomas responded than a pair of ships

rose from the planet's surface, their appearance surprising Thomas. They looked grown rather than built, their organic hulls rippling with patterns of luminescent energy. As they approached, he could feel the magical energy exuding from them through Excalibur's sensors.

"Are those ships made of wood?" he asked, amazed by the craft.

"Yes, unlike the Druid capital ship you saw at Caerlyon," Merlin replied. "They're living ships, cultivated from the time they're seedlings and imbued with magic during their growth. The only mechanical parts are the reactor, thrusters, and life support."

"That's amazing," Thomas replied, awestruck.

"Follow them exactly," Merlin advised. "The Druids won't hesitate to become aggressive if they suspect ulterior motives."

Thomas felt the pressure as he guided Excalibur into position between the escort vessels. He'd never had to fly the ship with any kind of precision before, and maintaining a matching course and velocity with the Druid ships triggered a wave of anxiety that threatened to derail the entire approach. Excalibur began to wobble in space, reacting to his mental state.

"Don't try too hard to control the ship," Amren said, noticing his distress. "Work with it."

Knowing how hard it was for Amren to follow his own advice was calming to Thomas. One area where he had excelled so far was not trying too hard to force his will on the ship, but rather working in conjunction with it. In that way, it wasn't all that different from riding his bike. He imagined lanes of a highway, with Excalibur in the center and the two Druid vessels on either side. All he had to do was drive straight.

In this way, he was able to match their deliberate

descent through the atmosphere. Unlike what he knew of Earth's sharp reentry, their passage felt smooth, as if the planet's magical field was cushioning their arrival.

They broke through the cloud layer to find a landscape that took Thomas' breath away. Vast forests stretched to the horizon, their canopy broken by massive trees that dwarfed anything he'd seen on Earth. These titans rose thousands of feet into the sky, their trunks wider than office buildings.

The escort guided them toward one of these megalithic trees. As they drew closer, Thomas could see platforms and structures built on top of its massive branches, connected by bridges that looked like they were woven from living steel. Their designated landing zone was at the topmost platform. There were currently no other ships on it, though Thomas saw a few scattered on other platforms nearby.

"Quarantine," he said. "Should we be worried?"

"No," Merlin replied. "It's standard procedure. An inspection team will board the ship on landing. You'll escort them to the damaged control board, and once they're satisfied that the emergency was real they'll allow us to remain long enough to make repairs."

"Without contacting the Draconites?"

"That remains to be seen. Life support issues are uncommon, but not particularly suspicious."

"But this is Excalibur. You don't think they'll recognize it?"

"Even if they do, we can pass it off as a replica design," Amren said. "Also uncommon, but not unheard of."

"I'm surprised the Draconite haven't banned ships that look like this one."

"Oh, they have, but like banning weapons on civilian starships, there's only so much the Draconite can control. And certainly, the Druids have little interest in providing support for relatively minor infractions."

"Precisely," Merlin said. "The Druids may be allied with the Draconite, but there are limits."

"And many oppose Morgana's rule in secret," Amren added. "Which is the reason we're here."

"But how will we know who to trust?" Thomas asked.

"We won't," Amren replied grimly. "That's what makes this dangerous. And fun."

Thomas guided Excalibur to the platform, again growing nervous—this time about landing—as he neared. He needn't have worried.

"Pass the controls to the core to allow the ship to land itself," Merlin advised.

Thomas sent a thought to the computer, and it took over the controls, guiding the ship the rest of the way to the platform. Rather than use landing gear or skids, the ship settled a foot above the platform, floating without a visible tether. A dozen armed guards carrying long staves circled the ship, while two additional guards waited to board with a Druid Thomas took as the inspector.

His body relaxed in relief, thankful he had landed without causing any collateral damage or strife. He was about to ask Merlin how the inspectors would get on the ship—and how they would disembark—when a panel opened in Excalibur's hull, lowering an oversized teleportal to the platform. It remained tethered to the ship by a semi-rigid cable.

"You should inform Control that you're ready to receive the inspectors," Merlin said.

"Okay," Thomas agreed, turning his thoughts to the comms. "Avalyeth Control, we're prepared to receive your inspection team at your convenience."

"Thank you, Longstrider," Control replied. "Inspectors are boarding now."

Thomas could sense in every direction around Excalibur, and he watched the inspector and his guards confidently enter the teleportal before opening the command pod's canopy and climbing out. He turned to Amren. "Let's go meet our new friends."

The man smiled. "I hope they will be friends," he replied, producing one of his blades seemingly from thin air. "But I'm ready if they aren't."

CHAPTER 43

Thomas and Amren met the Druid inspector and his guards at the teleportal closest to engineering. Thomas was immediately struck by how ordinary the inspector looked at first glance. He could have passed for human if not for his hair, which grew in thick, wild curls that reminded Thomas of brambles in an untamed garden. His eyes were an unnaturally pale green, almost luminescent in the ship's lighting. They stood in sharp contrast to his plain grey jumpsuit. An embroidered patch on his left breast pocket labeled him a quarantine inspector.

The guards flanking him were more obviously alien. Like their ships, their armor was grown rather than forged, with intricately carved layers of dark wood flowing over their bodies, obviously designed to allow them easy movement. Each guard carried a stave that glowed softly with magical energy.

"I'm Inspector Thornheart," the Druid announced, his voice carrying the crisp authority of someone used to being obeyed. "You will show me this critical system failure."

Thomas glanced at Amren, who gave him a slight nod.

"Of course," Thomas replied, trying to project confidence he didn't feel. "This way, please."

They led the inspection team through Excalibur's corridors toward engineering. Thomas could feel the inspector's eyes on him, studying him. He also couldn't help noticing how the guards' boots made no sound on the deck plates despite their obvious weight, adding to the tense and otherworldly atmosphere.

"Interesting design," Thornheart commented as they walked. "Rather... antiquated."

"She's old," Thomas agreed carefully. "But reliable."

"Hmm." The sound carried volumes of doubt.

"Life support is through here," Thomas announced. He was glad to have Amren with him, certain he would be a lot more nervous without the comfort of the warrior's presence.

The hatch slid open at their approach, revealing the complex machinery within. Thomas led them to the panel where Merlin had carefully staged the malfunction and opened it for the inspector to review.

Thornheart examined the damaged control board with obvious skepticism. "How did this occur?"

Thomas repeated the explanation Merlin had prepared for him. "A faulty transformer caused a circuit overload. It fried the whole board before the safeties could engage."

"The transformer. Show me."

"Amren?" Thomas said, turning to him.

Amren nodded and retrieved the deliberately damaged component from a nearby counter. Thornheart took it, turning it over in his hands with practiced expertise. His pale eyes narrowed as he studied the scorch marks and melted connections.

"This is consistent with your story," he said finally, though his tone suggested he remained unconvinced. "You have twenty-four hours to effect repairs and leave Avalyeth. You may enter the city to acquire necessary supplies, but your ship will remain under guard."

"Thank you," Thomas replied, relief flooding through him. "We appreciate your understanding."

"Don't thank me yet," Thornheart said. "We'll be monitoring you closely."

They escorted the inspection team back to the teleportal. As soon as they were gone, Thomas exhaled sharply. "That was intense."

"Indeed," Amren agreed. "Though not unexpected."

A soft scrabbling announced Merlin's arrival, his mouse-sized GOLEM approaching from the corridor. "Well done, though we shouldn't linger," the Advisor said as he scampered toward Thomas. "We have limited time to accomplish our goals." Thomas picked him up and deposited him in his pocket.

They entered the teleportal, emerging out on the platform. The inspection team was on its way to a second teleportal near the trunk of the tree, at the far end of the platform, while the dozen guards remained in a circle around Excalibur.

"Are they going to wait there for us to come back?" Thomas asked.

"If those are their orders, yes," Amren replied. "Druid warriors are extremely disciplined."

"Be sure to set your mind to the city when we enter," Merlin reminded Thomas when they neared the teleportal the inspector had used. He did as the Advisor suggested, and Thomas gasped as they emerged onto a second broad platform hundreds of feet above the ground. The Druid city spread out around them, a breathtaking fusion of nature and technology that defied his expectations.

Massive bridges wider than highways connected the titanic trees, while wooden and metal flying cars glided silently between levels, following paths marked by streams of floating lights. Buildings had been constructed into and around the branches, their metal and glass shapes flowing seamlessly into the natural architecture of the forest.

"This is incredible," Thomas breathed, watching as a group of Druids walked past. "I've never seen anything like it."

"The Druids have spent centuries perfecting the integration of technology and nature," Merlin explained, "though Avalyeth doesn't appear to have changed at all since the last time I was here."

"What would be the need?" Amren asked. "The Druids have been at peace for nearly a millennia."

"By aligning with whoever holds power," Merlin scoffed. "There's nothing courageous about that."

"Perhaps not. But it's the ruling class who have chosen that path. Maybe we can change that among the commoners if nothing else."

"We should find a tavern," Thomas said, doing his best not to gawk too long at anything or anyone. "That's usually the best place to start, right Merlin?"

"The Wizard's Guild would be more direct," Amren suggested.

"Wait, there's actually a Wizard's Guild?" Thomas asked, surprised.

"Yes," Merlin replied, amusement clear in his tone, "though the guilds don't tend to be too particular about who joins so long as they can pay the fees. In my opinion, approaching them directly would be unwise. They're too closely monitored by the Draconite, and probably more so these days."

"So the tavern it is," Thomas said. "Where should we start?"

They made their way through the city on foot, Thomas constantly distracted by the incredible sights around them.

A group of young Druids practiced levitation nearby, their instructor guiding them as they lifted small objects with hand gestures. A merchant's stall sold crystals that contained galaxies in miniature. Even the air felt different here, charged with enough magical energy to stand the hairs of his arm on end and tingle his skin.

"There," Amren said. "Tavern up ahead."

"I was starting to think Druids didn't drink," Thomas remarked, noting the holographic sign of an ale tankard a short distance away.

They started toward it, pausing only a few steps later as the Druids on the platform ahead of them hurried from the center of the thoroughfare to both sides. Behind them, a group of Draconite soldiers, similar to those they had encountered on Caerlyon, passed between them.

"A Draconite patrol? Here?" Merlin grumbled.

"They look like they just left the tavern," Amren remarked.

"And they're coming our way," Thomas said.

"In here," Amren said, motioning to a nearby doorway. They ducked inside, and he closed the door behind them, crouching low enough to stay out of sight through the shop windows. He positioned himself to look out onto the platform. "I don't think they spotted us."

"That was close," Thomas said as they passed by the shop's door.

"Can I help you?"

The voice behind Thomas caught him by surprise. He turned to find an elderly Druid woman regarding them with obvious amusement. Her hair was pure white, the sides braided and held by glossy wooden clips. Her green eyes pieced straight through him as if she could see his soul. She wore light robes that accentuated a figure more youthful than her face suggested, her feet completely bare.

"I apologize," Thomas said quickly. "We were just, uh..."

"Avoiding the Draconite soldiers," she finished for him. "A wise decision." She gestured at the window, where the guards could still be seen moving through the crowd. "They grow bolder with each passing season, don't they? They visit more often, and they're increasingly demanding. I can see the way their distaste for us grows. They don't care much for magic these days."

While the woman spoke, Thomas took a quick look around. The shop's interior was a riot of color and movement, filled with an assortment of strange objects that defied categorization. Shelves lined with bottles containing swirling, luminescent liquids stretched toward a ceiling that appeared much higher than should have been possible given the building's external dimensions. Mechanical devices that looked more like abstract sculptures rotated slowly on floating pedestals, each one humming with barely contained energy.

"You're no friend of the Draconite, then?" Thomas asked.

"That's a rather impolite question, seeing as we just met, don't you think?"

"We should go," Amren said. "We don't want to impose."

"Nonsense," the woman replied, moving deeper into the shop. "You're clearly new here, and looking for something. Perhaps I can help?" She paused, her eyes fixing on Thomas with uncomfortable intensity. "Though I suspect what you seek isn't something that can be found on my shelves. I specialize in oddities both magical and technological."

"They're all very interesting," Thomas said. "But you're right. Our ship needs repairs, and I doubt you have the parts we need."

"Did you use the 'emergency landing' excuse to get clearance to land here?" She smiled, revealing teeth that sparkled like crystals. "Such an old trick. Though I suppose the classics endure for a reason."

In Thomas' pocket, Merlin's GOLEM stirred, moving out of his pocket and up the back of his leg before the woman's eyes flickered toward the movement. Her smile widened fractionally. "My name is Sylana," she said, moving to a smaller branch of the tree they were in, growing through one wall and the floorboards to form a counter. "While I may not have what you're looking for, I might know where you can get it. I should warn you though, the Wyldentree can be…difficult for outsiders."

"I said we need starship parts," Thomas said. "You make them sound hard to get."

"I'm quite sure you aren't here for parts. I'm telling you where to find what you came here looking for, not what you're telling everyone you came here looking for."

"And how can you be so sure you know what that is?" Amren asked.

Sylana's laugh sounded like wind chimes in a breeze. "It's written all over you. You're looking for something specific. Something that requires a certain expertise." She paused, her eyes locking once again on Thomas. "Or maybe I should say, someone specific."

"And you can help us find them?" Thomas asked, trying to keep his voice neutral despite an increase in both excitement and apprehension. She couldn't know why they had really come to Avalyeth. That would be impossible. Wouldn't it?

"I already gave you a lead, though I should warn you things have changed here. The old alliances aren't what they once were. Trust must be earned anew."

"What do you mean?" Amren asked.

"The Draconite grow more suspicious by the day," she said softly. "They feel something coming. A change in the wind. Perhaps they're right to worry."

"We should go," Merlin whispered from where he'd crawled under Thomas' tunic and all the way up to its collar. "She's expecting trouble here beyond what the presence of those Draconite soldiers hinted at."

"Thank you for your help," Thomas said, heeding his advice.

"Don't be too hasty," Sylana said, reaching beneath her counter. She produced an oversized coin, imprinted with a relief of a gnarled tree. "Take this." She held it out to him. "When you reach the Wyldentree, show it to the keeper of the Whispering Vine. He'll know what it means."

Thomas accepted the coin, surprised by how warm it felt against his palm. "Thank you again," he said. "But why help us?"

Sylana's smile l centuries of secrets. "Let's just say I remember what it was like before. When magic and technology worked in harmony, when all of us lived together in peace. When Arthur..." She trailed off, glancing toward the window. "Never mind, such talk is dangerous these days. You should go. And be careful. The Draconite aren't the only threat out there."

Thomas swallowed hard at the comment, thanking her again before he and Amren left the shop.

"Merlin, what do you mean about trouble?" he asked quietly once they were outside.

"She's worried about the Draconite's increasing animosity toward magic. Avalyeth is a bastion of magic, even more so than Fendragel. When the enemy makes their move, it will be harsh and swift."

"Is there anything we can do to help?"

"Yes, head to the Wyldentree, collect our wizard, and be on our way."

"How do you know that's what she was talking about?"

"While she was speaking to you, she was also communicating with me. Today isn't the first time Merlin and Sylana have met."

"You mean the original, organic you?"

"Yes. Be prepared. Our quarry may not be as easy to retrieve as visiting a tavern, flashing that coin, and returning to the ship."

"What do you mean?"

Merlin chuckled. "You'll find out soon enough."

CHAPTER 44

The elevator platform hummed softly as they descended the massive trunk of the tree they had landed in, the city's gleaming architecture disappearing into the canopy above them. Like the buildings suspended by the tree, the elevator —a sleek capsule of polished metal and glass that rode magnetic tracks down the tree's ancient bark—was pure technology.

"How far down are we going?" Thomas asked, watching the mist swirl past the glass. The deeper they went, the more the pristine facades of the upper city gave way to something wilder and less controlled. Through gaps in the foliage, he caught glimpses of maintenance platforms and forgotten infrastructure, the hidden machinery that kept the Druids' world above running smoothly.

"All the way to the forest floor," Merlin replied from his pocket. "The Wyldentree stands apart from the others."

"I've heard stories about that place," Amren said. "It was originally home to a settlement of Fae refugees, but has since become a trash heap of sorts. A home to any of those who don't fit into proper Druid society."

"Every city has areas like that, I suppose," Thomas

remarked, remembering his childhood apartment in Bed-Stuy. "Some things really are universal."

They emerged from the mist into the perpetual twilight of the forest floor. Here, massive roots created natural archways and caverns, while bioluminescent fungi cast everything in an ethereal blue glow. The elevator, all chrome and softly pulsing indicator lights, docked with barely a whisper at a station that was jarringly high-tech amid the primal surroundings.

A sleek groundcar waited nearby, its dark metal surface reflecting the blue glow of the fungi. No driver sat behind the controls, but the vehicle's AI acknowledged their approach with a soft chime as its gullwing doors rose smoothly.

"Destination?" a soft voice asked.

"Wyldentree," Thomas replied.

"I'm not sure I understood," the vehicle's AI replied. "Destination?"

"Wyldentree," he repeated, the doors closing as soon as they were seated. The vehicle pulled away with incredible smoothness, following wide roads that wound between the titanic trees. "This is different from the upper city," he observed, watching the landscape flow past in amazement. Ancient roots larger than London buses created terrain around and overhead, where additional vegetation grew and a range of alien birds and small animals had made their homes. "More...primal."

The groundcar wound through the twilight forest for nearly twenty minutes, its quiet electric hum the only sound besides the occasional drip of condensation from above. Soon enough, Thomas caught his first glimpse of the Wyldentree rising before them like a dark monument to decay. Its bark was blackened and twisted as if by some ancient fire. Unlike the healthy trees supporting the city above, this one was slowly dying, its branches displaying dwindling volumes of leaves, reaching toward the canopy with gnarled fingers.

"What happened to it?" Thomas asked, unable to tear his eyes away from the unsettling sight. Even from a distance, something about the tree—as if it were in constant pain—felt wrong, its very existence an affront to the natural order. "And why didn't I notice it on our way down?"

"The upper branches are dwarfed by a healthy canopy from adjacent trees," Merlin explained. "Both the residents and the tree itself receive only secondary sunlight, leading to the tree's slow demise."

"I heard it was cursed," Amren said, his voice dropping to barely above a whisper. "Deliberately corrupted to serve as a haven for darker magics."

"Don't be ridiculous," Merlin replied. "The simplest explanation is the most accurate. Either way, it's stood like this for centuries, and will take thousands of years to fully decay."

The groundcar delivered them to another station near the tree's base. Where the one they had left was polished metal and spotless glass, this one looked worn and forgotten, its metal rusting and marred with graffiti sigils, its glass coated in pollen and dust.

"Wyldentree arrival complete," the AI announced, the doors opening to spit them out.

"Not exactly welcoming," Amren said.

"Remember," Merlin cautioned as they exited the car, "we're interested in the Whispering Vine. No distractions. No delays."

They crossed the station to the tree's elevator. It was as dilapidated as Thomas had expected, with more graffiti on both the inside and outside of the car, the surfaces worn and grimy.

"Do you know what level the Whispering Vine is on?" Thomas asked.

"No," Merlin answered. "Like you, I've never been in this location before."

"I'll go for the lowest level, then. We can ask for directions."

The elevator carried them up the trunk and into the branches. The lowest levels were delegated to machinery and engineering, unreachable via the public elevator. They were halfway up when they reached the first inhabited platform, stepping out into a dimly lit and dirty street.

Glancing around, Thomas immediately felt at home. The narrow walkways and suspicious glances reminded him of certain parts of New York he'd known well in his youth. But where those streets had been dominated by concrete, here everything was carved from the dying wood of the tree itself. It only added to the overall gloom.

The platform was more crowded than Thomas had expected, with many of the beings different from the ones he had spotted on Caerlyon. A group of shorter statured beings with thick hair and oversized heads haggled with a tall, willowy figure with greenish skin over glowing mushrooms.

A pair of slender, alien females drifted past. They appeared almost human at first glance, but there was an ethereal quality to them that no human could match. Their skin was so pale it practically glowed from within, while their silver hair floated down across their shoulders as though it was barely heavier than the air. Their movements were impossibly graceful, feet barely seeming to touch the ground as they walked. Their physical beauty stood in sharp contrast to their dirty dresses and scuffed slippers.

Another smaller humanoid with a sharply wrinkled face and yellow eyes watched them all from the shadows. He sized up everyone who passed, as if looking for weaknesses or opportunities.

"Excuse me," Thomas said to one of the thick-haired

beings, trying to sound casual. "Could you point us toward the Whispering Vine?"

The gnome's eyes narrowed, his long nose twitching slightly as he studied them. "Depends on who's asking," he replied, his voice surprisingly deep for his size. "Or how much gold they got."

Thomas produced the coin Sylana had given him. The gnome's expression changed instantly, though Thomas couldn't tell if it was recognition or calculation that sparked in his eyes.

"Ah," he said, suddenly more helpful. "Three levels up, follow the purple lanterns. Can't miss it." He hurried away before Thomas could thank him, vanishing into the crowd with surprising speed.

The next elevator carried them higher into the Wyldentree. Here, the platforms were wider, connected by rope and wood bridges that looked like they would collapse if too many beings walked across them at the same time. Shops lined the walkways, their dirty windows displaying items —potions that moved of their own accord, crystals that pulsed with unnatural light, and things he couldn't even begin to identify—that made Thomas' skin crawl.

The air was thick with competing scents—incense, herbs, and cooking food—mingling with sweat and garbage. Music drifted from various establishments, ranging from haunting melodies to pounding rhythms Thomas' ears couldn't find pleasure in.

"The Druids condemn this place," Amren remarked quietly as they walked, motioning to a group of young Druids exiting one business and crossing toward another. "But their wealthy youth come here seeking thrills and pleasure."

"What kind of pleasure?" Thomas asked.

"Drugs, alcohol, gambling," Merlin answered. "Fights, magic duels and the like."

"I'd love to see a magic duel."

"No, you wouldn't," Amren said. "Unless you're keen on seeing someone burned alive, or their limbs reduced to crumbling dust."

"Yeah, on second thought…"

They followed purple lanterns through increasingly narrow passages, where the wooden walls absorbed sound, creating pockets of unsettling silence. From behind closed doors came the complicated symphony of society's forgotten corner—bursts of laughter or argument, music or fighting or both. The deeper they went, the more Thomas felt like he was walking through the arteries of some vast, corrupted heart.

From shadowy alcoves, beings watched their passage with predatory interest. A pale-skinned woman lounged against a doorway, her silver hair cascading like liquid moonlight around shoulders left bare by a revealing dress. Her nearly-white eyes followed them with ancient hunger. Next to her, a goblin-like being cleaned wickedly curved claws with a silver pick.

"Stay close," Amren murmured. "The deeper we go, the more dangerous it becomes."

They passed a gambling den, its entrance marked by floating spheres of purple light. Inside, beings crowded around tables where dice clattered across surfaces marked with glowing runes. The air crackled with magical energy and desperation in equal measure.

A sweet smoke drifted from another establishment, where patrons reclined on floating cushions, breathing in colored vapor from ornate pipes. The customers' eyes glowed with unnatural colors, their expressions suggesting they were seeing things far beyond the confines of normal reality.

"Should we ask for more specific directions?" Thomas wondered aloud as they reached another junction. The purple lanterns lead in multiple directions now, their light creating confusing patterns in the ever-present mist.

"Not here," Merlin replied from his pocket. "The wrong question to the wrong person could be...problematic."

They chose a path that angled upward, the wooden planks beneath their feet creaking despite their apparent solidity. The walls pressed closer, threatening to disorient him.

Another group of young Druids stumbled past, their elegant robes disheveled, eyes glowing with artificial euphoria. They barely noticed Thomas and his companions, lost in whatever enhanced reality their purchased magics had granted them.

"This way," Amren said, indicating a narrower passage. "The lanterns are brighter here."

They had just started toward the new path when Thomas felt something brush his leg. The sensation was so light he might have ignored it, except for his familiarity with the sensation of being pick-pocketed and Merlin's sudden cry of alarm.

"No!" the Advisor shouted, but it was too late.

Thomas lunged for the thief, fingertips sliding along his cloak as he darted away through the crowds, Merlin's small golem clutched in one hand. He moved with impossible grace, barely seeming to touch the ground as he reached an alley and vanished into the darkness.

"After him!" Amren commanded, already moving to pursue.

They chased the figure into the alley, but he had a good head start, and Thomas barely got there in time to see him turn a corner up ahead. He growled as he skipped over garbage and tree branches, unwilling to let the thief escape. The pick-pocket was incredibly fast, but Thomas had spent years navigating urban obstacle courses as a courier. He vaulted over a stack of crates, rolled under a low-hanging branch, and kept pace despite the challenging terrain.

The chase led them into a marketplace where stalls sold everything from supposedly enchanted trinkets to questionable liquids. The thief weaved through the crowd with practiced ease, knocking over displays behind him to slow pursuit. Thomas followed, ignoring the cries of the angry vendors as he passed.

They burst into another dark alley, the thief ahead, but not by as much. Thomas could feel the wind behind the thief's rippling cloak, only a few feet ahead of him. And he was gaining.

The thief shot through a narrow gap between two stacks of old crates. Thomas followed him.

One moment, he was sure-footed and speeding along right behind the pick-pocket. The next, he was airborne, his legs yanked out from under him. He hit the platform hard, nearly biting his tongue as his chin painfully struck the wood. He slid to a stop, slightly dazed but already rising to his feet.

He glanced over his shoulder at a group of five thugs who had hidden behind the crates, and had lifted a rope across it to bring him down. They faced him now, glaring at him with menacing intentions.

"I'm gonna turn yer face to ground meat," one of them said, the entire group taking an ominous step toward him.

Thomas stood facing away from the thugs, his thoughts focused on the thief. How would he catch up now? There was no chance.

Then he noticed the half-shadowed face at the corner ahead, looking back at him. Waiting to observe his fate.

Thomas swung around, dropping into a fighting stance. Five against one, he had no chance. But he had nowhere to run, either. He'd been jumped before. He knew how to take a beating. "Let's get this over with," he said.

The thugs took another step toward him, grinning in anticipation.

That was as far as they got.

Thomas' attention was stolen by Amren, who vaulted to the top of one stack of crates in one leap. Pushing off, he slammed into the lead thug from behind, sending him stumbling toward Thomas. Reacting quickly, Thomas drove his knee into the falling being's head, wincing at the loud crack when he broke the thug's nose.

Amren rolled forward and to his feet, whirling to face the thugs, his daggers drawn. "Thomas!" he called out without taking his eyes off the thugs, "Stay with the thief. I'll handle this."

"Are you sure?" Thomas asked, though he was already preparing to run.

"Go!" Amren's daggers twirled threateningly in his hands, their edges beginning to glow. The thugs had taken a step back, reconsidering their life choices. "Find Merlin!"

Thomas didn't wait to see what happened next. He spun back around, searching for the thief, who had seen his fortunes turn and was once more sprinting away.

The sounds of combat faded behind him as Thomas pursued the pick-pocket deeper into the Wyldentree's maze-like passages. His feet splashed through puddles and leaping branches threatening to trip him up at every turn. He caught glimpses—the flutter of a cloak disappearing around corners, a shadow sliding between patches of darkness—of his quarry ahead. The thief was fast, but Thomas once more slowly gained ground, his heart pounding with exertion and adrenaline.

The chase led to the door of a random run-down building somewhere on the platform, deep inside the settlement maze. The thief slowed just long enough to yank the door open and duck inside. Thomas followed immediately, his instincts overriding his caution.

Reaching the door, he paused to grab the handle, half-expecting it to be locked. It wasn't. He yanked it open and threw himself inside without looking to see where he was going.

The moment he crossed the threshold, he felt it—a pressure against his skin like static electricity. Before he could react, invisible bonds seized him, lifting and holding him suspended a foot off the floor. He struggled against the invisible grip but couldn't overcome it, leaving him helpless as a figure stepped from the shadows.

He was young. Barely more than a child. His silver hair was cut short to his scalp, his pale skin revealing the veins beneath. There was something in his expression that sent a wave of fear through him despite his captor's age. A predatory calculation that reminded him of the cats that had stalked Manchester's alleys.

"Well," the boy said, his voice rougher than he expected, "what have we here?"

CHAPTER 45

Thomas hung suspended in the air, his muscles straining uselessly against the invisible magical bonds that held him immobile. The kitchen around him was dimly lit by magical braziers that cast everything in an eerie orange glow that made the shadows dance and shift unnaturally. Ancient wooden cabinets lined the walls, their surfaces scarred and stained from centuries of use. The wood itself captured what little light reached it. Pots and pans hung from hooks in the ceiling, occasionally swaying despite the lack of any breeze, creating soft metallic whispers that set Thomas' nerves on edge.

The silver-haired boy watched him with unnerving intensity, his unnaturally pale eyes reflecting the blue light like a cat's. His young face held none of the uncertainty or hesitation one might expect from a child wielding such power. There was something deeply unsettling about the contrast between his youth and the casual way he held Thomas helpless. He couldn't have been more than twelve, yet he maintained the complex spell with apparent ease, his fingers moving in small gestures that sent fresh waves of pressure through Thomas' immobilized form.

The interior door in front of Thomas creaked open slowly, the sound unnaturally loud in the tense silence. The thief sauntered in, still wearing his dark cloak. He pulled back his hood with deliberate showmanship to reveal delicate features and sharply pointed ears. An elf, Thomas realized with a jolt of recognition. The first he had seen on Avalyeth. The boy's appearance contrasted sharply with the cruel mockery in his expression as he grinned up at his captive prey.

"Look what followed me home, Halvy," the thief said, his voice carrying notes of cruel amusement. "Like a lost puppy." He reached into his cloak with theatrical flourish and produced Merlin's golem, holding it up to the light. "Though all he had worth taking was this weird little mechanical toy. Hardly worth the effort, really."

The boy—Halvy—frowned at the small automaton, his concentration on maintaining the binding spell never wavering. "What is it? Doesn't look like any mechanical I've seen before."

"No idea." The thief turned the golem over in his hands, studying it with exaggerated care. "Doesn't look particularly valuable, but something about it feels...different." He shook it slightly, the motion making Thomas wince. "Maybe we can sell it for parts. Or see what makes it tick."

"Please, let me go," Thomas said, fighting to keep his voice steady despite his precarious position and rising anger. "You can keep the device if you want. I just need to leave." He waited for Merlin to complain, but the Advisor remained silent. The GOLEM was an extension of the digital consciousness, not the consciousness itself.

Halvy's pale eyes narrowed dangerously, the air growing heavier with magical energy. "Can't do that. Orders are orders." A slight tremor entered his voice, betraying his youth despite his power. "And I'm not getting my hide tanned for letting someone go who followed Ryn back here. The boss was clear about that."

"Your boss? Who is that?" Thomas asked, but before either could answer, heavy footsteps approached from outside—deliberate, measured steps that made the pots overhead tremble with each impact. The door burst open with enough force to rattle the entire wall, admitting a blast of cooler air that sent the floating lights fluttering wildly.

A massive figure filled the doorway, so tall he had to duck to enter, his shoulders nearly brushing both sides of the frame. His wild black beard contained bits of what looked like wood chips, while his bare arms rippled with muscle beneath tattoos that Thomas could swear writhed and shifted in the light. He wore a leather apron covered in suspicious dark stains, and his hands looked capable of crushing stone. But it was his eyes that drew Thomas' attention. They burned with an inner fire that spoke of barely contained violence.

"What's all this racket about?" he demanded in a deep, rumbling voice. His gaze settled on Thomas still floating helplessly in the air. "And who's this?" The question carried a clear threat despite its casual delivery.

"He followed me," Ryn said quickly, his earlier bravado faltering slightly under the giant's harsh glare. "I nitched something off him in the market, but he gatched me. That's never happened before. Chased me all through the twisties."

"Why didn't you run him past Burl?"

"I did, boss. Burl knocked him flat on his face. Had him snooked for sure. I stopped to watch."

The giant's eyes turned to Thomas, a glint of respect in them. "How'd he get free?"

"He had another fellow with him. An Ursan. I didn't think he could keep up in the twisties. He was too far behind. Somehow, this one did, though. He bashed Burl real good, and then turned on the rest of the gang."

The giant grinned. "He's all but dead right about now then. Burl should be along any second."

"I wouldn't be too sure of that," Thomas said.

"Nobody told you that you could speak," the giant growled. Thomas silenced immediately, unenthused about the idea of one of the man's ham fists being introduced to his face.

"Anyway, he chased me all the way here before Halvy caught him." He held up Merlin's GOLEM as if offering proof of his actions. "All for this mechanical."

The giant's expression darkened dangerously, the tattoos on his arms seeming to writhe faster. His hand shot out with shocking speed for someone his size, grabbing Ryn by the front of his cloak and lifting him off his feet until they were eye to eye. "What's wrong with you, boy?" His voice dropped to a menacing growl that made Thomas' blood run cold. "Are you completely brainless? What's the first rule?"

"Never lead them home," Ryn gasped, dropping Merlin's GOLEM as he clutched the massive fist holding him aloft. "I'm sorry! But Halvy caught him, didn't he? No harm done!"

"No harm?" The giant shook him like a rag doll, his massive beard bristling with rage. "What if he'd been followed? What if he works for the Draconite? Did you think about that before you compromised our location?" Each question was punctuated by another shake that made Ryn's teeth rattle.

"I don't!" Thomas interjected quickly, seeing an opportunity to defuse the situation before it got worse. "I'm just trying to find the Whispering Vine. I don't want any complications, and you can have the GOLEM. If you let me go, I'll leave and forget this ever happened." He tried to inject sincerity into his voice despite his awkward floating position.

The giant turned toward him slowly, still holding Ryn off the ground with one hand. His eyes burned into Thomas with an intensity that made him wish he could shrink away. "The Vine? What business you got there?"

"Sylana gave me a coin for the keeper," Thomas replied carefully, watching the giant's reaction. "She seemed to think he could help me."

"Sylana?" The giant's eyes narrowed dangerously, his free hand clenching into a fist the size of Thomas' head. "And what exactly did that old witch think we could help you with?"

"We?" Thomas said. "Are you—"

Before Thomas could finish, the door swung open with devastating force. Amren burst through in a blur of motion, one arm wrapping around Halvy's chest while the other pressed a glowing dagger against the boy's pale throat. Blue energy crackled where the blade touched flesh, and the magical bonds holding Thomas vanished as Halvy's concentration broke. He dropped to the floor, barely managing to land on his feet.

"Don't move," Amren commanded, his voice carrying a deadly promise. The dagger in his hand pulsed with barely contained power, casting sharp shadows across his face. "I won't hesitate."

The giant slowly lowered Ryn to the floor, his expression unreadable beneath his wild beard. His massive hands remained loose at his sides, but Thomas could see the tension in his shoulders, like a coiled spring ready to release. "Well now," he rumbled, his voice carrying dangerous undertones. "This has gotten interesting. Let me repeat my question. Why did Sylana send you to me?"

"We need a wizard," Thomas said. "A good one."

The giant threw his head back and roared with laughter. "You need a good wizard? Not just an adequate one, then?"

"It's not a joke."

All of the giant's mirth vanished in an instant. His eyes locked on Thomas. "No, lad, it's not a joke. What would you need a wizard from me for, when the guild is back from whence you came? Why come to the Wyldentree?"

"I don't know. Sylana told us—"

"Yes, yes," the giant replied impatiently. "But why you? Why now? After all these years…"

"Because Excalibur has returned," Thomas said.

The tension in the room shifted instantly, becoming something else entirely. The giant's eyes widened slightly, while Ryn stumbled back against the wall, his ethereal features shocked. Even Halvy, despite the blade at his throat, turned his head slightly at the legendary name.

"Excalibur?" the giant said softly, the word carrying weight beyond its syllables. "Well I'll be. In that case, you can let my young and foolish apprentice go. There's no need for bloodshed among friends."

Amren hesitated, his blade unwavering against Halvy's throat. "You'll excuse me if I'm not quick to trust."

"Fair enough." The giant spread his massive hands, showing them empty. "But if I meant you harm, you'd be dealing with a lot more than two dimwitted children and an old wizard." His grin shifted, becoming more friendly. He turned his hands toward them, palms out. "My name is Grenyth. Welcome to the Whispering Vine."

CHAPTER 46

Grenyth waved them through the kitchen door. "Come on then. Let's talk somewhere more comfortable." He paused, turning to fix Amren with a fiery gaze. "After you let my apprentice go, of course. Poor lad's probably about to pass out from fear, though he's too proud to show it."

Amren hesitated, his blade still hovering near Halvy's throat. The boy's pulse was visible against the glowing edge, but his face remained carefully neutral despite his predicament. Finally, Amren slowly lowered his weapon, though his movements suggested he remained ready to strike if needed.

Halvy immediately darted away, rubbing at the faint mark the weapon had left on his pale skin. He shot Amren a look that mixed fear with grudging respect.

"That's a mite better," Grenyth said with a rumbling laugh that shook the pots hanging overhead. "Though I suppose it's only fair, considering they robbed you. Come. Let's talk properly like civilized folk."

The room beyond was larger than Thomas expected. Ancient wooden tables and chairs were scattered about in comfortable disarray, most showing signs of heavy use and careful repair. One particularly large chair had been specially reinforced to hold the large wizard's weight.

Shelves lined the walls from floor to ceiling, holding an eclectic collection that immediately drew Thomas' attention. Leather-bound books sat beside an assortment of scrolls. Mysterious devices hummed with barely contained energy, their purposes impossible to guess. In one corner, a small forge glowed with blue flames that cast strange shadows across the room.

"Have a seat," Grenyth said, dropping his massive frame into the reinforced chair. It creaked ominously but held. "Ryn, fetch us some ale. The good stuff, mind you. Not that swill they used to serve here." His beard twitched in what might have been amusement. "And try not to steal anything else along the way."

The elf nodded and hurried off.

"Is this really the Whispering Vine?" Thomas asked, still examining their surroundings. "I thought it would be a tavern, not a set from Harry Potter."

"Hairy what?" Grenyth asked. "I'm not sure I follow."

"Never mind."

"Well, to answer your question, this is the Whispering Vine. Or rather, what's left of it." Grenyth gestured at the surroundings. "It used to be quite the establishment in its day. The kind of place where deals were made, secrets traded, fortunes won and lost." His expression grew distant, as if seeing ghosts of patrons long gone. "Now we keep up appearances, but the tavern's been closed to the public for years."

"And now?" Amren asked, choosing a seat that gave him clear lines of sight to both doors. His hands remained close to his weapons.

"Now it serves a different purpose," Grenyth replied. "Though perhaps not so different from its original function. We still deal in secrets here. Just more important ones."

"Training young wizards, I'd venture," Merlin suggested as he climbed onto Thomas' shoulder. It didn't surprise Thomas that the GOLEM had followed them into the kitchen from where Ryn had dropped it. "Though not through official channels, I assume," Merlin added.

"What?" Halvy said from his place near the fire, watching the GOLEM with interest. "It talks?"

"I do much more than speak," Merlin replied. "This GOLEM is an extension of my consciousness, but the rest of me is on Excalibur."

Grenyth raised an eyebrow. "Merlin?" he whispered softly, though it still came out as a deep rumble. "Is that you?"

"It is," Merlin confirmed. "As long as Excalibur survives, I'll survive with it."

"And Arthur?"

"I'm afraid not."

Grenyth's face fell. "Excalibur returns, but without the king. I suppose it was always too much to hope for after so many years." He perked up again. "But your return is still a light in the dark. You're right in your observation. I train the magically gifted here. Someone has to. The Draconite have been systematically dismantling magical education for decades. Slowly at first, so slowly many didn't notice. A regulation here, a restriction there. Just enough oversight to make people feel safe rather than controlled." He accepted a mug from Ryn, who returned with a tray of drinks. "But they've grown bolder recently. More direct in their methods."

"Because of their nanites?" Thomas asked, remembering what they'd learned about the Draconite's technological advancement.

"That's part of it." Grenyth took a long pull from his mug, his throat working as he swallowed. When he lowered the drink, his beard was flecked with foam.

"They've managed to replicate many magical effects through technology. Makes them feel secure enough to start showing their true colors." He wiped his mouth with the back of one massive hand. "But there's more to it than that. They won't admit it, but I know the truth. They're afraid."

"Of magic?" Amren asked.

"Of what it represents," Grenyth replied. His voice dropped lower, though it lost none of its power. "Magic is...unpredictable. Wild. It can't be fully controlled like their precious nanites. And anything they can't control..." He trailed off, letting them fill in the implications.

"How many students do you have?" Thomas asked.

"Fourteen at the moment, though most are asleep at this hour." Grenyth glanced toward Halvy. "Mostly orphans and outcasts. Children born with the gift but not to Druid parents." He sighed heavily. "The Druids only train their own these days. Part of their arrangement with the Draconite."

"Some arrangement," Amren scoffed, reaching for his drink. "Trading their principles for protection. What happened to the proud Druids who helped keep peace in Avalon for centuries?"

"Don't be too hard on them," Grenyth replied, though his tone suggested he shared some of Amren's sentiment. "They did what they thought was necessary to survive. Made compromises they believed would preserve their way of life." His massive fingers drummed against his mug. "But now...well, the Draconite don't need them anymore. They've gotten what they wanted. A solid ally to keep their grip on power while they built up their strength. Now they're just waiting for the right moment to change the terms of their alliance."

"And the Druids can't see this coming?" Thomas asked.

"Oh, many do," Grenyth replied. "But they're caught in a trap of their own making. They've grown soft, comfortable.

The young ones have never known anything else. And those who remember..." He shook his head sadly. "Well, we're fewer every year."

"But surely there must be Druids who remain loyal to the old ways. To Arthur and Camelot."

Grenyth's eyes fixed on Thomas with an intensity that made him want to squirm in his seat. The giant wizard leaned forward, his chair groaning beneath him. "Aye, there are some. Myself. Sylana. A few others scattered about. But our numbers dwindle with each passing year." A spark of hope entered his expression. "Though with Excalibur back in Avalon…"

"Without Arthur," Amren said.

"Even so." Grenyth's massive hands clasped around his mug, making it look like a child's toy. "The ship itself is a symbol. One that might remind people of what once was. What could be again."

"That's why we're here," Thomas said. "And why Sylana sent us to you. We need a wizard. Someone who can help us begin to chip away at the perception of the Draconite's impermeability and strength."

"Excalibur is a symbol," Merlin added. "But in some cases, it's too identifiable."

"I see what you mean," Grenyth replied with a softer laugh. "You need someone who can disguise her. Not many wizards have that kind of ability."

"Do you?" Thomas asked.

"Aye."

"Will you join us, then?"

The giant wizard shook his head, his wild beard swaying with the movement. "I can't. My place is here, helping these young ones." He gestured at Halvy and Ryn. "They need guidance, protection. Training. Someone has to keep the old ways alive, even if we have to do it in secret."

"Sylana didn't know that?" Thomas asked, unable to

keep the disappointment from his voice. "Why would she send us to you?"

"Because I know exactly who you need." Grenyth leaned back in his chair, which creaked alarmingly. "There's a Druid. Kaelithan. Brilliant boy, but too curious for his own good. Started experimenting with magic in ways the Draconite didn't approve of." His expression grew grim. "They drove him out, of course. Now he works with some of my former students, trying to protect what's left."

"Protect what, exactly?" Amren asked, his interest clearly piqued.

"There's a cave system not far from here," Grenyth explained, his tone dropping to almost a whisper despite the privacy of their location. "A sacred site that few outside the Druid elite even know exists. It taps into the magical energy that flows through this world like blood through veins." He traced a pattern in the air with one thick finger, leaving a trail of sparkling light. "The Druids built collectors there ages ago, devices that help channel and distribute that power across the planet. It's what powers their defenses, among other things."

"And Kaelithan is guarding these collectors?" Thomas asked, fascinated by the implications.

"Him and a handful of others. Those who refuse to accept the Draconite's increasing control." Grenyth's eyes darkened. "It's risky, dangerous work. But we believe they mean to sabotage the collectors."

"If they succeed," Merlin interjected, "it would leave Avalyeth vulnerable."

"More than that," Grenyth replied. "It would be another nail in magic's coffin. Another step toward their dominance." He fixed Thomas with an intense stare. "I should warn you though. Kaelithan may take some convincing to join your cause."

"Why's that?" Thomas asked.

"He's dedicated to his current mission, and despite his parents disavowing him and his banishment from the rest of Druidic society, he loves this place, as he should. He believes protecting the collectors is the most important thing he can do." Grenyth smiled slightly. "He's not wrong, but perhaps there are other ways to fight back that he hasn't considered."

"I can be very persuasive," Merlin said.

"I'm sure you can." Grenyth's smile widened. "Though I wonder if he'll believe you're who you claim to be."

Before Merlin could respond, heavy footsteps approached from outside. The door burst open, admitting Burl and his thugs. They looked considerably worse for wear—one nursed a pair of black eyes, another limped heavily, and Burl's nose was heavily swollen from being broken, his face bruised around it. They froze upon seeing Grenyth sitting casually with their recent opponents.

"Boss?" Burl said uncertainly, glancing between the giant wizard and Amren. "What's going on?"

"Ah, Burl." Grenyth's grin widened. "Perfect timing. How do you feel about a little adventure?"

The thug's eyes darted between his employer and the warrior who had so thoroughly defeated his gang. "I...what?"

"These fine folks need guides to the sacred caves. Ryn and Halvy are going to show them the way, but since you're here, I'm sure a little extra muscle couldn't hurt." He studied Burl's companions critically. "Though your friends look a bit too banged up for the journey."

"You want me to help them?" Burl asked incredulously. "After what that one did to us?"

"Consider it a learning experience," Grenyth replied. "It could have been much worse. To be honest, I thought perhaps he'd killed the lot of you."

"My father taught me not to kill unless there's a need," Amren said. "There was no need."

"And who's your father, then?" Burl asked, still scowling. "You fight like a rabid tree skart."

"Sir Bedivere," Amren replied. "One of King Arthur's Avalonian Knights."

The entire group of thugs reacted with shock, gasping and stiffening, suddenly thankful to be alive. Burl's entire demeanor shifted from indignant to utter respect.

"My apologies, Sir…"

"Amren. But there's no 'sir' ahead of it. I'm no knight."

"Not yet, anyway," Thomas said, unsure of how the young warrior would actually become a knight.

"My apologies, Amren," Burl said. "If I had known…"

"How could you?" Amren said. "No harm done…to me, anyway." He smiled. "You have a lot of power, but you lack finesse. It can be learned."

Burl turned to Grenyth. "I'd be honored to go with them, boss."

"Good lad." Grenyth turned back to Thomas, his expression growing serious once more. "My students will show you the way. Ryn knows the forest paths, and Halvy's magic might come in handy."

"And the caves themselves?" Amren asked. "What should we expect?"

"The magical energy fields can play tricks on the mind if you let them, make you see things that aren't there." Grenyth's voice dropped lower. "And lately, there have been rumors of Draconite patrols in the area. They claim they're just maintaining security, but…"

"They're planning their attack," Merlin finished.

"Aye. That's our belief as well." Grenyth rose from his chair. "Which is why time may be of the essence. Do they know you're here? With Excalibur?"

"Excalibur?" Burl gasped, along with the other thugs.

"If you think that's amazing," Thomas said, motioning to the GOLEM, "meet Merlin."

"What?" Burl looked at the small GOLEM with reverence. "I've heard all the stories about you. About Excalibur. The Draconite, they've tried to erase them but…"

"We have copies of datastores tucked away," Grenyth explained. "Keeping a history of the truth the Draconite want everyone to forget."

"We should get moving," Merlin said. "Grenyth is right. The Draconite know Excalibur has returned, which means time is not on our side."

Thomas stood, noticing how Ryn and Halvy immediately moved to gather supplies. "Thank you," he said to the giant wizard, offering a handshake. "For everything."

"Don't thank me yet," Grenyth replied, shaking his hand and placing his other enormous hand on Thomas' shoulder. "You still have to convince Kaelithan to join you. And even if you manage that..." He trailed off, his expression growing distant. "Well, the path ahead won't be easy."

"It never is," Merlin said from Thomas' shoulder.

They gathered their unlikely group. As they prepared to leave, Grenyth caught Thomas' arm.

"One more thing," the giant wizard said softly, his voice barely above a whisper. "Remember that what you carry isn't just a ship. It's hope. Something many of us had feared lost for all eternity."

Thomas swallowed hard, the weight of the wizard's words pressing on him. The hope of a galaxy was a heavy hope to bear. One he still lacked confidence he could handle, but he gave the big man confirmation of his understanding with a sharp jerk of his chin before following everyone out of the hidden tavern and back into the Wyldentree's shadowy passages.

Thomas couldn't shake the feeling that they were embarking on something far more significant than simply recruiting a new crew member. He glanced at their unusual companions—the nimble elf thief, the young wizard who'd held him immobile with casual ease, and the bruised enforcer who eyed Amren with unbridled awe.

"Well," he said quietly to Merlin. "This should be interesting."

"Indeed," the Advisor replied. "Though I suspect 'interesting' may prove to be an understatement."

As they made their way through the dying tree's twisted corridors, Thomas couldn't help but agree. But then, nothing had been simple since he'd first set foot on Excalibur.

He had a feeling things were only going to get more complicated from here on out.

CHAPTER 47

The dense canopy blocked most of the sunlight, leaving the forest floor bathed in an ethereal twilight broken only by patches of bioluminescent fungi that cast everything in ghostly shadows. The air was thick with moisture and the rich scent of decay as ancient leaves broke down into new soil. Massive roots, each one larger than the largest tree Thomas had ever seen on Earth, loomed all around them. Strange birds and small creatures called from the shadows with unfamiliar voices that echoed through the perpetual gloom.

Thomas wiped sweat from his forehead as he carefully picked his way between two giant roots. The bark beneath his feet was slick with moisture, forcing him to watch every step. "Why can't we just take another groundcar?" he asked. "Seems like it would be a lot faster than hiking through all this."

Ryn glanced back at him. "The Druids track the movement of every ground vehicle," he explained. "They'll know if anyone goes to the caves, and since the caves are supposed to be secret…"

"It's suspicious as anything," Halvy finished for him.

"How far is it to these caves, anyway?" Amren asked, deftly climbing over a smaller root.

"A few hours," Ryn replied, pausing to examine what looked like claw marks on a nearby trunk. "Assuming we don't run into any trouble."

"And how likely is that?"

The elf's silence wasn't particularly reassuring.

They walked in silence for a time, their footsteps muffled by centuries of accumulated leaves and moss. Thomas noticed how easily their guides moved through the forest, their feet finding purchase on treacherously slick surfaces. Even Burl, for all his size, managed to move with surprising grace through the ancient woods.

"Amren, sir," Burl said finally, breaking the comfortable quiet. His voice carried an almost childlike reverence despite his rough appearance. "What was it like? Growing up as the son of one of Arthur's knights?"

Amren glanced at the enforcer, something guarded entering his expression. "My father was already retired by the time I was born," he said. "Most of what I know comes from his stories, and from the training he gave me."

"What kind of stories did he tell?" Burl pressed eagerly. "Did he ever talk about the Battle of Camlan? Your father was there, wasn't he?"

Amren's jaw tightened in response to the questions. Even the forest grew quieter, as if sensing the weight of the moment.

"He was there," Amren said finally, his voice tight with carefully controlled emotion. "Though he rarely spoke of it directly. The loss was...too personal."

"I've heard so many stories," Burl continued, seemingly oblivious to the tension. "They say it was the greatest space battle ever fought. That the galaxy burned with energy weapons and magic. That if Arthur had been there..."

"If Arthur had been there, things would have been

different," Amren interrupted sharply. "But he wasn't. He was already gone, lost somewhere in the vastness of space. And without him..." He paused, visibly gathering himself. "Without him, we didn't stand a chance. Not really. My father commanded one of the heavy cruisers in the fleet. They thought they had positioned themselves perfectly and had the tactical advantage."

"What happened?" Halvy asked softly, his youth showing through his usual careful control. The boy's pale eyes reflected the bioluminescent light around them, making them appear to glow from within.

"Mordred had spent years preparing," Amren explained, his voice carrying the weight of history, "building his forces in secret, gathering allies. When he finally struck, it was devastating. The Draconite fleet emerged from multiple vectors simultaneously, a force larger than any of our operatives had seen. Larger than anyone could believe possible. More than that, their technology had advanced beyond what we expected. My father..." He trailed off, his shoulders tense with remembered pain. "...his ship was badly damaged in the initial assault. He nearly died."

"Why wasn't Arthur there?" Halvy asked, turning to look at the small mechanical form. "Why did he abandon his people?"

"He didn't abandon them," Merlin replied. "He was betrayed, his ship damaged. We crashed on Thomas' planet, called Earth, and wound up buried deep beneath a mountain. Unable to help when our people needed us most. We wanted to be there. Believe me."

"I do believe you." Halvy turned to Thomas. "What is Earth like? Is it anything like Avalyeth?"

Thomas considered this as they walked, trying to find the right words to describe his home to beings who had never seen it. The comparison was almost impossible.

"Parts of it are similar," he finally said. "We have forests, though nothing like this. Our trees are much smaller, and they don't pulse with energy the way these do. We've built massive cities of metal and stone, stretching toward the sky." He thought about Manchester's crowded streets, the constant rush of vehicles and people. "It's...busier. More chaotic. And we don't have magic."

"No magic at all?" Halvy asked, clearly shocked by the concept. "How do you manage?"

"Technology," Thomas replied. "Though compared to what you have here, it's primitive. We have spaceflight, but we can't travel between the stars."

"That must be strange," Halvy mused. "A world without magic. Like a body without blood."

"I don't know. It's hard to miss something you've never had."

"Would you miss it now, if you went back?"

"I don't know if I'll ever go back," Thomas replied, suddenly feeling homesick. "I was in some trouble back on Earth."

"What kind of trouble?"

"Halvy, it's none of your business," Burl grumbled before Thomas could form a reply. "Leave the man alone."

They continued through the forest, their conversation dying off as the light grew dimmer. Thomas noticed their guides becoming more cautious, moving more carefully between the massive roots. Even Burl sensed the change in atmosphere, his unconcerned swagger replaced by careful attention to his surroundings.

Ryn had moved ahead to scout their path, slipping through the shadows like a ghost. He returned now, his expression grim in the green-tinged light.

"There's a camp ahead," he reported in a whisper, gathering them close. "About twenty beings. Mixed group—Draconite, Druids, some Fae. They're set up in a clearing between three of the larger roots."

"Soldiers?" Amren asked.

"I don't think so. They're armed, but not wearing proper military gear. Their equipment looks...unofficial. Mismatched. They're carrying energy weapons, but I also spotted traditional blades and some magical implements."

"Mercenaries," Merlin said from Thomas' shoulder, his mechanical voice carrying clear concern. "But why are they out here?"

"I can find out," Ryn offered. "Stick around longer, give a listen."

"Be careful," Thomas warned, remembering how easily the elf had lifted Merlin's GOLEM from his pocket. "If they're mercenaries, they might be more alert than regular soldiers."

"Don't worry. They won't even know I'm there. It's what I do."

They waited for Ryn's return in tense silence, using the time to find better cover among the massive roots. Thomas kept his eyes on the direction the elf had gone, straining to catch any sign of movement in the perpetual twilight. His heart rate had picked up, that familiar surge of adrenaline that came with knowing danger was near. The forest grew quieter around them, as if the local wildlife also sensed the strain.

"These mercenaries," Thomas whispered to Burl. "Are they common here?"

"More so lately," he replied softly. "The Draconite use them for operations they want to keep officially separate from their military. Gives them deniability if things go wrong. Important when trying to muck things up on Druid territory."

Amren moved closer to them. "If they're mercenaries, they're likely here about the caves. "

"Which means Kaelithan could be in danger," Thomas replied.

"If he isn't already dead," Merlin added grimly. "Though I doubt it. From what Grenyth said, he's not an easy target."

Movement, a whisper of shadow against shadow, caught Thomas' attention. Ryn emerged from the gloom like a ghost, something held carefully in his hands. As he drew closer, Thomas recognized it as a rifle of some kind.

"They got word from their boss," Ryn reported, slightly out of breath despite his apparent ease of movement. "Something about a timeline shifting. They're planning to move on the caves immediately. I snatched this to show you how they're armed."

"A coward's weapon," Amren snorted. "What exactly did you hear?"

"Not much. They were being careful with details. But they looked nervous. Like something big has changed and they need to adapt quickly."

"How well armed are they?" Amren asked, studying the weapon Thomas now held.

"Energy weapons like that one," Ryn replied. "Plus whatever magic the Druids with them can manage. But they're not expecting trouble. Their guard is down."

"Overconfident," Burl growled softly, cracking his massive knuckles. "That makes them vulnerable."

"We should move now," Amren suggested. "While we have surprise on our side. They'll likely call in reinforcements once they begin their assault on the caves."

"It's risky," Merlin cautioned. "We don't know their full capabilities. And we can't risk Thomas. Right now, he's the only one who can command Excalibur."

"Are you any good with a sword?" Burl asked Thomas, tapping the broadsword on his hip that he'd collected at the Whispering Vine.

"I've never used one before." He glanced at the gun Ryn still held, nervous to admit the truth after Amren's earlier comment. "I've used something like that before." He nodded at the rifle, then slipped a look at Amren. "It's a coward's weapon, and I'm not a coward."

Amren clasped Thomas on the shoulder. "Regardless of my opinion on the weapon, if they use fire, then we have every right to use fire and not feel lesser for it."

Thomas nodded. "I'm not eager to use one again, but we can't let them reach the caves. If we want any chance of recruiting Kaelithan, we need to help stop the attack."

"Ryn, give the rifle to him," Burl said.

Ryn held out the weapon to Thomas, who hesitated before taking it. The grip felt wrong in his hands, bringing back memories of New York he'd rather forget. But this was different, he told himself. This wasn't about gang violence or proving himself tough enough to belong. This was about protecting people who needed help.

"Let's all take a moment to consider our options," Merlin said. "If we're going to do this, we need a proper plan of attack."

"I could try to get closer," Ryn offered. "Maybe create a distraction."

Halvy shifted nervously beside them. "I could help with that. I can conjure some pretty convincing illusions."

"No," Amren said firmly. "You're both too young to risk in direct combat."

"We're not babies," Ryn protested. "We can hold our own."

"What about this," Burl suggested quietly. "Ryn and Halvy create a distraction from one side. While the mercenaries are looking that way, the rest of us hit them from behind. Hard and fast."

"That could work," Amren agreed. "But we need to coordinate perfectly. If the timing is off..."

"Halvy, how convincing can you make your illusions?" Thomas asked, studying the weapon in his hands.

"Pretty convincing," the young wizard replied. "Especially in this light. Why?"

"Could you make it look like there's a full squad of Druid guards approaching their camp? Maybe make it seem like their operation has been discovered?"

"I think so," Halvy said, though he sounded uncertain. "But they'll figure it out pretty quick when their weapons pass through the illusions."

"They won't have time," Amren said, catching on to the plan, "because we'll hit them from behind while they're distracted."

"And I can cause some real chaos once they're focused on the illusions," Ryn added. "Add to the confusion."

Thomas turned to Burl. "How good are you in a scrape?"

The big man's bruised face split into a fierce smile. "Better than I looked earlier. Amren caught me by surprise. It won't happen again."

"Alright," Thomas said, trying to project more confidence than he felt. "Here's what I think we should do..."

He laid out the plan quickly, each member of their group adding suggestions and refinements.

"Remember," Amren said when they'd finished, "these aren't Draconite soldiers. They're mercenaries, and they aren't as well outfitted. Hit them hard and fast, and they'll likely break rather than stand and fight."

"Unless they're truly loyal to their employer," Merlin cautioned.

"Mercenaries are loyal to coin," Ryn scoffed. "And coin don't spend well when you're dead."

They split up, each moving forward toward the camp from opposite sides. Soon enough, Thomas could hear the movement of the mercenaries as they packed up their gear and prepared to advance on the caves.

"You've done this before on Earth?" Amren asked quietly as they crept forward. "Led people into battle."

"Not exactly," Thomas replied, keeping his voice low. "But I've had to think on my feet a lot."

"It shows. You have good instincts."

"Let's hope they're good enough," Thomas muttered.

He lost track of how much time passed before they came into view of the camp. He shivered slightly at the sight of the mercenaries, predominantly Draconite but including other beings. From the looks of things, they had nearly finished their preparations, and were about to move out.

Amren ducked behind a root. Burl and Thomas joined him there, Merlin's GOLEM still perched on Thomas' shoulder.

"Now we wait for the signal," Amren said softly.

Thomas nodded, his grip tightening on the stolen weapon. He didn't know how much of his nerves were from the idea of getting hurt himself, and how much came from the idea of hurting someone else. He forced familiar fears to the background, eyes up to where Ryn's signal would appear once Halvy was ready.

The forest held its breath, waiting for chaos to erupt.

CHAPTER 48

The first shouts of alarm from the mercenary camp cut through the forest's eerie silence like shattering glass. Thomas pressed himself tighter against the ancient root, its rough bark digging into his shoulder as he strained to hear the chaos unfolding ahead. Voices rose in confusion and fear, overlapping in multiple languages as weapons were hastily readied. The sound of power cells charging filled the air with an electric whine that set his teeth on edge.

"Now?" he asked, eying a switch he assumed would activate the rifle.

"Hold," Amren whispered beside him, one hand gripping Thomas' arm with almost painful intensity. "Wait for Ryn's signal. Timing is everything."

Through gaps in the massive roots, Thomas caught glimpses of the mercenaries scrambling to respond to Halvy's illusions. The young wizard's magic—his phantom Druid guards looked terrifying in the forest's dim light, their wood armor reflecting the glow of their staves as they approached the camp—had exceeded expectations. Some mercenaries took up defensive positions, their weapons trembling slightly as they trained them on the approaching figures. Others were more interested in gathering their equipment, clearly considering retreat. Their sudden fear was palpable, crackling through the air like static electricity.

A Druid mercenary started chanting something in a language that made Thomas' skin crawl, his hands weaving patterns that left trails of sickly green light in the air. Beside him, a pale-skinned warrior drew twin blades.

Thomas' heart hammered as he waited, every second feeling like an eternity. The stolen weapon felt slick in his sweating hands. He had been in fights before, but nothing like this. These weren't street thugs or rival gang members; these were killers for hire, armed with weapons that could reduce him to atoms and with magic that could do worse.

A silver light suddenly burst above the camp. Ryn's signal, cutting through the gloom like a shooting star.

"Now," Amren cried, already moving with deadly grace.

Thomas burst from cover alongside him, adrenaline flooding his system. The first mercenary he saw was so focused on the illusory guards that he never saw the real threat coming. Thomas squeezed the trigger, the weapon's lack of recoil surprising him. The energy blast caught the mercenary square in the back, dropping him without a sound. The smell of ozone and burned flesh filled the air, making Thomas' stomach lurch.

All hell broke loose as their small force attacked from multiple directions. Amren moved like a deadly wind through the camp, his daggers leaving trails of blue fire. Each strike found vulnerable points—a gap in armor here, an exposed throat there—with surgical precision.

Burl crashed through their lines like an enraged bear, his massive broadsword swinging in wide, powerful arcs. A Draconite tried to engage him with a longsword, only to have the weapon shatter against Burl's blade before it cut deep into the enemy's gut.

"Contact!" someone on the right shouted in panic. "We're surrounded!"

"It's a trap!" Another voice cracked with fear. "Fall back!"

The mercenaries' formation dissolved into chaos as they tried to face threats from multiple directions. Some fired frantically at Halvy's illusions, their energy bolts passing harmlessly through the ghostly figures. Others turned to face the real attackers, but their responses were uncoordinated and increasingly desperate.

A wild burst of gunfire passed close to Thomas. He dove behind a fallen log to avoid the energy bolts and returned fire. His shots weren't particularly accurate, but in the confusion it hardly mattered. The mercenaries were too busy trying to figure out what was happening to mount an effective defense.

The Druid mercenary he'd noticed earlier raised his hands high, beginning to weave some kind of complex spell. Energy gathered around his fingers, forming patterns that hurt Thomas' eyes to look at. Before he could complete whatever horrific magic he was preparing, a bolt of reddish-hued magical energy struck him from behind. The competing magics collided in a shower of sparks that left the man staggering and cursing.

"Their morale is breaking," Merlin observed. "But watch for desperation. Cornered animals are the most dangerous."

He was right. Several mercenaries had already fled into the forest, abandoning their employers at the first sign of serious resistance. Others were throwing down their weapons, raising their hands in surrender. Victory was within reach.

Then everything went wrong.

"ENOUGH!" a voice boomed across the clearing with enough force to shake leaves from the branches overhead. "Stand down or the boy dies!"

Thomas spun toward the sound, his blood turning to

ice. A massive Draconite held Ryn, one clawed hand wrapped around the elf's throat while the other pressed blade against his pale skin. The mercenary captain stood head and shoulders taller than his compatriots, his scaled hide rippling with what Thomas took to be nanite-augmented muscle.

"If you value his life, drop your weapons!" the captain commanded. Every word dripped with lethal promise.

The blade pressed harder against Ryn's throat, drawing a thin line of blood. The elf's face remained eerily calm despite his predicament, but one wrong move and that dagger would do far worse than scratch.

"I won't ask again," the captain growled, his reptilian features twisting into a cruel smile. "Drop them. Now."

Thomas' mind raced. The captain's position gave him a clear view of most of the clearing. Any attempt to flank him would be seen. A direct shot risked hitting Ryn. Even Amren had frozen in place, his deadly daggers hanging uselessly at his sides.

Ryn's eyes met Thomas' across the clearing. Despite the blade at his throat, despite the very real possibility of imminent death, the young thief managed to wink.

Then reality glitched.

One moment Ryn was there, solid and real in the captain's grasp. The next, he was simply gone. "What the—" he started to say, stumbling back in an awkward half-step that left him vulnerable for a crucial second.

Ryn materialized behind him like a ghost stepping through a wall, moving with fluid grace as he drove a stolen dagger into the back of the captain's knee. The Draconite roared in pain and rage, trying to spin around to face this new threat. By then, Amren had reached him. The warrior's daggers flashed in the dim light, their enchanted edges finding vital points with ruthless efficiency. The captain managed one more strangled cry before collapsing, his scaled hide no match for weapons forged to kill his kind.

"Clear!" Burl called from the other side of the camp, his massive form emerging from the shadows. "The rest have fled into the forest."

Thomas lowered his weapon, his hands shaking as the adrenaline began to fade. They had won, and somehow no one on their side was seriously hurt. His legs felt weak, and he had to resist the urge to puke. He had killed. Again.

"You acted in response to an unjust threat," Merlin said as if reading his mind. "It was a noble kill."

"I shot him in the back," Thomas replied.

"And he would have done the same to you. I told you things wouldn't get any easier here."

"Maybe I'm afraid that they will get easier," Thomas answered.

"Taking a life should never be a thoughtless endeavor. But it sometimes is a necessary one."

Thomas exhaled his faded adrenaline, sitting on a tree root as the others regrouped around him.

"That was some trick," Amren said to Ryn as the elf approached. "The disappearing act. How did you—"

"Trade secret," Ryn replied with a grin, though Thomas noticed he looked paler than usual. "Though I have to admit, that blade was a bit too close for comfort. I felt my skin slit. Any longer and..." He trailed off, touching the shallow cut on his throat.

"It's not a secret," Halvy said. "I created an illusion around him so the big ugly thought he disappeared. His mind told him he was gone, even if the weight hadn't changed, and he loosened his grip so Ryn could get away from him."

"Clever," Merlin praised, impressed with the young pairs' action. "Grenyth has taught you well."

"We should search the camp," Amren said. "See if they left behind anything useful."

"Already on it," Ryn replied, holding up a datapad. "Found this on the dead captain. It might take some time to crack the security, but—"

"Quiet," Merlin interrupted sharply. "Listen."

They fell silent. Soft popping sounds echoed in the distance, suddenly replaced by a deep boom that echoed through the forest.

"What is that?" Thomas whispered.

"It's coming from the caves," Ryn replied.

"Run," Amren commanded. "We need to get there! Now!"

CHAPTER 49

They raced through the ancient forest, their feet rustling through fallen leaves as they did their best to avoid roots threatening to trip them with almost every step. Pushing himself to keep up with the others, every breath burned in Thomas' lungs. More explosions echoed through the trees, the flashes of light casting strange shadows through the perpetual twilight. The sounds of energy weapons grew constantly louder, along with the crack of powerful magic and screams that made his blood run cold.

"How much further?" he gasped, ducking under a low-hanging branch.

"We're close," Ryn replied, leading them along paths only he could see. "The cave entrance is just ahead."

Another explosion rocked the forest, shaking the ground. Thomas stumbled but managed to keep his feet under him. The rifle felt heavy in his hands, a constant reminder of the death surrounding him. Would he have to kill again? The possible answer to that question rolled around in his stomach like a thunder storm.

They burst through a final screen of vegetation into a small clearing. The cave mouth gaped before them like an open wound in the ancient rock. But it was the scene outside that brought them to a halt.

A half-dozen bodies lay sprawled on the blood-stained ground. Their robes marked them as wizards, death having stolen whatever power they'd once commanded. Their mercenary killers were still stepping over their bodies and disappearing into the cave's dark maw.

"Where are the security forces?" Thomas whispered, pressing himself against a massive root. "Shouldn't there be guards here?"

Burl spat quietly. "Paid off, most likely," he growled. "Enough gold can make almost anyone look the other way. Don't matter if you lose your job when your pockets are already full."

"We need to move," Amren said, his daggers already in hand. "Before they get too far ahead."

The entrance was roughly circular, its walls unnaturally smooth as if melted by intense heat. Thomas tried not to look too closely at the dead wizards as they too stepped over their bloody bodies.

They moved quickly, exploding from the darkness into the torch-lit cave entrance, surprising two guards left by the mercenaries, one posted on either side of the opening. Before the guards could even register the threat, Amren's daggers found one's throat while Burl's massive blade nearly severed the other's head from his shoulders. They quickly dragged both bodies into the shadows before following the sounds of the mercenaries deeper into the cave system.

The passage twisted and turned, branching occasionally into smaller tunnels lit by strange crystals embedded in the walls. Their light pulsed in time with the magical energy that flowed through the rock.

"The collectors are drawing power from the entire planet," Merlin explained softly. "These crystals are part of the distribution network."

They reached an intersection where three tunnels converged. Thomas was about to ask which way they should go when movement caught his eye. Too late, he realized they had walked into an ambush.

"Down!" Amren shouted as energy beams cut through the air where they were standing. Thomas dove back around the corner, blindly returning fire. Beside him, Halvy's hands waved as he started a spell.

Ryn didn't move fast enough.

An energy bolt caught him squarely in the chest, burning through his light armor as if it weren't there. The young elf's eyes went wide with surprise as he stumbled backward. His mouth opened as if to speak, but no words came.

"No!" Thomas screamed as the youngster crumpled to the ground, smoke rising from his horrific wound.

Rage and grief overwhelmed Thomas as the world narrowed to a tunnel, the mercenary who'd killed Ryn standing at the end of it. Thomas shifted position, targeting the Draconite, the rifle steady in his hands as his two quick shots dropped the killer .

Halvy's spell—a wave of bone-crushing force—slammed two more mercenaries into the cave wall, their weapons clattering to the ground as they collapsed, leaving trails of blood on the stone walls.

Amren burst from cover to join the fray. The remaining mercenaries barely had time to register his approach before he was on them, slipping away from their clumsy sword swings and rifle fire, his blades flashing as he stabbed and sliced. One mercenary fell, then another. Blood sprayed from the throat of a third as Amren ducked low and behind a fourth, slicing through his lower leg and dropping him to his knees. Without looking, Amren stabbed him through the back of the neck, toppling him to the ground. Out of opponents, he spun, eyes locking on Ryn.

Thomas lowered his weapon and rushed to the boy's side, where Halvy already cradled his friend in his lap, tears streaming down his pale face.

"He was just a kid," he whispered, his voice breaking as he stared down into the elf's eyes, all life having fled from their depths. "A damn kid."

He knelt beside Ryn's body as Halvy looked up. "We'll make them pay," the young wizard promised, his voice hard with grief and rage. "We'll make them all pay."

Burl placed a massive hand on Halvy's shoulder. "Aye," he growled. "That we will. But we need to keep moving. There'll be time for proper vengeance later."

Thomas knew Burl was right, but it felt wrong to just leave Ryn's body there. The elf died trying to help them, trying to protect his home. He deserved better than this.

"We'll come back for him," Amren promised, reading Thomas' expression. "But right now, we need to stop the mercenaries."

Their steps heavier now—weighed down by grief and determination—they continued deeper into the caves, the passage winding back and forth as it descended. It opened occasionally into larger chambers, where they found more bodies—mercenaries and wizards alike—marking the defenders' fighting retreat.

The sounds of combat became audible ahead, echoing off the stone walls. They came within visible range soon enough. Flashes of light were accompanied by the crackle of powerful magic. They quickened their pace, the tunnel opening into a vast chamber. Massive crystals rose from floor to ceiling like frozen waterfalls, their surfaces rippling with barely contained power. At the center stood what had to be the collectors—three towering obelisks of black stone covered in glowing runes.

A shimmering barrier of pure energy surrounded the collectors, maintained by a lone figure in blue robes. Two other wizards fought desperately to keep nearly a dozen mercenaries at bay, but they were clearly losing ground.

"That wizard won't be able to hold the shield much longer," Merlin observed from Thomas' shoulder. "We need to act now."

"Thomas, Halvy, you two stay here as our backup," Amren replied. "Burl, you and I will move in close."

"Gladly," Burl answered, still furious about Ryn's demise.

Thomas and Halvy remained where they were while Amren and Burl quietly advanced, crouching and careful not to be seen, toward the mercenaries. When Amren signaled he was in position, Thomas balanced the rifle on the crystal and glanced over at Halvy. The boy's hands were already moving to prepare a spell.

"Now!" Amren shouted, drawing the shocked attention of the mercenaries as he rushed them, daggers in hand and ready to draw blood.

Thomas squeezed the trigger, his first shots catching a mercenary squarely in the chest. Either he didn't have an energy shield, or it was already spent. The rifle blasts burned through his light armor like it was paper, dropping the enemy before he could even register the new threat. His body hit the stone floor with a dull thud, his weapon clattering away into shadow.

Beside him, Halvy unleashed his spell, a bolt of pure magical force that put large holes in two more mercenaries. The young wizard's face was tight with concentration as he immediately began weaving another spell.

The defending wizards reacted instantly to the unexpected aid. One swept his staff in a wide arc that left a trail of crackling lightning in its wake, forcing several enemies to dive for cover. Another gestured sharply, causing a mercenary's weapon to explode in his hands in a shower of superheated sparks and fragments. His scream of pain was cut short as Amren's dagger found his throat.

Amren moved through the chaos like a deadly wind, his enchanted blades leaving trails of blue fire. A mercenary tried to bring his rifle to bear, only to have one of Amren's daggers slip between his ribs while the other opened his throat. Another enemy managed to block his next strike but left himself open to a devastating counter that sent him sprawling.

Burl charged straight into the thick of things with a roar that echoed off the chamber walls. His massive sword cleaved through a mercenary's hasty guard, the blade continuing through flesh and bone with terrible efficiency, blood spraying across nearby crystals. Burl wrenched the weapon free, already turning to face his next opponent.

The mercenaries found themselves caught between two forces. Those who turned to face the new threat left themselves vulnerable to the defending wizards. Those who kept their attention on the wizards were easy targets for Thomas and his companions. In their desperation, the last mercenaries remaining alive turned their attention to the collectors, peppering the magical shield around them with energy bolts.

"Those are no mercenaries," Merlin uttered somberly. "They're more interested in completing the mission than saving their own lives."

Thomas shifted his rifle toward the mercenaries targeting the shield. His aim wasn't great, and most of his bolts missed, but they served as a distraction and delay, giving Halvy time to hit them with his magical missiles. Two of them dropped, one after another, but the attack on the shield continued.

"The shield is failing!" Merlin warned as fractures appeared in the barrier protecting the collectors. The wizard maintaining it had fallen to one knee, sweat streaming down his face as he fought to maintain the protective magic. The barrier rippled and flexed like a soap bubble about to burst.

A mercenary got close enough to engage Burl directly, blade sparking against his massive sword. The big man grinned as he battered aside their guard and simply ran them through. Nearby, Amren danced between two opponents, his daggers moving almost too fast to follow as they struck again and again.

The defending wizards pressed their advantage. One conjured a swarm of burning projectiles that sought out targets like hungry wasps, while the other's staff crackled with electrical energy that arced between mercenaries with devastating effect. The air grew thick with ozone and the copper smell of blood.

The battle reached its crescendo as the remaining mercenaries realized their position was untenable. Three tried to flee toward the tunnel entrance, but Thomas caught one with a lucky shot while Halvy's magic ensnared another. The third made it halfway to safety before one of Amren's daggers zipped through the air and caught him between the shoulder blades, the enchanted knife sinking deep into his back.

The final mercenary dropped his weapon and raised his hands in surrender, only to be cut down by a blast of pure force from one of the defending wizards.

The chamber fell silent except for heavy breathing and the constant thrumming of magical energy from the collectors.

Thomas moved from cover, taking a moment to survey the carnage. Bodies lay scattered across the chamber floor, their blood seeping into cracks in the ancient stone. He felt sick, but pushed the feeling aside. The violence was justified, but that didn't make it any less gruesome.

The wizard who had maintained the shield finally slumped to the ground, clearly exhausted. The barrier around the collectors flickered and faded, but the danger had passed.

Before anyone could move to assist him, one of the other defenders approached. He was older, his gray hair shot through with traces of silver, his face lined with experience. Despite the signs of recent combat on his robes, he moved with steady purpose, his staff still crackling with residual energy.

"Who are you?" he demanded, his voice carrying both authority and wariness. "How did you find this place?"

"Grenyth sent us," Thomas replied, lowering his weapon as he approached the man. "We're looking for Kaelithan."

The older wizard's expression shifted at the mention of Grenyth's name. He studied them more carefully now, his eyes lingering on Merlin's mechanical form perched on Thomas' shoulder. "That's quite an interesting construct," he said finally, his tone suggesting he suspected it was far more than a simple mechanical. "And you say Grenyth sent you specifically to find Kaelithan?"

"Yes. We need his help."

The older wizard gestured toward the exhausted young man by the collectors. "Well, you've found him. Though he's not in any shape to help you at the moment."

Kaelithan managed to climb back to his feet, though he still looked shaky. His blue robes were damp with sweat, and his hands trembled slightly from exhaustion. But there was something in his bearing that spoke of both power and resolve.

"What kind of help?" he asked, his voice hoarse but steady. "And why would Grenyth send you to me?"

"Because we need a wizard," Thomas replied. "Someone skilled enough to help us fight the Draconite. Someone who can hide a starship. A very particular starship."

The young wizard's eyes narrowed in suspicion. "What ship?"

"Excalibur."

The word hung in the air like a physical thing. The wizards stared at Thomas with expressions of shock and disbelief.

"Impossible," the older wizard breathed. "Excalibur was lost a century ago."

"And yet here we are," Merlin said, his mechanical voice carrying clear across the chamber. "Returned at last, though perhaps not in the way anyone expected."

"By the ancient powers," Kaelithan whispered. "Are you..."

"Merlin. Yes."

"This changes everything," the older wizard said, finally lowering his staff. His expression shifted from suspicion to wonder. "I am Master Crom. And if what you say is true…" He glanced at Kaelithan. "You have to go with them."

"I…I can't," Kaelithan said firmly, though regret tinged his voice. "You saw what just happened. The collectors are too important. Avalyeth is too important. This isn't the end of the fight. It's only the beginning."

"Precisely," Master Crom agreed. "And would you remain here defending a single planet, when you can go with them and perhaps guide the fate of the entire galaxy?"

Kaelithan sighed. "I understand what you're saying, but…"

"But what?" Merlin pressed. "Grenyth told us you were the best equipped to help us in our quest. If we're to succeed in challenging the Draconite grip on Avalon, we need you."

"The whole galaxy needs you," Amren added.

Thomas watched the internal struggle play out across Kaelithan's face. The young wizard clearly felt torn between his current duty and this new possibility.

"The collectors are vital," he said finally, turning to Crom. "But they're only one part of a larger system. If Excalibur has truly returned, if Merlin is calling me to action." He straightened, coming to a decision. "We'll need to return to the Whispering Vine so I can gather my things. And say goodbye."

"Of course," Thomas agreed. "But we need to hurry."

"What about the caves?" Burl asked. "Do you think that's the end of the mercenaries?"

"For today, at least," Crom said. "But when you speak to Grenyth, have him send reinforcements. Our defenses won't hold forever, but we'll do what we can to hold them long enough."

"I will," Kaelithan promised. "Thank you Master Crom, for all your teaching and advice." He turned to the other wizard. "Thank you, Master Heryld, for your kindness and support." He embraced them both quickly, leaving their eyes moist.

"Go on, Kaelithan," Crom said. "I've always known you were meant for bigger things. And now I know what they are."

"Indeed," Heryld agreed. "Farewell, young master."

Kaelithan turned to Thomas and the others, his face set with determination. "I'm ready."

CHAPTER 50

The journey back through the winding tunnels was subdued and quiet but for the sound of their footsteps echoing off the ancient stone walls and the somber hum of power flowing through the crystals embedded in the rock. The occasional drip of water provided counterpoint to their movement, each drop a reminder of the passage of time. They had helped foil the attack on the collectors. They succeeded in locating Kaelithan, and had convinced him to join them.

But at what cost?

Thomas' chest felt tight as they approached the spot where Ryn had fallen. The young elf's body lay where they'd left him, one arm stretched out as if reaching for something just beyond his grasp. His eyes remained open, staring sightlessly at the crystal-studded ceiling. The wound in his chest had stopped smoking, but the damage —a perfect circle burned through clothing and flesh alike— was horrific.

Halvy made a choked sound and turned away. The young wizard's shoulders shook slightly, though he remained silent. Magic crackled around his clenched fists, sparks of raw power betraying the emotions he struggled to contain.

"Ah, Ryn," Kaelithan said sadly. He approached the boy's body slowly and reverently before kneeling beside him. "The finest young rascal I've ever known. Though I doubt many of Wyldentree's citizens would have said the same."

"Yeah, since he robbed most of them," Burl agreed with a soft chuckle.

Kaelithan whispered over the body, his hands waving as he weaved a spell. Soft blue light flowed from his fingers like water, wrapping around Ryn's body in gentle waves.

"What are you doing?" Thomas asked.

"A preservation ward," Kaelithan explained, his concentration never wavering. "It will keep his body from..." He trailed off, unable or unwilling to finish the thought. "It will preserve him until we can give him proper rites."

"He was so young," Amren said, his voice heavy with regret. "Too young for this kind of end."

Burl moved forward, his massive frame somehow diminished by grief. "I'll carry him," he said gruffly. "It's the least I can do." He paused, looking down at Ryn's still form. "I didn't even know his full name."

"Rynalaes," Halvy said, his voice barely above a whisper. "His name was Rynalaes. But he always said it was too fancy, too proper for a street thief." The young wizard turned back to face them, tears streaming down his pale face. "He just wanted to be Ryn."

Thomas placed a hand on Halvy's shoulder, feeling the tremors running through the boy's frame. "How long did you know him?"

"Three years," Halvy replied. "Since Grenyth found me. Ryn was already there. The only non-gifted in the Whispering Vine. He told me Grenyth took him in because he was so good at sneaking around, it was like magic. He..." A sob caught in his throat. "...he showed me how to survive in the Wyldentree. Taught me which merchants would cheat me, which alleys to avoid. Said I was too naive, too trusting." A bitter laugh escaped him. "Guess he was right."

"This isn't your fault," Amren said firmly.

"Isn't it?" Halvy demanded, anger flaring in his eyes. "I always promised him we would protect one another, like I did out in the forest. But then I failed." He broke down into sobs again. Thomas put his arm around the boy, who cried into his shoulder.

"You did your best," he said. "That's all anyone can do. I know that doesn't help, but it's true."

The blue light settled into Ryn's body like frost, creating a subtle shimmer across his skin. "A sad end to die for a king that disappeared a hundred years ago. A king who abandoned his people, and left us to the Draconite."

"Is that what you think happened?" Merlin asked from Thomas' shoulder. "That Arthur abandoned you?"

"Isn't it?" Kaelithan challenged. "It's been a hundred years, and even when Excalibur returns, it's without Arthur. Without the one person who could truly unite the people against the Draconite. Instead we have..." He gestured at Thomas. "No offense, but you're hardly what the stories promised."

"That's enough," Amren snapped, stepping forward. "Thomas was chosen by the ship itself. That has to mean something."

"Does it?" Kaelithan's voice carried both bitterness and fear. "Look around you! Look what following that choice has already cost us! And for what? So we can chase some impossible dream of rebellion?"

"Sometimes dreams are all we have," Burl said quietly. He knelt beside Ryn's body, gathering the elf into his arms with surprising gentleness. "Sometimes they're worth dying for."

"And sometimes they're just dreams," Kaelithan countered. "While reality bleeds out in our arms."

Silence fell over the group, broken only by the soft hum of crystals and Halvy's muffled sobs. Thomas felt the weight of their gazes, the unspoken question hanging in the air: Was this worth it? Would there be more deaths like this, more young lives sacrificed on the altar of resistance?

Of course, there would.

"I didn't ask for this," he said finally. "I was in the wrong place at the wrong time. Or maybe the right place at the right time. I still don't know which. I didn't ask to be chosen, or to be thrown into someone else's war. But here I am, fighting for a galaxy that isn't even my own and for no other reason than because it feels like the right thing to do. The thing I was fated to do." He glanced at Merlin's GOLEM, who nodded approvingly before he looked at each of the rest in turn. "Here we all are. And we have a choice to make."

"What choice?" Halvy asked, wiping tears from his face.

"Whether we let Ryn's death mean something, or nothing at all." Thomas squared his shoulders. "Whether we fight back against the Draconite and try to end their tyranny, or accept things just the way they are. A kingdom ruled by fear, where young boys live in run down taverns learning magic in secret."

"Big words," Kaelithan said, but there was less bite in his tone now. "The Draconite have had a century to consolidate their power. They've crushed every attempt at resistance, eliminated every threat to their rule. How do we stand against that?"

"From what I've seen of the Draconite so far, they aren't that tough," Thomas answered.

"Those mercenaries were nothing compared to Mordred's elite forces."

"He's right," Amren said. "We can't compare mercenaries and guards to true Draconite warriors, and especially not to Mordred's Claws. That's what they're called. Warriors selected for their potential, then transformed by nanites." He shuddered slightly. "My father told me about them and never without a quiver of fear in his voice. They're not just stronger or faster. The nanites change them on a fundamental level."

"Like Mordred himself," Merlin added grimly. "Though I suspect even his own Claws may fear what he's become."

"What do you mean?" Thomas asked.

"The Mordred I knew was ambitious, yes. Ruthless, certainly. But he was still recognizably organic." Merlin's mechanical voice carried genuine horror. "From what we've learned, he's pushed the boundaries of what nanite enhancement can do. He may be more machine than anything now, a being of pure technological might who also wields that which he seeks to destroy."

Burl shifted Ryn's weight in his arms. "So we face an empire led by a hybrid monster and his mother, enforced by enhanced super-soldiers, with resources we can't hope to match." He smiled grimly. "Sounds like proper odds for a legend."

"You're mad," Kaelithan said, but there was a hint of admiration in his voice. "All of you."

"Perhaps," Amren agreed. "But madness might be exactly what we need. Along with the hope brought about by Excalibur's return. A few small victories will quickly add up to growing resistance. At least, that's the plan."

"And how many more will die in the process?" Kaelithan demanded, gesturing at Ryn's body. "How many more children will we sacrifice?"

"As many as choose to fight," Halvy said suddenly. His voice was steady now, though tears still stained his cheeks. "Ryn knew the risks. He chose to come anyway, because he believed in something bigger than himself." The young wizard straightened. "I choose to fight too."

"Halvy..." Kaelithan started.

"No," the boy interrupted. "I'm not a child anymore." His eyes blazed with internal fire. "If Ryn can die for this cause, then so can I."

Thomas felt something shift in the air. He looked at their unlikely group–a young wizard burning with righteous fury, a massive enforcer cradling their fallen companion, a warrior trained from birth for a destiny that had almost passed him by, and a Druid whose cynicism couldn't quite hide his desperate hope.

"Well?" Merlin asked Kaelithan. "Have you changed your mind? Will you still help us? Or will you return to your collectors, pretending that protecting Avalyeth is enough?"

The Druid wizard was silent for a long moment, studying Ryn's peaceful face. Finally, he sighed. "I think you're all insane," he said, "but I'll still help you. Though I suspect we'll all regret it eventually."

"That's the spirit," Amren said.

The group continued through the caves, returning to the chamber just inside the opening. Their mood remained somber, but tinged with a greater sense of hope and purpose.

They were halfway to the cave exit when a figure appeared ahead of them in the mouth of the cave, his form silhouetted against the twilight beyond. The stranger's presence made the very air grow heavier.

"Hold," a commanding voice ordered, carrying both authority and threat. The word echoed off the cave walls, seeming to come from everywhere at once.

Thomas felt his blood run cold as he and the others came to an abrupt stop. Something about the voice triggered him at a primal level. A sense of familiarity and fear.

"Who are you?" he demanded, though he feared he already knew the answer. "Show yourself."

The figure stepped forward into the light cast by the crystals, his head down. Then he raised it. He was older than Thomas expected, his thick white hair and lined face suggesting decades of hard living, though the wrinkles and creases only added to his rugged handsomeness. His body remained powerful, muscles clearly visible beneath shimmering chain-like armor. His eyes gleamed silver and gold, locked onto them like a falcon to a fish. But it was his bearing—the easy grace of an apex predator, the absolute confidence of someone who had mastered every discipline he sought to excel in—that truly commanded attention.

"Lancelot," Merlin breathed, his mechanical voice carrying centuries of complex emotion. "What are you doing here?"

"I'm here for you, old *friend*," Lancelot replied, his voice hard and dripping with disdain. "I'm here to destroy you."

Thank you for reading! I hope you enjoyed the book! For more information on the next installment in the series, please visit mrforbes.com/thestarshipinthestone2

OTHER BOOKS BY M.R FORBES

Want more M.R. Forbes? Of course you do!
View my complete catalog here
mrforbes.com/books
Or on Amazon:
mrforbes.com/amazon

Starship For Sale (Starship For Sale)
mrforbes.com/starshipforsale

When Ben Murdock receives a text message offering a fully operational starship for sale, he's certain it has to be a joke.

Already trapped in the worst day of his life and desperate for a way out, he decides to play along. Except there is no joke. The starship is real. And Ben's life is going to change in ways he never dreamed possible.

All he has to do is sign the contract.

Joined by his streetwise best friend and a bizarre tenant with an unseverable lease, he'll soon discover that the universe is more volatile, treacherous, and awesome than he ever imagined.

And the only thing harder than owning a starship is staying alive.

Wraith (The Convergence War)
mforbes.com/wraith

A retired captain. An experimental starship. A war like no other.

When the research starship Galileo vanishes without a trace, the powers-that-be are quick to bury the incident, eager to prevent escalating tensions that could lead to war. As a former POW, Soren refuses to give the ship up for lost.

His daughter is one of the missing.

Taking matters into his own hands, Soren starts pulling strings and calling in favors, determined to launch a clandestine mission to bring Galileo home. When an old friend offers him a ship for the operation, he expects a rusty relic headed for the scrapyard.

Instead, he's given the Wraith—an unfinished, experimental starship with plenty of potential and just as many problems. A marvel of engineering...if his crew can keep her running.

They'd better.

Because Galileo's disappearance is just the beginning. War is coming to the Federation from the most unlikely of places.

And Soren may be the only one who can stop it.

Forgotten (The Forgotten)
mrforbes.com/theforgotten
Complete series box set:
mrforbes.com/theforgottentrilogy

Some things are better off FORGOTTEN.

Sheriff Hayden Duke was born on the Pilgrim, and he

expects to die on the Pilgrim, like his father, and his father before him.

That's the way things are on a generation starship centuries from home. He's never questioned it. Never thought about it. And why bother? Access points to the ship's controls are sealed, the systems that guide her automated and out of reach. It isn't perfect, but he has all he needs to be content.

Until a malfunction forces his wife to the edge of the habitable zone to inspect the damage.

Until she contacts him, breathless and terrified, to tell him she found a body, and it doesn't belong to anyone on board.

Until he arrives at the scene and discovers both his wife and the body are gone.

The only clue? A bloody handprint beneath a hatch that hasn't opened in hundreds of years.

Until now.

Man of War (Rebellion)

mrforbes.com/manofwar
Complete series box set:
mrforbes.com/rebellion-web

In the year 2280, an alien fleet attacked the Earth.

Their weapons were unstoppable, their defenses unbreakable.

Our technology was inferior, our militaries overwhelmed.

Only one starship escaped before civilization fell.

Earth was lost.

It was never forgotten.

Fifty-two years have passed.

A message from home has been received.

The time to fight for what is ours has come.

Welcome to the rebellion.

Hell's Rejects (Chaos of the Covenant)
mrforbes.com/hellsrejects

The most powerful starships ever constructed are gone. Thousands are dead. A fleet is in ruins. The attackers are unknown. The orders are clear: *Recover the ships. Bury the bastards who stole them.*

Lieutenant Abigail Cage never expected to find herself in Hell. As a Highly Specialized Operational Combatant, she was one of the most respected Marines in the military. Now she's doing hard labor on the most miserable planet in the universe.

Not for long.

The Earth Republic is looking for the most dangerous individuals it can control. The best of the worst, and Abbey happens to be one of them. The deal is simple: *Bring back the starships, earn your freedom. Try to run, you die.* It's a suicide mission, but she has nothing to lose.

The only problem? There's a new threat in the galaxy. One with a power unlike anything anyone has ever seen. One that's been waiting for this moment for a very, very, long time. And they want Abbey, too.

Be careful what you wish for.

They say Hell hath no fury like a woman scorned. They have no idea.

ABOUT THE AUTHOR

M.R. Forbes is the mind behind a growing number of Amazon best-selling science fiction series. Having spent his childhood trying to read every sci-fi novel he could find (and write his own too), play every sci-fi video game he could get his hands on, and see every sci-fi movie that made it into the theater, he has a true love of the genre across every medium. He works hard to bring that same energy to his own stories, with a continuing goal to entertain, delight, fascinate, and surprise.

He maintains a true appreciation for his readers and is always happy to hear from them.

To learn more or just say hello:

Visit the website:
mrforbes.com

Send an e-mail:
michael@mrforbes.com

Check out his Facebook page:
facebook.com/mrforbes.author

Join his Facebook fan group:
facebook.com/groups/mrforbes

Follow on Instagram:

instagram.com/mrforbes_author

Find on Goodreads:
goodreads.com/mrforbes

Follow on Bookbub:
bookbub.com/authors/m-r-forbes

Printed in Great Britain
by Amazon